Valentina Goldman's Immaculate Confusion

MARISOL MURANO

For information or requests please contact

info@HipsoMedia.com
www.HipsoMedia.com

Fiction/Humorous.
ISBN-13: 978-0-9840556-9-2 • ISBN-10: 0-9840556-9-X

Also by

MARISOL MURANO

The Lady, the Chef, and the Courtesan

Deliciously Doable Small Plates from Around the World

For Clara, for coming to meet me, despite Henry's death.

For Azucena, for trusting me with your firstborn.

"Dreams? . . . But I don't need dreams, Doctor, that's why I hardly have them—because I have this life instead. With me it all happens in broad daylight!"

Portnoy's Complaint

Philip Roth

CONTENTS

I. PUBIC RELATIONS

LIES DOWN IN THE TROPICS

"Marriage is a gyp. Marriage is a gyp. Marriage is a gyp," is my sister Azucena's favorite refrain. So why does she take offense whenever anyone suggests she divorce Carlos Upstairs, the man who upon returning from their honeymoon took residence in the upstairs part of the house and proceeded to devote every waking hour to playing with his Game Boy? That a man who held so much promise has been happily unemployed for years very much annoys Azucena—being annoyed is my sister's only hobby. It's a strange thing to say, but it might be the contentment rather than the unemployment that causes our father to ask on a relatively regular basis if the *chulo* upstairs is also a cripple. *Chulo* is Spanish for "gigolo," even if, according to Azucena, the words *Latin lover* and *Carlos Upstairs* should never be used in the same sentence. Unfortunately for Azucena she has, with this man my father calls *un chulo de mierda*, not one but *two* children, which makes sending him packing a little trickier than dialing a divorce lawyer.

One of the most insistent images I have of Azucena is her telling me at her thirtieth birthday party—champagne flute in one hand—that she was done with Carlos being upstairs. On that very special day, Carlos surprised family and friends by coming downstairs for the occasion and giving Azucena a very thoughtful, if unusual gift—a free liposuction, compliments of a plastic surgeon who happened to be a friend of his. Azucena finds it hard to believe that a man who hardly ever leaves the house can have so many devoted friends while she, who works at a trendy magazine downtown, has a hard time getting people to return her phone calls.

At any rate, ever since that prophetic birthday, the word *liposuction* cannot be uttered in front of Azucena. She's the only one who can bring it up, in fact. And then, strictly for the purpose of torturing herself. When she's not at work, my sister practices self-torture the way some women practice Pilates. As for me, after staying away for years and vowing never to return to the tropical paradise

2

where I was born, I flew in for the aforementioned birthday bash, which Azucena insisted on throwing for herself, although not without agonizing in the months leading up to it about whether it was or wasn't socially acceptable for a woman in Caracas to plan, pay for, and otherwise arrange the details of her own birthday party.

It is unfortunate, really, that despite all the advances in drilling oil from the Amazon, feminist rhetoric has still not found its own clearing in the jungle. In the end, what choice did my poor sister have? Carlos Upstairs routinely forgot her birthday. But even if he had been the kind of creature inspired by Hallmark moments, it wouldn't have made that much difference. My sister is one of those people whom everyone inevitably disappoints, no matter how hard they try.

She herself will tell you that "trying" is not the same as "achieving." (Perfection, that is). Thus, managing the details of this important milestone was a kind of insurance for her against disappointment. Had Azucena been familiar with the finer points of beating egg whites to soft peaks, she would have whipped her own birthday cake, I'm sure of it. But it's tough enough as it is to be a working mother with a penchant for perfection, so it fell to a *pâtissier* named Mozart to put the icing on the cake.

By that point in her marriage Azucena did not give a macaroon that Carlos Upstairs was within earshot when she told me she had had enough of him. As a matter of fact, she had started referring to him as "the sperm donor" in public. That's probably why all of us close to the situation thought it was only a matter of time before Carlos Upstairs became Carlos Outside.

"Does that mean you're finally going to leave him, Azucena *querida*?" I asked. That's when Azucena went mute. Holding an android stare in absolute silence until a person feels like solid waste is one of Azucena's specialties. When she finally did speak, it was to say, "Things are different when you have kids, Valentina."

So, rather than hiring a divorce lawyer to get rid of the extra weight, my sister did what any reasonable unhappily married woman would do. She cut a patch of her pubic hair and stuck it to her husband's favorite bar of soap. And she waited.

Did I mention that patience is one of my sister's virtues?

SHOPPING AS ECO-TOURISM

The secret to happiness, Emily *mi amor*, is to keep moving. So convinced am I of this that whenever I get to a place—say a bookstore or a restaurant—the first thing I do is to locate the nearest exit sign. I've always been wary of emotional landslides. It isn't your standard phobia, I realize, to be mortally afraid of bumping into someone you intensely dislike in the Romance corner of your local bookstore. And you just never know when a child with the face of a cherub will throw a tantrum at your favorite sushi restaurant. So I've found that the best way to survive these debacles is to know in advance where the exits are. "Cut your losses," is one of my favorite refrains.

I can't remember how many times I've moved since emigrating to this country, though I do remember moving after each divorce. I know you thought your dad was the first, *mi amor*. Unfortunately, he wasn't. But given what he has done, what else do I have to lose? Now I get to do the back and forth. I get to wonder if when we were having coffee that morning Max was telling me good-bye in his mind. He was sitting right where you are.

Azucena has always accused me of not taking marriage seriously. And, from her point of view, I suppose she's right. My little sister believes it's preferable to live under a state of siege in one's own home than to get a divorce.

Does any sane woman you know set out to move to another country, marry a series of losers, get a stepdaughter and a set of twins in the process, and go on to spend the rest of her days feeling like she's part reptile, part fish? These things just happen. And who has a crystal ball to see them coming? Sometimes when I wake up, even after all these years, I don't remember where I am until after I have my coffee. And there are days when I can hardly believe that my own life has turned out the way it has.

Do you remember the time when you won that prize for playing the violin? When the woman running the show asked you to

4

introduce your parents and you said, "That's my mother in the front and that's my stepmother in the back," I couldn't believe my ears. Step-what? I thought we were friends! "This is your chance, Valentina," I thought. "Run for the door." The reason I was sitting all the way in the back in the first place was that I'd planned my exit strategy, just as I told you I do. Why deny it anymore? Your mother has always been one of these potential emotional landslides. So I knew I had to be prepared for anything. Anything except "That's my stepmother in the back."

What possessed you to insult me this way? And on that day, of all days? Step-ladders, step-children—everyone knows that step-anything is bad news. Give me a good friend over a stepmother any day of the week. Who wants to go through life being a constant reminder of being forced to peel potatoes? You know that scene in *Cinderella* when the sisters are getting ready to go to the ball and the stepmother makes Cinderella stay behind to do kitchen work? Well, I can't say that that woman was ever someone I'd want to resemble. But the minute you unleashed the word *stepmother* in that tone full of affection, not only was I myself deeply confused—because I'd never imagined anyone loving me as a "stepmother"—but on top of that I thought your mother was going to get up and slug me!

I had been warned from the start that she was bipolar, given to sudden mood swings, possibly schizophrenic, more than likely borderline. I should have listened to my own mother, who is, after all, an expert in schizophrenia. Still, it doesn't take a Harvard degree to know that *bipolar* is one of those "terms of endearment" that people are still hurling at each other even after the divorce lawyers have made out like bandits and moved to Hawaii. Apparently, though, I was supposed to take some of the warnings about your mother seriously.

I still remember the day when I asked you for her phone number so that I could invite her out for a cup of coffee. "A cup of coffee with Mom? Ha-ha-ha. Naive Latina," you said. But if one can't even have a cup of coffee with the new wife to discuss the daughter, what is to be done about the real enemies? If the "enemy" is on the other side of the city, what to do, for instance, about all those people walking from Mecca to Medina? Bomb them, I guess.

When he was alive, your dad used to tell me that you were the only person in the world who could get me to do something I didn't want to do. I guess I was susceptible to smart little girls who use the word *naive* in conversation. That's how I ended up at that violin recital in the first place—because you asked me to go. I didn't know you were planning to drop the stepmother bomb in front of a hundred strangers and a probable borderline.

When I picked up your dad at the airport later that night and he asked me how your recital had gone, I barely let him finish the sentence. "She called me a stepmother in front of everyone, Max!"

"What?"

"You heard me."

It took me a while to get past the insult. Afterward, all I could think about was this: the day you called me a stepmother, you gave me a job. From that day forward my job was to try to sleep eight hours in a row without waking up in the middle of the night with the startling thought that I had an IRS dependent who liked maraschino cherries. All those years when we were just "friends," I slept through the night just fine. After you called me a stepmother, though, there simply wasn't enough Paxil to ease my step-maternal anxiety.

"What if her boyfriend breaks up with her, Max?"

"Valentina, Emily doesn't have a boyfriend."

"Fine, Max. But in the future! And what if she eats too many maraschino cherries? Did you know they've recently been linked to cancer?"

And do you remember the time you texted me to ask, "V-dog, what does it mean when u cant donate blood cuz u r a carrier?"

It made me yell out, "Max!!!!!!!!!!!!!! Emily might be a carrier!"

I can't remember exactly when or why you started calling me V-dog. Your dad insisted it was a teen's way of expressing love.

"Really, Max? Calling someone a dog? In my country, darling, the only *perros* are men who cheat on their wives."

That's when I started having nightmares. Well, maybe that's not entirely true. The day I really started having nightmares in earnest was the day after I set foot in this country. It's not the country's fault. Some repotted plants experience similar dislocation. Better soil. Bigger pot. Plenty of sunshine. But despite all that, they still suffer from the transfer.

How to forget, for instance, my first experience of eating a meal in a moving vehicle? Or what it was like to first set foot inside a place called Banana Republic? Everything was on sale! If you ask me, shopping as eco-tourism has not gotten its fair shake. It's only through this kind of exchange that one can have one's views of the world expanded. How else is a non-cognoscenti supposed to find out that government-sponsored death squads in Central America have their own flagship store in the Northern hemisphere?

I know what you're thinking: that I'm incapable of silence. I can't say I disagree. But that's why I've always suspected I might be adopted. My parents are practically deaf-mutes, and Azucena speaks only when the elegant insults she rehearses in her mind become too tempting to keep to herself.

My *tía* Zulay, my mother's sister, once told me I once jumped from my crib when I was a baby. Apparently, my parents had been trying to teach me restraint, so they locked the door to my room and let me cry myself purple. They claimed I was crying for attention. I was too young to argue. So I jumped out. *Tía* Zulay, a devout Catholic, says it's a miracle I'm still alive. But miracle or no miracle, the point is that I survived the jump from the crib. And in the same way, I survived the move across the Atlantic, the Darling Spuds, the Happy Meals, the "snack attacks," the strange notion of living without compromise, and the directive to never be without great coffee. The trick to surviving this country, *mi amor*, is to look at your own face in the mirror every morning and resist the temptation to hate yourself for turning into the person you swore you'd never become.

That's what happened to Azucena.

NEVER TRUST A MAN WHO WEARS
STRONG COLOGNE

It was the cologne that did it. Azucena met Carlos Upstairs during a winter break, which, if you ask me, was really a break from a near-nervous breakdown induced by culture shock after living in a place called Charlotte, North Carolina. I only have Azucena's word for it, but apparently Chapel Hill—the place where she was getting her MBA—was experiencing an upsurge in Arab migration at a time when Azucena's biological clock started ticking in earnest.

Now, Azucena has always been fond of expensive perfumes. But men wearing John Varvatos cologne to school—that was more than she could bear. She considered it just plain vulgar that the classroom where she was trying to study futures smelled like a boardroom in the United Arab Emirates. "Where are the Americans?" I asked, on more than one occasion. "Take it from me, Azucena *querida*, American men make great husbands, trained as they are to fold the laundry, to treat women the same way they treat men, and to mind their own business—that 'business' being sports."

But no one is a prophet in his own land, *mi amor.* American women themselves fantasize about Italian men who eat, pray, and love all day. To hear Azucena tell it, though, there were no Americans to be found in all of Charlotte, which means, in Azucena-speak, that there was no one in the MBA program who looked like Roger Federer or who wore linen suits to class. Yes, I know Roger is Swiss, of course. "Only Arabs and Chinese," said Azucena. "Oh, and there's this Greek guy whose name is Demosthenes," she sighed. "It's a small tragedy, Valentina. Who wants to move to Greece?"

"Who said anything about moving to Greece, Azucena?"

But that's how my sister thinks: that if you kiss a man, you have to marry him within the week. Slim pickings, then, when you considered both the language barrier and the cost of flying our entire family to either China or Greece. The Gulf region wasn't even an option.

To make matters worse, at twenty-five Azucena was still a virgin, which is why, whenever she called me to discuss curriculum choices, I told her that her priority should not be her grade-point average but to lose her virginity at her earliest convenience. You have to use subtlety with Azucena. Otherwise, she might take offense. Being the youngest, she always thinks people are trying to boss her around and to tell her what to do. Ever since I became aware of this paranoia of hers, I try to use the words "at your earliest convenience" when I'm telling her what to do. It never works.

We couldn't be more different—both inside and out. The lovely Azucena has the kind of virginal complexion often vilified by the makers of Hawaiian Tropic. As for me, maintaining a seamless tan has always been a priority. Speaking of virginity, I can't fathom how Azucena came to be in such a predicament at twenty-five. The only reasonable explanation for my sister's dormant hymen is that while we were growing up, our mother instilled a number of fears in both of us, fears that I overcame by moving abroad as soon as I was of fleeing age, and that Azucena is now passing on to her children as one does family heirlooms.

The list of fears includes, but is not limited to: roller coasters, swimming, gonorrhea, the mall, bicycles, and animals, dogs in particular. After years of living in the States, though, I no longer believe that I will be paralyzed at the amusement park, drown in a swimming pool, or die from gonorrhea for kissing a stranger. But some fears are more difficult to eradicate than others. Being murdered at the mall, for instance, is not just another random trauma passed on by a neurotic mother but a daily reality in Caracas. Just last week my mother called to tell me that while she and my *tía* Lula were at a mall called El San Ignacio, two gunmen killed a young woman for her miniskirt, in full view of other shoppers. My mother took care to point out that the miniskirt was genuine leather. What to say about the Miniskirt Murder? One might say that leather sells well in the secondary market in Third World countries. Or that these were no ordinary killers, but killers who can tell leather from pleather. And what of the incorrigible Catholicism—the fact that even malls are named for saints. Despite that, where was Saint Ignacio while an innocent girl was murdered at his mall?

The fear of bicycles is something else altogether. I'm positive I would die from a head injury were I to learn to ride a bike. As for Azucena, she has expanded on my mother's list of fears, which now includes donating blood, among other barbarities. But what I find truly amazing is how my sister managed to lose her virginity without our entire family having to attend a wedding in Athens. The wedding we ultimately attended is the one that led to a clean bar of soap being soiled with pubic hair as a way of getting revenge for the unwelcome mention of the word *liposuction*. On more than one occasion during my sister's marriage to Carlos Upstairs my mother has wished aloud that Azucena had married the Greek with the bleeding penis instead.

PLAYING WITH LEGOS

Let's take my husbands in the order in which they were received. The first one was named Jean-Pierre Joste. It's not as exotic as it sounds. But I will admit that when I first met him, his name sounded like an exotic alliteration of sorts. Everything about him, in fact, seemed exotic. That's how it usually is before you meet the mother.

On first acquaintance, Jean-Pierre's mother, Philomène, seemed poised. She turned out to be a narcoleptic. Jean-Pierre's sister, Chantal, seemed chic. Come to think of it, Chantal *was* chic. She smoked Belmont cigarillos and draped scarves in interesting patterns around every part of her body—her head, her waist, her hips. She was also narcissistic. And by this I don't just mean Chantal's excessive admiration of herself in mirrors, though there was that, too.

As for his father, Monsieur Gérard Joste, when Jean-Pierre and I announced we were moving to the United States, he just stared at the wall, puffed hard on his cigar, and said, "*Américaines* ahrr babies." "What is *that* supposed to mean?" I wanted to ask. But I was only eighteen at the time, which means I listened to what my elders said and rolled the pair of secret eyes hidden in the back of my head.

More importantly, though, my only objective after living under the same roof with the narcoleptic, the narcissist, and the Francophile, who suffered bouts of involuntary urination, was to get to the airport. It didn't matter where I moved. I would have moved to Bhopal at that point. But we didn't move to Bhopal, *mi amor.* We moved to Melbourne. No, not Melbourne, Australia. I wish. We moved to Melbourne, Florida—population sixty thousand. I'm sure it has grown since then.

The move was supposed to be temporary. But isn't that the problem with life? You think something is temporary and all of a sudden you're shopping for tombstones. What to say about Melbourne? The place was named after its first postmaster, an Englishman who had spent much time in the real Melbourne, the one in Australia. The two things I remember about Melbourne are that I

11

had never seen so many oranges and that it was within driving distance from Epcot and Disney World. After a few weeks in Melbourne, eager for a horizon expansion, I finally convinced Jean-Pierre to go to Epcot one weekend. I was hoping for a *"Mais oui, ma chérie."* I got a sneer, instead. That should have been a warning sign. Come to think of it, it was a warning sign. But what newlywed actually bothers to read a sign that reads D I V O R C E during the honeymoon?

Our day at the amusement park was far from amusing. After getting our hands stamped with invisible ink I headed straight to the information booth, where there was a girl who looked like a living doll. When I asked her what "EPCOT" meant, her face became instantly animated. It was her job to hand out brochures and to repeat in the chipper voice of a cheerleader, "Experimental-Prototype-Community-of-Tomorrow-have-a-nice-day!" I had to take Jean-Pierre away so he wouldn't burn the girl's tongue with his cigarette. In the end, the overeager Disney girl turned out to be the least of our problems. The fact that Disney's rendition of Europe could be walked in all of fifteen minutes simply depressed Jean-Pierre.

I didn't yet know what depression was, but after our weekend at Epcot, Jean-Pierre got seriously, clinically depressed. And as everyone knows, the only cure for depression of the clinical variety is to have an affair. *Oui. Oui.*

The other problem we encountered that day was that we had a perfect crêpe Suzette, and that I made the mistake of praising it as the best crêpe I had ever had. For some reason this got the best of Jean-Pierre, who dispatched a swift *"Merde"* and called me "an ignorant *señorita*," upper-lip quivering included. I hadn't yet learned to leave well enough alone, so I told him that just because we had to eat the crêpe standing up and it was served on a plastic plate didn't necessarily mean that it was a bad crêpe. But to say, "I've been to Paris," is not the same thing as, "I was born in Paris." Is it?

Still, I remember being very impressed that day. No, not with a sugary pancake served on a plastic plate. I'm not that easily won over. Think about it: to build a Lego-set model of half of Europe in your backyard and to charge Europeans to come see it! Isn't that brilliant? Well, Jean-Pierre didn't think so. That weekend at Epcot pretty much sealed our *au revoir* to Melbourne. A few months later we were living in New Orleans. Or as Jean-Pierre called it, "Nu Orléans."

NOT ALL GREEK GODS
ARE CREATED EQUAL

The day Azucena finally decided to part with her virginity, she ended up at a hospital in Charlotte, North Carolina—in the ER, no less.

There comes a time during adulthood when it's all right to regain consciousness, if only to say, "I am no longer a child." But how many people actually make an effort to put those lowly years behind them? Certainly not Azucena. You see, Azucena was born anemic. And the simple fact that she was a little low on hemoglobin for two weeks during the first year of her life completely defined her.

For starters, due to the anemia, my parents made a number of concessions that ensured that every perverse, childish, or thoughtless act on Azucena's part would always have a built-in answer. "Mamá, how come Azucena doesn't have to go to Grandma's house on the weekends?" "She was born anemic, Valentina." "Mamá, why does Azucena sit around all day reading Oscar Wilde?" "She was born anemic, Valentina. Leave your poor sister alone." "Mamá, how come no one can say the word *shit* in front of Azucena?" "Because, Valentina, she might have a relapse."

Apropos of relapses, I once made the mistake of buying Azucena a second cup of coffee. I was experiencing the rare pleasure of a two-sided conversation with my sister and it occurred to me to prolong the occasion with a second cup of Java. Imagine my surprise when, after a mere sip, Azucena announced, each pupil the size of a nickel, "The anemia is back."

"What do you mean the anemia is back?"

"I'm feeling light-headed, Valentina."

"It's the caffeine, silly. Trust me on this. I have two American-size lattes every morning; your body gets used to it."

Odd as this might seem, the exact same thing happens when Azucena comes within breathing distance of a guy who gets her going. Whenever her heart rate goes up, and she feels light-headed or short of breath, her first thought is, "The anemia is back!" In order to avoid complications, Azucena tries to steer clear of guys who quicken her pulse, lest they give her a heart attack—a symptom of anemia.

So how did Demosthenes the Greek get through Azucena's anemia screen? Well, for starters, he didn't wear John Varvatos cologne to class. Secondly, he didn't cause Azucena to be short of breath, which is another way of saying that Demosthenes did nothing for her. As a matter of fact, after the inauspicious visit to the ER, Azucena confessed that the reason she had selected Demosthenes to "do the deed" was that she felt nothing for him. She found him a little repulsive, as a matter of fact. Don't all women surrender their hymen to men they find repulsive? I thought so.

I should also mention that because she was born anemic, my sister has always had a somewhat pale complexion. This has only compounded her sexual problems in the sense that whether Azucena is in a state of virginity or not, she always looks like a virgin. And, as some people of the opposite sex have been kind enough to point out, the porcelain skin framed by the long, black hair, makes her seem untouchable, something of a deity.

Whenever Azucena bemoans that rather than ripping her clothes off, men are moved to pray to her instead, I've always been quick to remind her that it could be worse. She could live in my skin, for instance. Whether I'm quoting from Kant's *Critique of Pure Reason* or discussing the thinkers of the Enlightenment, men are convinced that my one lonely thought is to unzip their pants and get on my knees. Albeit not to pray. I don't think Azucena realizes how frustrating it is to constantly try to explain that Kant is not a sexual slur. I'd much rather have men prostrated at *my* feet.

But if there is a way in which Azucena does *not* resemble a virgin, it is in the fact that she has no mercy. My sister is quick to point out that my predicament is wholly self-inflicted; that when shirts are missing sleeves and buttons, men can't help but get the wrong message.

"Really, Azucena? Since when do men need any assistance in thinking the wrong thing?"

At this, her expression turns ever more judgmental as she proceeds to accuse me of playing a hand in my own objectification. Indeed, even before the objectification of women as a cause had a full-time congresswoman in Washington, D.C., Azucena sneered at women who favor satin over cotton.

What really happened on the night when she decided to offer her virginity to Demosthenes the Greek was that Azucena was wearing Fruit of the Loom panties, which is another way of saying that there was no rapid heart rate, not even an anemic heart murmur, on either of their parts. The fact that there were no Victoria's Secret tags anywhere in the room is one of the reasons Azucena and Demosthenes the Greek ended up in the emergency room in the first place. Everything was as dry as a pumice stone.

As luck would have it, Demosthenes turned out to be a virgin as well, though he hadn't bothered to mention it. Surprise, surprise! I guess no man with a head on his shoulders would start an otherwise promising evening owning up to a shortcoming with his "little head." So when Azucena called me from the hospital to tell me that Demosthenes' penis would not stop bleeding and that he might die from a hemorrhage, I had to put her on hold so I could recover.

But that was hardly what was bothering her. Owing to our respectable upbringing—and before the intern in the emergency room had a chance to explain Demosthenes' "condition"—it had crossed Azucena's mind that either she or her Greek god might have gonorrhea. Going to class the next day to discuss macroeconomic theory with a guy whose penis you caused to rupture the night before had to have been a little sticky. That's why when a few months later Azucena met Carlos—not yet Upstairs—at a cocktail party in Caracas where men were wearing tuxedos and holding champagne flutes, the bubbles got to her head. She had returned to civilization, at last.

BRAINS AND TESTICLES—NOT
NECESSARILY IN THAT ORDER

Moving to another country to save your marriage is like getting pregnant to save your marriage. By the time you finish painting the walls in that pukey baby-yellow, you're still unhappy, and now you have a baby and the stretch marks to prove that you do, indeed, have the brains of a primate.

New Orleans might be the worst mistake I've ever made. But it's too early for such sweeping statements. Sometimes all a woman needs is a little time so she can outdo herself. And New Orleans itself has much to recommend it besides. It isn't all reptiles and hurricanes, as they make you believe on TV. There's Mardi Gras. There's Jazz Fest. And there were the Saints, always marching in. There was also, of course, Café du Monde on Decatur Street.

Jean-Pierre did admit that the beignets from Café du Monde were the genuine article, even if he thought the French spoken in South Louisiana should have been reported to The Hague. Two things to know about the French, *mi amor*: the bit about their being good lovers is pure marketing, and the bit about their being aloof is propaganda. Neither is true. What the French are is discerning. Jean-Pierre knew his crêpes and his beignets. He was a frustrated Toulouse-Lautrec, a wannabe poster maker, so he became a food snob. See the connection? I don't either. I can't tell you how many restaurants we left with Jean-Pierre shutting his eyelids as if someone close to him had died, and saying, "You can't call this Soupe a l'Oignon. You can't call this Crème Brûlée." On and on he went.

As you know by now, *mi amor*, your step*madre* can't even boil water. How can I be fond of the kitchen when my own mother used the refrigerator merely to store her perfumes? Not Jean-Pierre. His idea of a honeymoon involved going shopping for offal—brains, testicles, tripe, that sort of thing. Our fridge always contained something or other that had been alive quite recently. And I'm afraid that after finding a cow's tongue or coiled tripe in the fridge, when all you wanted was the cow's milk, it's easy to lose your appetite. Let's say I have a slightly different take on French food than most people. Don't get me wrong. We all owe a bow to Pommes Frites. Your very own McDonald's has turned French fries into a national symbol of culinary excellence. If you ask me, the good people of Michelin ought to award McDonald's a star or two.

Jean-Pierre's dream was to move back to Paris one day and to open a bistro inside an art gallery. It wasn't the worst idea I had ever heard. The bistro would be called—what else?— Jean-Pierre's. My mother always thought he had a bit of an ego. Maybe, maybe not. Many restaurants in the world are named after the people who own them. And drugstores, too, like Walgreens, for instance. I think Mr. Walgreens' first name was Charles.

When it comes right down to it, though, isn't that the curse of divorce? A name that once sounded to you like poetry now sounds like a racial slur. The clothes you once called "bohemian chic" now make you think you married a careless slob.

That's exactly what happened with Jean-Pierre. Once I'd translated Jean to John, I thought, "What's so glamorous about John? I mean, other than the fact that John is one of the characters in the book with the largest circulation ever." And once the name Jean-Pierre Joste became part of a once-upon-a-time nightmare, when I translated his name further into Spanish, I said to myself, "*Chica tonta*, his name is Juan! So is the name of every Mexican *carnicero* in the United States."

I don't think you realize the gravity of that realization. To see yourself for the fool you are is never a reassuring feeling. So, Juan was the first one. For the sake of moving on, it's better for me to remember him that way. Because, let's admit it really fast, there's something very romantic about the French. You've read your Flaubert. I remember giving it to you. Who else but a Frenchman can make you pine for a stuffed parrot the way Flaubert did in his little book about a simple heart? *¡Por favor!*

NO PLACE LIKE HOME
(EXCEPT FOR THE HOLIDAYS)

After the parlor fiasco with Demosthenes the Greek, Azucena went home for the holidays. I can't remember why I didn't go home that year. Maybe it was because at that point I was confused as to where home was. But I was pretty sure it wasn't a place where you might get murdered at the mall for wearing a leather mini. Who says civilization isn't catching? In less than a fashion season I was afraid of leaving U.S. territory. The irony is that I had once called those types of people "provincial." The point is that it was during the Christmas I failed to go home when Azucena met Carlos Upstairs. He wasn't upstairs yet. And he didn't yet own a Game Boy. At some point or another all of us in the family have wondered what attracted Azucena to *el chulo de mierda*. On that matter, at least, our family has been able to reach consensus. Carlos Upstairs was tall. Carlos Upstairs was handsome. Carlos Upstairs liked sushi. He was also partial to expensive bars of soap.

The following spring Azucena got her MBA. My parents and I flew to Charlotte for the occasion. I can't remember whom I was married to at the time. It is possible that I was single again. I don't remember anyone sitting across the table from me to whom I could express the full extent of my surprise when Azucena said during dinner that she was engaged to be married. What? When? How? She delivered the news in the same tone one might ask, "Do you have any Advil in your purse?" We didn't yet know that the man Azucena was going to marry had read and mastered a book called *The Importance of Being Idle*.

DIGS LUSTILY INTO LARD

Besides the image of my friend Cecilia on top of Jean-Pierre in my bed, what comes to mind when I remember New Orleans is the rain, the alligators, and the forty pounds I gained from eating beignets at Café du Monde once it started to sink in that I was a fugitive lost in a swamp. If anyone tells you it is possible to hide your unhappiness beneath forty pounds of fried dough and sugar, you need to trust that person. Only my mother has what it takes to dismiss so round a truth.

The plan had been to go to Melbourne in Florida, learn English, return home, have babies, and die. So when I enrolled at Tulane instead, my mother, in particular, began to doubt I would follow the little plan she had secretly outlined for my life. The final blow came when she saw me at the airport in Caracas sporting my forty new pounds. I think that finished her. She walked straight past me as one suffering from aphasia. I'm as tall as it gets for a girl. There's no way she didn't see me. But my mother is the kind of person who believes that if you avert your eyes when you see something unpleasant, then the thing didn't happen. I've met other people who think that way, too, that if you look past a beggar, for instance, then poverty does not exist.

That particular Christmas wasn't exactly what the Three Wise Men had in mind. The Three Wise Men are big in South America, except we don't call them "wise." We call them *los Tres Reyes Magos*—the three king magicians. We may be cross-bearing Catholics *in saecula saeculorum*, but we're open to the possibility that Caspar, Melchior, and Balthazar were not wise at all. There's a lot of Barnum & Bailey in the Bible, *mi amor*. The truth is that nobody knows who these men were. The "wise men" were a sect called the Magi and traveled in groups of thirty. The only reason people think there were only three of them is because only three gifts were offered—gold, frankincense, and myrrh. But you were raised under that "no proselytizing" clause in your parents' divorce decree, so you probably don't even know where Bethlehem is, who Jesus was, or why that matters.

In any case, despite the obvious Darwinian advantages, there's a price to pay for adaptation of any kind, which is to say that after speaking English almost exclusively for two years and getting consistent migraines as a result, my Spanish started to suffer. I'd be in mid-sentence, trying to say something and I'd go, "What's the word for 'umbrella' in Spanish?" My father thought I was being ridiculous. And in order to teach me a lesson he gave me a Spanish dictionary from the Academia de La Lengua as a Christmas present that year. That's also when he started calling me "our *gringa*." He simply couldn't grasp what it was like to have these foreign bullets being fired inside my ears from the moment I set foot outside until the moment I came home, where I'd find Jean-Pierre blowing smoke out of his mouth, ready to correct my comatose French.

Speaking of Jean-Pierre, he insisted on staying in New Orleans that Christmas . . . all by himself. At first, I was disappointed to be going home alone. But the mere thought of watching him puff on one Gauloise after another while my mother fluttered her hands in the air as if she were fending off a bat infestation, was enough to tell myself, "Let him stay in Nu Orléans and listen to Aznavour as if he's terminal with something." You have to wonder about a man whose favorite song is *"C'est Fini."*

That Christmas has gone down in memory as "the Ghost of Christmas Odd"—my husband in New Orleans in bed with my best friend, my father calling me "our *gringa*," and my mother materializing in the kitchen out of nowhere to say, "Gaining forty pounds is inexcusable, Valentina." It may sound strange, but when it comes to certain rights, a South American mother has her North American counterpart beat. She can, for instance, search for *and* read your secret diary; she can go through your closet and throw away any clothes she doesn't like; she can give you unwelcome advice on any subject in front of your friends; she can talk to your boyfriend behind your back and tell him he's not what *she* had in mind for you; she can choose the food you will eat and veto any classes you might want to take in college, and she can do so on any grounds. And once you marry, she can show up at your home, unannounced, and stay for an unspecified period of time. She also has the right to pick the name for your first-born, no matter what you and your husband have already decided.

It's a little different than growing up a measly hemisphere over, where your mother might have seen the syringes in your room, but she'd first have to consult a lawyer to see if it's all right to bring up the matter with you because the mere insinuation that you might be a heroin addict might infringe on one or more of your constitutional rights.

You can see how your calling me your "stepmother" at your violin recital that time gave me pause. Now I was going to have to start reading your diary, going through your personal belongings, and phoning your boyfriend behind your back. That the word *privacy* has no meaning whatsoever to a Latin mother should come as no surprise. But it does explain why closing my bedroom door during that ill-fated Christmas after taking a shower was such a big mistake. The fact that by then I had been married for two and half years and that I had lived abroad for most of that time did not hold any water with my mother. It wouldn't have done to say, "Mother, I've seen a condom. Don't you think I have the right to some privacy?"

She might have laughed. And then she would have said, in the tone of a serial killer, "You are still *my* daughter, Valentina." No matter what anyone tells you, South American daughters are the sole possession of the mother—something akin to state property.

I still had a hand on the door handle and a towel wrapped around my body when my mother pushed the door open, put a little pressure on the doorstop with her foot, and said, "I will not let you disrespect me in me in my own home, Valentina." A cold shower in the Tropics, if there ever was one! This happened many years before I met you, *mi amor*. Still, I can't help but wonder what my mother would have done that day you went into your room with that boy whose name only you knew and shut the door behind you. She would have called 911, I'm sure of it.

A doorstop buried into the carpet in Caracas means what it means. In my case it meant that the door to my room was to remain open for the remainder of my stay, another two weeks. I thought I had landed on Pluto after a stopover on Uranus. The only thing I still recognized was the furniture. It was scarier than Hitchcock looking you in the eye and saying, "All breasts must fall." Can you blame me for wanting to return to New Orleans a little earlier than I was supposed to?

From time to time I wonder how my life would have turned out had I been willing to negotiate with my mother about the doorstop.

But no one will ever accuse me of being a negotiator. And besides, I have this thing about exit signs. When I have the urge to leave, nothing can stop me. I'd even jump from my crib if necessary.

THE CREATOR'S MISCARRIAGE: OR, MORE SPECIFICALLY—*UN CHULO DE MIERDA*

It is true that Carlos Upstairs has done everything in his power to earn the nickname my father gave him. But what does it matter? The rest of the world seems to be infatuated with the guy. What everyone, absolutely everyone, likes about him—particularly women, children, and valets—is the fact that he is such an *admirador*. I think the closest expression in English to describe Carlos Upstairs might be "ass-kisser." What happens when you are in his presence is something very close to magic. You might be stupid, ridiculous, or missing a few teeth, but for the duration of your time with Carlos Upstairs, you feel special. Carlos Upstairs has that *je ne sais quoi* that the nuns at the Catholic school where I was "enlightened" called "a gift from the Lord." If Azucena, the untouchable, is the ultimate outsider, Carlos Upstairs is her exact opposite—very accessible, the consummate insider.

Take, for instance, the time we all went on vacation to some island or other and I asked Carlos Upstairs if he liked sailing. All I had to do was ask him the question. The next thing you know we're on a sailboat. For one, it wouldn't be Carlos Upstairs who would admit that he had never even seen a sailboat except on television. As for me, I deserved what I had coming for being such an empath. After learning that he was studying to be a maritime lawyer I thought I'd talk boats with him. Unfortunately for both of us, I had never been on a sailboat either. After several failed attempts to fight the angry winds and the rising tide, and nearly drowning in the middle of the ocean as a result, my mother called him evil. Azucena called him a liar. To be fair, he had never actually said he had been on a sailboat. He had just said, "What a great idea!"

I'm pretty sure Carlos Upstairs hates canned sardines. I'm also positive that if anyone were to offer him some—after swallowing a little bone or two—he'd say something along the lines of, "Hey, these sure are different! Where did you learn to eat these?" By way of contrast, if anyone is ever brave enough to put anything fishy under my sister's discerning nose, it's almost a cinch she'll turn pale. She was born anemic, after all. And therefore, feeling like scum is something many people report when in her presence. Meanwhile, all it takes is for Carlos Upstairs to show up anywhere—a tennis club, a restaurant, it doesn't matter where—for people to flock to him. He himself can't tell a joke to save his life. But in a world where everyone is starved for a little attention, Carlos Upstairs is happy to laugh at other people's jokes.

And it is because of this quality—which, I might add, caused Azucena to fall in love with him—that Carlos Upstairs can get just about anything he wants from just about anybody. His three aunts— a group of women Azucena has always referred to as *las tres tías*—still did his laundry for the first couple of years of their marriage. Because Azucena worked and was always rushed, she had little time for starching things. And as anyone who is anyone knows, starched shirts are de rigueur for would-be attorneys at law. So once a week Carlos Upstairs made the effort to go downstairs to collect his dirty laundry and take it to his *tías*, three spinsters who simply could not get over the fact their nephew had married someone like Azucena—a woman who insisted on leaving their poor baby alone all day pining for baked *plátanos* while she selfishly went to work to bring home the bacon.

All told, Azucena has been a big disappointment to the Contreras family. What with her MBA and flamboyant ideas about equality, my little sister has brought disgrace to their great name.

BY THE TIME HE WAS ERECT . . .

Azucena's wedding was memorable for so many reasons. But two things in particular pop out of my scattered memory for their peculiarity. The first one is that as my father was about to deposit the lovely Azucena into the arms of her future husband, Carlos Upstairs whispered something to the priest and disappeared. The groom's untimely departure caused a chorus of hushed voices to echo throughout the sacred walls of Santa Capilla. Even the good Padre Solano excused himself a couple of times to test the sacramental wine behind the altar. I was the *madrina* for their wedding, so I had a front row seat from which to better observe the comings and goings of very cold feet, and to hear the charitable murmurs of horror-stricken socialites. As for the bride, I've always admired Azucena's incredible capacity to channel the Mona Lisa in times of duress. It's difficult to predict what one might be inclined to do in a similar situation, but I'm pretty sure I wouldn't have smiled impassively at the statue of Christ in full view of two hundred gossiping souls the way Azucena did. In the end, it turned out to be nothing more than a case of bowels moving in the wrong place at the wrong time. But still, what bride do you know who wants to hold a sweaty palm in her virginal hand?

The second odd thing that happened that day is that a group of strapping young men showed up at the reception carrying small boxes that all turned out to be soap. Never mind about the soap, the offense was so much greater than that. Who would be so crass as to carry a wedding gift into a place like the Caracas Country Club? Azucena was dismayed. After observing the inexcusable faux pas with her Mona Lisa eyes, she pulled me aside to a little corner hidden from scrutinizing country club stares to say, "Can you believe this? Why did I bother to register us at Iskia?" As befits an MBA-carrying bride marrying a man who one day might become an attorney-at-law, Azucena registered at Iskia, an upscale establishment which, were it

25

not located inside a Third World mall where murder is the *plate du jour*, would most certainly belong on New York's Fifth Avenue.

But perhaps the worst calamity of all was that by then the maid of honor had been living abroad for too long, that is to say, I had completely forgotten that carrying a gift in one's hands to a country club wedding is "unconstitutional." Acclimation elsewhere and the accretion of strange beliefs made it impossible for me to feel my sister's pain. I doubt Azucena would survive watching me bite into a burrito in the company of sweaty construction workers sporting tool belts at a place called Chipotle, where forgoing utensils and eating Tarzan-style are part of the dining experience. In the end, I failed to be sufficiently distraught for Azucena's taste. When instead, I asked, "Why soap?," she shook her head ever so slowly and said, "You can be so trivial sometimes, Valentina."

It turned out there was an explanation for the bars of soap— even if it would not come until after the wedding. What was more certain on that day was that Carlos Upstairs had a wealth of striking, if ill-mannered friends and that all of them possessed a great sense of humor, a quality that Azucena had praised during their rushed courtship but that at some point during their marriage caused her to start calling her husband "an indiscriminate wanker." In all her life Azucena has very much admired the English, going so far as to refuse to share her stitched-leather copy of *The Importance of Being Earnest*. But unlike the protagonist in the trivial comedy for serious people, thus far Azucena has been unable to escape the burdensome obligations of marriage.

GETTING TAPEWORM WILL GET YOU FIRED

Growing up, I had a hamster. His name was Pablo. He wasn't any ordinary rodent; he was a hard-won hamster. It wasn't Pablo's fault that he came to our house carrying so much baggage.

My mother, having obtained her degree as a psychotherapist, went on to do a specialty in schizophrenia. I don't know all the particulars involved, but I do remember visiting the lab at the university where she was doing the equivalent of an internship on the subject. Mostly, I remember the rats. They were absolutely gorgeous and they were drinking milk. Their bodies were covered with soft, white fur and their tiny noses looked like pomegranate seeds. It was only natural that I should want to take one of these live stuffed animals home. My mother should never have taken me to visit those beautiful rats. The only reason she did was that my dad was in Germany at the time, and Mecha, our maid, had been fired for getting a tapeworm. It wasn't Mecha's fault that a three-foot worm decided to roll up cozily around her intestines. All the same, my mother couldn't bear it. Being a single mother for a week, she had no choice but to take me to work with her. I never knew why Azucena wasn't with us. Maybe it had to do with her being anemic.

In any case, after a day at the lab, there was no forgetting the furry rodents suckling milk out of little straws. I wanted one. When I got home that night and told little Azucena about the rats, she said, nearly vomit-stricken, *"Cochina*, get out of my room." Capable of calling her big sister a pig at the tender age of eight, little Azucena would grow up to send chills up other people's spines. I find it mystifying that two people can grow up in the same household yet experience completely different realities, remember different childhoods even.

After my father returned from his business trip in Germany, I waited a day before I began lobbying for my own rat. My mother would not hear of it. And this I know not because she said anything along the lines of, "Valentina, a rat is out of the question." My mother has never favored the overt. Whenever she hears something crass or unpleasant, she kindly changes the subject. She herself was raised by two elegant people of very small gestures. As a result, our childhood was shrouded in mystery.

Neither Azucena nor I ever heard our parents argue. The way the shit hit the fan at our house was that my mother would press her lips together—so tightly you were afraid they might bleed—and then she'd say, "Reynaldo, we have to talk." At this, my father would follow her into the study, where the door would remain locked for hours on end. Nothing ever rose beyond the level of a whisper in the study except the words, *"Por favor,* Reynaldo." Sometimes I pressed my ears against the door, hoping to hear something horrible, or at least remotely interesting. That's how I heard my father say, *"Valentina es sólo una niña,"* arguing on my behalf, telling my mother that I was only a child and that it was natural that I should want a pet. That's when my mother said, *"Por favor,* Reynaldo," and unlocked the study door all of a sudden, causing me to dash to Azucena's room. Mercifully, my sister's room was next to the study and Azucena wasn't there. Otherwise, I would have gone down in history as a pig *and* a snoop.

GROOMING A *CHULO*

On the day of Azucena's wedding my mother found it strange that instead of the eight musicians she had hired, only four showed up to play at the reception. A different kind of woman might have been open to the possibility of a misunderstanding. But a scrupulous psychotherapist who knew how many rats were caged in the lab where she was studying schizophrenia is nothing if not precise in her instructions. She'd said eight, not four. So after the last crumb of wedding cake had been eaten, and once the newlyweds were in the Bahamas, she called the manager at the entertainment company to discuss the musician shortage.

That is how she learned that a few days before the wedding the groom had showed up at the very place to request a smaller band, as well as a partial refund. In fact, the man who answered the phone remembered Carlos Upstairs so well he even praised my mother for having such a charming and generous son-in-law. "Your daughter is so lucky, *señora!*" It turned out Carlos Upstairs had tipped the man for his trouble.

"Excuse me? That wasn't his money you refunded, *señor*. It was mine." Azucena was still on her honeymoon when my father started calling his new son-in-law *un chulo de mierda*.

AN INCITEMENT TO FREEDOM

In time I got my hamster. I will never forget the day my father took me to the pet store. Pablo and I found each other right away. He had kind eyes, and his fur was the color of warm caramel. My mother never agreed to Pablo. It's not like she said, "You can have a hamster, on one condition . . . ." It was more like, "If a hamster wants to rent a room at our five-star hotel, he must abide by our rules." The rules were that Pablo must live inside this plastic globe, where he had no choice but to run in circles all day. I don't know if hamsters get headaches. But watching Pablo rolling inside the miserable globe was enough to give me one. On my mother's directive—lest we all get infected with the bubonic plague and die—every few days I had to let Pablo out of the globe and clean it with Clorox. That is why, *mi amor*, to this day I keep two bottles of Clorox under the kitchen sink. That is also why I don't consider anything to be really clean until I have Cloroxed it. Pablo was the beginning of a lifelong affair with verbs that find their roots in cleaning fluids. "Have you 409'd the toilet? Have you Windexed the windows, Valentina?"

It doesn't take a neurologist to figure out that Pablo got tired of going around in circles inside a plastic cage. So one day, as I took him out to Clorox the globe where he lived, Pablo scurried out of my grip and scuttled as fast as he could toward the top of the stairs. He contemplated it for a few seconds, his hamster suicide. But when Pablo realized that this was his last chance, that if he didn't jump off the banister at that moment he'd have to go back inside the globe to the dizzying smell of Clorox, he made a decision that put an end to his life and to any desire on my part to have a pet ever again. It wasn't until I met you and the twins, that memories of Pablo came back with a vengeance.

Do I think that's what happened to your dad?

Ay, Dios, mi amor . . . Who can say what was going through your dad's head that day? *Sólo Dios sabe.* Only God knows what really happened. And your mom, of course. I wish I knew why she refuses to talk.

CRUCIBLES OF PASSION—MARRIAGE AS A TORTURE DEVICE

Marriage is such a great lab for the incubation of eccentric behavior, isn't it? Learn the other person's phobias and passions. Store them in your memory for future use. And you have all the ingredients for homemade Abu Ghraib. Carlos Upstairs had a thing for soap. Azucena made a note of it. In the end, his love of soap almost cost him his Game Boy.

Azucena herself has always been partial to liquid soap. Both Azucena and I have always been wary of things that can be potentially infectious. Real soap, as we all know, is a sponge for bacteria, bodily fluids, and pubic hair. And let's face it—marriage isn't a solid enough institution to change any ingrained beliefs about soap, or to correct any flaws from the factory. Everyone knows that a marriage is an idyllic paradise where two people go to have fun together, not some sort of reeducation camp where people are trained to go from obstinate bitch to sweetly accommodating. To think that signing a piece of paper can effect such changes of character is to be, at best, naive. And Azucena cannot be accused of being naive.

So what did Carlos Upstairs do when he came across the patch of black curls on his favorite bar of soap? I still find it hard to believe that the trial of pubic matters at my sister's house would be the thing to bring the solid institution of marriage to its knees.

THE BIG SLEAZY

The image of Cecilia on top of Jean-Pierre was enough to make me reach for a copy of *Sybil.* Not too long afterward I shortened my name to Val. But no split-personality disorder can be complete without the requisite hairstyle. To match the new name, I went to a hairdresser in the French Quarter and asked him to dye my black hair the color of fresh cranberries. It was he who referred me to the optometrist with the catchy slogan: "If you don't see what you're looking for, you've come to the right place." The blue contacts were all I needed to ensure that Valentina Viloria remained the passport impostor she was.

Why didn't I see it before? Messy red hair and seductive blue eyes—is that a Swedish model strolling down Poydras Street? As for the Joste, I kept it because it was short and because it was something of a neutral name. Sometimes, all you need is a shorter name that melts easily inside a melting pot. And even if anyone were to place the name's etymology as French, so much the better. The French have an unimpeachable brand. Mention the word *French* and two images immediately come to mind: the Eiffel Tower and a warm croissant. That's not the case with a name like Chávez, for instance, which immediately places you as a first-rate *tonto* in a Third World country. And with a damning Spanish accent to set you back! And besides, Joste wasn't my real name, so I wasn't emotionally attached to it. If anyone ever said they liked it, my first thought was, "That's like praising breast implants." In a couple of years I would have another name. And then another. I don't think any of the names I've had in this country actually suit me. Mostly, the name changes have been tough on the IRS, although I have to admit that filling out job applications is by far the worst. There's a little space where potential employers ask you to list other names you have used. Well, let me tell you, there's never enough room to explain everything that's happened. But at least my name isn't Cecilia.

Did I mention Cecilia was from Bolivia? Such an ordinary name, really. Well, it was ordinary until I heard Jean-Pierre calling her Cécile. My antennae should have gone up when I introduced them. Jean-Pierre kissed her hand and Cecilia blushed. *¡Por favor!* Here was this insipid woman from a country whose claim to fame is that its people powder their noses, blushing because a guy named Juan kissed her hand. *¡Qué ridiculez!* I should have never brought Cecilia home.

My mother disagrees. She thinks Cecilia was put on my path by the Holy Spirit. Because thanks to Cecilia, my mother no longer had to abide the Gauloise-sucking creature who corrupted her daughter to the point of making her believe that smoking was chic. But my mother had weightier reasons for disliking Jean-Pierre. Apparently, her father died of lung cancer when she was a teenager. And I say apparently because after what happened with Jean-Pierre and the Bolivian hussy, my trust thermometer was shattered for good. Never again could I get an accurate reading on anything. And ever since, I've been using the word *apparently*, a bit excessively perhaps.

Say someone tells me, "Zebras are not horses with stripes." I reply, "Apparently, Zebras are not horses with stripes." "Soybeans prevent cancer, a study proves." And I say, "Apparently, soybeans prevent cancer." "Angelina Jolie is a peace ambassador." And I say, "Really?"

It's not as bad as it seems, losing your trust. It makes you discerning and appreciative. Of all the things one can lose while making a run for the grave, losing one's trust in humanity isn't even in the top ten. There are worse things you can lose, like your hymen (which you'll never get back); your taste buds (which would make eating pointless); your eyesight; your house to a hurricane (though I suppose you can always build another one, so long as you have insurance and are not a victim of Katrina); one of your children (which happened to my neighbor); your passport in Moscow (which happened to me); faith in God (if you ever had it); and your mind, of course. I could name a few more, but you get the idea.

Apparently, whenever my mother saw Jean-Pierre, she saw only a pair of tarred lungs. Not his—mine. And my mother's position on this was that divorce was preferable to cancer. Some people think that cancer is preferable to divorce. Those are the ones who stay married to people they'd rather see dead before breakfast, like Azucena. Not me.

The day I found Cecilia arching her back on top of Jean-Pierre, I headed straight to the cemetery. I had nothing to my name, except some scholarship money and the courage I had gathered since jumping out of my crib as a baby. Perhaps you've heard that in New Orleans all the tombs are above the ground. It's an eerie sight, particularly at night. So I walked inside the cemetery, picked a grave at random, and dropped my wedding ring on the ground. Then I gave it a little push with my shoe, the way my mother did with the doorstop that time. Bye-bye, Juan-Pedro. My only hope is that a poor little raccoon, innocent about us creepy humans, didn't choke on that cheap piece of gold.

Yes, I promise to take you to New Orleans one day, *mi amor*. And don't let me forget to tell you about the alligator that escaped from Bayou Lacombe.

MY FIRST JOB IN AMERICA

The thing to do after Jean-Pierre was to get a divorce, a new place to live, and a job. A woman named Barbie Boudreaux gave me two of the three things on my wish list. "Two out of three ain't bad," goes the song.

The divorce was a little tricky. Jean-Pierre wanted to marry Cecilia right away. But how to oblige him at his earliest convenience when he and I were still legally married in Venezuela? Sometimes it helps to have your father on your side. My father was only too eager to have our marriage annulled on account of adultery. To this day, *mi amor*, I can't tell you if I actually got divorced from Jean-Pierre or if our marriage was annulled by some high priest in Caracas. For all that, cutting ties with Jean-Pierre was certainly a lot easier than your mom getting rid of your dad, or vice versa. There were no lawyers, negotiators, court dates, court fees, or court orders to speak of. In politically evolved countries like Venezuela we have what are called *palancas*. Everything is much easier if you know someone somewhere—friends, or friends of friends, who can expedite things for you, navigate through the brain-numbing bureaucracy. My dad, being a well-known psychiatrist, had many *palancas*. He knew lawyers, judges, you name it. It is only in TV shows called *Law & Order* that doctors and lawyers can't seem to see eye to eye. In the end, all I had to do was to sign a power of attorney that my dad's secretary faxed me to the nearest Kinko's and it was done. I can see by the look in your eyes that you have a certain admiration for the efficiency of this process. It took all of five minutes to exhume the remains of Valentina Viloria. Bye-bye, Val Joste.

Well, I say five minutes, but that was only the paperwork. The initial phone call to my parents—when I had to tell them I found a Bolivian hussy doing a balancing act on the Eiffel Tower —that phone call made AT&T's stock set a record high in the New York Stock Exchange. We were on the phone for hours. As I've told you, South American parents can get very involved. So during that phone call, my parents, each on a different phone in the house where I grew up, proceeded to outline what I would do with my life next, which, they both agreed, would be my immediate return to Venezuela.

Well, not so fast. "First," my dad said, "I will kill him." Yes, *mi amor*. Our patriarchs are not quite like the Muslims with their silly honor killings, but pretty close. Every culture has its little barbaric rituals. Let me tell you, it took no small amount of sweet talk to convince my parents that I was an adult.

"No one is an adult at twenty, Valentina," said my mother.

But my father set her straight: "She was adult enough to marry a *cretino*."

You would think they would have asked if I was heartbroken, or something along those lines. But that would have been undignified— to let a cretin upset you. So my father said, in a tone of voice that could slice prosciutto, "You need to get us a fax number, Valentina." And let me tell you, Emily, if you know what's good for you in South America, you don't argue with a patriarch. So after we got off the phone, I headed to Kinko's to get my father a fax number. I hadn't lived in the States long enough to know about Judge Judy, the woman who could have helped me handle both a divorce from my parents and a divorce from a cretin. Had I been willing to appear on television free of charge.

II. COCKS AND COCKFIGHTS

WHAT A KING MUST SUFFER

My father, the first of eight, was baptized Reynaldo because his mother, much like the Virgin Mary, had been expecting a king rather than a son. So she named him Reynaldo, and from that day forward proceeded to call him *mi rey*. As fate would have it, the newborn came out of the womb in as perfect condition as a child can. And in the same way that the women of ancient Athens planted gardens of Adonis to celebrate the god, Reynaldo was worshipped in visible ways by his adoring mother, a woman named Chocha. This included the making of delicious cakes that were only *"para mi rey."*
Cakes were Chocha's specialty. After an entire childhood spent eating cakes, sweets became my father's favorite food group. Touch Reynaldo's cakes at your own peril. Any arrogance on my father's part as an adult was wholly understandable.

Many times I had to remind Azucena how lucky we were that Reynaldo didn't become a dictator, at least not outside the home. Unfortunately, some of the arrogance spilled over to my sister, who resembles him in more ways than one—what with her perfect nose and those alluring dark eyes that give off vampiric vibes.

As so often happens in the comedy of life, we are repelled by people who remind us of ourselves. I, for instance, am a little guarded among amiable people who like to bond. I call it the Natural Theory of Redundancy. As for Azucena, she is easily appalled by her own father, shoving, as King Reynaldo does, a mirror to her face.

KNOTS

A childhood memory of mine includes arriving at my grandparents' house and watching one of the maids dumping a giant mound of knotted socks on the long kitchen table for sorting. As it turned out, more than a king was to come out of Chocha's womb. There's no telling what will crawl out of certain places sometimes.

Did I not like my grandmother? An incisive little question, that. Would you mind pacing yourself a little, Emily? I can't tell you when it started, because I don't know. What I do know is that I was never moved to call Chocha *yaya*—a term of endearment we reserve for our favorite *abuela*. I just called her Chocha.

Azucena was a little more discerning. Whenever she saw Chocha tending obsessively to her rosebushes, my sister would tap her head lightly and would mouth to me, *"Está tocada."* That's Spanish for "touched," as in a touch of madness. Still, I don't think Azucena knew half of what I knew. My sister just happens to have a great nose. That's why she's so good at what she does. Azucena just knows—in her bones—that at this time next year there will not be a trace of fuchsia in anyone's closet in Caracas because O'Keefe prints will be in. It would be Azucena who remarks at a dinner party, "New vintage, same old grapes." My sister knows where everything special is made, how it's made, and how to enjoy it to the fullest. Me? I can't tell you what I'll be wearing tomorrow. And if you want the absolute truth, I find it stressful to the point of madness sometimes that I don't have what it takes to make a fashion statement. Sometimes I wonder if I'm not a little "touched" myself, if madness isn't hereditary.

Your dad leaving the way he did, that has certainly made me question who's who and what's what. It's still a mystery to me that we were able to receive a shock of that magnitude without going a little insane. I wouldn't be surprised if the only reason we're still going about brushing our teeth and so on is because we're still stunned. It's one thing to know something as a fact and quite another to have to absorb the details pore by pore.

I remember studying the Amazon in high school. Our teacher described the rainforest as "dense." Let me tell you, "dense" doesn't begin to cover it. I'm pretty sure she had never actually been there. She was never in the thick of the rainforest right before twilight, looking through the web of a disturbingly large tropical spider while the approaching rustle of a snake made you feel there were stalkers lurking underneath your feet. Being taunted by a two-faced squirrel monkey that keeps dropping in front of you like a wicked puppet will crush any vanity that humans are superior to animals. And all those eerie sounds, coming at you from everywhere and nowhere at the same time. My father is "dense." The Amazon I remember was remote, merciless, and mean. If you weren't careful, it would swallow you whole. I haven't tasted anguish like that since. And I can't say I'm looking forward to it.

But I was telling you about Chocha.

It took some time, but the house where I lived for the first eight years of my life, and that one day we had to flee like fugitives, eventually was taken over by knots of mismatched socks and the constant recycling of the daily needs of seven men and the various creatures they brought home. I often think of that house as a giant meat grinder with rusted blades. Things went in whole and came out in unrecognizable chunks. And if King Reynaldo captured everyone's hearts for being the first, it was his brother Anibal, the third, who hogged all the attention. How come it's always the bad ones who get all the attention? Anyway, there was also a girl squeezed in among the seven brothers—my *tía* Lupita. It was from her that I first learned about bows and arrows.

My own mother was seven months pregnant with me when Anibal—unaccustomed to being ignored by timid women named Serena put an arrow to my mother's belly and vowed to ram it through if she didn't smile. It is, admittedly, a way to get a shy woman to show her teeth. It was my *tía* Lupita who later told me this story. It was also Lupita who interceded on my mother's behalf by placing herself between the pregnant belly and the sharp edge of her brother's arrow. By her own admission, the young girl who would soon become my *tía*, saw my mother, the first of many wives of her many brothers, as a kind of savior. And what a savior to have, a woman who has only three smiles per year and rarely exhales. Back then, my mother was studying to become a psychotherapist, even if by the innocent act of getting married to my father she had also unwittingly signed up for a minor in zoology. Sometimes I have trouble picturing my mother, the meticulous Serena Serrano, voluntarily setting foot inside a place where chaos reigned from dawn to dawn.

In addition to the mound of mismatched socks at the kitchen table I also remember the smells of that house, which, owing to the variety of fauna that rotated through the place, smelled mostly of soiled socks and zoo. If it is true that opposites attract, then my mother must have grown tired of the smell of Lanvin perfume at her own house and become explicably attracted to wild life. That is the only plausible explanation. That might also explain the eventual mutation—Azucena, the Wolfdoodle, and Valentina, the Bullhound—two offspring with incompatible traits.

WHAT'S EVEN MORE GOLDEN
THAN SILENCE?

It takes the bow-and-arrow episode to understand why, when Azucena and I were born, my mother made the visits to that side of the family brief, and few and far between. But while the reasons were obvious to her, they were far from clear to us. That's the problem with someone who is being so good at keeping secrets. The entire time growing up neither Azucena nor I ever understood why my mother sat us down at the kitchen table right before leaving for work in the morning and said, with angst in her voice, "*Niñas*, if any of your uncles ever comes here after you get home from school, please don't answer the door."

"Bueno, Mamá."

Then she would add, for good measure, "*Niñas*, I've already given instructions to Luisa" (or Tita, or Petra, or whoever happened to be our nanny at the time). "*¿Está claro, niñas?*"

"*Sí*, Mamá, that's clear." But "clear" and "makes sense" are not the same thing. My mother used to call the place where my father grew up "*esa casa.*" But it isn't so much the pejorative—"that house"—that I remember as much as my mother's tortured grimace when she said it. It is true that *esa casa* always looked vandalized. It is also true that the three, unevenly split levels made it look unstable from the outside, and that the two main entrances side by side seemed to have been built for the sole purpose of confusing visitors. But in the end, it was the sprawling rocky hill in the backyard that camouflaged the creepy secrets hidden inside *esa casa*.

There's this instance that Azucena swears never happened but that, were I to live another hundred years, I'd never be able to get out of my mind. It was a Saturday afternoon, which I remember because after abruptly moving out of *esa casa* when I was still a child, we started visiting my father's side of the family on Saturdays. This was so that after five minutes my mother could politely excuse herself

and say, "*Señora* Chocha, *las niñas* and I have so many errands to run."
And then we'd run out of there.

This particular Saturday stands apart because, after ringing both
doorbells several times, no one came to either front door. This was
very strange. With six men—my dad was no longer living there—plus
their friends, plus the shifts of girlfriends (at least twelve shifts,
because the brothers all cheated), plus Lupita, plus her friends, there
was always someone at that house. So many women cycled through
the place over the years that it was silly to even try to remember their
names—an artist, an angel, a hippie, a vamp, and at least two Miss
Venezuelas; skirts of every ilk went through both front doors of *esa
casa*. Save for the firstborn (my father) and the baby (who died
young), the brothers married at least twice each.

As for the wives, I liked the comedienne, Fabricio's first wife.
Her name was Neli. She had uneven, buck teeth, which made you
smile just from looking at her. She was married to Fabricio for a year
or so, long enough to collect new material and return with it to the
stage, where she could actually cash in on the dysfunction. Neli was a
smart woman. Some of the others considered it something of an
achievement to have a claim on one of these rough-hewn bachelors,
even if only for an afternoon.

On the Saturday when no one came to the door, my mother
accidentally let slip one of her three annual smiles and said, "*Vamos,
niñas,*" so relieved was she. But as we were walking toward the car, we
heard convulsed fits of laughter coming from one of the patios. That
house had several patios. There was *el patio del frente*. There was *el patio
de atrás*. There was *el patio de abajo*. There was a confused architect
somewhere. We were turning back around when we saw a nest of
yellowish hair standing on stilts, high on something more than
laughter. One look at the girl and my mother said, "We'll come visit
Grandma another time, *niñas*."

"Come join the party," said the girl.

"Is *señora* Chocha home?" my mother asked reluctantly. Maybe it
was the drugs, or perhaps it was the oddity of hearing a polite term
like *señora* so utterly out of context that gave the girl a bad case of the
giggles. Chocha was standing right behind her, wearing an apron
splattered with cake batter. She motioned with her spatula for us to
come in, and returned to the kitchen without even looking at the
half-naked girl.

My mother followed Chocha into the kitchen, stealing glances at us over her shoulder. I went straight to the *patio del frente,* where the laughter was growing louder, and was followed by a wary Azucena. My sister has always had a great nose. It's a wonderful asset, particularly at wine tastings.

When we arrived at the patio, we saw Anibal, Fabricio, and a handful of their friends playing volleyball. Oddly enough, there was no ball. The image of the yellow frog issuing a sticky serum as it went up in the air is forever fixed in my mind like Dali's suspended rose. Frogs tend to spaz when they are mishandled, and their skin is very slippery, so the guys kept picking up the freaked-out frog from the ground and throwing it back up in the air every time it slipped out of their hands. That's what caused the fits of laughter. I'm pretty sure that by the time Azucena and I arrived on the scene, the poor frog was very close to dying.

Fortunately for Azucena, she inherited the gift of ignoring all things unpleasant. That's why she was able to effectively block out this particular Saturday from her childhood memories. On the few occasions I've asked her if she remembers the yellow volleyball frog—if only to check on my own sanity—Azucena looks at me and says, "You must be adopted." Whether this means that I *should* be adopted and removed from the premises at once, or that I *was* actually adopted, it's hard to say. It's always hard to tell with Azucena; she's nearly overdosed with Oscar Wilde.

As for my mother, who had left Chocha to her cakes by then, one sticky drop of frog serum was all she needed in order to say, "You didn't see that, *niñas.*" But I did see it. And because I did, sometimes I think I will reincarnate as a yellow frog, just for having witnessed the ordeal.

I once told your dad this story. Afterward, he said, "That explains it."

"Explains what, Max?"

"Why you're such a gullible cynic."

"But that's an oxymoron, Max. You can't be gullible and a cynic at the same time."

"Precisely," he said. "You want with all your heart to believe that people are good. But you know too much."

It wasn't just the frog, *mi amor.* Your dad knew I had seen much more than a group of men rushing the coming of the Apocalypse. Sometimes I wonder if that's why he went to your mom's that day. . .

. I wish she would talk to me. I know. I know. I hear what you're saying, Emily. I know Helen wouldn't talk to me if my name was Mary Spaniel and I ran a leper-dog hospital. Still, she's keeping something we have a right to know. Unless she's told you and you're not saying. . . .

LEAVE IT TO CLEAVAGE

I fired my first gun at sixteen. Way before the Kardashian sisters discovered there was money to be made in overexposure, there were financial advantages to being a well-endowed sixteen-year-old in the Tropics. One of them is that your twenty-year-old uncle can show you off at the shooting range without having to pay cover. Another plus is that the male attendant at the shooting range is happy to give you the ear guards without asking for a bribe for your being underage. Boobs as bribes—the not-so-brilliant idea of distracting men from their aim with a silicone substance—wasn't sanctioned in North America until very recently.

But what good does it do to wish you'd been born elsewhere? Or wrapped in a different package, for that matter? The mere thought is oppressive—to wish I had spent my teen years going to Walmart in my flip-flops rather than risking life and limb at the shooting range in Caracas. And besides, there's much to be said for a woman who knows how to shoot a gun and aim for the heart.

I don't know what I was expecting, but the first time I shot a gun, I fell flat on my ass. Part of the problem was that I was wearing high heels. The other problem owed entirely to recoil. I wish my uncle would have warned me. My uncle Frasquito, the baby of the brothers, always packed a gun. He was only a handful of years older than I, so I always thought of him as a brother. As for my mother, if she ever finds out that I was a regular at the shooting range, she would kill him again.

HOT YOGA POSES LEAD TO WISDOM

Azucena has always had a knack for calling at the wrong time. Thanks to specialized features such as Caller ID, these days I'm warned, the moment I see the numbers 58-212-963, that if I choose to answer the phone, I will be short at least two hours by the end of the day.

Unfortunately, on the day you were having your wisdom teeth pulled, I made the mistake of answering the phone. I thought my sister was calling to wish me luck. Azucena knows how much I dread going to the dentist, even if it isn't for my own cavities. For one, the reading selection in dentists' waiting rooms leaves so much to be desired—magazine covers picturing swollen gums and rotting teeth, among others even more offensive. Anyway, it only takes two seconds to say, "Good luck, Valentina." Five seconds if Azucena were thoughtful enough to say, "Good luck to Emily." But what's even more reprehensible is that Azucena is well aware that North American dentists don't wait. Here, it is the patients who have to be patient.

It was a balancing act, to be sure, to try to hurry the call along without my sister noticing it. As it turned out, just as I had expected, the rest of our time on the phone after the brief *hola* was devoted to Azucena's favorite topic: Carlos Upstairs. "Has he said anything about the pubic hair on the soap, Azucena?" I asked. What was I thinking? My prying too soon about pubic matters put me further behind schedule. An interruption, or the wrong question at the wrong time with Azucena, automatically remands you to a lower court, that is to say, the beginning of the conversation.

"How about asking me how I'm doing first, Valentina? Is the soap all you care about?"

"No. No. No, Azucena. It's just that Emily has an appointment that took months to get, and well . . . you know. . . . You remember wisdom teeth, Azucena, don't you? So-what's-up?"

"What do you mean what's up, Valentina? I can tell when you're trying to rush me. If you don't want to talk to me, just say so. Do you like that Emily girl more than your own sister? She's not even your flesh and blood."

That's when I remembered yoga. I really don't know how we're supposed to survive in this country without Bikram. Those Indian people sure know how to sweat without giving themselves away. So I exhaled quietly over the phone, letting the air in my lungs out very, very . . . slowly as I said, "Oh, it's not . . that . . . Azucena . . . of course I . . . want to talk to you. I always . . . want to talk to you, especially when the privilege is going to cost me five hundred dollars for a dentist appointment I won't get to keep!! Tell me, Azucena, how's the weather in Caracas today?"

Mercifully we were interrupted by Sofía. Sweet little Sofía, like her mother, is devoted to the study of the self. She's only six years old. But they've been six years well spent. In all that time Sofía has become intimately familiar with the terms *self-appointed, self-centered,* and *selfish.* "Mamiiiiiiiiiiiiiiiiiiii," the wail echoed through the phone.

These ear-splitting wails are standard sound effects whenever Azucena calls. I used to dread them. Now the wails give me an opportunity to say, "Better rush and see if Sofía is all right, Azucena."

But does she listen to me? Noooo. She's listening to Sofía, who has also mastered the use of cadence for effect. *"Mami . . . aquí hay un bicho."* Sniffles.

"Oh, is just a bug," says Azucena, speaking to both me and Sofía at the same time.

And Sofía, who is morbidly jealous of anyone who holds her mother's attention for more than five seconds, says, "Come kill it, Mami."

So Azucena, channeling Oscar Wilde as only she can, proceeds to tell her daughter, "The only thing worse than having to kill a bug, Sofía, is being one."

"I have a question before I let you go, Azucena: If you're upstairs with Sofía, where is Carlos Upstairs right now? Did he get a job?"

"Don't make me laugh, Valentina. Even God rested on Sundays."

"Today is Monday, Azucena *querida.* You're working way too hard."

FELIZ NAVIDAD

My uncle Frasquito was born with a body that had special features. He could move his ears independently of one another. He could peel his eyelids backward and show only the whites of his eyes. After one of these tricks he was usually able to put everything back together, but sometimes his eyelids stayed pinned; I was afraid he wouldn't be able to close his eyes ever again. "Isn't Frasquito amazing, Azucena?" I might ask.

And Azucena would say, "He's a freak."

When he wasn't at the shooting range, the baby of the brothers was home practicing new ways of vying for attention. Because of that, we saw more of him than we saw of the others. It was Frasquito, as a matter of fact, who broke the news about Christmas.

When I was growing up, Christmas was an extravagant affair. Well, maybe that doesn't quite paint the picture. The truth is we had two Christmases on the same day, not unlike the two Thanksgivings you and the twins started having after your parents got divorced. And here I'm going to expand on Tolstoy's remark about all unhappy families being unhappy in their own way. And I'm going to include dysfunctional families as well. As you know from experience, all dysfunctional families are screwed up in their very own special way. So let me tell you about *Feliz Navidad!*

Every Christmas around mid-afternoon my mother would dress Azucena and me in identical white dresses, carefully put the presents for that side of the family inside a white satin bag, and drive the us to my normal grandmother's house, where we would have an elegant dinner on a white tablecloth in the company of highly educated people who believed that laughter was something that happened only at trailer parks. Afterward, we carefully unwrapped identically wrapped presents under my mother's watchful eye, lest Azucena or I get possessed and attack our gifts, thereby ruining Christmas for everyone.

Meanwhile, my father was at *esa casa*, where large quantities of rum were being consumed since mid-morning by friends, friends of the family, and friends of friends of the family, to the beat of music so loud that the police had to be invited to keep them from ruining the mood. Whenever I saw men in uniform at *esa casa* upon arriving from our cartoon Christmas at our normal grandmother's house, I always assumed it was for security reasons and not for holiday merriment. But what really made Christmas so extravagant at my father's family home was not the drunk policemen on duty, but rather the fact that there were so many presents under the tree. You see, all of my father's brothers, who had married a few times each, and all of their former wives and the children from each of those marriages—they'd had, on average, three children with each—meant there were always abundant packages under the tree.

That Christmas tree at my grandfather's house almost always reached the twelve-foot ceiling, and the presents beneath it were at least three feet deep. For me, Christmas was always an opportunity to meet new cousins and women whose names there was no need to bother to learn. That's why, *mi amor*, it's simply beyond my comprehension that your mother refuses to sit down for a cappuccino with me when my uncles' ex-wives were all so game to participate.

During one such *Feliz Navidad*, an hour or so before the opening of the hundreds of presents was to begin, Frasquito and I went outside to light sparklers. Wherever there was fire or danger, even the remote possibility of danger, you could count on Frasquito to be there. He had a box of sparklers and a neon-green lighter, which he handed to me as he said, "Want to know a secret?" This was years before our visits to the shooting range; I might have been, at most, eight years old to Frasquito's twelve. And it might have been that very Christmas that I developed my distaste for secrets and surprises.

Perhaps you think that strange, since most people take me for an insatiable extrovert. But having an effervescent spirit doesn't mean that one enjoys being splashed with untimely truths such as "Valentina, there is no Santa Claus." Many years later, as an adult living elsewhere, I happened to read a reprint of the famous editorial "Is There a Santa Claus?":

Dear Editor, I am eight years old. Some of my friends say there is no Santa Claus. Papa says, "If you see it in The Sun, it is so." Please tell me the truth, is there a Santa Claus?

Sincerely, Virginia O'Hanlon.

Frasquito was dead by then. Still, the memory returned to me whole by the time I finished reading the editor's response to the inquisitive Virginia. Frasquito had been standing under the streetlamp outside my grandfather's house watching me play with a sparkler that was about to go off when he had the urge to break the news. "I don't believe you," I said. "Santa Claus is coming tonight." To prove it, he suggested that once I got home, I should stay awake and then sneak downstairs at midnight. I did as Frasquito told me: Battling sleep, I managed to stay up until I saw my mother's slim figure tiptoeing down the stairs. When I surprised her by the Christmas tree, her face was contrived in the grimace of grimaces. And when I called her a liar over and over, with tears streaking down my cheeks, she just sat on the floor, hugged her knees, and shook her head.

"Which one told you?" she asked. My father's brothers were too much for her. There was so much they lacked. So much she could not forgive.

My friendship with Frasquito, and what happened on that Christmas in particular, might help explain why as an adult, I've always worked hard to empty my head of garbage such as fairy tales. All the while wishing that someone would come to me and say, "Valentina, there's a red elf dancing in the backyard." By the time I met you and the twins, I had already torn up the baby's rattle to see what made the noise inside. But as that editor so wisely said to Virginia, "The most real things in the world are those that we can't see." And because I didn't see your dad actually going into your mom's kitchen that day I still want to believe that he didn't do what he did.

LIPOSUCTION OF THE BRAIN

A couple of months ago Sofía brought her report card home to Azucena. Notice I didn't say, Sofía brought her report card to her parents. Sofía knows that were she to bring the report card to Carlos Upstairs, he wouldn't even bother to lift his head off the pillow. My little niece is smart enough to realize that a mere report card is no reason for her father to stop paying attention to his Game Boy.

This particular report card, though, was of special significance. It was the first time in her short life that Sofía got an "A" in spelling. That's because, until recently, the little sweet Sofía, taking a page from her mother's book, always left a few words blank in her homework assignment just to piss off the spelling teacher, whom she dislikes for reasons known only to her. Stranger still is the fact that Sofía's teachers claim that she intimidates them.

"A six-year-old who intimidates the people who hold the pencil with which she's graded wouldn't last long in this country," I keep telling Azucena. Teachers in North America have Ritalin at the ready, a slow-motion lobotomy of sorts, which works wonders with insufferable little people like my niece. As for Azucena, she believes her daughter is being maligned by envious teachers. "Envious of what, Azucena *querida*?" Call her crazy, but my sister believes that because Sofía is extremely tall for her age, her female teachers are envious of her long legs.

"Of a six-year-old, Azucena?"

"Yes, Valentina."

I feel for Azucena. Ever since Carlos Upstairs gave her a liposuction as a birthday present, she's convinced that the desire for slim, long legs—whether by man, woman, or pre-school teacher—knows no limits.

It's entirely possible that the situation at school might have to do with Sofía's talent for holding a stare longer than it is comfortable. "I wonder where she learned that?" asks Azucena, mystified. It wasn't until my poor sister spent an undisclosed sum of money on a child therapist that Sofía finally decided to let go of her maladaptive behavior toward her spelling teacher and finally got an "A." Proud of her accomplishment, Sofía wanted to celebrate. So she said to Azucena—fresh out of school, her uniform still on—"Mami, there's a boy in my class whose father dances around the house whenever he gets an 'A.'"

"I'm so happy for both of them," replied Azucena.

"Aren't you going to dance around the house with me, Mami?"

At this, Azucena grabbed a picture of my mother from the side table in the living room, and speaking strictly to her daughter's hopeful eyes, said, "Take a good look at this woman, Sofía. Does she look like someone who raised people who dance around the house?"

DIGITAL CONTRACEPTION

On more than one occasion Azucena has threatened to send her children to me. She doesn't see it as a threat, of course. She simply says, "Now that you're free, Valentina . . ."

That's how most conversations begin these days. The only reason Azucena can afford to make a callous remark like that is because my little sister is only able to see the world through her own eyes. And in a perfect world, Carlos Upstairs would be gone. Not just gone outside, mind you. But gone, gone—as in: no reincarnation privileges.

She has no idea what that would do to me—sending her children my way. You spent part of your childhood and adolescence with me, *mi amor*, long enough to know that I'm not a monster, just someone who wasn't given the necessary equipment, nor the manufacturer's instructions, to tolerate noise levels currently being tested at NASA. I'm probably the only person alive who admires Steve Jobs not for the obvious advance that blasting new decibel levels through one's ears obviously is, but for the fortuitous advantage of the iPod as a child-canceling device.

What keeps me up at night these days is that I might get a call from the airport before dawn one day, and that it will be a representative from United Airlines on the other line, saying, "I have your niece and nephew here, Miss Goldman." If that ever comes to pass, *mi amor*, you know that I will move to another country and change my name. I've done it half a dozen times already. To me, a name change is like going to Love Culture to shop for a new pair of glasses.

And when that happens, *mi amor*, Sofía and Lucas Enrique won't even know what hit them. Being raised by a United Airlines representative. Ha! They have nooo idea how rough life can be. Those aloof flight attendants from the friendly skies won't put up with half of what Azucena's maids are made to endure. I'd love to be nearby when Sofía asks the woman for milk, if only to hear her reply in that nasal drone that has become so integral to the United Airlines brand, "I'm sorry, we no longer carry milk on board. Unless you buy the cereal."

IN THE TIME OF CHOLERA

An occasional Sunday feature at *esa casa* involved boxing matches among the brothers. These were occasions for their friends to drink *cerveza fría*, place bets, and fondle anything within gawking distance. These were times when teeth were knocked out, ribs were broken, and blood was spat out. Fortunato, my grandfather, was rarely there. Chocha, on the other hand, rarely left the house, which is to say, she was one of the spectators.

The boxing matches took place in the *patio del frente*, which was in full view from the kitchen where Chocha continued to beat cake batter as her sons' friends bet on their lives. She always beat her cakes by hand; modern appliances were not to her taste.

In extreme circumstances, after hearing a particularly loud, "OH-FUCK," my mother might be inclined to remark, "*Señora,* I think someone might be hurt out there." I'd be sitting at the kitchen table, watching the maid *du jour* unknotting socks, trying to keep a neutral expression as Chocha observed, "It's not cholera. It's not typhoid. It's only blood," adding a little more vanilla extract to the batter.

Tragedy is a cosmic matter, so merriment reigned outside as Chocha put another cake inside the oven. I don't know when my mother realized it, that she was looking at a special case.

PARADISE OF SNAKES

Fabricio, my father's second brother, grew up to wear tuxedos. Which reminds me: Did you ever read the story of King Midas? I know I gave you a lot of books growing up. But I don't remember giving you that one. For starters, I hate avarice. Still, there's much to learn from a man ambitious enough to turn his own daughter into gold. And yet, the man had *nothing* on Fabricio. Fabricio is a cross between King Midas and Vito Corleone from *The Godfather,* except that he's as handsome as Michael Corleone.

It's always tempting to paint people who remind you of the devil in a bad light. To say, for instance, that Fabricio had a crooked nose. But that wouldn't be true. It also wouldn't be very Christian. Ever wonder why that's the one that actually stuck? Ever wonder why it isn't groovy to say, "That wouldn't be very Buddhist"? Or, "That wouldn't be very Muslim"?

But anyway, as my grandfather was on his deathbed, Fabricio took a day off to go to the bank that was holding the loans and tell the loan officer that the business was insolvent. And boom, by the time clots of mud were falling on my grandfather's coffin, the business went into bankruptcy, just like that! Afterward, Fabricio took all the clients. Still, Fabricio was at the funeral. Wearing a tuxedo, I might add. And he did cry. It would be interesting to find out who those tears were for. But I've never been good with money, and terms like *financial receivership* are too complex for me.

For all that, it was nice of my father to ask me to dust off my MBA a few years later so that I could go back home and give the business a shot in the arm after Fabricio ran it into the ground. I almost welcomed the challenge. But saving a plumbing business from going down the tubes inside an even bigger toilet? No, thank you. And besides, I think the reason my father called me was because by then he had grown tired of clogged pipes. But that's just a wild guess.

Anyway, by the time my grandfather was snoring next to Saint Peter, Neli the comedienne had already left Fabricio to return to the stage for better company. So Fabricio remarried. The woman at my grandfather's funeral, Fabricio's second wife, was a woman named Tamara. She, too, was funny, albeit in a totally different way. Tamara married Fabricio, not for his money, but for the money *he would make* one day. She was a kind of clairvoyant, a futures expert, if you will. I think in this country you call people like Tamara gold diggers. But I can't think of a good translation for "gold digger" in Spanish, because in Spanish, "gold digger" would roughly translate as *minero,* "someone who digs for gold," not as a hobby but as a job. And besides, it wouldn't be polite to go around calling my second *tía política* "a *minera.*" My mother would disapprove.

As luck would have it, right around the time I was marrying Jean-Pierre, Tamara and Fabricio had a daughter. Using her powers as a clairvoyant, Tamara saw in her mind's eye that Jean-Pierre and I would make excellent godparents to her baby girl, Veronica. What an honor, to be asked to be someone's godmother! Or rather, it would have been an honor, except that whenever I hear the word *mother* associated with my name, for some strange reason, I invariably feel nauseated. It's ridiculous, really—the way former and current spouses want to stick others with their kids. But no one suspected that I was feeling nauseated at that moment. I was only eighteen, besides. And what eighteen-year-old has the necessary vocabulary to say to her pressuring parents, "This is total bullshit." My mother might have reached for the bottle of Clorox under the kitchen sink and start spraying my mouth in earnest. So, rather than saying that, I rolled my eyes in the back of my head, put on a pretty dress, and smiled when the priest poured the water over the head of the bundle that was Veronica.

I think the only reason Jean-Pierre agreed to be the godfather of the kid of a complete stranger was because there would be champagne at the reception. But it hardly mattered. A week after Veronica's baptism, Jean-Pierre and I were leaving for Melbourne, Florida, anyway. I suspected I'd never set foot in paradise again, even if that meant picking oranges in Melbourne for the rest of my days. I wasn't counting on the fact that this bundle of white lace would grow up to be a woman one day. I also wasn't counting on Facebook, or on snoopy people abusing that poking feature. Nor was I counting on Jean-Pierre meeting Cecilia. Come to think of it, I had no clue! Because how do you say to someone, "If I don't want to be your godmother, what makes you think I want to be your friend on Facebook?"

Some people just don't get it. Just last year, in fact, Veronica called to invite me to her wedding. Immediately, of course, I got on the phone with my sister.

"How did this woman get my number, Azucena?"

"Ask mother," she sighed. . . .

"Great! And how am I supposed to tell Veronica that I have no interest whatsoever in going to her wedding?"

As always, my sister was happy to oblige. "How about telling her the truth, Valentina?—that her father is a thief and her mother is a whore."

"Hmm. . . ."

People always want to know why I left an exotic place like Venezuela, *mi amor*. I never tell them about the boxing matches. I never tell them about the volleyball frog. I'd hate for anyone to get the wrong impression. Instead, I talk about my life in New Orleans. Most people find the Big Easy irresistible.

1X1

Her name was Lakeesha Gaines. We had taken a microbiology class together. It was Lakeesha who opened her home to me after Jean-Pierre and Cecilia changed the locks at my place.

It was at her house that I understood for the first time what it really means to be a parent: Give a kid your sweat and he will milk your blood. There was more blood involved in getting Lakeesha's three kids to bed every night than anything Bram Stoker could have ever put down on paper. And it was while observing the horrors of working motherhood that I had my first real epiphany: Go on the pill! There are so many things one can learn by keeping both eyes and ears open. It took only three days of sticking earplugs so far up my ear canal I might be permanently deaf, to propel me into action. On day four I walked to the Circle K down the street to buy Lakeesha a bag of Kraft caramels to thank her for her hospitality and to escape the madness of trying to convince a two-year-old to swallow a Cheerio before going to work.

My mother would have wholly disapproved of my choice of gift. To properly thank my friend for her hospitality in a time of so urgent a need, I would have needed to buy Lakeesha something from Tiffany's in a little blue box with a blue-ribbon bow. But my mother has never been in the position to have to buy a gift with one's last three dollars and having to donate plasma afterward to cover the shortage. That day I skipped calculus and went to see a handful of apartments I had circled in the classifieds, all of which read, "Immediate move-in." That is how I met Barbie Boudreaux, the woman who gave me my first job in the United States.

Barbie Boudreaux was the manager of a place called Maison Blanche apartments, though there was nothing White House about the place. It was a complex of three hundred plywood boxes within walking distance from campus, surrounded by giant oak trees, one of which later crashed through one of the apartments during a hurricane, killing one of the residents, who had refused to be evacuated.

My first impression of the place is that it had once been a jail. Think Alcatraz on the Bayou. It was at Maison Blanche that I became familiar with the term *eviction proceedings*. But we'll get to that later.

Meeting Barbie made me take seriously the notion that we become our names. She must have been in her very late forties, though she still wore bright blue eye shadow, pink rouge, and pink lip gloss, which made her look like a Barbie doll. I just realized you've never seen a Barbie doll, *mi amor.* "Barbie" was a doll made by a company called Mattel—something like a plastic version of Paris Hilton. But what am I saying? Paris is the plastic version!

Anyway, I walked into Maison Blanche, filled out an application, and asked Barbie if I could move in that day. "If your credit check is clean," she said. I didn't know what a credit check was, but I nodded and smiled. That's always a good trick when you don't know which end is up—to nod and smile. It doesn't commit you one way or the other, and as a bonus you come across as polite.

I'm embarrassed to admit that up until that day I believed the government paid for the electricity in Venezuela. The "government" was for me, of course, my father, though these days, that's not too far from the truth. At any rate, Barbie glanced over the papers I had filled out, grabbed a set of keys with which I would become very familiar, and we both left the office to look at what's called in leasing lore a "1X1"—a one-bedroom, one-bathroom apartment. Now that I think about it, it seems a little cruel to reduce heartbreak to a 1X1.

Anyway, I don't know what I was expecting for two hundred dollars a month and immediate move-in. All I remember is that the moment Barbie turned the door handle, I got a bad case of nausea. The place smelled of rotting bologna sprayed with Lysol. But that wasn't the worst part—you could always open the windows at least.

The apartments at Maison Blanche had been built in the sixties. Now, let me tell you what that means in two words: lime green. The oven door was lime green. So was the carpet, which was so worn out it looked like a lime-green cat splayed on its deathbed. I bore it well, I thought. When Barbie apologized for the carpet, I brushed her apology aside and said, "You can always buy one of those nice area rugs. " I'd used the word *you* as if I were a broker scouting the place for someone else. And so, it was the timely use of the second person that earned me my first job.

"Have you ever considered being a leasing agent?" Barbie asked.

"A what?" That night I had a place to sleep, even if I didn't own a bed. Some people claim that sleeping on the floor is good for your back. That might be. But what do they do about the bugs? The next day I started my job as a leasing agent at Maison Blanche. It was the first in a string of jobs that had nothing to do with my undergraduate degree in psychology, or with the MBA on which I would later waste my time. But maybe I'm wrong about that. "Psychos doing business" isn't exactly an oxymoron.

DOMESTIC FOWLS

Over the years many animals went in and out of *esa casa*. But the one everyone remembers is a big black rooster that my grandfather, Fortunato, brought home one day and introduced to everyone during dinner as *mi gallito,* his little rooster. Fortunato's *gallito* was nature at its most efficient. A rooster crowing *kickerykeee* at the same time every morning is nature working as intended. And Fortunato liked that. My grandfather had an appreciation for that on which he could count.

After a hard day at *Fortunato Inodoros* (Fortunato Toilets), my grandfather could count on two things: Chocha baking a cake, and his *gallito* crowing *kickerykeee* at daybreak. Roosters elsewhere might crow *cock-a-doodle-doo,* but South American roosters really know how to roll their *r*'s. Because Fortunato's *gallito* was so reliable a creature, it got special treats. Many days right after work Fortunato would stop at an empanada stand right around the corner from his shop to buy a fresh empanada for his *gallito.* That's probably why the *gallito* was always so happy. He pecked on soiled socks all day until the man who appreciated him more than he did his own wife fed him an empanada by hand. Many in the house envied the *gallito.* But they shouldn't have. Chocha was always around to make sure there was plenty to eat. She never left the kitchen, as a matter of fact. It was obvious she cut her own hair. And I'm pretty sure she never left the house to buy a dress, either. She wore these toga-type things she made herself out of threadbare sheets.

As for my grandfather, I remember him as a man who was fond of rare pets and who enjoyed spoiling them. The *gallito* wasn't the only lucky one. Fortunato was a very generous man, and not just with fowls. Vivid in my mind is the Saturday before I was to turn fifteen. A *quinceañera* is a big deal in South America. And I was the first among twenty-odd grandchildren to do the honors. Naturally, my grandfather was proud.

So he asked my mother to drop me off at his house in the morning and to pick me up later that afternoon. He also told her that he had a surprise for me. That day is another reason I don't like surprises. My mother dropped me off reluctantly and only after giving me a thorough warning about anything that might happen, which is, of course, impossible. Wasn't she a psychotherapist? Didn't she know that no one could have predicted what might happen when a fifteen-year-old girl leaves a demented household in the company of a man who feeds empanadas to a rooster? But never mind.

As we approached *esa casa*, my mother said, "You know what to do, no matter what happens, right?" But "no matter what happens" is such vast territory, almost without limits. My mother's most fervent wish has always been that life be preventable. It is a fantasy like any other, I suppose.

When I asked my grandfather where we were going, he just said, "It's a surprise, *niña*." I hated being called *niña* when everyone knew full well I was an adult at fifteen! Calling me *niña* was like handing me the kid menu and telling me I should order the noodles with butter. But I smiled. It's a trick that seems to work—to smile when you have the urge to smack someone. My mother calls it "grace."

SEEING IS NOT BELIEVING

Around mid-morning my grandfather and I entered a jewelry store. That was a surprise. You don't usually associate people whose way of making a living is toilets with jewels. And yet, there we were. It turned out my grandfather wanted to give me a special gift, something lovely I'd be proud to wear at my upcoming *quinceañera* ball. Suddenly I felt bad for having had mean thoughts a few minutes earlier. The jeweler greeted Fortunato as one does an old friend, and after the pleasant preliminaries my grandfather told me to pick out anything I wanted.

"Anything?" I asked.

The jeweler, one of those men with a wink at the ready, said, "You're a lucky girl. What's your name?"

"Valentina," I said.

"Well, Valentina, what are you in the mood for?" Suddenly I wished Azucena had come along. She would have known how to answer such an ambitious question. She might have said, "I'm the mood for emeralds . . . from Cartier." I had no idea what to say. So I smiled. And upon my smile the jeweler locked up the shop, to lead thieves not into temptation, and proceeded to take out a number of small cases with sparkling things in them.

As it turned out, all I needed was to know what my options were. As a child, given a choice between two cereals, I was never one to pull on my pigtails and say, "Oh, no! What now? I can't decide!" Making a decision is as expedient for me as foreplay is for some men, a quick move to get elsewhere. This has always worked well for me, except maybe in the husband department. Here's the way I look at it: even if I choose the wrong thing, then I know I don't like it, and now I'm down one in the process of elimination. So I picked a pair of silver earrings that caught my eye—two tiny leaves with two green gems encrusted in them.

"That's it?" asked the jeweler. I nodded. He praised my good taste and asked my grandfather if he should wrap the earrings.

"Not yet," he said, and asked me to pick out something else.

"But I don't want anything else, *abuelo*."

"Just do it for me, *niña*."

The second time around I picked out something entirely different. It was a bracelet with two types of gold twisted together, a sort of gold braid. My grandfather inspected the bracelet through his glasses and told the jeweler to wrap it up, along with the emerald earrings.

"Thank you, Grandpa," I said. I didn't know what else to do before such generosity, so I started making mental notes for Azucena. She always liked it when I came back from being out in the world and told her stories. She sincerely enjoyed telling me that she didn't believe me. So I snapped a mental photo of the jewelry shop, to better show her that there was money in the toilet business. Once the gifts were wrapped, we left the jewelry shop with two little velvet boxes in hand.

One of the things I'd planned to tell Azucena was that no money had been exchanged in the process. I'd gone inside a jewelry store with my grandfather, picked out a couple of things, and come out half an hour later carrying two little boxes, for which no one paid a thing. At that point I thought we were headed back to *esa casa*. But nooo. The jewelry store had not been the real surprise, after all. Do you see?

Despite her cozying up to crazed rats in a maze for a living, my mother could never have predicted what my grandfather had in store for me on that very special Saturday.

WHEN HARRY MET VALENTINA

At the time I showed up looking for a place to live at Maison Blanche apartments in New Orleans, Barbie Boudreaux had not had a vacation in three years. This was due to a series of small complications that turned out to be huge complications after all, starting with the fact that the previous leasing agent had left without giving notice, and ending with the fact that Barbie's son, Jess—who was ten years old at the time—had accidentally shot and killed his best friend with his dad's gun in a place called Jackson, Mississippi. When I met her, Barbie was understandably on edge.

All this to tell you that I hadn't been working at Maison Blanche two weeks when Barbie Boudreaux announced she was going to Jackson to see Jess, who had been staying with her parents since the accident. She then handed me a set of keys and closed the office door behind her with the words, "You're in charge."

This turned out to be unwise. Many unusual things happened at Maison Blanche while Barbie Boudreaux was in Jackson, Mississippi, trying to convince her son that he wasn't a serial killer. But the one thing that stands out above the rest is the couple making love with the TV on. This shouldn't have happened. The reason I was standing at their doorstep with a would-be resident, which caused the occupants to lunge for their clothes in horror, was that in her rush to cross to get to Mississippi, Barbie Boudreaux forgot to tell me which of the three hundred apartments at Maison Blanche had people living in them and which did not. How was I supposed to know? Enter Ricky and Harry.

Ricky and Harry were known to all the residents as "the maintenance men." That is to say, it was their job to fix anything that broke, which meant lifetime employment for both of them. Excluding during the hurricanes, something broke at Maison Blanche on an hourly basis. Ricky and Harry were the Laurel and Hardy of the place, or, as we know them in Spanish, *el gordo y el flaco*. Harry was the stout one. Ricky was the rail. I have many Ricky and Harry stories, but I'll tell you the two that stand out, one of which involved my being held at gunpoint at the office. Now that I think about it, guns figure a lot in my life in this country. Thank God for my uncle Frasquito and the shooting range.

But anyway, after showing the man the apartment where the naked couple had been watching the Saints game, the potential resident was no longer potential. He was disgusted. There went my first commission—twenty-five dollars—all on account of not knowing which of the apartments were vacant.

Right after the man left, Harry came into the office and told me we needed to have a chat. My English was still too new for me to know that the words, "We need to have a chat," really mean, "You fucked up and I'm here to drill you a new one." And so that you get the full picture, *mi amor*, I should probably tell you that Harry was a large bearded man from a place called Mobile, Alabama; that he had been a maintenance man all his life; and that he believed—to put it in his own words—that you can never trust no niggers or spics.

It turned out I was in this latter category, but how could I take offense? The only other time I had heard the word *spic* was in a Procter & Gamble commercial. I'm a neat freak, as you know, and I love Spic and Span. That commercial spoke directly to me. So when Harry called me an ignorant spic, I thought he was saying I was clean, which I am. It was the "ignorant" part that pissed me off. What allowed someone of Harry's intellectual caliber to call me an ignorant spic is something I will have to leave to Steven Pinker. He's the psycholinguist, the one who knows how certain words creep their way into the brain and crawl their way out of some people's mouths.

At any rate, you'd be amazed at the number of things that break down in an old apartment complex made of plywood. Half the time, when people called to report something, I didn't know what they were talking about, let alone how to spell it. It's one thing to read *Huck Finn* cover to cover. And quite another to try to figure out what someone means when they say their "acey" is acting funny. It's the same in every language, isn't it? They never teach you what you really need to know. So Harry marched into the office, work order in hand, and looked at me as if he were looking at goat shit.

"What's thess supp'ose to mean?" he said, slapping the piece of paper with the back of his hand.

"Let me see," I said, reading my own handwriting. "I don't know, Harry. That's all the woman told me when she called—that her 'acey' was acting funny."

"What's thaaat supp'ose to mean?" he asked, louder this time. It was at that point that I told him I wasn't deaf, just unfamiliar with the term "acey."

"Isn't that your department, Harry, to know what things are called? I thought *you* were the maintenance man."

Yikes! I hardly need to tell you that no stiletto-wearing spic was going to tell Harry what his department was, or wasn't. Just as he was raising a warning finger to my face, a woman came in to pay her rent. I took her check, and while I was recording the amount in a little log Barbie kept on her desk, it occurred to me to ask her if she had an acey in her apartment. "You mean air conditioning?" she asked, a little puzzled.

"There you go, Harry. Have a nice day." Wham! He slammed the door on his way out. By the time the next A/C started acting funny, I had been invited to a crawfish boil where people were toe-tapping to the catchy rhythm of Hank Williams's "Jambalaya and a Crawfish Pie and Filé Gumbo."

You should add that song to your playlist, *mi amor*. It's a hoot.

ACCESSORIES

Her name was Bianca Solano. The first thought I had on meeting my grandfather's mistress was that my mother would like her. Everything about this woman reminded me of my mother. She was elegant. She was tall. She was poised. The only way in which Bianca Solano did not resemble my mother is that I don't think my mother would have been game for lunch with a teenager at an expensive restaurant. Come to think of it, my mother wouldn't have been good at playing the amiable mistress anywhere. But of course Bianca wasn't introduced to me as "my mistress," but rather as "my friend, Bianca Solano." I liked her even more after we ordered the same thing for lunch—breaded chicken. After the Austrians introduced schnitzel to the world, chicken with bread crumbs and a lemon wedge was perfected at the restaurant where I first met my grandfather's mistress.

So we had lunch over lust. My grandfather was very, very proud, he said, as he regaled the smiling Bianca Solano with details about my upcoming *quinceañera* ball— details he had obviously made up. But I didn't say anything. When Azucena and I were growing up, my mother used to tell us, "Never invalidate an adult in public, *niñas*." So I never invalidate adults in public. Now, in private . . . anything behind closed doors always changes the name of the game. As for Azucena, she simply neutralizes people with her stare. It's so much more efficient to do it the Azucena way; I waste a lot of time pretending to be polite. So I ate my breaded chicken and I smiled. For dessert my grandfather ordered something flamboyant. It was called a baked Alaska. I had never heard of a baked Alaska. I had always thought Alaska was an iceberg the Russians sold to the Americans for seven million and change.

During dessert, my grandfather said we had much to celebrate and winked at Bianca Solano. I couldn't have put it into words back then, why that wink made my stomach turn. But now I can. I felt like an accessory. So after the ice cream was set on fire, and we'd all had a piece of baked Alaska, when my grandfather asked me to give Bianca her present, I gave *both* boxes to her. I wanted nothing to do with either of them. Bianca was delighted. By the time she opened the second box and cooed, it was too late for my grandfather to say, "Bianca, there's been a mistake."

EL POBRE GALLITO

Roosters are nature's alarm clocks. As soon as a farmer hears the unmistakable *kickerykeee*, he's supposed to jump out of his hay cot and say, "Time to milk the cows."

It was Toño, son number four, who betrayed his father. And he did it before the rooster crowed a third time. Just like Peter in the Bible, once Toño betrayed his father, he never forgot that sound.

Most people associate betrayal with Judas Iscariot. *Bueno, mi amor,* I have two things to say to those people. The first is that they didn't go to a Catholic school in the Tropics, where Fridays were reserved strictly for brainwashing and the Apostles. The second is that after what happened with Jean-Pierre, I became something of an expert on betrayal. If this were *Double Jeopardy* with Alex Trebec, the person who would win the jackpot would be the person who answers: "Both, Judas and Peter betrayed Jesus." The only difference between the two men is that Judas sold Christ to those who wanted to kill him for thirty pieces of silver—the price of a slave—and then, wracked with guilt, went home, got a piece of rope, walked to a nearby field, spotted a tree, and put the rope around his neck. Peter was a little smarter. After betraying Jesus, Peter said to himself, "Oh, shit, what if this guy really is the Messiah, after all?" And so he said to Christ, "We believe and know that you are the Holy One of God." Please! Everyone knows Peter didn't even go to the crucifixion. But he did go to heaven. That's because even before State Farm said it was so, insurance has always been a smart idea. That's why so many jokes begin like this, "So Peter is at the pearly gates of heaven, when . . ." It's also the reason that, to this day, many people continue to name their kids Peter. Tell, me, *mi amor,* did you go to school with any boys named Judas? It seems the names Adolph and Judas have lost popularity, despite the fact that Judas and Peter were basically identical people. As a matter of fact, Peter might have been a little worse. Besides being a traitor, he was also an ass-kisser, and a hypocrite. But we were talking about Toño, son number four.

It was a Friday morning *en esa casa* when Fortunato's *gallito* crowed and woke everyone up. It was unusual, but for some reason the *gallito* crowed a second time. Sometimes roosters do that; they crow in alarm, say, if someone turns on a light at the wrong time. Roosters are sensible animals. And that day there was trouble in the coop.

Toño had heard his father's *gallito* crow many times before. But of all the times he had heard it, he was only to remember that one Friday morning. My grandfather never let him forget it. After Toño went to Chocha and told her that he had seen his father with a woman named Bianca Solano at a bar, his fate was sealed. The malicious gossip also sealed the poor *gallito's* fate. It was thanks to Toño that Fortunato's *gallito* ended up in the crockpot. People who know their way around the kitchen know that a crockpot is the only way to get rooster meat tender enough to eat.

The night when Fortunato came home from work and asked Chocha, "Where is *mi gallito*?" became a sort of family legend, embellished with additional details in the retelling.

It was *the way* Chocha did it, too. After Fortunato left for work that morning to attend to whatever was currently clogged up at Fortunato Inodoros—the plumbing business that made enough money to buy emerald earrings for one's mistress—Chocha followed the *gallito* around *el patio de atrás*. When she finally caught up with it, she wrung the bird's neck.

Wringing a rooster's neck is slippery business. It takes some strength. And sincere determination. When she first pulled its neck, the bird went limp. But just as some women fake certain things—say, maternal love, for instance—the *gallito* must have been faking. Chocha strung it up, but just as she was about to cut its throat and bleed it out, the *gallito* ran off. After she caught up with it a second time, she tried again. But at that point it didn't look dead enough for her. So she whacked its head with a rock until it squawked. Chocha was experienced. She had grown up in a place called Villa de Cura, after all. She had killed a rooster before. And she knew full well that the only way to do this properly is to hold both feet firmly with one hand, then put the other hand under the beak, tilt the head back, and twist until you hear a pop. Chickens do indeed thrash around without their heads, but only if you allow them to do so. That's why you have to hold the head—to control the neck for the bleed-out. But no one ever said anything about hitting the poor *gallito* with a rock.

Later that night, when Fortunato asked about his *gallito* during dinner, Chocha said, "Let me tell you how I fixed it."

Anibal the third was also at the table that night, which was unusual. When he wasn't aiming the arrow at his sister's throat, Anibal was playing the tyrant elsewhere.

Toño the traitor was there, too. Everyone in the family remembers Toño as "the traitor." But I always think of him as "the sulking one." It made an impression on a young girl, a grown man sulking all the time. But that night around the kitchen table, he wasn't sulking. That night Toño must have had the same sticky feeling that Peter had after speaking of Jesus to the servant girl in the courtyard by saying, "I don't know that man." Toño knew he had betrayed his father. So he wasn't very hungry.

Lupita was there, too, sitting next to her mother. Lupita always sat next to Chocha. It was understandable. Lupita always assumed—wrongly—that staying close to her mother might help keep Anibal from pointing arrows and other sharp things at her. But Chocha wasn't that kind of mother; she didn't appreciate clinging. Even as an adult, my *tía* Lupita continued to follow her mother around the house. I always wondered if I was the only one who found that strange.

Apparently, on the night the *gallito* ended up in the crockpot, my father was out with his friend José Luis. Fabricio—the one with the Corleone DNA strand—was not home either. There was no telling where Fabricio was. Men who love imported guns, vampy women, and Cuban cigars cannot be expected to be around the dinner table every night. Everyone knows that learning how to say to your father, "It's not personal. It's strictly business," takes some getting around.

As for Narciso, the misplaced intellectual, he was at the table, reading as usual. Narciso always read during meals, as if the other people around the table were unrelated to him, as if he were staying at a cheap *posada* somewhere and these people where guests and he just wished he had a little more money to stay at a decent hotel. That was my uncle Narciso—smart, striking, and disgusted by his surroundings.

Lelo, the middle child who loved trains more than anything else in the world, was playing with a new toy train that night. Had Lelo lived in an industrialized country, he would have been diagnosed with Attention Deficit Disorder, *y pronto*. But he was born in a tropical paradise, so no one ever minded him playing with trains for eighteen hours in a row, or his going psycho-ballistic when his trains were not allowed in the shower. That's one of the advantages of calling the Third World home. There aren't enough teachers. And the doctors are so busy with malaria and yellow fever that they hardly know how to spell the word Ritalin.

As for Frasquito, the moment Chocha said, "Let me tell you how I fixed it," her youngest son stopped playing with his eyelids for once, to better look at his father's face. And then Chocha said, "If it were my bird, what would I do with it? Is that what you're asking, Fortunato?" And she smiled. Chocha didn't smile very often. She, herself, would tell you that life didn't give one much to smile about. The only times I remember seeing a sincere smile on her face was when she was tending to her rosebushes. Chocha loved roses. Despite the chaos, the transient floozies, the boxing matches, and the perpetual mound of knotted socks, *esa casa* was surrounded by gorgeous rosebushes. So Chocha said, "Well, Fortunato, you have to scald it before you pluck it. The water had to be really hot. But your *gallito* was so big I had to use a ten-gallon pot. It took a while for the water to boil, but once the water boiled, it only took about five minutes. I held it by the feet, and in it went. As you know, Fortunato, you have to keep swishing the roo around so it doesn't get too hot in any one spot and ruin the meat. So I tested it by pulling on the big tail feather. It came out with no trouble. That's how I knew it was ready to pluck. As for the recipe . . . what you're tasting in the sauce are the herbs. I ran out of sage. But I had some extra thyme. I know how you always want seconds."

GUNNING FOR IN THE BAYOU

Barbie was still in Jackson, Mississippi, when I caught sight of a guy chasing Ricky in the parking lot at Maison Blanche. It isn't every day one has the opportunity to witness a gun chase at work, so I stepped outside to better believe my eyes. Not knowing the details of the situation, I immediately sided with Ricky. He was the maintenance man, after all. And he was wearing his uniform. People in uniform are always principled and upright, except, of course, when they aren't.

At any rate, I'm pretty sure my normal grandmother would have called Ricky "a sack of bones." Then she would have made him a hearty chicken *sancocho* with the hope of putting some meat on those bones.

It seemed nothing wanted to sprout from Ricky. His pathetic mustache looked like an ant trail, and his eyes looked like pale garbanzo beans. On Ricky's behalf I will offer that he knew how to tell a joke, knew a great many of them, and managed also to keep people laughing long after he was gone.

The man chasing Ricky with the gun, on the other hand, looked like Arnold Schwarzenegger. When Arnold saw me standing outside, he stopped chasing Ricky and put the gun to my head instead. It was a quiet moment. For the better part of my teen years I had been a regular at the shooting range with Frasquito. And save for Lelo, the train lover, every last one of my father's brothers packed a gun. Why was I speechless all of a sudden? For his part, Ricky used the moment to try to get away. But there was no escaping Arnold. He was possessed, his eyes bulging with mad rage. So enraged was he, in fact, that he moved the gun from my head and fired at the steps, missing Ricky's foot by a hair.

"Hey . . . what's going on, guys?" I asked, aiming for that natural tone of voice you hear in pimple commercials. Got a pimple? No problem. That's why God invented Clearasil! After the first shot, we all froze in place. A second or two went by before I suggested we take the problem inside. Staying outside in full view of potential passersby might have been a smarter move, but I kept thinking about the button under my desk that automatically dialed the sheriff's office in case of an emergency. A gun to the head qualified as a bona fide emergency. As we were walking into the office, Ricky's eyes were frantically searching for a way out of range of Arnold's gun, which was now aimed at Ricky's crotch.

"What kind of joint you running here, bitch?" Arnold asked at that point. I thought of asking him what the word *joint* meant, but on second thought I decided to keep the superfluous to a minimum. A loaded gun is a loaded gun, and Frasquito used to say that a loaded gun wants silence. Seeing that I was willing to listen—or perhaps because he knew I couldn't go anywhere—Arnold relaxed his grip on the gun long enough to tell me that he lived in apartment number such and such and that Ricky was banging his wife. I didn't know what *banging* meant either, but for once I didn't need to ask, or to reach for my Webster's dictionary to look up the meaning of a new word. *Banging* sounds like what it is. Doesn't it? In fact, I almost told Arnold that just a few months before, *the exact same thing* had happened to me, this banging. And in my very own bed, of all places. But something told me Arnold wasn't the empathetic sort, so I told him I was very sorry and then turned to Ricky.

"Is this true, Ricky, that you are . . . banging Mrs. . . . ?"

"The name is Conner, you bitch! Sam Conner. And she ain't no Mrs., she's my girlfriend."

"Ahem . . . didn't you just tell me she was your wife?"

"Never mind . . . . D'you even know who you got shacking up in this God-damned joint, you bitch?"

"I'm sorry, Mr. Conner, this shouldn't have happened. Would you like to register a formal complaint?"

Before rushing to Jackson, Mississippi, Barbie had told me about this system of formal complaints. When I was finished laughing, Barbie asked me what was so funny. "I'm sorry, Barbie, it's just that . . . " How to tell her that formal or informal, complaining isn't something that's well received South America? You could complain all day long, of course. But who would listen?

It turned out Sam Conner didn't want to register anything. He wanted blood.

"Your ass is grass, you little swamp weasel," he told Ricky. Everything Sam Conner said that day I meant to look up later. I've forgotten most of it. It's been years. The only reason I remember about the ass being grass is because it rhymes so nicely.

At any rate, once it sank that some of us might not live to tell the banging story, I pretended my high heels had failed me, and leaned my body against the desk. I was about to push the button that rang at the sheriff's office when the light bulb went on. What had I been thinking? I was working at Maison Blanche without a work permit. The last thing I needed was a sheriff in South Louisiana asking to see my green card and, after realizing I didn't have one, telling me that my ass was grass and that he was shipping me back to Venezuela as a divorcée, a social standing that, other technicalities aside, is regarded the same as being a whore. In the end I had to put my faith in psychology.

"Hey, Sam, you drop the gun, we don't press charges—what do you say . . . ?"

"I'm gonna beat the crap out of you," he said, staring at Ricky.

Who knew Ricky could run so fast?

RISKING DEPORTATION

A couple of weeks after the gun incident Barbie Boudreaux returned from Jackson, Mississippi. And I was soon to be rich. Almost half of Maison Blanche had been vacant when she left. Now the place was full. A quick glance at the occupancy report and Barbie Boudreaux declared, "Sweet darlin,' you got a knack for sales."

"That's not exactly a compliment," I thought. Still, I had some three thousand dollars in commissions coming my way.

Barbie asked me how things had gone in her absence, and immediately I sensed that unless I said, "Smooth sailing," she would have a nervous breakdown. Practically overnight my job title went from Leasing Agent to Resident Therapist.

I was almost half Barbie's age. Still, it seemed that merely as a result of having visited my mother's rat lab as a child, a knack for nut cracking had rubbed off on me. Hour after hour I sat in the office with the depressing lime-green carpet, taking in Barbie Boudreaux's life, including the details of the day her son, Jess, shot his best friend with his dad's gun. To be sure, Barbie had more than a formal complaint to get off her chest. Compared to hers, my life was a mere walk in the basin.

I won't go so far as to say that Barbie and I became friends. What I felt toward her was immense gratitude. That's why the longer I stayed at Maison Blanche the more remorseful I grew about not telling her that I wasn't supposed to be working there.

The whole work-permit ordeal was a full-blown catch-22: it was illegal to work while attending school, but if you were not enrolled in school, you had to go back to your home country immediately. All the same, taxes were coming out of my illegal paycheck. The only reason that could happen was because the IRS and the INS weren't on speaking terms back then. Mostly, I remember living in a constant state of expectation, the expectation being panic. So whenever the sheriff came to the office—which happened every time we started eviction proceedings, or whenever someone skipped out—I grabbed the stapler on the desk and headed to the supply closet. Refilling a stapler is very tricky, this is something on which everyone agrees— you cannot rush the refilling of a stapler. You will not soon see a reality TV competition based on who can refill a stapler faster, I'm positive about this. All this to tell you that no one ever knocked on the supply closet's door while I was there with the stapler and my heart was beating like the heart of a greyhound. I knew what penalty I'd get for working without a permit. The words "IMMEDIATE DEPORTATION" are nicely printed on every scrap of paper you receive upon setting foot at the airport, where all the signs pointing to customs say, "WELCOME TO THE UNITED STATES."

What was less clear was what kind of punishment Barbie Boudreaux would receive for having hired an illegal alien. God knew she had enough problems trying to convince her son that he wouldn't burn in hell for killing his best friend. So I promised myself that after the next paycheck, I would collect my commissions, quit being a leasing agent, and return to school full-time.

Then came Halloween.

IN MATTERS OF HEART AND STATE

My grandfather had a violent temper. You knew his temper was about to flare up when you looked at his neck and saw little red map-like lines growing all over it.

On the night his *gallito* ended up in the crockpot, he didn't look at Chocha. Instead, he surveyed the table and searched his children's eyes, one pair of eyes at a time. Then he got up, went around the table, and calmly removed each plate. As everyone understood it, they had practically eaten a family member—that is to say, the mood was somber. Anibal was the only one who was still eating. Playing with a bow and arrow tends to work up an appetite. Even Narciso put his book down, which is saying volumes. Rarely was anything interesting enough in the world of the living to merit averting his eyes from Kafka or Chekhov. Lupita did what she always did. She looked up at her mother, waiting for a reaction so she could measure her own reaction accordingly. But since Chocha just sat there with her hands on her knees, Lupita must have thought that nothing of great consequence was happening.

When Fortunato removed Toño's plate, he noticed the sweat on his son's forehead. Fortunato wasn't a mind reader, mind you. But when remorse works as it should, even a blind man can spot a traitor in a crowded room. So Fortunato finished collecting all the plates and carefully put them in the sink. He then looked out the kitchen window, to better remember the tropical sunset on that memorable day. It was as he was contemplating the view that the red map started growing on his neck. All eyes, including Chocha's, were on the growing lines. She was many things, but she wasn't stupid. What Fortunato had in mind when he opened the big kitchen drawer was anyone's guess. The one thing that was clear was that he was looking for a sharp object.

I'll never forget that drawer. It was a drawer of great depth. An entire toolshed might have been crammed in there. I myself don't own any special tools. One pan. One pot. A wooden spoon. That's about it. Not Chocha. She had a fully stocked kitchen. She owned a few whisks, spatulas, and those types of things. But where Chocha showed her mettle was in her choice of scissors. Chocha knew her shears well. She owned all kinds of scissors: sewing scissors, trimming scissors, and whatnot. But Fortunato wasn't a clippers connoisseur, just a man in the throes of rage. So he grabbed a pair at random, left the kitchen, and walked to the front yard of *esa casa*.

As he was decapitating every single one of Chocha's rosebushes, he was careful not to prick his fingers with the thorns. After a while he returned to the kitchen with all the decapitated roses inside a large bucket and poured them on top of her head. Beautiful, colorful roses issuing out of a gardener's bucket might have been a lovely sight . . . had it not meant what it meant.

That's when Toño started sobbing. Then he ran upstairs. Everyone present understood that a change of magnitude had taken place. But having been born to a dedicated baker, they also knew that even though cakes might have a different texture from then on, there would still be cakes.

TREAT OR TRICK?

You'll have to agree with me that Halloween is a weird little holiday. *Bueno. Bueno.* We have Día de los Muertos, I'll grant you that. But those people are truly dead, *mi amor.* They're not plastic skeletons from Walmart. Ours is a religious holiday—which is a separate tragedy—not a get-rich-quick scheme by the makers of corn syrup.

Of course, *mi amor.* Of course I remember that Halloween when you dressed as an M&M. How can I forget? The moment you left the house to beg strangers for candy, which Max and I could have easily bought for you, I started seeing flashes of the headline "Murdered M&M" as I cleaned away all those pumpkin seeds.

What a mess! I still dream about those sticky pumpkin seeds sometimes. As a matter of fact, when Azucena cut a thatch of her pubic hair and stuck it on the soap, I remembered those pumpkin seeds.

In any case, on that Halloween of long ago, Barbie Boudreaux arrived at the office ahead of me, which was rare. We both lived on the property, practically ten steps from the office. This wasn't our choice: both our jobs specified that we had to live on the property, to better be tortured by our neighbors/residents at unseemly hours. Barbie usually carried the pager, which allowed her to come into the office later in the day. But that Halloween was different. That Halloween, Barbie came in early to decorate the office and then went back to her apartment. I didn't know this, of course. So when I unlocked the door and turned on the lights, I saw there was blood on our desk. There were also knives and other weapons. My first thought was, "Oh my God! Arnold killed Ricky for banging his wife!" That's when I screamed.

Mercifully, Ricky was still with us, even if he did have a black eye from the beating. All of a sudden, Barbie came charging out of the supply closet yelling, "Trick or treat. Trick or treat!" Harry was right behind her. And because he hated spics, seeing how confused I was, he said, "You got 'er good. You got 'er good, boss."

That might help explain why when you and I met years later and you asked, "Do you know how to carve a pumpkin, Valentina?" I looked at you and said, "You like pumpkins, Emily? Really?"

The following week, after all the blood had been cleaned up and there was nothing left of Halloween but those tricolor candies no one ever wants, we got paid. I had promised myself that I'd get my paycheck and then get out of there. But now that Barbie and I had a blood bond—even if it was fake blood—I felt I owed her an explanation. So I invited her to lunch.

We walked to the French Quarter to grab a couple of po' boys. Those are sandwiches, *mi amor*, extremely large sandwiches, as in a foot long. No, I don't know why they're called that. They're probably named after the poor boys who eat them—construction workers, streetcar conductors, people who can't spell *Châteaubriand*. But that's only an inference, a little better than a guess, but not by much. No, I've never seen a po' boy outside of Louisiana. But, as they surely would tell you, "tha' don't mean they don't exist."

After the second bite of my sandwich, I started to thank Barbie for everything she had taught me, and told her how much I had enjoyed working at Maison Blanche. All I can say to explain what happened next is that Barbie must have heard her share of breakup speeches in her time. She knew her preemptive strikes. Just as I was about to say the words "two-week notice," she told me I had been a God-send and that I was due for a promotion.

"Wait, Barbie. There's something I need to tell you."

"Sweet darlin', I'm sure whatever you need to tell me can wait. Now, eat your po' boy and let me tell you what it means to be an Assistant Manager."

"Barbie, I can't; you can get in so much trouble for this."

"Honey bunny, you got no idea what trouble is."

MI TÍA LUPITA

My *tía* Lupita was friendly with the people next door. She used to call them *los vecinos de al lado*. She was friendly with all of them, but her best friend was their daughter, Idoya, who was her same age. Lupita always invited me along when she went to see Idoya. Because my father was the first of eight, I ended up having a couple of uncles— and an aunt—who were very close to my own age. I was ten years old to Lupita's fourteen, and was thrilled that she welcomed me among her friends. Still, it was odd to hear Lupita introduce me as *mi sobrina*; strange to be called "my niece" by someone so young.

Whenever Lupita brought me along, she stood very close to me. It showed in different ways, this desire to protect me. To this day, whenever I think of Lupita, I see her standing very close to me. I think of it as a desire to protect me. But who can divine that sort of thing? Maybe she stood so close because I didn't have any scratches on my skin, and she thought that some of my innocence would rub off onto her.

Idoya's family was from Spain. Everyone in the family had identical blue-gray eyes with specks of yellow around the iris. An entire family with the same eye color—to me that was proof enough that they were strange. But something a little stranger eventually happened to all of them. Idoya's brothers, Imanol and Carlos Eduardo, both played soccer and were hardly ever around. Idoya and Lupita both dabbled in art. Idoya dreamed of making sculptures. *Tía* Lupita was fascinated by glass.

One Saturday afternoon when the two of us went to visit, Idoya came to the door and said, "Wait till you see what I've done." Idoya was always very mysterious. She was also very graceful. Her hair, which was straight and hung down to the middle of her back, swayed a little as she waltzed in front of us. "Are you ready?" she asked. She then made a brief curtsy, opened the door to her study, and turned on a lamp. The lamp consisted of strings of nylon to which round ivory petals made of soap were attached. The nylon was so very thin, it gave the impression that the petals were suspended, the way stars seem suspended from the sky. I thought the lamp was beautiful. That is, until it started to melt.

Lupita was very shy, always smiling awkwardly at situations she could not read well. She was never one to say, "Look, the soap is melting!"

That was me. I was the one who said, "Idoya, your lamp is melting!"

"Oh, oh," she said. "I guess I didn't think about that." She looked calmly at the lamp and then turned off the light to stave off the complete meltdown of her sculpture.

"Maybe it's just for decoration," I offered. "Maybe you don't ever turn it on, Idoya." Leave it to me to offer consolation to the people of Pompeii.

Idoya had worked for months on her soap lamp. But as I said, she was graceful. So instead of saying, "There's no point to a lamp without a light bulb, you nitwit," she said, "I'm glad you came along, Valentina."

After the sculpture meltdown, the three of us went up to Idoya's room, where I watched my aunt and her best friend play with lip gloss for a while. Neither wore much makeup; they didn't need it. Idoya looked like a virgin goddess from an old Spanish village. And my *tía* Lupita could have passed for Sophia Loren's twin. I sat politely on Idoya's bed while the two of them sampled little tubes and different containers of lip gloss, testing for stickiness, shine, and staying power. Everything was going well until Idoya told Lupita that she had a boyfriend and swore her to absolute secrecy. Just then, the moment got suspended. On hearing about Idoya's boyfriend, my *tía* Lupita froze. So I froze.

"What's wrong with you guys?" Idoya asked. And just like that our playdate was over. A few minutes later, Lupita and I were headed back to *esa casa*. We usually walked side by side, but that day Lupita rushed ahead of me. I did what I could to fall into step while making sure I didn't get so close she might never invite me to play again. It was my *tía* Lupita who taught me how to patch a running stocking with clear nail polish. But sometimes there's no catching a run.

WHO ARE THESE PEOPLE?

"We don't swim in your toilets, so don't pee in our pools." This was printed on an ashtray that was in the home of Gerald and Virginia Wilson, the two people who had delivered Barbie Boudreaux into this world before she traded the Wilson to marry the Boudreaux with the gun. Over a generous Thanksgiving dinner, Gerald Wilson told me he had been to the war. I didn't ask which one. Maybe Korea. Most likely Vietnam. Certainly not 1861, though he hadn't forgotten. Instead, I asked him where he'd gotten the ashtray and what the little slogan meant.

I know. I know. Your dad used to say, by way of loving advice, that sometimes, although not always, it's better to keep one's mouth shut. I'm still trying to figure out when to do one and not the other. The ashtray with the catchy slogan turned out to be a souvenir that Mr. Wilson had picked up in the French Quarter when he and Virginia "had gun up to Lucy-Ana to visit Barbie."

"But what does the phrase mean, Mr. Wilson?"

"Means we don't want no niggers around here, *siñoreeda*."

"I see, Mr. Wilson. Now tell me about Thanksgiving. What's the meaning of this holiday?

On our way back to Louisiana a few days later, Barbie apologized for her father's remark during Thanksgiving and told me he lived in a different time in his head.

I think that's probably why when you came home from school that time and told Max and I that you wanted to be a rap singer, I suggested you take pictures for the school newspaper instead. Still, I never told you why I said that. But now that your dad is gone, well . . . . I want to explain why I thought it was bad idea for *you*, in particular, to audition as a rap singer. Mind you, this is only *my* view of things. Just because I lived a handful of years in South Louisiana and read *Huckleberry Finn* doesn't mean I can get a job working for Kofi Annan. I'm sure the man can tell you stories about Ghana that would make my swampy tales seem like bayou shrimp by comparison. But for whatever it's worth, this is *my* take on why a blond person with blue eyes in this country saying she wants to be a rap singer might be considered a little gluttonous.

You're a smart girl, Emily. I wouldn't waste my breath on a moron. To say to the people who were once enslaved by the majority of which you are a part, "I raped your children. I raped your soul. Now, I want to rap." . . . Am I the only one who thinks that's a little insensitive? I'm just a foreigner here. What do *I* know? For all I know, your black friends at that all-inclusive school were flattered by the idea of Emily Goldman the rap singer. Some people might even say that this is what freedom of expression is all about in the land of opportunity. And that Emily Goldman has as much right to become a rap singer as Beyoncé Knowles has to be a Country-Western singer. It seems a little off, that's all.

Mostly, I've been confused since the day I set foot on American soil. And the day of the rap singer episode did little to assuage my confusion. I still remember how upset you got when I suggested you try out as a photographer for the newspaper. You're a great photographer. Why not? Then all of a sudden you started crying as if I had suggested you be inseminated by a goat. Still, it wasn't until you screamed at us, "I *hate* white people who skiiii," and ran to your room that I got really, really confused.

"Max, help me here, isn't Emily 'white people who ski'? I thought so." But what do I know? Our very own Shakira confused an entire hemisphere when she dyed her hair blond and started singing in English. You laugh now. But on the day you thought you might have blood ties to the Jackson family, all I could think was, "Pour me some rum. Who are these people?"

HOLIDAY HANGMAN

My first New Year's alone in this country I went to Pat O'Brien's with some friends. Right around midnight, almost everyone was throwing up Hurricanes on the sidewalk. After the Hurricane party, I went back to my unfurnished place at Maison Blanche and sat on the lime-green carpet, trying to convince myself that the end of a calendar year was not of special significance. Whose calendar is it, anyway? Try to convince anyone in Medina that it's not the year 1433 A.H. Try to convince the guy with the long beard walking the length of the Wailing Wall that he's not living in the year 5772 A.M. and see what he has to say. Just because someone named Gregory decided in 1582 A.D. that he didn't feel like moving Easter around anymore should not mean the rest of us should go Gregorian, should it?

But trying to convince myself that the end of a calendar year was just another day was like trying to convince you and the twins come Thanksgiving that your parents had not actually split up. There was never enough cranberry relish at either house to make up of the absence of the other parent. As for that first New Year's in New Orleans, there wasn't enough alcohol in a Hurricane to overcome the magnitude of the emotional landslide.

I've already told you that the secret to surviving these is to move and keep moving. *Moving* is one of those words that means exactly what it means. Moving is the opposite of sitting around and waiting for something to happen. Even sitting in a plastic chair at the Department of Motor Vehicles in a new city, waiting for your little number to be called, means you will soon be driving away to a new place where you will have to spend some time filling out an application of some sort and having your credit checked. And who can dwell on divorced parents, the people who cheated on you, or the evil boss from your last job when filling out an application demands so much from you? And don't forget the bank—the trials involved in having to prove all over again that you are who you say you are—that process alone can make you forget you have family in another country.

The following year, after finally getting my MBA from Tulane University, I no longer had to be afraid of holiday hangman, or of being eaten alive by fugitive crocodiles. I was living in Scottsdale, Arizona, where I discovered, to my surprise that "What you know, coon-ass?" and "How's it hanging, brother?" were not standard greetings throughout the country.

SILENCE

The year she turned thirteen, *tía* Lupita was unexpectedly yanked out of school and sent to a school in Montreal for a year. I never learned why Montreal. Lupita's sudden departure set many strange things in motion. All of a sudden everyone started moving very fast.

Literally overnight we moved out of *esa casa*, though no one explained why my mother packed so frantically, as if she were a fugitive on the run. I watched in silence absolute as she pulled clothes from hangers and emptied drawers, throwing everything into boxes fast, fast, very fast. My mother, an otherwise measured woman, was acting like a lunatic all of a sudden.

And then Rosa, my babysitter, left. Years later I learned that Rosa had been fired for not having kept a proper eye on me, for letting me wander around *esa casa*. An image stitched to my head is Rosa and me painting a portrait of Snow White on a paint-by-number canvas. And the next thing I knew, Snow White was in the trash.

After we moved out of my grandparents' house and into our own place, my mother became sullen and somber. I missed Lupita all the more. The time she was away in Canada passed the way sand passes through an hourglass. As soon as the sand falls through, you have to turn the glass and start waiting all over again. As for my mother, she had always been one to coo, to sing, to read to us at bedtime. My mother had such a lovely voice. Now she sat in bed all day reading Agatha Christie mysteries. To this day, I'm wary of mystery novels, young women living with dwarves, and any kind of child tale. Between my head and the pillowcase I whispered, "Why did Lupita leave?" But asking that out loud would have been like raising your hand in class and having everyone stare at you.

When I finally learned the truth, I wanted to throw it away.

A RARE STRAND OF SILENCE

The year Lupita and Idoya turned sixteen, a different kind of mystery was layered on top of the other mystery. For her sixteenth birthday, Idoya's family planned a vacation to Spain to visit the grandparents who still lived in Girona. The only one who did not go on that vacation was Imanol, the oldest son, because he had a soccer tournament that could not be missed for anything in the world. That is the only reason Imanol was spared. Even after all these years the banality of it overwhelms me, the fact that something as routine as a soccer tournament would be the one thing that makes a person's life turn out to be dramatically different than it might have been.

On the way back from visiting the grandparents in Spain, Idoya's family stopped in Malta. And by the time they returned to Caracas, they were all deaf and mute — every single one of them. The mother, the father, Idoya, and Carlos Eduardo could no longer hear or speak. It was inexplicable. After their return, they visited doctor after doctor. No doctor in Caracas could offer a logical explanation for what had happened. Not one could offer even an illogical explanation. From then on, whenever Lupita and I went to Idoya's house, we had to communicate through writing pads. There were pads of every size all over the house. At some point they all enrolled in sign-language classes, including Imanol, who at first thought his entire family had been putting him on for not going on vacation with them. But no. They went to visit the grandparents and came back speechless.

Azucena used to wish that I had gone on that vacation.

SKINNY WOMEN SHOULD NOT BE TRUSTED

The first wave of wives kept everyone busy for a few years, especially Chocha, who now had a fresh crop of regulars for her cakes. After the first four brothers married—my father, Fabricio, Anibal, and Toño—Chocha started experimenting with new cakes. There's no denying that Chocha had a talent for batter. The wives, even the anorexic redhead who married Toño—a woman named Jizela— found Chocha's cakes irresistible.

Chocha always kept an eye on the skinny Jizela; the baker in the house did not trust skinny women. I don't think she trusted my mother, either. But at least Chocha was afraid of my mother. Why deny it? Fear is so much more effective at inspiring respect than other lame, benign emotions. I don't think my mother liked Chocha, but she would have thought it crass to give voice to such a cheap sentiment. Still, she didn't have to say a word. My mother has a gift, which she passed on to Azucena: the ability to speak volumes by pushing a little plate of cake away and leaving it untouched time and time again. Chocha knew not to insist.

REASONS TO REMARRY

Even the fastidious Narciso got married in due time. Bookworm that he was, he must have realized that there's only so much to laugh about in *The Book of Laughter and Forgetting*. The thing to do after combing through the classics, then, was to find a wife.

Narciso's first wife was a schoolteacher. Her name was Maria Celeste. My mother and Maria Celeste were like two flowers in the same vase. They were both pregnant at the same time. Both came from good families where no one had ever heard the word *shit*, and both shared the unique talent of space travel. In family pictures they're usually sitting next to each other, apart from everyone else, looking at each other's pregnant bellies—my mother pregnant with me, Maria Celeste pregnant with my cousin Gustavo.

Maria Celeste and Narciso were married for several years, until the day Narciso could take her dwelling spirit no longer. He, who had traveled in his youth to other lands via Milton, Cervantes, and Saint-Exupéry, had an itinerant soul, after all. Maria Celeste was a homebody. Such differences are rarely survived in peace.

So with all the knowledge Narciso had gathered from Milton et al, he decided to become a lecturer on cruise ships in order to better admire the paradise that might be forever lost to a stale marriage. When he arrived at La Mancha, Narciso wanted to be able to tell like-minded souls all about the crazy knight tilting at windmills and pining for a village woman whose pastime was to look out the window in a place called El Toboso. And for those skeptics who discount the power of literature to alter the course of history, the town of El Toboso was the only town spared by Napoleon as he proceeded to shred Spain to pieces. The only reason he spared it was because it had been the birthplace of Dulcinea, who, as everyone knows, existed only in Don Quixote's imagination.

Life being stranger than fiction—that's what Narciso was betting on. In the beginning he invited Maria Celeste to come along to exotic locales. At least that's what Maria Celeste told my mother. She also told her that she had married so she could stay home with the many children she hoped to have. Narciso, on the other hand, had married so he could travel. And who better to mediate such conflicts of interest than a bikini model?

Eventually, Narciso divorced Maria Celeste and married the model he had met on a trip to Brazil. I have vague childhood memories of Maria Celeste. But the woman I can see quite clearly is the woman Narciso proudly referred to as "my second wife." Her name was Anya. Anya liked to travel. Anya liked to tan. Anya thought Émile Zola was a clothes designer, that naturalism meant going topless, and that *J'Accuse* was a large tub where topless people gather to make a splash. Better for Anya to bring naturalism down to the level of Jacuzzi water. Left to his own devices, Émile Zola might ruin someone's vacation with all that talk about poverty, prejudice, prostitution, and filth.

My mother took Maria Celeste's departure to heart. The only truly devout Catholic among them, my mother believed divorce was a sin. My uncles, on the other hand, always thought of divorce as a form of absolution. And what was there for a specialist on schizophrenia to talk about with a comedienne, an anorexic, and a bikini model, besides? To take them as patients would have been my mother's only option.

She always warned Azucena and me not to call any of these women *tía*; we never knew how long they'd be around. Her desire to protect us showed the weight of the love she carried inside. It also showed that despite her spending so much time in the company of rats, my mother knew surprisingly little about them.

III. SELF-DEFENSE

NATURAL BORN K _ _ _ _ _ S

The year I turned nine, my mother enrolled us in self-defense lessons. This, like many other things she did, came out of the blue, accompanied by a restrained grimace of terror on her face and without any explanation. Practically overnight Azucena and I were yanked from piano lessons and left in the charge of a man who wore a braided ponytail and knew all about killing people with your bare hands.

I never learned our teacher's name. All the students had to call him sensei. In the Japanese tradition of martial arts a sensei is a kind of master. But this man was not Japanese. He was from Norway. In retrospect, that, too, makes little sense. Why would anyone leave a civilized country like Norway to move to a paradise of snakes like Venezuela? I remember two things about our sensei: his blond warrior ponytail and his huge feet.

During our first class, I was surprised that Azucena and I were among the oldest there. Most of our classmates were five and six years old. At eight and nine, Azucena and I could practically be these kids' parents. All of a sudden I felt very tall and very awkward. It turned out I was tall. And I was awkward. As my sister and I were to learn, when you're not petite, it is to your disadvantage to be a good killer. The boys who were our classmates were not only small, they were also very nimble. What were Azucena and I supposed to do? We had missed our peak. But not to worry, each of us had very different ideas about overcoming our handicap. We were allied in one thing, though: we wouldn't take this lying down.

For her part, Azucena shot an upward glance and trained it in the direction of our teacher's pale blue eyes. It is a rare gift of hers, to make people feel like scum not by looking down but by looking up at them. So she made the sensei feel ill at ease; she made the man feel that he wasn't as good as he thought he was at the art of seamless killing. In all other respects a warrior, the sensei always made it a point to smile at Azucena at the beginning of each class.

Our first lesson was devoted to learning about the vulnerable points of the body, spots where one might make an easy kill without going to a lot of trouble or spilling a lot of blood—the temples, the windpipe, that sort of thing. Who knew that the art of suffocation could put one under a spell? Already I liked this so much better than piano lessons. Compared to seamless carnage, scales seemed infinitely boring.

In no time at all the weekly self-defense lessons turned into my own personal horror show with the Norwegian warrior called sensei. And this was before he showed us his *katana*, a kind of Japanese sword that had a blade longer than the sensei's torso. In just a matter of weeks I learned to appreciate the advantages of being the oldest in a class of agile little whiners. I could walk past them and make them be silent and still, as befits a person learning to kill with her bare hands and feet. There would be time for *katas* and other elegant demonstration moves. The first order of business was to learn the basics.

"All strength comes from your mind," said the sensei, "and from your stomach." Let's face it, if you have weak abs, how are you supposed to jump up and kill the enemy with your feet while suspended in mid-air? To better illustrate his point, after a few weeks of excruciating sit-ups, our sensei lined us all up on the cold cement floor and proceeded to test our strength by walking across our bellies. That's why I remember his feet. They were so pale. Yuk! I had never seen veins show through skin like that before.

Self-defense lessons were not for people mindful of thread counts on Egyptian cotton. They were not for formerly anemic youngsters like Azucena, who would grow up to call death "an involuntary misadventure." These lessons were for people who called toilet paper "toilet paper" rather than "hygienic tissue."

Now that I'm older, I think what my mother was trying to tell us was, "I'm enrolling you in self-defense lessons so you can better defend yourselves from people like your uncles." But she didn't say that. So we misunderstood.

That February, at the start of the carnival, our neighbor Guillo made the mistake of throwing some water balloons in our direction as Azucena and I were coming home from school. Throwing water balloons at innocent passersby is a carnival tradition in some parts of South America. It is, admittedly, a little savage. As luck would have it, one of the balloons hit Azucena's leg as she was going up the steps to our house. For some reason, this made Guillo laugh. But what was so funny about that? Unfortunately for him, I was fresh out of a new lesson with the sensei.

Just at the beginning of the week, he had taught us to identify conventional objects in a room, ordinary objects that were commonly thought of as harmless by most normal people. He asked us to look at a lamp, for instance, and to evaluate its full potential as a weapon. I paid close attention. I found it fascinating that you could make someone's eyes bleed just by breaking the innocent light bulb beneath a decorative lamp shade. I've always been a good student, and I was eager to put my newly acquired knowledge into practice.

So after Guillo's water balloon hit Azucena, I walked up to him. I did it calmly. The sensei told us never to lose our temper before a kill. Losing your temper is counterproductive in such cases. I had a temper. I had so much to learn. Few people know that you can't properly asphyxiate another if your mind is crowded with angry thoughts. Most people think just the opposite, as a matter of fact. But true violence demands Zen-like calm.

So I walked up to Guillo, who was a couple of years older than I, and I asked him, "Is that what's in your balls, Guillo? Water?" And I smiled. And Guillo smiled back. His little flirtation with water had paid off! You aim a water balloon at a girl and the next thing you know, she has approached you and asked you about your balls. So as Guillo fantasized an answer, I pushed him against a large boulder that my mother had gone to great pains to have an expensive landscaper position at the entrance to our house. Then I banged his head against the jagged edge of the rock a couple of times. Blows to the head, our sensei had warned, were not the easiest way to kill anyone. Blows to the head must be accompanied by the enemy's exhaustion and attending loss of will. The trick is to have the brain rattle a little bit inside the head. Then you can actually knock somebody out, cause some real damage.

Even Azucena was impressed. Azucena is not easily impressed. Looking at Guillo pinned against the rock, she didn't do that upturn thing with her eyes. Her eyes had finally focused on something she could not so easily dismiss. What can I say? Teach an innocent nine-year-old to kill and she will do it to the best of her ability. Luckily for Guillo, a hard head is hard to break. But I tried my best.

In a few short years I would earn my black belt.

HAMSTER PACKS BAGS

That was around the time when my hamster, Pablo, committed suicide. I've already told you about Pablo. I've already told you I was cleaning his cage with Clorox when he decided he would take neatness no longer. My mother was at work that day. I was at home with the maid when I saw Pablo jump off the banister. So why did my mother, who wasn't even there at the time, insist on explaining his death as, "Pablo no longer lives here."

"Mami, why do you think Pablo jumped?"

"Would you like some mango, Valentina?" That's another of my mother's gifts, her ability to subtly change the subject.

The truth is Pablo should never have entered our house. Since the day of his arrival, that innocent hamster divided the family into two camps: the people who were *for* and the people who were *against* my mother.

Azucena was disgusted by him; she hadn't been to the schizophrenic-rat lab, after all. So she was *for* my mother. My father, having grown up with flying frogs and *guacamayas*, which call their owner *puta*, welcomed Pablo with open arms. Pablo himself was against my mother, even if he didn't know it. My first and only pet was the subject of many a conversation between my father and my mother behind closed doors in the study. A potentially infectious rodent in the museum that was our house—this was a subject important enough to have been discussed at Davos.

BLOWN GLASS

The year I turned seventeen was a very busy and strange year *en esa casa*. But then again, every year *en esa casa* was busy and also strange. By then my *tía* Lupita was twenty-one years old and she was in love for the first time in her life. To help her with her dream of becoming a glass artist, my grandfather had sent her to Murano, Italy, the birthplace of blown glass. So Lupita left home in pursuit of all things fragile. While living in Murano she met a young opera singer.

His name was Maximiliano. In addition to being an opera singer, Maximiliano was a heartthrob. And that is saying a great deal. I grew up calling a version of Sophia Loren *"tía,"* and observing a rare assortment of women part with their panties for various versions of Marcello Mastroianni. It took a lot for a man like Maximiliano to stand out among Lupita's brothers. But he did. Maximiliano was charming. None of them were. Maximiliano knew opera. None of them did. Maximiliano spoke Italian. None of them could. Maximiliano and Lupita were engaged to be married. She had brought her fiancé all the way from Italy to introduce him to the family. I had never seen Lupita so happy.

Maximiliano, too, came from a large family, he said. To Lupita's version of seven brothers, he had six sisters. He, too, had a mother in the kitchen, except his mother made pasta instead of cakes. He, too, had a father who had pulled himself up by his bootstraps. His father had been a stonecutter, and now he owned a company that sold marble. These two were perfect for each other.

The only problem with Maximiliano was that everyone in the family was afraid he might intimidate Anibal. So everyone hoped that while Maximiliano was visiting, Anibal would stay away. It was possible. Back then Anibal was very busy. But then again, he had always used that house as a kind of hotel. He came and went unexpectedly, always unannounced.

Since Lupita's departure for Italy three years earlier, Anibal had gotten one of the maids pregnant. In the end, Chocha fired the maid.

It had been the maid's fault, of course. Everyone knows that young, uneducated women are nothing if not eager to welcome sadists into their midst. In any case, with the arrival of new, younger wives, there were more people to spread gossip *en esa casa*. Strange things still went on. But now they were out in the open. Apparently, Anibal had married a woman in the nearby city of Valencia. He had two children with her. He also had a wife in Caracas. So he had two wives. The two women did not know of each other. He had kids with the one in Caracas, too. But we had never met them. Nor did we ever learn their names. My grandfather, despite his fervent desire to have a large extended family and a giant Christmas tree filled with presents for twenty-odd grandchildren, never allowed Anibal's kids in his house. They were strictly forbidden to be there. Even the mute neighbors knew that.

It was also around that time that my grandfather's mother, a crumpled woman named Ñoña, moved into *esa casa*. Ñoña, too, was from Villa de Cura. The problem with Ñoña was that she had favorites among the brothers. For Chocha, this was a capital sin. Until the day she died, Chocha maintained that she loved all her children equally. "They are *all* my children," she once told Fortunato in the kitchen in front of everyone. None of us ever knew what prompted the sudden outburst. Well, maybe that's not entirely true. My mother knew.

As for Ñoña, she loved Toño, the traitor, who was already married to the anorexic Jizela by then. Narciso, she despised. Even after divorcing Maria Celeste, Narciso still carried a book around everywhere he went. Ñoña used to call him "pretentious" to his face. The long kitchen table where knotted socks were sorted was Narciso's favorite place to read in the entire house. As luck would have it, the kitchen table was also Ñoña's favorite place to sit and count the coins she carried around in a little silver purse. Whenever Ñoña happened to be at the table, even if she was sitting at the farthest end from him, Narciso would get up to leave. It happened in an instant—the minute Narciso got up, Ñoña would say to Chocha, "Your son is being disrespectful."

And right before leaving to read elsewhere, Narciso would walk up to her and say, "Look who's talking, the village slut." It was a little unusual, I must admit, to hear one's uncle call one's great-grandmother a slut time and time again. Perhaps what made their encounters so hilarious was the fact that Narciso looked so distinguished and was so erudite that it seemed he was talking through a ventriloquist. I only laughed once, though. The one time I burst out laughing, my mother gave me one of those looks that can stop a moving train on its tracks.

Because life is full of little ironies, Narciso's second wife, Anya, the bikini model, and the anorexic Jizela, who was married to Toño—Ñoña's favorite—became best friends. So it was tricky to navigate Ñoña's preference for one of the brothers. But in the end, it hardly mattered. These weren't women of allegiances. Both of them were given to sudden fits of laughter in Ñoña's face. Quite openly they discussed the crazy old lady from the village.

But Ñoña's predilections mattered immensely to Chocha. Favoritism was the one thing that had the power to bring the beating of a cake to a complete halt. That she thought of her children as equal was, of course, a load of batter. Everyone knew that my father, King Reynaldo, was her favorite. And everyone knew that she covered for Anibal when his wives called the house looking for him. I happened to be sitting at the kitchen table one day working on my trigonometry homework when the phone rang. Anibal was sitting at the kitchen table too, though he wasn't working on his trigonometry, of course. He was polishing a switchblade with some tarnish-guard liquid or other. I still remember my confusion when Chocha answered the phone and told one of Anibal's wives, as one under oath, "No, *m'ija*, Anibal hasn't come by in days. Have him call me when he gets home."

When Anibal had given enough shine to the blade and it was time to leave, Chocha went to the *patio de atrás* and returned holding a wife-beater T-shirt. "I washed your shirt, *m'ijo*," she said, inspecting it. But I couldn't get out the bloodstains."

Excuse me? To this day, I will always associate trigonometry with murder.

THE VILLAGE PEOPLE

Batter went stale inside a mixing bowl while Ñoña and Chocha had it out about the sticky business of playing favorites. The only thing I wished for during the incredible tirades between the two women was a bowl of popcorn, to better enjoy the entertainment. The new crop of wives was younger. And with youth came impudence and disinterest in the haranguing between old village women. Most of them passed through the kitchen and looked at Ñoña and Chocha the way people look at chairs that are in the way.

There were also girlfriends intermingled with the new wives. Frasquito had a girlfriend who walked through the house in a red bathing suit on her way to the backyard, where she preferred to sunbathe. Sometimes Frasquito went with her. On the rare occasions when he wasn't practicing swallowing gas for his flamethrowing somewhere, he followed closely behind Lilia, slapped her bottom, and said, *"Culito rico."*

On hearing Frasquito praise his girlfriend's succulent ass, Chocha would look at him and say, *"Más respeto, muchacho."* And she shook her head in disapproval. I was never quite sure if she was asking him to respect her—his mother—or to respect Lilia, the girlfriend whom Chocha herself allowed to parade around her house in various degrees of undress. It was confusing, sometimes.

As for Azucena, by the time she was fifteen, she already understood what good company was and was not. On the weekends, when we visited *esa casa*, she made sure she had other plans. Azucena was rarely seen *en esa casa*. My father's side of the family always referred to her as *"la frígida."* When I first told her that they called her "frigid" behind her back, Azucena said evenly, "The only thing worse than being a barbarian is listening to one, Valentina." And the only thing I wish for Azucena is that Oscar Wilde were still alive. And that he liked women instead of men. I shouldn't worry, though. Oscar Wilde might be long gone. And he might have preferred men. All the same, Azucena still calls him Oscar. Ever since I can remember she's been on a first-name basis with the sharpest tongue in history.

Though she has never told me why, my little sister intensely disliked Lelo. Maybe it has something to do with his running trains on the expensive dining table *en esa casa*. Whatever it is, we shall never know. Azucena keeps her predilections to herself. All I have to go on is her saying in front of Lelo, "The older the boy, the younger the toy" while staring at the ceiling. In her estimation barbarians are not smart enough to recognize an insult when they hear one. One has to look at the ceiling for the remark to have its full effect.

THE ITALIAN JOB

There was a small open area in the back of my grandparents' house, right outside the study where Narciso spent the better part of his adolescence. Save for Narciso, no one ever went back there; it wasn't chaotic enough for any of them. At one point, my grandfather had gone back there to read the newspaper after a busy day at Fortunato Inodoros. The décor consisted of an old leather couch, a red ottoman that had been slashed across the top, and a scrawny floor lamp with a skull for a shade. There was also a Picasso hanging on one of the walls. The paint was still wet. So it couldn't have been a Picasso. It didn't matter. What mattered is that everyone believed it was. And because any belief, outlandish or not, eventually becomes the reality of the believer, no one ever said that Fortunato's painting wasn't a Picasso. In fact, everyone called it "the Picasso." Why, it was even signed! And what's more, the painting looked every bit like *Guernica*. It is a widely accepted belief that *Guernica* is hanging on one of the walls at the Museo Reina Sofía in Madrid. But no matter. Picasso made an extra one for my grandfather—and made it smaller, so it would fit on the wall. In fact, the one hanging at Fortunato's house was the original.

It was in this intimate, peaceful area where Maximiliano and Lupita asked me if I would serve as the maid of honor for their wedding. They planned to get married in a place called Verona and they were very excited. After they went on and on about San Zeno Maggiore, Piazza delle Erbe, and Casa di Giulietta — Oh, she of *Romeo and Juliet* — I, too, was ready to say, "Good night, good night! Parting is such sweet sorrow . . . ."

Lupita and I were browsing through a bridal magazine when Anibal blasted through the back door that led to the backyard. Maximiliano, who was sitting right under the Picasso, immediately turned his head when the metal door hit the wall. Lupita's hands froze on top of the magazine when she saw Anibal.

As for me, I was still studying with the sensei. And after nearly eight years I had earned a brown belt and had a stomach that was almost as hard as the door. The sensei approved when he walked on my stomach in those days. Hard as he tried, his foot would not sink into my belly. By then I had also earned trophies for my stealth, for my ability to bring the side of my foot to someone's neck, distract them, and then quickly knock them to the ground with the other foot by destabilizing their stance. All this to say that when I saw Anibal, I was more observant than scared. My eyes went from him to the skull lamp. I also wondered how heavy the ottoman was. It was probably Anibal who'd slashed it. I'm pretty sure it hadn't accidentally become dissected. Still, the ottoman was out of the question. Heavy, round objects covered in fancy fabric do not make good weapons. Afterward, I wondered if that had been the moment my mother had anticipated for years.

As for Maximiliano, he was a gentleman. Despite the unseemly entrance, he got up to shake Anibal's hand. I had no idea what, if anything, Lupita had told her fiancé about her brother. So Maximiliano got up, this tower of a man, and trained his best stage smile on Anibal, who suddenly looked small, though he wasn't. Not physically, anyway. At that point, Lupita and I locked eyes. What happened next happened very fast. After Anibal refused to shake Maximiliano's hand, he took a step back and pulled out the switchblade he kept strapped to an ankle holster. He then sent it flying in Maximiliano's direction, the way knife throwers do in circus acts. And for some strange reason, this made Maximiliano laugh. It must have been all that opera. He must have thought he was in the middle of *Il Trovatore*, playing Manrico's part. But no. The only reason Anibal missed his throat is because Maximiliano moved. Otherwise, he would have become another casualty, right under the fake *Guernica*. The switchblade ended up pinned to the Picasso instead.

Lupita was mortified. Never mind that her fiancé had nearly died at the hands of the brother who had hijacked her childhood. Never mind that the painting wasn't even a Picasso. "Papá is going to be so mad," she said, looking at the painting. "Anibal, *por favor*," she pleaded. As if my grandfather, who loved her more than anything in the world, would have her head for her brother's little stunt.

A few weeks later, during a visit to the other side of the family, my grandmother asked my mother, "So when is the wedding, *hija?*"

And my mother said, "Oh, I forgot to tell you, Mamá. The wedding has been called off." Upon returning to Italy, Maximiliano broke up with Lupita.

As for my mother's mother, a wise and practical woman whose name was Isabel, she wasn't one to mourn averted disgrace. "Smart man," she said. "He doesn't know what he missed."

I was sad for my *tía* Lupita. But in the same way that it's difficult to say to someone who's had a miscarriage, "I'm sorry about your dead baby," I didn't know what to say. "I'm sorry, *tía*," seemed so paltry after she'd lost the love of her life to the one who owned every waking thought she had. Not to mention every nightmare.

PREGNANT PAUSE

Something was bound to happen sooner or later. There were too many weapons in the hands of too many men. But *men* is probably too strong a word for a group of people whose first decision in the morning was to go back to sleep.

The thing that stands out in my mind about Frasquito's funeral is the number of people there who were so close to my own age. I particularly remember Lilia, his girlfriend. She was nineteen years old. Everyone at the funeral kept whispering, "Poor thing, she's only nineteen." Lilia was and wasn't there. Her body was there. But she was drugged out of her mind. That it wasn't a good idea to use drugs when you were pregnant was not wisdom anyone passed on to her. After Frasquito's daughter was born, she, too, became my father's responsibility. He didn't want it, but my father inherited the plumbing business in the end. Now he had two more people to support: Frasquito's girlfriend and her daughter, a girl I only remember as a baby and whose name I never learned.

"It's not cholera. It's not typhoid. It's just blood." That's what Chocha used to say. I wonder what she said on the day she found her youngest son charred to a crisp in the *patio de atrás* while the scarlet macaw named Panchita repeated *"Puta, Puta, Puta."* So used was the bird to hearing the word "Whore" that it now repeated it indiscriminately.

Frasquito had loved to perform. He also liked to test the limits of things. On the day the gasoline he had in his mouth for his flamethrowing trick backfired, there was nothing more to be done. Everything caught on fire: his mouth, his throat, his lungs, his stomach.

On that day, Chocha had to stop beating egg whites to peaks to call an ambulance. I hope she didn't say, "It's just gasoline." As for Azucena, despite my mother and father telling her she had to, she refused to go to the funeral. After we got home that night, I went up to her room to tell her about it. And what did Azucena do? She shut her eyes really tight, put one finger inside each ear, and did not open her eyes until she was sure I was gone. Some people hate the circus. Others watch the animals in disbelief.

DANCING THE FLAMINGO
ON A BAD-HAIR DAY

Ultimately I had to get out of New Orleans. Having to choose between Vagisil and Monistat whenever I went grocery shopping, when all I wanted was the Campbell's soup, was more than irritating. Who knew that bacteria loved clammy legs? I know, I know this is somewhat personal, *mi amor.* But how are you supposed to trust me if I don't come clean about Monistat?

By now you know that trust is the protagonist of this story. I'm also trying to untangle things a little. And by then I had started to figure out that if you move enough times, it is possible to find something true and beautiful in the vastness of this world. I was betting that it is possible to wake up one day and smell something soft and fragrant. As long as you keep holding your nose, of course.

By the way, do you know how to tell if someone is lying? Apparently, the eyes have it every time. With the exception of some serial killers, no matter how accomplished the liar, the nervous blinking is always a giveaway. I got this tip from my mother one day when I asked her how she knew if her schizos were telling her the truth. From then on I started looking people straight in the eye. Color contacts also give you an edge.

But why am I telling you this? Oh, yes. How I met your dad. I met Max long after I had left New Orleans, after a series of jobs so uninspired the only thing I remember is having quit them so I could move. Anyway, I know we told you that we met at his office when I went to apply for a job. But that's not true. What we told you then is what is known as an emergency lie. An emergency lie is basically a temporary lie used to put the truth on hold until a better time, for safety reasons—to protect the person hearing it. Divorce and its aftermath require many more of these emergency lies than people realize at first. The number of lies one might have to tell, as a matter of fact, is impossible to predict. But for your information, an emergency lie is not the same as a white lie. A white lie is a lie that if uncovered would cause relatively minor damage. Some people will tell you that a lie is lie. Saint Augustine, for instance. But I no longer care what Saint Augustine thinks about me, or about anybody else, for that matter. There are many practical considerations to daily existence that masochistic men in robes who've had too much to drink simply can't get their little heads around, *mi amor*.

Now that your dad is gone, I have to ask myself, What were we protecting you from? A little embarrassment? So here's the truth. Your dad and I met at a Zumba class. See? You're laughing now. But what would you have done with the truth back then? What was a smart man holding a Yale diploma doing playing Richard Simmons in Scottsdale, Arizona? Your dad wouldn't have been caught dead entering a giant glass cube with a plastic banner hanging over the door that read, "Ditch the Workout. Join the Party!" But there he was.

It was both of our first time at Zumba, and we were both there to get over our respective heartbreaks. I had just been fired from my job; Max was recently divorced. I don't know how recent, *mi amor*. You know your dad. He just said "recent," which meant, "Don't ask." But I knew something fishy was going on with this guy the moment I saw him walk through the glass doors. He was the only guy at Zumba, for one. But that's not the fishy part. I mean, here's this white guy with these crazy Einstein curls dressed in brand-new workout clothes. New shoes. New socks. New shorts. Oh, and the aqua blue bandanna with the little black checkmark on it. That's why your dad and Azucena always got along—such suckers for anything with a logo. And if all new clothes at a trendy dance studio don't scream, "I'm starting over!!!!!!!!!," I don't know what does, *mi amor*.

Zumba was new to me, too. I was there for completely different reasons, though. You can say that being fired without an explanation makes one crave a little different air. But there was more to it than that. I had just turned thirty earlier that month. And who would have thought that thirty would hit me with all its wisdom? I know you're only seventeen and that thirty probably seems ancient to you. But trust me on this. Thirty is like skydiving. Nothing quite compares to that sense of freedom you get from being able to look down on the world. It was great to finally be done with the all the self-consciousness and indecision of my twenties and to be able to say, "I think I'll drop in at a Zumba class. Who cares that I just got fired?

Who cares if I can't follow the steps?" I can't say the same thing about thirty-seven. But anyway, I was also curious about this so-called revolution in fitness. You have to pay attention to something which has fifty thousand followers per month and counting. That's more than a trend, *mi amor.*

So I went to Zumba. And what did Zumba turn out to be in the end? You have to remember we were in Scottsdale, Arizona. I don't know if this has always been the case, if the place has always been a Botox mecca, but all the faithful were there that afternoon. All those women beset by botulism were in class, including the teacher, who wore a very, very tight pink shirt to go with her tightened cheeks. Quite frankly, it was a little unnerving to watch her dance. Whenever she moved, we all held our collective breath and checked the mirror to see if one of her boobs had escaped.

So there they were, all these white *chicas* wearing Zumba shirts and shaking their hips to the Latin rhythms with which I grew up. You name it—merengue, salsa, vallenatos, cumbia. But it was the teacher's explanation of cumbia that took my breath away. Before starting the music she gave us a little history about the dance and went on to explain that cumbia was a courtship dance from Colombia once practiced by slaves. That is true. Then she told us that way-back-when the slaves' legs were literally bolted to the ground as they danced, which is also true. And then she said—and I swear I'm not making this up—"Do me a favor everyone! When I start the music, I want you to keep those slaves in mind and drag that leg. Now, let's party!" And the next thing you know, this aching music that once symbolized a cry for freedom is blasting out of the speakers. Every once in a while our teacher adjusted her microphone to say, over the music, "Drag that leg, drag that leg. I want to see everyone drag that leg." There was only one way out of that room, and she had locked the door. So I couldn't escape.

After the cumbia she came to a complete standstill and said, "I'm gonna stop the music for a sec so I can teach you guys a new dance called the flamingo."

"Great," I thought. "A new dance might be worth the fourteen dollars I paid to drop in." Max and I were both drop-ins that day, which is to say that we weren't actually members of the club. We were there to check it out, as it were.

When the music started again, the *chica* put her arms above her head, arched her back just like a flamenco dancer, and started to clap.

That's when I started to laugh. That's also when everyone in class stared at me as if I were having a seizure. I was laughing to keep myself from screaming, "You dilettante! The Flamingo is a hotel in Las Vegas. It's also a bird, pink as your shirt!" But I didn't scream. I laughed and laughed. And when all those scrutinizing eyes were fixed on me from the big mirror, I said, "I'm such a klutz. I don't think I get the steps to the Flamingo." It works every time—put yourself down and people suddenly feel superior. "Oh, that poor girl at Zumba; she couldn't even do the Flamingo." Ever since then I've done that kind of thing to get me out of a jam—talk fast, mix up the slangs, pretend I don't speak three languages. Let's face it, no bona fide citizen wants to admit that some stupid immigrant can locate Ho Chi Minh City on a map, when all along they thought it was a Chinese restaurant in downtown Chicago. When you're an immigrant, it makes life so much easier just to play dumb. You don't incur anyone's wrath or envy that way. It really works . . . . It works until you start to believe your own lie. Mind games are a little dangerous that way. You may wake up one day and really believe that you're the Manchurian Candidate.

Earlier that day, right after getting fired without so much as an explanation, I had considered moving back home. But only for the time it took for me to say, "Maybe it was my hair color. Maybe they don't like spics here either."

Instead, I realized, it was time to bring Val back. Why sulk when you can go to a salon and dye your hair strawberry blond? It seems I've spent a lot of time in hair salons since moving to this country. The only problem with changing your hair color is that sometimes you end up—for purely economic reasons—at cheap haunts called something like Curl Up and Dye, and instead of the color you wanted, you come out looking like a vampire at Halloween. So I'd gotten what I paid for: burned cherries instead of strawberries. Still, the bad color was good enough to dupe everyone at Zumba into believing I was white enough not to be able to get the steps to the Flamingo.

Everyone except Max, who walked up to me afterward and said, "What was so funny?"

"The Flamingo," I said.

"I know," he responded. "I lived in Granada for a while."

He hadn't ever seen my luscious black hair, and he liked me anyway. Maybe it was because he had his own hair issues to deal with.

HOLIER THAN THOU

Bianca Solano was at my grandfather's funeral, the year I turned eighteen. She had been his mistress since at least the death of the *gallito*.

As it turned out, it wasn't just Toño who knew about her. He was just the only one smart enough to betray his father. I myself had had lunch with the woman the week before my *quinceañera* ball. But I never told a soul. One dead *gallito* per family was good enough for me. What if Chocha decided to skin the tiger that came to replace the *gallito* and serve Grandpa stewed tiger? I was always a quick study. So I kept that Saturday lunch with Bianca Solano to myself.

At the funeral she looked very alone, standing all the way in the back of the church. There was no trace of the welcoming smile of three years before. Still, she made it a point to acknowledge me with her eyes. And what did I do? I went up to her in full view of everyone. I was three years wiser, after all. When I got closer, I saw that she was wearing the emerald earrings I had picked out for myself at the jewelry store that time. I thought they went nicely with the elegant black suit she was wearing that day. Up until that point, everyone had been silent and somber, all eyes on God. But my little greeting seemed to wake both the living and the dead. All of a sudden all eyes were on us. That's when Bianca Solano said, "You're daring, just like him. I don't want you to get in trouble." And she left the church.

Later that night my mother told me it had been in poor taste to say hello to the mistress in front of the wife. "You are so right, Mamá. But it would have been fine to say hello behind the wife's back, right?"

"It's inexcusable, Valentina." Case closed. No words ever came after my mother said the word *inexcusable*. Everyone knows "inexcusable" is a tough act to follow. Everyone in the family knew about Bianca Solano, including my father, though no one, except me, was crass enough to humiliate the wife in front of the mistress. And inside a holy place, of all places! What had I been thinking?

BLOOD STAINS

On the day my grandfather died, I was the last person out of his hospital room. But everyone thought it had been Anibal. That's what happens in large families; too many people coming and going for anyone to notice any one person. That might explain why women who bear more than they should bear start saying all of a sudden, "It's not cholera. It's not typhoid. It's only blood." That's why when Anibal went into the room and I stayed behind the curtain, no one noticed. We all knew that my grandfather was very close to taking his last breath, because the doctor had said so.

My grandfather might have been close to kissing this world good-bye, but he was clear on one thing: there would be no forgiveness forthcoming for Anibal. He even forgave Toño for causing the death of his *gallito*. Out in the hallway everyone heard him growl, "You're a fool, Toño. But you're still my son, and there's nothing I can do about that now." In the end, there turned out to be a whole lot that my grandfather could do nothing about. But it was the death of his favorite son, Frasquito, that made a man as strong as Fortunato decide to call it a night when there was still light to be had. After Frasquito's terrible accident, my grandfather started smoking and drinking as if it were the end of times. And for him, it *was* the end of times. Lupita was still alive, but there's a way in which Anibal had killed her. So when Anibal asked him on his deathbed, "Would you forgive me, Papá?" my grandfather asked him for some water instead. And when Anibal asked, "Did you hear me, Papá? my grandfather said, "You're not my son." For a minute or so, time froze on the words "You're not my son." Then whose son was he? That's when Anibal started to cry. This made an impression on me. But Anibal's tears didn't impress my grandfather. As Anibal sobbed and begged for forgiveness, my grandfather gathered every bit of breath left in him to push this out: "May God forgive you, Anibal . . . because . . . I can't."

All I can I say is, thank God for the sensei. Had it not been for the Norwegian who toughened my belly, I might have gasped right along with my grandfather and given myself away behind the curtain. I wasn't hiding on purpose. My going behind the curtain had been purely a reflex. But now that Anibal was in a state, I couldn't very well come out and say, "Hey, Anibal, what's with the tears?" This wasn't a moment for people easily lured by gum ball machines. Before the sensei, I used to be impressed by gum ball machines. I used to imagine I was the colorful ball that traveled through the little groove and showed up at the other end. As far as I was concerned, that was magic. Now I had to stay alert. It was anyone's guess what Anibal might do if he saw me standing behind the curtain in possession of his secret.

Most people think that hospital rooms are antiseptic. And there is that, of course. But bacteria aren't the only weapons. Take needles, for instance. If you studied with the sensei, you'd know that needles are underrepresented in the weaponry department. Guns, swords, and knives get all the glory. But a needle with a little bit of electricity is all it takes to kill hair at the root. *Tía* Zulay used to boast about the merits of electrolysis. A tiny needle that dissuades a follicle from turning into an ugly hair sticking out of your chin is definitely worthy of respect. So as Anibal grew more agitated, I started to panic. I wanted to leave the room. But I knew that moving would be a mistake. That's when I thought, "Needle on tray versus switchblade in ankle holster." Would the needle even have a chance? And where to stick the needle, besides?

Most killers fail because they see the situation as they wish it were, not as it is. That's what the sensei said. I saw the problem now. I was wasting valuable time by wishing the situation were different. I was failing in my appraisal. I kept wishing I were not there, witnessing death and its sticky aftermath. But I was. "What's more important, Valentina, life or death? Death in progress always seems more urgent. But life wins every time. Life is ice-cream melting on the sidewalk. Death is ice cream already melted." That's what the sensei used to say to make sure his point got through to six-year-olds. And as he prepared to walk on our bellies, he told us there are only two ways out of close-contact combat: dead, and bring the death certificate.

But there was a problem with the needle on the tray. I couldn't have foreseen it, but I saw it quite clearly then. The problem was called "intent." When it came down to it—tears of atonement or not—Anibal would always outdo me when it came to intent. And what would the sensei say to that? He'd say, "You're dead, Valentina." He'd say lack of intent is no different than getting hot-blooded before a kill. There's a reason they call it "cold-blooded murder." And there's a way in which I'm grateful that my blood has always been body temperature. That was my little epiphany on the day my grandfather died, that after years of training with the sensei, all I had to show for it was that I owned a black belt. I didn't have it in me to hurt a fly.

The day my grandfather died, I grew up in less than a quarter of an hour. While my mother was in the hallway, just a few feet away, I was growing up. At the funeral, I wanted to forget, wanted not to belong to such people. But I did. I wasn't there to forget. I was there to remember.

A few days after the funeral, on a day when everyone seemed more anchored than they had been in a while, I told my mother about the conversation I had overheard. She took a sip of her coffee. She was quiet. But then again, my mother has always been quiet. So I asked, "What is it that my grandfather could not forgive, Mamá?"

"Valentina, *por favor*. Not now. I can't talk about this right now." By then I was too old for her to say, "*Niña*, you didn't hear that." I heard what I heard. And I heard that some things are unforgivable. Can you amend your life with one sentence?

YOU SHOULD NEVER MARRY FOR ____

On the day I was to marry Jean-Pierre, my father made me an interesting offer. As he was walking me down the aisle inside a church crammed with people down to the last pew, he asked me if I wanted to run out the back door. Trust me, I realize that's not standard wedding-day issue by the father of the bride in most parts. I think my father suspected I was marrying for the wrong reasons. In response to the generous, if unusual offer, the young bride said, "Dad, to express something in one note is to define your style." I had read that—or something very close to it—in one of the bridal magazines. I had no idea what it meant. Or why it came to mind at that moment. It just sounded good. Then I squeezed my father's right arm and said, "Let's see how I feel after the Ave María." But my father *knew*. He wasn't both a father of the bride and a psychotherapist for nothing.

My wedding day is the only time I ever saw my father wearing a tuxedo. You can see a lot through a veil. I saw women fainting to the right and left of the aisle. "Papi, doesn't Jean-Pierre look good waiting? He hates to wait, you know . . . ." My dad smiled and shook his head a tiny bit. If the priest only knew about the conversation we were having behind our infidel smiles. "Excommunicated! Both of you!"

"Let's keep walking for now, Dad."

"Are you sure, *mi vida?*"

"I'm sure, Papi. But wouldn't it be fun to see mom's face if we turned our backs on all these people now?" My dad smiled really broadly then. More women fainted.

Sometimes I wish I had taken him up on his offer. But I couldn't have stomached dealing with both Azucena and Oscar Wilde. I didn't want to hear anyone say: "The only thing worse than not getting what you want is getting what you want." At least now I have the experience. And I'm so much wiser for it. What was I doing there in the first place, wearing an uncomfortable fluffy white dress? It would have been much more in character for me to marry on an island, with a bathing suit for my wedding dress. Or to marry in a Gypsy cave to the beat of Zambra music. That's how I married your dad. But eloping didn't count. As you know, we had to have a staged follow-up wedding in order to make our families happy. The things we do for love . . . .

SNOW IN THE TROPICS

There ought to be a law against marrying on the rebound. Think of the years that might be spared. It was only a few months before marrying Jean-Pierre that I had broken up with Miguel, my boyfriend of three years. I've often wondered how my life would have turned out had I not gone to that party with him. Miguel and I had been inseparable. Miguel gave me my first kiss. Miguel and I planned to get married and have two children, a boy named Miguel and a girl named Valentina. But he ruined everything by befriending people who liked mirrors.

The day after the party where they had been passing lines of cocaine on beautiful beveled mirrors of all shapes, Miguel came to visit me. I gave him a hug, asked him to wait in the *antesala*, and headed upstairs. I despised him even more for not suspecting what he had coming to him. On the way up to my parents' room I kept seeing flashbacks in my mind of naked people entering and leaving various rooms at the party the night before. I also saw flashbacks of Miguel and the girl whose crotch he was fondling as I was leaving the party. Miguel didn't know that I had seen him. I myself left the party with someone else—she was the only other person who still had her clothes on when the clock struck midnight. It was strange, the way that girl and I had not known each other before that night, and how we found each other in the kitchen of that huge house and said, without saying a word, "Which way is out?" It turned out the girl had a car. And she offered me a ride. Afterward the only words that passed between us were "What's your name?" and "Thanks." What else was there to say?

Now Miguel was downstairs waiting for me. And my dad was upstairs. He had just taken a shower and was doing what he always did after a shower. He was in his robe holding a small towel he used to dry each and every one of his toes. To my knowledge he has followed this little routine every single day of his life. Once he was absolutely sure each toe was drier than toast, he proceeded to sprinkle talcum powder between each one. Men talk about women being finicky and so on, but I've seen enough fussiness in men to invalidate that claim.

"Can I borrow your talcum powder, Papi?"

"What for?" My father knew me well enough to be suspicious.

"I just need a little bit," I said." I promise to bring it right back." So I headed back downstairs, went into the kitchen, and sprinkled a little talcum on a spoon. By the time I was out of the kitchen, my father was downstairs talking to Miguel. "Sorry to interrupt," I said. Then I walked up to Miguel, forced his mouth open, and said, "How about a little powder?"

My father was horrified. "What are you doing, Valentina?"

"Did you know Miguel likes powder, Papi? Here's your talcum back."

A couple of weeks after the talcum episode, my best friend, Mariela, invited me to a private discotheque that had just opened in the trendiest part of the city. Private discotheques exist in countries like Venezuela for practical reasons, such as avoiding pesky kidnappings, and also to avoid accidentally bumping into any undesirables outside your social circle, which might increase your chances of not marrying well. The number of private discos is somewhat small. They couldn't be called "exclusive" otherwise. To paraphrase a very smart economist, most of the problems in South America stem from the fact that there are many more people whose last name is Chávez than there are people with hyphenated last names trying to keep them from trendy discos and such.

That's where I met Jean-Pierre, at the private discotheque. He was French. He smoked. He thought only barbarians lived in the Tropics. Going down there had been the worst mistake he'd ever made. He couldn't wait to leave, he said. I had him at *très bien*.

Jean-Pierre and I were no longer living in the country when Azucena called to tell me that Miguel had died of a drug overdose. "It was in the paper today," she said.

Along with the privilege of being part of the elite, comes the privilege of being front-page news. Dead, or bring the death certificate? I wonder if my parents realize how much they owe to the sensei.

DO YOU SMOKE AFTER SEX? I DON'T KNOW. I NEVER LOOKED.

How to put this in a way that doesn't cause friction? Whereas Azucena lost her virginity in a civilized country and proceeded to get proper medical attention, I was deflowered by a surgical razor in the Third World and proceeded to get scolded. There might be some truth to the notion that the firstborn gets more photos in the family album than the next in line. But it is also true that the firstborn undergoes many more experiments.

Still, I try not to take sides. It's dangerous to take sides when it comes to your own life. When it comes to someone else's life, it's a lot easier to answer the question "Whose side are you on?" In the interest of vouching for my own sanity, though, I offer that in most places outside of Eritrea and surrounding areas, a girl's hymen and surrounding area is hers to do with as she pleases.

Something strange happened on the days following my announcement that I was going to marry Jean-Pierre. My mother and father locked themselves in the study, as they usually did when they had to discuss weighty matters. Flimsy as it was, my hymen—like my hamster—turned out to be a weighty matter. Why was a little piece of film, which many women surrender to a guy named Tampax, so important to them? After a few days of secret conferences—to which neither Azucena nor I were invited—my parents emerged from the study and called a family meeting.

"This is what we've decided," said my mother.

"Decided about what, Mamá?"

"You need to see a doctor. *Un doctor*, Mamá? But I'm not sick. Why?"

"To make sure you don't get pregnant right away."

"Who said anything about getting pregnant right away, or ever?"

My mother looked at my father. They locked eyes. My father wanted to have a conversation. I could tell by the way he said, "Let's hear her out, Serena." Fat chance!

Whenever my parents discussed something "as a couple," they were as good as the Soviet Bloc. The better to avoid the confusion, mixed feelings, or petty misunderstandings so common in households where everyone has a say, they presented a united front. It didn't matter. I was confused anyway.

"It's been agreed," my mother said.

"What has been agreed, Mamá?"

It was my father's turn to speak. They always took turns. "Your mother and I have already discussed it. And to make it easier for you, we've made an appointment with a friend of ours."

"An appointment for what, Papi?"

"Don't worry," said my mother, smiling maternally, "I'll be with you throughout."

"Throughout what?"

"The procedure."

"What procedure, Mamá?" Meeting adjourned.

I have to hand it to them. My parents were always very good at entertaining questions. In the end, no one could accuse them of being unreasonable. I had had my day in court. They had heard me out. A week later my mother and I were sitting in the waiting room of a Doctor Larrazabal. He was well respected for wearing kid gloves when it came to shoving pieces of copper between the legs of unsuspecting virgins. How do you get a reputation for such a thing, anyway?

And how to bring this up with Jean-Pierre? How to tell a Frenchman, of all people, that he wouldn't get to do the honors? "Here, Jean-Pierre, have a cigarette, *before* sex."

And because our family has always been very open, Azucena was invited to our little *tête-à-tête* about my hymen. She was only seventeen. I can't blame her for waiting to marry until curtain call; and then again very reluctantly so, and only because her biological clock would not accept the snooze setting. That was before she realized that children sometimes crave ice cream and are rarely mindful of the costs of the clothes on which ice cream is often spilled.

WHICH WAY OUT?

Only in retrospect is one able to say about certain situations, I should have put up a little more resistance. It is only afterward that one has accumulated the necessary trauma to give voice to such a sentiment.

When the nurse in Doctor Larrazabal's office called my name, I was a little guarded. You'd think that after years with the sensei I would have been very much at home in any situation involving knives and other metal objects. What can I say? I've never been that comfortable doing splits before strangers. Let alone a stranger holding a surgical knife.

"It will be just a little prick," said the doctor.

"Just a little prick is what you are, Doc!" That's what I wanted to say. Well, it wasn't a little prick after all. First the knife, then the piece of cold copper. I screamed. Then I fainted. And in much the same way as I had humiliated the entire family by shaming the wife in front of the mistress the year before, once I came to, and came tottering out with an intra-uterine device, which made me waddle like Daffy Duck, my mother said, "Everyone in the waiting room heard you scream, Valentina. Would it ever be possible for you to be a little more elegant?"

Now it was my turn to use the word *inexcusable*. But I didn't. I smiled at my elegant mother. In her own way, she had been trying to spare me. I can only imagine how far she had had to bend by setting her Catholic beliefs aside, turning a blind eye to every chapter and verse of the Bible she had all but memorized—forcing fornication with a scalpel, imposing contraception, and hoping for an eventual divorce—all for fear that her daughter might bear a child while still a mere adolescent.

Why deny it? A cold, sharp razor between your legs feels like a betrayal. True, the sting was over in the time it takes to say, "I hate you." Yet, it was the thievery that devoured everything. But it wouldn't do to go insane. In my mind, I was already packing my suitcase. As for the soreness between my legs, the wedding was a few of months away. I had time to recover. I even had time to break the news to Jean-Pierre. And to prepare for his befuddled, *"Pardon, chérie?"*

But I wasn't worried. I had read about it in *Cosmo Latina,* about women who fake orgasms. How hard could that be? And for me, who wasn't even elegant? Faking an orgasm through scabs and scars just might turn out to be a sneeze. All of a sudden my skin grew as thick as a coconut shell.

The following week, once I was again able to walk without giving myself away as a duck relative, I headed to the American embassy. Sooner or later, anyone who's anyone in Caracas ends up studying English in the United States. It's a status symbol, to speak the tongue of your trade partners. "Well, make that sooner"—that's what I said.

It was at the American embassy that I saw a brochure about a place called Melbourne, Florida. The rows of Florida oranges on the cover looked familiar. Melbourne looked like a colorful, tropical paradise, except that they spoke English there. So I asked one of the clerks about it. She told me they were accepting applications and giving out some scholarships at the university there. But you had to have excellent grades. So I applied. I never dreamed I'd be accepted. So I never told anyone about it. Melbourne as a honeymoon locale took Jean-Pierre by surprise. It happens a lot, my taking people by surprise, even if that's never my intention.

Years later, when I was no longer called an alien resident, and had my own driver's license to prove it, people asked the inevitable: "Where are you from?" And then, "How come you left an exotic country like Venezuela? And at such a young age?"

"I didn't leave my country," I would say. "Countries are places with trees, rivers, mountains, that sort of thing. You can find that anywhere."

IV. THE MYSTERY OF THE MAIDS

STORK FEATURES

For Lucas Enrique's birth I flew to Venezuela with a box of Godiva chocolates in my luggage, risking arrest and risking the chocolates being confiscated by a gluttonous customs official. Venezuela grows its own cocoa. Still, most of it ends up in Godiva boxes elsewhere. When I bought them I didn't know who the chocolates were for, the baby or the mother. All I knew was that if I didn't bring something imported for the occasion, Azucena might not recover from childbirth. So I arrived at the Clínica Metropolitana de Caracas, the Nordstrom of hospitals, with my Godiva box in hand. And I might add, wearing a super-cute red miniskirt, as befits someone who is about to become an aunt in the Tropics. Who could have predicted what was to come? Now that I'm telling you this, I realize that my life has been a series of unsuccessful attempts to control the uncontrollable.

The minute I got there, I found my mother pacing outside Azucena's room because the doctor who was supposed to attend to her was in the emergency room with a woman whose baby had taken all the wrong turns. Meanwhile, Azucena proceeded to go into labor. And before I had a chance to say, "I brought some chocolates," a nurse poked her head out and said she needed a hand. A hand for what? And for reasons explained only in *The Secret*, once the nurse put her request out into the universe, it couldn't help but materialize. That's when all eyes turned in my direction. If a red miniskirt and a box full of expensive bonbons doesn't say, "I don't do births," then I don't know what does. Midwife, anyone?

Mere seconds later, I was in the room with Azucena, presiding over Lucas Enrique's birth. As luck would have it, Lucas Enrique was sideways inside of Azucena. My theory on this is that Azucena had spent too much time sitting at Marketing Committee meetings when she was pregnant. But that's just a theory. To add to the dilemma, Lucas Enrique was not breathing as he was supposed to. All this intelligence came courtesy of a machine to which Azucena was hooked and that read the vitals for both the mother and the unborn child. At some point, the numbers on the machine turned bright red. As if childbirth weren't stressful enough. I think what the machine was really saying was, "Get a fucking doctor!"

But there was no doctor in sight. So the nurse looked at me and told me to tell Azucena to push. For some strange reason, at this very urgent moment, the nurse saw it fit to use an interpreter. Maybe she thought the sister's word carried more weight than hers. So I said, "Azucena, you need to push." And Azucena, who was limp as a noodle because the nurse had given her too much of whatever that thing is they feed you through your spine, said to me, "I don't feel anything."

That's when I said, "Well, you'd better start feeling something because if you don't push, the kid dies." Instead of pushing, Azucena proceeded to cry, perhaps for the first time in her life. What can I say? My sister's sense of timing has always been impeccable.

So I was forced to say, "*Hermana*, this isn't a time for tears. You need to push!" From that point on things started getting more and more complicated. The numbers in the machine were now blinking. It was at that point that the nurse told me she had to go get a doctor, any doctor, because she was in over her head. As if I hadn't realized it! So she left the room. But life is very stubborn. Life doesn't wait for missing doctors, or for nurses going MIA. The moment the nurse left the room was the moment Lucas Enrique decided to come out. I only had a chance to say one more, "Push," when out of the blue— more like out of the black—I see this thatch of black hair peeking out of Azucena. Oh, my God! I had no idea they came with hair.

As bad luck would have it, I had just had a manicure before getting on the plane. I really hoped the kid could get out by himself. Playing midwife was not something I had ever considered. I hardly need to tell you that it wasn't a pretty sight. I kept looking at Azucena's teary face, then at the mess squeezing out of her legs, thinking, "Where do they keep the Clorox?" That was a defining moment for me. Childbirth is one of those things that the good people of Hollywood have not yet captured to the best of their ability. Nothing I have seen on the big screen compares to the real deal. What choice did I have but to kiss the manicure good-bye? So here comes this blob, this purple mass of a thing, and now I'm holding him, it, whatever it was, when an intern, a doctor-in-residence, walks in just in time to cut the umbilical cord. Watching that part of the process made me wonder why we're not connected to our mothers by the elbow, or by some part of the anatomy less disgusting than a string of bloody sausage.

That's when Azucena, spending the last little bit of breath she had left, asked me if it was a boy or a girl. I wasn't sure what it was. "I don't know, Azucena . . . . It came with hair. The problem is . . . how to put this? I'm not sure it's normal; it has a cone head." That's when she passed out. I had no idea all babies came out that way.

Anyway, that's why I have two people in the world calling me "the other mother." You call me a stepmother and Lucas Enrique, once he learned the story, started calling me *"mi otra mamá."* Life has a way of dealing you these cruel little blows. Nothing ever seems to want to stay on plan.

Take for instance, Azucena. She leaves a foreign country where she's called an alien, thinking she's going back to a tropical paradise where everyone can spell her name, and where does she end up? She ends up in a polluted oil well where the only distractions are beach robberies and murder at the mall. As far as I know, street executions are still free down there. Still, I'm sure Azucena would much prefer to issue the following message from her BlackBerry: *"Ce message a été envoyé depuis un terminal BlackBerry de Bouygues Telecom."* Instead, she has to issue an unglamorous message like this: "You're lucky to have gotten this message from me and not from one of my kidnappers."

WHAT'S IN A NAME?

At the posh hospital where there were no doctors to be found, my sister was registered as Azucena Viloria Serrano de Contreras. But way of cultural peculiarity, the longer the name in South America the higher the social standing; this is another way of saying that the poor maids who work for Azucena have only one name. I simply know them as Pipa, Cuca, Ula, and so on. But what I find more peculiar still is why all these women keep leaving my sister's employ – every single last one of them.

I wish I knew why, *mi amor.* I don't know why poor people in the hotter of the two hemispheres are the ones with the shorter names. Sociology is not my department. Still, it's a very good question— good enough to give one pause. My guess is that it has to do with living conditions. I mean, I've never visited the *ranchos*, or anything. The squatter settlements are very dangerous. The maids at our house used to say so. From the very little intelligence I've been able to gather, in the *ranchos* where Azucena's maids live it's pretty much the norm to have six, seven, ten people to a room—brothers; sisters; cousins; the men who rape them, beat them, and sometimes kill them; and their dingoes. No. I'm not making this up. It's too sad, really. No, *sad* is not the right word. The right word for some of these happenings is *sordid.*

The reason I know some of these stories is because, as you know, I like to talk to people. Occasionally, I also listen. Like when you used to tell me stories about your evil girlfriends in high school and I just sat there, incredulous about what some of these girls were capable of doing. To this day it breaks my heart, the way that girl Lisa uninvited you to her birthday party after you had bought her a present and everything.

But evil high school girls in North America are small potatoes compared to the lives of some of the maids who worked for Azucena. My guess why they generally have short names is that many times these women end up getting pregnant without even knowing who the father is—through no fault of their own—and then, well, they have no choice but to have their babies and go to work to support them. By the time they totter to the bus and arrive at the gate of my sister's gated community to iron her Gucci skirt, well, can you blame them for not having any energy left to think up a longer name for their child? But that's just a theory. I really don't know.

Some things about South America are inexplicable. How to explain, for instance, so many mango trees and half the people starving down there? Meanwhile, I can always find fresh mangoes at Whole Foods, and with little stickers on them, even—cute, little stickers that say, "Made in Ecuador."

Other things are explicable, but very difficult to explain, if that makes any sense. Wait till you hear about Pipa, the maid who stole Azucena's beauty tomatoes. But I suppose no one who was raised going to Costco can grasp the concept of ten people to a room; any more than anyone hungry enough to steal my sister's tomatoes can grasp the concept of Costco. Though I will say it is easier to get used to Costco, even if you do find the place obnoxious. That's just logical. Abundance is better, any day of the week.

So let me tell you about Pipa, the first in an illustrious line of maids to whom my sister gave the boot. Back then, Azucena had started buying tomatoes because she read in some *chica* magazine that tomatoes are good for you. Apparently, something about the substance that makes tomatoes red also makes them good for your skin. Or so Azucena read. So even though no one in our family eats tomatoes, Azucena started buying them to teach herself how to eat them, so that in turn she could have better skin.

I've told you that Azucena looks like a virgin. This means that her skin is as perfect as the flower after which my parents named her. Azucena neither wants nor needs any tomatoes. But one can't argue with her. Just to prove you wrong, she might say, "I do too have ugly skin!"

So this is what happened. While Azucena went to work as editor of the magazine *Caracas Spectator: How the Rich Live Now*, Pipa stole the tomatoes, which were going bad anyway. The only reason I know about the tomato smuggling is that on the day Azucena fired Pipa after finding the rotten tomatoes inside her jute sack, my mother called me to tell me that my sister was being unreasonable and asked me to talk some sense into her. My poor mother knows that every time Azucena fires one of her maids, Grandma has to move in and take care of the kids. This is no routine babysitting job, mind you; my niece and nephew are extremely particular, having been raised on only the best. They are the kind of children who start conversations by saying, "When we were at the swimming pool at the Ritz Carlton in the Caymans . . ."

So I called Azucena, if anything to spare my mother the trouble of having to make another brioche with melted Brie, the only cheese Azucena's children eat. After a while it gets expensive, *mi amor*—trying to talk sense into a stubborn person long-distance. And besides, there's no talking sense into Azucena. This is a woman who once glared at a sommelier for recommending a 2004 Châteauneuf-du-Pape. Adding, for good measure, "That's child abuse." I have no idea if that was too young a wine to drink, *mi amor*. All I know about wine is that it comes from grapes and not from mangoes. But the next time she calls, I'm going to tell Azucena that here in the States people are so rushed that her favorite wine is called "CDP" at the liquor store. It doesn't have the same ring to it, does it? Châteauneuf-du-Pape is a mouthful.

But to finish the tomato story, the way my mother saw it, knowing that Pipa was stealing tomatoes was far better than having to hire a new maid with God-knows-what vices yet to be unleashed on the unsuspecting Viloria Serrano household. My mother's logic had something to do with the idea that it's better to keep the devil you know than the devil you don't know, or something along those lines. See? It's all perfectly explicable. However, just because something has an explanation, *mi amor*, doesn't mean you can get your head around it. I mean, there are think tanks in Washington working on some of these issues as I speak.

BANANA SPLITS

For our first date your dad invited me to a place called Camelback Mountain, a type of slope right in the middle of the city that looks like the back of a camel from a distance. I remember it being very hot that day. Come to think of it, Arizona in the summer ought to be reserved for camels only. It was so hot, in fact, that the only thing fit to wear was a miniskirt and skimpy sandals. How was I supposed to know that when Max said, "Let's meet at Camelback Mountain," he meant we were going to climb it? That's something you only see at the Imax: people hauling backpacks, trying to get to the top of Kilimanjaro after eating a can of Spam. I thought he meant we were going to walk around . . . you know, a nature walk at the base of the mountain. So when I saw him dressed to the hilt in mountaineer gear, I thought, "Hmmm, there must be some kind of misunderstanding here." I had heard the expression before. And as I understood it, what that expression really meant was, "You must be out of your fucking mind."

It wasn't an auspicious start. But Max was always very resourceful. When he saw what I was wearing, he told me to get in his car and drove us to a place where they sold hiking shoes. How to explain to this eager near-stranger that there are more *zapaterías* in Caracas than there are Super Bowl fans in this country, but that none of them sell shoes without a heel? The places that sell shoes to go spelunking and to go look at spider monkeys are called "adventure outlets." So when we arrived at a place where the attendant brought out a pair of hiking boots that gripped my ankles, I had to tell her that I hadn't suffered from polio as a child.

That's when I asked Max if he liked banana splits. To my complete shock, he said no. Who doesn't like banana splits? It turned out that Max had a personal vendetta against both bananas and avocadoes. They made him gag, he said. All the same, we ended up at Baskin & Robbins, where I had a banana split and Max had a cone with a ball of coffee ice cream on top. He shouldn't have had the coffee ice cream. He was nervous enough as it was.

An hour or so later we drove back to the mountain to get my car. Imagine my surprise when at the conclusion of our date, Max leaned over and planted a kiss on my lips. "What? Did you think you hired a whore for the afternoon?" I know. I know. It's a little confusing sometimes. Down in the jungle we are raised to dress like little sluts, but to behave like virgins. The reason we're not as confused as people named Mary Jones is because our choices are really straightforward: virgin, whore, or both. And also because, mixed signals or not, we're all clear on one thing: You have to buy the cow. You can't just get free milk. Or however that goes.

YOU HAVE THE RIGHT TO REMAIN SILENT

I didn't think it was possible to top the first date. But there you have it. For our second date Max invited me to go on a picnic. I remember we drove for what seemed ages to finally arrive at a very remote place where there were neither phones nor bathrooms. Uh-oh. Still, I could tell that Max was in his element. He was smiling as if he had a million dollars in the bank when he took a picnic basket out of the trunk of his car, complete with a red-and-white-checkered tablecloth for us both to sit on. The entire time I was watching Max with the basket, I kept telling myself, "Don't think about the wilderness, Valentina. Focus on the positive. Look how organized he is . . . ."

Inside the picnic basket was a box of Kentucky Fried Chicken, which I'd told him I had always wanted to try. "Are you sure?" he'd asked me. He was a little incredulous, at first. "Valentina, I can go to a deli and pick up a couple of sandwiches."

"No, no, I really want Kentucky Fried Chicken, Max." I had seen the commercials: "crispy, golden-fried chicken" looked like something everyone ought to try before they died. As it turned out, I nearly did.

But anyway, picnic basket in hand we start walking, talking, walking, talking, until we came to a river. And Max says, "There's a great spot on the other side of the river."

And I'm like, "Where's the helicopter?" The moment I set eyes on the roiling waters, I wondered if Max had ever seen any English films. I wondered if he knew that picnics take place in meadows, in the shade of huge, lush trees. It's not a picnic when it involves crossing a river.

So we changed course and started walking in a slightly different direction, toward a place where there was an actual tree and not a cactus, which is a rare sighting in Arizona, a tree that isn't a cactus. It wasn't an oak or anything that substantial, mind you, just a little better than a shrub, but not a cactus. So we sat there and ate our fried chicken. Or maybe I should say that Max observed a rare bird from

South America proceed to eat a bucket of Kentucky Fried Chicken. It was really delicious, but I think Max was grossed out by it. He ate a chicken wing and then told me he'd had a late breakfast, or some such excuse.

Afterward, there followed the inevitable interrogations that make up most second dates. City of birth? Population? Brothers or sisters? Beach or mountain? It was too soon to touch on childhood traumas, former sleeping partners, phobias, or pet peeves. We played it safe, aided by that unspoken understanding that anything you say in an unguarded moment of bucolic bliss, can and will be used against you. It was all smooth sailing until Max told me that he had three kids. Uh-oh. Then he pulled out his wallet. *Ay-ay-ay.* To this day, I don't know if it was the pictures or if it was the chicken that didn't agree with me, but right after asking him, "What are their names?" I threw up. Date over! And then, "Oh . . . it's not you . . . I'm just . . . a little sick."

Who could explain? Perhaps my parents could. That's how those things usually work. Say a pipe bursts at your house. You call a plumber and what does he tell you? He tells you that you need a new pipe. You call an architect and what does he tell you? He tells you that you need a new house. You call an engineer and what does she tell you? She tells you that you need a new foundation and that this is why the pipe burst in the first place. Being psychotherapists, my parents always told me that I had psychosomatic responses to the world, which is another way of saying that it was all in my head. I suspect that when Max showed me pictures of his adorable children I proceeded to throw up a bucket of Kentucky Fried Chicken because my child-averse subconscious could not absorb the shock. It might have been the chicken. But then again, I'd never expected to be a stepmother, or a mother of any kind, for that matter. So it was probably a little of both. That picnic was excessive in every way.

Several months went by in this way. Max would invite me to one thing after another and I'd make up an excuse, or else I went along and then had a miserable time. To tell you the truth, it wasn't his fault. I wasn't ready to have a good time, neither with him nor with anyone. I didn't know what I wanted to do with my life next. And besides, Max and I were just too different. His idea of a good time involved pitching a tent in the middle of the wilderness, lighting a fire, and waiting for the animals to come. As for me, sleeping in the woods and waiting for animals to knock on my tent is the plot to a horror film.

How to bridge the differences? Move, of course! As I told you, moving is really the best way to stay a step ahead of any potential emotional landslides. I didn't move right away, however. But I did take an important step in that direction: I acknowledged in the back of my mind that life in Arizona had already happened to someone else.

Meanwhile, I called my friend Ana in Miami. Ana was from Nicaragua. We had met at Tulane. By the time we got off the phone, Ana had already said, "You'll love my friends!" It was on the plane to Miami that I sat next to the guy from Canada. His name was Marc. I wish I remembered his last name. After all, Marc asked me to marry him. And I said yes.

YOU HAVE THE WRONG NUMBER

Since moving to the States I've carried the following in my purse: a Band-Aid, two Advils, and a safety pin. Up until the iPhone revolution, I also carried a quarter in a separate pocket of my wallet. These objects served a single purpose: disaster insurance. No cut would ever be larger than my finger-size Band-Aid. No headache would last longer than four hours. And no shirt would ever expose me in public by popping more than one button, preferably not the one keeping the boobs in check. As for the quarter, I have no idea whom I planned to call in case of emergency. You can't call anyone in this country without making an appointment first. And pay phones are now in museums, anyway. But that's beside the point. The point is I had nothing in my purse when the call came in—other than the Band-Aid, the painkiller, and the safety pin. Why those items in particular? Why not, for instance, carry a pair of scissors? Why not learn to change a tire? How come I wasn't carrying a vibrator in case of emergency? Insurance or no insurance, when the dreaded moment comes, it still finds you jerking your head sideways and asking, "Who, me? You have to be kidding!" Sometimes, though not always, it pays to be prepared. I've used the safety pin. I've used the Band-Aid and replaced it. I've used the Advil and returned to Walgreens. But what was I supposed to pull out of my purse when the guy on the phone asked, "Is this Mrs. Goldman?" Excuse me? I don't like the sound of that. Nobody ever calls me, "Mrs."

"Is someone dead, Officer?"

But let's not go there just yet, *mi amor*. I'd like to think that Max is still upstairs, about to come down and say, "Pizza and a movie, baby?" I don't want anything more.

A *SEÑORITA* BY ANY OTHER NAME

Lucas Enrique and Sofía, my nephew and niece, are being raised as a prince and princess at a time when monarchies are going out of style. This is going to be a problem, I keep telling Azucena, to no avail. Not content to give her firstborn the name of a dead king most remembered for the fate of his six wives—divorced, beheaded, died, divorced, beheaded, survived—Azucena threw in the name of a prophet to make sure that Lucas Enrique would never be beset by self-esteem issues. As for Sofía, my little niece only needed one name; what with Sophie of Greece, Sophie of Württenberg, and Queen Sofía of Spain, she's covered.

And why all this talk of kings and queens all of a sudden? Because, *mi amor*, Venezuela is a crumbling monarchy of sorts, a place where people with names like Lucas Enrique Contreras Viloria will suffer at the hands of people named Nea. As you might have guessed, Nea was one of my sister's maids. Now let me tell you why Nea was fired.

One day Azucena comes home from work a little earlier than usual and finds Lucas Enrique in front of the television, except the television is off. This surprises Azucena, given that Lucas Enrique is addicted to telenovelas. Apparently, that's what he does after school. Rather than doing his homework, Lucas Enrique watches the reasons for the demise of South America unfold before his young eyes in dramatic form. That's where Lucas Enrique hears things such as, "It's impossible, Isa! Our love is impossible! I have to marry Maria Fernanda," says the man on the screen, then gives Isa a two-minute French kiss. Isa is, of course, the maid. Maria Fernanda is, of course, the poor rich girl the man will marry. He will have an illegitimate child with Isa. The illegitimate child will be president one day. End of story.

So Azucena finds Lucas Enrique on the couch as if he's coming down with dengue fever and she asks, *"¿Qué pasa, mi rey?"* *Rey*, meaning, of course, "king."

And Lucas Enrique says, sulking as only he can, *"Mami, Nea se comió mis palmitos."*

"What? Nea ate your hearts of palm? Nea, you and I need to have a talk. You cannot continue to eat Lucas Enrique's hearts of palm. If this doesn't stop, I'm going to have to let you go."

So guess what happened? You guessed it. Nea was hard of hearing. She ate Lucas Enrique's hearts of palm one last time, and then she was gone. I hadn't noticed this pattern, this thing with the maids until I told Max the hearts of palm story and he asked, "Why do all the maids keep getting fired? You should write a book about that."

And I'm like, "Max, I know I've had a lot of different jobs. I know how you might think I'm due for a change of scenery. But you have another thing coming if you think I'm going to lock myself in the basement like one of the wives of Henry the VIII and try to compete with people called Joyce, whether James or Carol."

Still, since the day Max first asked me about why Azucena's maids kept leaving, I started listening more closely to our Sunday phone conversations. I used to put the phone on speaker and tune out her stories, because they were always the same. "Valentina, I had to fire the maid today." Every once in a while, Azucena would ask, "Are you there? Did you hear what I just said, Valentina?"

Then I would pick up and say, *"Claro,* Azucena, of course I'm listening. Go on."

But for all the mangoes in Venezuela, *mi amor,* I could not muster any sympathy for Azucena, or for any of the incorrigible maids for that matter. It all seemed so trite. However, once I started paying close attention, I started to notice a pattern. And the pattern broke my heart. Then I felt sorry for both Azucena and the maids. Maid or not, it isn't easy to find a job in Caracas. Let alone trying to find a job and raise children at the same time. Down in the jungle, day care boils down to finding a poor woman from the slums who will cook, clean, do the laundry, and watch your kids. When the woman arrives at your house, she realizes that compared to her, you are a multimillionaire, if only because you can afford to have a spare can of hearts of palm. Almost immediately, she starts to see you as her oppressor. At first, she eats the hearts of palm, not because she's a thief but because she's hungry. If that's all she does—eat the hearts of palm—you need to consider yourself lucky.

How best to put it? A poor maid has other options. She has the option to start robbing you blind. She also has the option to tell one of her boyfriends when your house is empty so he can perpetrate a state-of-the-art robbery that will never be reported to the police. Or she might abduct your children and then have a friend call you at work to ask for ransom. Or she might decide to abuse your children in exchange for your oppression. Thus far, the biggest price Azucena had to pay for being practically a single mother in the Tropics while Carlos Upstairs played with his Game Boy was a half-dozen rotten tomatoes and one can of hearts of palm. I kept telling her how lucky she was. That was until she hired the woman from Medellín, the one with the STD.

The best way to learn the history and geography of South America and its oppressors, *mi amor,* is through the lives of these maids. There is a Medellín in Colombia. There's a Medellín in Spain. An important battle was fought in Medellín, Spain, in 1809. A French guy named Claude Victor defeated the Spanish army, trying to gain territory from the kingdom of Spain. There it is again, the word *kingdom.* The maid my sister hired was from Medellín, Colombia. For this to have its full impact, you need to know two things: that Colombia is next door to Venezuela, and that a woman from Spain would just as soon slit her wrists than press shirts for Venezuelan "monkeys," who were once under her ancestors' thumb. See? Who's king and who's not king is only a matter of a few hundred years.

So when the maid from Medellín, Colombia, arrived at Azucena's house, there were problems immediately. For starters, her name was Cuca, which in Venezuela means "pussy" but in Colombia is just a name like any other. And because Azucena simply could not bring herself to say the word *pussy* in front of Lucas Enrique and Sofía, she started to call Cuca *"señorita."* But you have to remember that Azucena is sending Lucas Enrique and Sofía to a very expensive private school where only the best and brightest are admitted, and that *all* children are more perceptive than adults ever give them credit for. So one day, Princess Sofía asks, "Mami, how come the new maid doesn't have a name?" And Azucena, who has picked up a tip or two from my mother's dealings with schizophrenics, says, "Let's see what's on TV, *mi reina.*" There it is again, a word for royalty—*queen.* Most of these details I learned not from Azucena but from my mother. South American mothers can get very involved in their daughters' lives. Do you realize how lucky you are in this regard, Emily? If I were you, I'd start counting my blessings right now.

Sometimes, there's no telling where a kid will pick up a bad habit. One day, when Princess Sofía was left with Grandma because Azucena was in Marketing Committee meeting yet again, Sofía started scratching her crotch. And my mother, in that calm demeanor that is not really calm, but horror-under-control, asked, "What are you doing, *preciosa?*"

And Sofía said, "*Señorita* says it itches down there."

So it fell to my mother to conduct a proper investigation, which led to the discovery that the person my sister went to such pains to call *señorita* was carrying something else that starts with the letter *s*. Cuca's venereal disease was discovered by our family doctor when my mother sent her to get tested, pleading for the matter to be kept "hush-hush." Cuca is probably back in Medellín taking revenge on a drug lord by sleeping with him. But I have no way of knowing that. I just know she's no longer in my sister's employ.

ULA THE SAINT

After Cuca, there were no maids for a while at the Viloria Serrano de Contreras headquarters. Those were difficult times for Azucena. Pretty soon I started to wish a maid would fall from the sky on her lap, because due to the amount of stress Azucena was under, I heard from her not only on Sundays but via e-mail and surprise text messages. These included such musings as, "The kids are home alone. What if they get murdered?" Unfortunately, Azucena is one of those people who cannot keep her fears to herself. You tell me, what can I do, thousands of miles away, with a text message that includes the word *murder* in it? Barring war zones, the word *murder* is not part of the dinner conversation in most places in the world. In Caracas, it is served for breakfast, lunch, *and* dinner. So after months and months of receiving messages with the word *murder* in them, help arrived at last.

The next maid in my sister's employ was an older woman. No more unstable young women carrying STDs for Azucena! Her name was Ula. It was going to work out. Ula's food was delicious. Ula starched my sister's shirts just so. There were no lines on the clothes Ula ironed. Ula did not bicker. Nor did she sleep with my sister's chauffeur. Ula vacuumed in only one direction, the way Azucena prefers. Ula did not get her feathers ruffled when she got one instruction from my sister and the completely opposite instruction from my mother, via telephone, within a five-minute time span. Ula was, in a word, a saint.

But on the day her only son was murdered in a shoot-out at the Plaza Bolívar, Ula had a nervous breakdown. Azucena pleaded with her, even offered to pay for the funeral, which Ula gratefully accepted. But after the funeral, she left. I never learned where Ula was from. A safe bet might be Margarita, Coche, or Cubagua, the three islands off the coast of Venezuela. And this I say because Azucena once mentioned that Ula made a fish *sancocho* that would wake up the dead. Unfortunately, her *sancocho* was not good enough to bring back her only son.

MAN DIES

After Ula's aborted stay, my niece and nephew were left in the charge of the chauffeur, a man named José, whom Lucas Enrique and Sofía adored. But José had been hired only to drive Azucena to work and the kids to school. José could not cook, do the laundry, iron, vacuum, and drive a car on top of that! Only women are brainwashed from early on to take on such feats of multitasking.

José had two favorite pastimes: singing and whistling. His dream in life had been to be Carlos Santana. The next best thing was to sing and whistle whenever he could, which was usually in the car, usually while driving Azucena's children to and from that private school I told you about. I learned about José not from my mother or from Azucena but from the children themselves. Whenever I called to say hello to the kids—lest Azucena have my head for not being a good aunt—Sofía would say, "*Tía*, guess what José did today?"

"Tell me, Sofía, what did José do today?"

"Today, José took us to school and was drinking *cuba libres*."

"Really, Sofía?"

And then Lucas Enrique would say, "*Tía*, guess what José did today?"

"Tell me, Lucas Enrique."

"José rolled down the window and taught me to whistle at pretty girls."

"And you did, Lucas Enrique?"

"*Sí, tía*, I whistled and I hooted, just like José."

"Sofía, *mi vida*, is that true that your brother hooted at girls?"

"*Sí, tía*, José is teaching us a song, too."

"Have you told your mami any of this, Sofía?"

"No, *tía!* Mami is in Marketing Committee."

"I see . . . ."

"Guess what José did today, *tía*?"

"Tell me."

"José took me to the club for my tennis lesson and afterward we went to visit one of his friends."

"And what happened there, Lucas Enrique?"

"His friend gave him a supermarket bag filled with money, just like in the movies, *tía*."

"Really, Lucas Enrique?"

So I called Azucena at work to tell her she's giving half her salary to a drug dealer who drives while intoxicated, and Azucena said to me, "Valentina, you are so cruel. As if I don't have enough to worry about for you to torture me like this. You know very well I have Marketing Committee on Thursdays."

Luckily, Azucena didn't have to get that call from the morgue telling her that her children had died in gunfire related to a drug deal gone sour. She had to call the morgue, instead. One afternoon, while waiting for Lucas Enrique to get ready, José fell asleep on one of the "good" chairs, which he wasn't supposed to do. He was neither supposed to sit on the "good" chairs nor was he supposed to fall asleep while on duty. But José did more than that: he died in his sleep. It turned out José was a snorer and suffered from something called sleep apnea. It was my mother who found him. Given that José was the kids' favorite person in the whole world I thought I'd ask my mother what she planned to tell the children. And my mother, drawing from her experience with the mentally unstable, said, "There's no need to traumatize children with the truth, Valentina."

"I see . . . ."

The next time I called, just because I can't leave anything alone, I asked Sofía where José was, and she started to cry. "What happened, Sofía?"

"*Tíaaaa*, José got another job." (Major sobs). "He left us!!!! He left us, *tíaa*!!!!"

"Sofía, *mi vida*, you need to stop watching telenovelas. José didn't mean to leave you. I'm sure he just got a better-paying job, that's all."

It's better to tell a child she's been abandoned, than to ruin her day with something as sour as a dead chauffeur. Don't you agree? And while all this commotion was going on downstairs, Carlos was Upstairs, twiddling his Game Boy.

BY THE SHORT AND CURLIES

And whatever happened with the offending bar of soap at Azucena's house? The safe thing to assume was that the minute Carlos Upstairs set foot in the shower, he was, at least, curious. A more inquisitive man than he might have wondered, "Say, what's that little mound of black curls doing on my soap?" A brighter bulb than he might have been instantly on the alert: "I wonder if I'm in trouble. Pubic hair doesn't grow on oatmeal soap, after all." Another man, any man, might have been outright provoked: "Pubic hair on my favorite bar of soap is the last straw!" Any breathing creature of the male species, as a matter of fact, might have done a number of things that Carlos Upstairs did not do. And why didn't he do anything? Azucena was mystified.

So I ventured a guess. "Here's what I think, Azucena *querida*: people who have it made go quietly about collecting their benefits. To rock the boat, to engage in unnecessary, petty bickering about pubic hair on oatmeal soap is to have your video games taken away. And who wants his Game Boy confiscated?"

Since dropping out of law school to marry Azucena—a full-time job, apparently—Carlos Upstairs has not worked a day in his life. It's possible he never worked a day in his life *before* marrying Azucena, but that would be a calumny. I didn't know him then. All I know is that since marrying my sister, Carlos Upstairs has not lifted a finger around the house, or elsewhere, for that matter.

So, what does a woman who lives to provoke, who provokes others constantly, and who has turned provocation into an art she believes is widely unappreciated do when her pubic provocation goes unacknowledged? Azucena was inspired. This was, after all, a well-thought-out, premeditated provocation. And besides, she hadn't provoked just anyone. She had provoked a man prone to stomachaches when food looked sloppy on a plate, a man who refused to change his own children's diapers, claiming diapers smell bad and that it wasn't his job to change diapers in the first place. In short, she had provoked a finicky creature. So to better speculate about her husband's unresponsiveness, Azucena called me up.

Since my moving to the United States a few years before, Azucena and I had a scheduled phone call on Sundays. Scheduling it had been her idea. The only reason I agreed was because I got tired of hearing her say, "How come you never answer the phone? "Over the years our Sunday call has become a kind of therapy for Azucena. I hardly need to tell you that it isn't therapy for me to hear about maids with STDs, children who might get murdered after school, or the showering habits of a *chulo* in the Tropics. "Do you think he didn't notice the pubic hair, Valentina? I cut *a lot* of it off. Or, do you think he noticed and is plotting his revenge? Maybe he removed the hair, showered, and put it back on the soap," my sister mused out loud.

"I doubt it, Azucena. If the man can't even bring himself to change his son's diapers without saying *"¡Qué asco!"* and making a face, do you really think he's going to rub soiled soap on his body? So we stayed on the phone for the better part of an hour, speculating. And, I should add—long-distance.

Seeing that we were getting nowhere, and as we were about to hang up and the mystery before us still remained unresolved, Azucena asked, "What should I do now, Valentina?" My sister's mind is an intricate maze. Her thought process is beyond the reach of most normal people. The only reason I dare even venture a guess as to what she meant, is because over the years I've heard her ponder similar riddles. What Azucena meant was, "Now that pubic hair didn't do the trick, should I try something a little stronger?" That is how Azucena thinks, that if a given provocation fails to achieve the desired effect, something is fundamentally wrong with the provocation. "I'll bet he didn't notice," she sighed.

"What's next, Azucena? Are you willing to go bald down there just to see if he notices?" As a last resort I said what I always said whenever Azucena shared charming stories about the man who nearly left her at the altar. I told her to divorce him. But *divorce* is one of those words that refused to enter my sister's ears. I even said it a second time, and with emphasis: "DIVORCE THE *CHULO*." But do you think she heard me? In the end, my sister's pubes remained stuck to the soap for days, weeks, months . . . until the day Azucena discovered that Carlos Upstairs had started using her liquid lavender soap.

WARNING: THIS E-MAIL MIGHT BE TOXIC

TO . . .

Just last week I got another cheerful e-mail from Azucena. The thieves seem to be getting cleverer than ever in Caracas.

"Valentina, if you get an egg aimed at your windshield, do not turn on the windshield wiper. The thieves are betting that you will. If you do, you'll end up making a cake on your windshield, which means you'll have to stop your car due to zero visibility, and when you get out of the car, the thieves will kill you, execution style, and then will steal your car. So be careful, hermana, please. Azucena."

What to say to so much thoughtfulness? I had to think hard before hitting the Reply button.

"Azucena querida: You need to get out more. Here, where I live, people might wear ugly shoes made for evolution-shaped human feet, but they use eggs for other things. Besitos, Valentina."

LA CASA DE LOS ESPÍRITUS

As if an egg on your windshield were not sticky enough, Azucena now had a new maid in her midst. This one thought the house was haunted.

She was from Ecuador, from the village where they make the Panama hats. I know it makes no sense that Panama hats are made in Ecuador. There's no logic either to authentic Yankee T-shirts made in China. But they are. In any case, I told you that the best way to learn the history and geography of South America is through the maids. It was the good people of Hollywood who started the Panama-hat story after American movie stars went to Ecuador—to either Cuenca or Montecristi—and came back wearing fashionable Panama hats. Another story is that the workers building the Panama Canal wore Panama hats to protect themselves from the sun. But that is unlikely. These little masterpieces take about six months to make, each. Each hat is handwoven. Each costs about five thousand dollars, sometimes more. And what were Ecuadorians doing in Panama in the first place? It doesn't matter. Now Panama is known for both the hats and the canal. All those poor villagers in Cuenca and Montecristi breaking their backs weaving all that toquilla straw, and Ecuador doesn't even get the credit. But then again, Ecuador has Mount Chimborazo, which, thanks to a bulge on the earth, is the highest mountain on the planet. I know you thought it was Mount Everest, *mi amor.* Many people think that. But Chimborazo is actually one-and-half miles higher than Everest. And who said the earth was round, anyway? The earth is an oblate spheroid; it's a little pregnant just below the equator. You need to know these things if you're planning to move down there. And when you have something as mind-blowing as Mount Chimborazo, maybe you don't need to brag about some little hats. Let the Panamanians have them. All they have is that little creek, after all. And it's not even theirs; they just manage the traffic.

But let's get back to the maid from Ecuador. Her name was Ika. As luck would have it, Ika was illiterate. That is to say, Ika was unable to read the instructions Azucena always wrote for her maids every morning before going to work at *Caracas Spectator*. I've seen some of Azucena's notes, and even if you're not illiterate, *mi amor*, they're hard to understand. And I'm not talking about the handwriting. Remember, we both learned calligraphy from the nuns. A note from Azucena to one of her maids might read, for instance:

Mondays bathrooms, iron, meet the gardener, <u>never</u> open door, kids, snack not fattening, flowers dining room change water, vacuum, kids tennis, late dinner, coq au vin—easy salt—meetings all day, emergency only, Carlos upstairs.

Carlos Upstairs is the only constant in Azucena's notes, which I might add, come from a box bearing a label that reads, "100% *lino fino.*" And just in case fine linen doesn't cut it, every single one of my sister's notes has the following embossed across the top: *"Azucena Viloria Serrano de Contreras."* This is in case the maids get confused, in case they don't realize who's leaving them all these little notes. I should probably bite my tongue. Azucena might stop speaking to me after this. At any rate, at the time of Ika's arrival, Carlos was still upstairs. But by then he was alternating between his Game Boy and Batman and Robin, fascinated as he was—albeit so late in life—by all the goings-on in Gotham City. As for Ika, she might have been ignorant, but she wasn't stupid. When she noticed the *señor* upstairs all day, day in and day out, while the *señora* was at work, well . . . can you blame a maid from a traditional village in Ecuador for asking the *señora* if the *señor* was a cripple?

"No, he's not a cripple," explained Azucena, "just a loser of Notre Dame proportions." Yes, *mi amor.* Of course I realize that *that* particular Notre Dame is having a winning season. Azucena was talking about the real Notre Dame—the Catholic cathedral in Paris, the one with the organs inside. That's because Azucena is something of a Francophile. That's why she used the Notre Dame analogy with Ika, to make sure Ika understood what she meant, and to teach a village woman something about Gothic architecture while she was at it.

So while Azucena went to work to fight the demonic traffic of Caracas, the random street closures, and the antigovernment demonstrations, Carlos Upstairs read Batman comic books in their bedroom. He got up to pee every once in a while, of course. And some days he even had enough energy to play tennis at the country club, where he was admitted despite the fact that he didn't have a membership. As luck would have it, his father was dating a rich socialite at the time, a woman who could afford to pay the astronomical dues at the Caracas Country Club. And besides, because Carlos Upstairs is the ultimate insider, all he needed to do was to put on his Nadal tennis whites, shake a few hands at the door, and waltz toward the tennis courts. ¡Y listo! Azucena might not approve, but being a sinecure of sorts is more work than meets the eye at first—to say nothing of the advantages of being endowed with that kind of charisma.

But anyway, when Sofía and Lucas Enrique got home from school around mid-afternoon, Carlos Upstairs would yell the name of the maid du jour at the top of his lungs. In this case, we were talking about Ika, the illiterate maid from Ecuador. So Carlos Upstairs yelled, "Ikaaaaaaaaaaaaaaa, the kids are home!" And then he turned the page to find out what happened to the Joker.

Reliably idiotic as he was, Carlos Upstairs turned out to be the least of Ika's problems. One day, while the poor woman was dusting in the master bedroom and Carlos Upstairs was at the country club, the alarm radio went off. Unfortunately for Ika, the alarm radio in Azucena's bedroom has always been set to the highest volume because since she was a little girl, Azucena has been prone to sleeping in. All this to tell you that the station on which the radio was set could be heard all the way from Caracas to Cuenca. Naturally, Ika was startled. That's understandable. Sometimes, many times, I'm startled by the microwave and I wonder why a mere object is impatiently telling me over and over, "Your food is ready. Your food is ready," until I open the door. More than once I've been inclined to say, "You don't know anything, you're just a microwave!" But on risk of being called crazy for talking to an inanimate object, I keep my mouth shut. But Ika, not having had the benefit of a degree in psychology from Tulane University in the States, concluded that there were angry spirits in Azucena's bedroom and that the house was haunted. So after staring at the alarm radio in alarm, she proceeded to kneel down as one heeding a muezzin call in Mecca and went on to pray in earnest to the radio announcer on the other side of the city.

That's how Azucena found her, prostrated on the carpet in the master bedroom, saying, "*¡Los espíritus! ¡Los espíritus!*"

Need I tell you how frustrated Azucena was? "Have you made the *coq au vin*, yet, Ika? I'm expecting company for dinner." Never mind that Ika could not tell *coq au vin* from coconuts. And because Ika was now crying, Azucena did that thing she does with her breath, she started to breathe in and out, slowly, the way they teach you in yoga to calm your nerves, except in Azucena's case the slow breathing is meant to let people know that she's tolerating them. And then she said, "Ika, please collect yourself."

The ignorance, *mi amor*, the ignorance! Ignorance spares no one. Because, guess what? Ignorance turned out to be the topic of discussion during my Sunday call with Azucena. "I just don't understand it, Valentina," she said. "I even left a copy of Martha Stewart's *coq au vin* recipe on the kitchen counter. But do you think she even bothered to look at it?" Now we were talking ignorance *and* negligence. It was simply inexcusable that instead of looking to Martha Stewart for guidance, Ika made fried plantains, just because the green tubers had vestiges of the familiar. All the while, Azucena was stuck in Marketing Committee meeting with her new boss at the magazine, a man who thought that a PMS chart was some type of warning about premenstrual syndrome at the office.

"Can you believe it, Valentina? The man doesn't even know his varnishes!"

"And what exactly is a varnish, Azucena *querida?*" All told, there was too much ignorance going around for my poor sister. Mere days after the *coq au vin* fiasco, Ika was shipped back to the Ecuadorian village with no alarm clocks to resume making Panama hats. "You'd swear we live in the middle of the Amazon jungle," Azucena said, so dumbstruck was she.

And I said, "You do, Azucena. Just because you have enough snake oil to set Texas on fire doesn't mean you don't." My little sister has such a great capacity to deceive herself.

KEEPING UP WITH RAMBO

Not too long after the illiterate Ika returned to Cuenca, Ecuador, to resume making Panama hats, a snake showed up in Azucena's backyard. That was around the time that Lucas Enrique thought that he was John Rambo. It's not just people in industrialized countries who are caught in the trappings of aspiration. People in Caracas, too, want to look at a poster that reads, "It's not just coffee. It's Starbucks." People in Caracas, too, want DirecTV. It wasn't bad enough that Lucas Enrique was now watching telenovelas made in Brazil because the telenovelas made in Venezuela simply did not include enough women wearing thongs. Now Azucena—who was working harder than ever while Carlos Upstairs continued to use her lavender soap—had to donate not an insignificant portion of her earnings to the people of DirectTV.

Understandably, the period after Ika was shipped back to Ecuador was a period during which the children were stationed in front of the television by Carlos Upstairs so that he could play with his Game Boy in peace. That's how someone named Sylvester Stallone was able to colonize Lucas Enrique's mind. So one morning, as Azucena was brushing her teeth, she walked over to her bedroom window because she heard a frantic barking and caught sight of Lucas Enrique whacking a snake with a stick, just as he had seen Rambo do to an entire squad of Burmese soldiers on Spike TV. The only difference between the two incidents was that Lucas Enrique didn't have a jeep-mounted .50-caliber machine gun to do the trick. As if a snake from Venezuela, a *mapanare* or worse, would be deterred by the insignificant blows inflicted on it by a six-year-old and the annoying barks of a bonsai dog.

That's when Azucena, who belongs to a church called "Money Solves Everything," enrolled Lucas Enrique in piano lessons. That was her plan: for Rachmaninoff to scare Rambo out of her son's mind. The Sunday after the snake showed up in her backyard, Azucena called me to say, "I have to get out of here."

And I said, "You had your chance and you blew it." I was, of course, reminding her of the time when she had lived in Charlotte, North Carolina; those blissful years of her MBA when she met a Greek god named Demosthenes and ended up in the emergency room with someone she thought had gonorrhea but who turned out to be a virgin after all. It was at the tip of my tongue to ask her if the Arabs wearing John Varvatos to class were really that offensive. But I didn't. Memory can be such a fickle thing.

THE PRISONER'S DILEMMA

After Ika, she of the angry *espíritus*, Azucena vowed never again to let ignorance squeeze in through the doors of her gated home. So after the spirits who had spoiled the *coq au vin* remained only as a memory of a brief nightmare, Azucena called her best friend, Cristina, someone who knew where, how, and whether one might find a person reliable enough to handle Carlos Upstairs, feed your children, and lay hands on your new bras from the Victoria's Secret in downtown Caracas. The reason Azucena had to call a friend was because there are no employment agencies for maids down there. Despite the painful labor involved, I'm afraid that a woman who cleans toilets is simply not considered skilled labor in many parts of the world. So the only way to find a maid in Caracas is through the offices of a good friend like Cristina, someone who can tell you whether the woman who will spend nights two doors down from your own bedroom steals only the basics—such as tomatoes and hearts of palm—or if you need to lock up your Cartier watch in a bank vault, or if you need to resort to something a little stronger, say, praying she's not a murderer on the run.

That's how Azucena found Esmeralda, the maid with aspirations, who could not only read, and spell *coq au vin*, she knew enough math to be able to double or even triple the recipe as needed so that Azucena could invite six, eight, or ten people to dinner at a moment's notice. That was Esmeralda. Notice the polysyllabic name. Esmeralda might even have had a last name, though I can't remember offhand if Azucena ever mentioned it during one of our Sunday calls. The problem with Esmeralda was that she was going to night school. And as everyone who has ever heard of night school knows, well . . . school is at night. Everyone, except Azucena. Because, "Where is Esmeralda tonight?" became one of Azucena's recurring refrains during that time. Where would Esmeralda be, Azucena, if not in night school, learning about wine pairings for *coq au vin*, as befits a maid with aspirations?

In the end, night school turned out to be the least of Esmeralda's problems. Esmeralda's days were numbered the moment Azucena found out about the grilled-cheese sandwiches. Unfortunately, after Esmeralda's arrival, neither Prince Lucas Enrique nor Princess Sofía were able to watch the Brazilian telenovelas after school without a grilled-cheese sandwich by their side. Even Carlos Upstairs—on the whole averse to peasant foods such as bread and cheese—liked Esmeralda's sandwiches. Apparently, putting a slice of cheese between two pieces of bread was one of her talents. Even I, thousands of miles from the Caribbean, heard from the children that Esmeralda made sandwiches so succulent that news of them reached Azucena's ears one day at Marketing Committee meeting.

So one Sunday during one of our scheduled calls Azucena said to me, "I had to let Esmeralda go."

"Why on earth, Azucena? I thought you liked her."

"The children were practically in love with her, Valentina. I was about to lose my entire family to a maid. Even Carlos Upstairs liked her. And you know how picky he is!"

"How about leaving work a little earlier, Azucena? Or learning how to make a grilled-cheese sandwich yourself? I've never tried to, but how hard can it be to stick a piece of cheese between two slices of bread and turn on the oven?"

"You're always criticizing me, Valentina. I *need you* on my side."

Working-mother's guilt can be such a tough nut to crack.

The thing to realize about Esmeralda is that she upset the order of things. She came to shine light on something slightly more perverted than a working woman's fear of grilled-cheese sandwiches—the bedeviling notion that we tend to demonize that which we don't want to believe. And there was more to it, besides. Esmeralda entered Azucena's life at a time when history started coming to us faster and faster, it seemed, at a time when someone of Theoneste Bagosora's reach cannot even hope for Warhol's fifteen minutes of fame. And if the man who said "ShamWow" to one million Tutsis in Rwanda can be forgotten overnight, overshadowed by the glare of the next day's YouTube videos, how can someone like Esmeralda—a modern maid of, by, and for the moment—ever hope to rise from the banalities of everyday life? The only thing Esmeralda had going for her was the threadbare tale of trying to rise out of poverty by going to night school, a tale she tried to patch to her torn dresses while perfecting putting a slice of cheese between two pieces of bread. And where did all that ambition get her?

In the end, Azucena didn't know how good she'd had it. The next maid to enter her house would be the one to make my poor sister truly delirious with apprehension, the woman who came to show Azucena that she could no longer afford to live in a world that was given its meaning and dimension by the length of the title on her business card. I'd never thought I'd hear Azucena say that it was preferable that Carlos be upstairs in their bed, shorts to his knees, fiddling with his Game Boy in reverie until all that tugging and stroking finally freed him of his preoccupations, while Sofía and Lucas Enrique got a true education from Brazilian telenovelas downstairs. Why are children's smiles so pure? Maybe it's because children can't look back, so they have no memory of what life has cost them.

TANGO CONSPIRACY

After the ambitious Esmeralda, there followed a growth period during which Azucena started to make peace with the notion that a maid with a degree from Le Cordon Bleu was not necessarily a priority for people living in a paradise of snakes. That's how a woman named Alicia Muti, the first maid with a last name, came to be in her employ. Alicia Muti, whom my sister called simply, Ali—so used was Azucena to the mini-syllabic names—was from Argentina. But before I tell you why Ali, too, had to go the way of luggage on a conveyer belt a few highlights about Argentina are in order.

Argentina is the cradle of civilization. Argentina is the Paris of South America. Argentinean Malbecs are the best in the world. Don't even look in Chile's direction! Argentina gave the world empanadas. Argentina introduced the world to Carlos Gardel, an unerring baritone who wrote enough tangos to make the entire Southern Hemisphere weep until the end of times, *y volver, volver, volver*. Never mind that Gardel was from Uruguay. Carlitos Gardel suffered from the same misappropriation as the Panama hats from Ecuador. Argentina gave the world Eva Perón, as well as *Evita*, one of the longest-running musicals in Broadway's history. But, come to think of it, it was Andrew Lloyd Webber who did the musical. For her part, Eva Perón, the second wife of Argentinean president Juan Perón, went to bat for women's suffrage before the Second World War was over, and before a woman named Gloria won that spelling bee in Toledo for spelling the word *feminism* and teaching it to the women of North America in a magazine called *Ms*.

But back to Argentina for a second. Argentina gave the world Bariloche, the Cortina of Argentina. Cortina is in the Dolomites, the Italian Alps. Anyone who's anybody in Argentina might be spotted either in Cortina d'Ampezzo or in San Carlos de Bariloche, skiing Cerro Catedral. But that was before a man named Fernando de la Rúa took Argentina to the cleaners and was driven out of the Pink House. Why is their White House pink, *mi amor*? You're always asking these questions, Emily. And I'm afraid now I have to give you one of those explanations that make people think that South America is crawling with monkeys. The reason the official seat of the Argentinean government is pink is because the original paint mixture contained cow blood. Apparently, cow blood prevents humidity. When in doubt, we who live near the Tropic of Capricorn always go for the natural remedy. Who knew cow blood had such properties? If you're really curious about it, *mi amor*, put the question to the good people of DuPont. I have no idea if it's true. As you know by now, there's a lot of legend issuing from the bottom half of the Americas. Why do you think García Márquez is our idol? The thing that is definitely not legend is that Fernando de la Rúa is considered to be the most uncharismatic president Argentina has ever seen. And that, *mi amor*, is like receiving the Nobel Prize for being an asshole.

You see, people in South America are raised to be charming—not quite as charming as the English, but pretty close. From a very early age we learn not to use words like *asshole* when in the company of others, so we say "uncharismatic," a kind of emergency euphemism reserved for people who remind us of places where the tropical sun does not shine. I would be very surprised if one of your Facebook friends hasn't already sent you a video of Fernando de la Rúa's son, Antonio. Antonio is a lawyer. And after his brief engagement to Latina superstar Shakira, Antonio de la Rúa became paparazzi fodder and made news among "the sushi set," a group of influential young men from Argentina who have a predilection for expensive Japanese cuisine. The sushi set is a group of men Carlos Upstairs would like to belong to, except that he never finished law school. And without a law degree, I'm afraid that many things in this world simply refuse to materialize, especially sashimi-grade maguro.

All this to tell you that Shakira's fiancé's dad was directly responsible for Alicia Muti's presence at Azucena's house. This is a roundabout way of saying that there is simply no way in hell that a woman from Buenos Aires would ever set foot in Caracas of her own free will, least of all as a maid. You can see how Alicia Muti might have arrived at my sister's house with a touch of petulance. And that, *mi amor*, is putting it mildly.

OPUS 1: THE ARGENTINEAN MALBEC CRISIS IN D MINOR

The arrival of Alicia Muti at Azucena's house coincided, as I mentioned, with Azucena's understanding that knowing how to stuff a snail was not all that crucial for a maid and that it was enough for the woman who watched over your children not to be wanted for murder. So much had Azucena grown in that department, in fact, that by the time Alicia Muti arrived at her house, my sister was already buying the meals for the children and Carlos Upstairs from a caterer and *pâtissier* whose name was Mozart, the man who had made the canapés for Azucena's thirtieth-birthday bash.

Tragically, it is *pâtissiers* named Mozart who give Venezuelans a bad name. They are the reason other countries in South America consider the Venezuelans gluttonous. Venezuelans, not content with boasting about Angel Falls, the tallest waterfall in the world; not content with boasting about Canaima, where the rarest varieties of orchids grow; not content with having oil gushing out of everyone's backyard; they have to have pastry shops named Mozart, as well, where the women who control the Miss Universe pageant go to bite on éclairs in punishingly short skirts. Surely you can see how people with last names such as Chávez—people on the other side of the mountain who haven't even heard of the real Mozart—might want a bite of the éclair, too. Even if on first biting the éclair they thought to share it with other people whose last name is Chávez, say their cousins, and with friends of their cousins and friends of friends of their cousins. *Mais non!* Everyone knows éclairs are too delicious to share. Jean-Pierre used to say so.

I used to ask, "Can I have a bite of your éclair, Jean-Pierre?"

And he would say, *"Mais non, chérie!"*

And what exactly was Mozart's culinary connection to Salzburg, you might ask? I'm not sure. . . . I think the caterer in Caracas just found the name chic, so he appropriated it. As it turned out, the man could cook. How I know this, of course, is from Azucena's children.

"*Tía*, have you ever had an éclair from Mozart?"

"No, Lucas Enrique, I thought Mozart was a composer."

"*Tía*, have you ever had Gnocchi alla Carbonara from Mozart?"

"No, Sofía, I thought only the Italians made Gnocchi alla Carbonara."

"*Tía*, have you ever . . . ?"

Well, apparently, Mozart was costing Azucena a small fortune, so thank God for the promotion she got at work. But as it often happens with these types of things, the only person not enjoying Mozart's culinary masterpieces was Azucena herself. For one, she was rarely home. For reasons she herself was unable to explain, she was always the last person to leave the office. So by the time she got home at night and opened the fridge, she realized that so delicious was Mozart's food that neither Carlos Upstairs nor her children ever stopped to think that the person buying them all these treats could possibly want to taste them. So the fridge was usually empty.

By the time Alicia Muti arrived at Azucena's house from Buenos Aires, the only chores the woman had to tackle were answering the phone, letting in the gardener, dusting, and taking care of Carlos Upstairs. And that she did! Given she was from Argentina, that she was educated, that she could tell her Malbecs from her pinot noirs, and her beef Burgundy from her beef Bourguignon, she also understood silk pashminas—Azucena's favorite accessory.

So one night, Azucena comes home from work a little earlier than usual and finds her entire family sitting around the table, having dinner with Alicia Muti, who was, to add insult to injury, wearing one of Azucena's pashminas. I wish I could tell you that a maid wearing Azucena's favorite scarf was the worst thing that happened that night. But no.

The worst part is that no one got up when Azucena got home. So used were the kids to being with Alicia that when Azucena got home that night, she heard Sofía say, "Would you tell me that story about the tiger again, Alicia?" But children are sly as foxes and learn from early on the downturns of their parents' mouths, the nearly imperceptible frowns of disapproval. So, Sofía had refrained from mentioning to Azucena that while she had been busy wrapping up Marketing Committee, Alicia was regaling her with stories about *tío tigre*, the fabled tiger with magic powers that Sofía had grown to love.

In fact, she had learned to keep this information tucked away, like shoes in a closet, for fear of ruining her mother's life. Because what child wants to ruin her mother's life and be made to pay for it with interest during adulthood?

As for Carlos Upstairs, so used was he to getting that call from Azucena around five or so in the afternoon, telling him that she had to work late, that on the evening in question he, too, stayed glued to his chair, listening to some skiing story Alicia Muti was telling him. And because Alicia Muti wasn't really supposed to be a maid—that is to say, she didn't curse, she didn't scratch her crotch, nor did she pray to radio announcers on the other side of the city—she had opened up a bottle of Opus 1 to go with the story she was telling Carlos Upstairs. Opus 1, apart from being one of Mozart's early sonatas, is one of Azucena's favorite wines, not because of her fixation with all things Mozart, but because it is a very special wine that she'd been saving for her next birthday.

And that's the tragedy of the oppressed, isn't it? Sooner or later they start to identify with their captors. When Azucena called me the following Sunday, it wasn't to tell me that she had fired Alicia Muti. Strange as it might seem, she called to ask me if I thought she was being paranoid.

"Haven't you learned anything from our parents being psychotherapists, Azucena *querida*? Don't you know by now that a paranoid is a person who has *all* the information? I can see why you might be inclined to keep Alicia Muti around. But just because she can tell Malbec from Mozart doesn't make her a good person."

SLUMMING IT

Alicia Muti was the last maid to enter and to leave Azucena's house. There were no maids from Bolivia, Brazil, Peru, or Paraguay, or from any other country, for that matter. These days she has a woman named Rita, who comes, as they say down there, *por día*, then goes back to the slums at night to curse and scratch her crotch.

V. BOYFRIEND IN A BOX

RELATING FOR DUMMIES

There was a time when I thought I was Jackie O. Well, I didn't think I was her exactly. I just thought I resembled her a little. Turns out I don't. That's part of what I call my New York period.

Never in a million years would I have guessed I'd end up in New York. But some emotional landslides carry more sludge than others and can drag you down farther than you might think. My New York period came after a misguided visit to Miami and after a brief stay in Canada, which included the word *marriage* in it. Here's how it happened. I boarded a plane that was going from Arizona to Miami, where my friend Ana lived at the time. I took more than one bathing suit with me, that is to say, I was planning to stay with Ana for a while. Subconsciously, I was going to check out the scene in Miami to determine if I might actually like living there, Miami being the Rosetta stone of Latin culture.

But I didn't articulate it this way. I just said, "I'm going to visit my friend Ana in Miami." In Spanish, we call what I was doing "one for the Devil and one for God"—that is, when you're at peace with both of them, you can sleep well at night. So that's what I was doing on that plane, going to visit Ana. I was also writing a letter to my parents, informing them of this temporary change of venue so that they wouldn't call the Gestapo after dialing my number in Arizona and finding that no one answered. Yes, of course it would have been easier to call them, *mi amor.* Well, not really. Some people respond better to letters. People who indiscriminately want to have the last word every single time are ideally suited to receiving letters. But if you find pen and paper are too Gutenberg, an e-mail will do. My parents, God bless them, are trained to argue people out of their decisions. But, to my knowledge, they're not trained to argue with a piece of paper. They might argue with the contents of the letter all day long, of course. But what good does it do to argue with a piece of fifty-percent cotton?

And it was as I was writing this letter to my parents on the plane to Miami that the guy sitting next to me said, "You have such elegant handwriting."

And because I do, because I have that immaculate calligraphy I picked up from the nuns, I didn't take his comment as a pickup line. As far as I was concerned, he was speaking the truth. So I said, "Thank you. What's in Miami?"

"A friend," he said. "How about you?"

"A friend," I said.

And he smiled. Then he asked, "You always do that?"

"Always do what?"

"Mimic people."

"Mimic people?"

"See? You're doing it again."

Why deny it? I am a kind of mimicking expert. I first learned to mimic people at a sales seminar taught by a guy whose name was Guy Malloy. That's one of the hidden benefits of living in this country, which no one ever tells you about when you're standing in line at Immigration—that eventually everything here becomes a technique, a program, something with ten easy steps anyone can follow and easily obtain for $9.99, or put on layaway. I, myself, secretly hope that this tragic story becomes a how-to manual for confused immigrants with stepdaughters on their way to Ecuador.

So that's what I was learning from Guy Malloy: "How to Use Mimicking People as an Effective Relating Technique"—that was the title of the seminar. I actually had no idea what I was doing at that seminar. I hadn't thought that I needed to learn how to relate. I've always thought relating is one of those things that comes naturally. But apparently not. As I was to learn from Guy Malloy, there are Embracers, and then there are people who cut you short.

My presence at that seminar had been due to yet another boss, one who thought that relating was at the center of gravity of things. In the end, mimicking turned out to be quite simple. It works like this: Say someone is a Pauser—you hit your own Pause button, slow down a bit. Say someone is a Nodder—you introduce a nod here and there in the conversation. Say a person is a Frowner, someone who always looks puzzled—you put on your puzzled face and do that thing with your eyebrows. Altogether, there are seven types of people—that's how many Guy Malloy told us there were, anyway. And by then, what did I care? I had been fired once, and I had learned my lesson. You want me to learn how to relate? Tell me when and where. Have a nice day!

As you might imagine, this business of relating can be done very effectively. It can also be taken too far. Use mimicking in moderation, that's what Guy Malloy said. That's how I use it these days. But on that day on the plane, I was just flirting with the guy from Canada. You can say I was mimicking for effect. And it worked. By the time the plane landed, I had given Ana's phone number to Marc. He said he was from Vancouver, told me he'd be in touch. I didn't believe a word he said. Well, that's not entirely true. I believed him when he said that my handwriting was elegant. Because it is. But I knew I'd never hear from him again.

That night, as I was getting ready to go out to meet Ana's friends, the phone rang. "There's a Marc on the phone for you," Ana yelled from the kitchen. "Marc, who?"

AMERICAN *CHICA*

Later that night while at a bar in South Beach, a guy who had drunk too many mango Mojitos came up to me and said, "I want you."

"*¿Qué?*" I was soooo confused. Seeing there was a woman with him, I said, "I didn't notice a Walmart on Lincoln Road. That's the only place I know where you can get two for the price of one." The girl burst out laughing. But who could know why? Laughter is too bedeviling a thing to even try to venture a guess. They left.

The next guy in line took off his wedding ring the moment he spotted me at the bar.

"Expecting a call?" he asked, looking at my phone on the counter.

"As a matter of fact, I am."

"Give me your number," he said.

"Excuse me?"

"Give me your number," he repeated, much louder this time around.

"Is that an order?" I smiled.

At this, he fished out his cell phone from the same shirt pocket where he had dropped his wedding ring and waited for me to give him my number. He entered each number carefully as I said it, even pausing in between to say, "Speak slowly." Finally, he pressed one of the buttons on his phone and looked at me. But don't you know it? My phone wouldn't ring. When he realized I had given him a bogus number, he said, "You fucking slut!"

I told him I'd be right back.

The bouncer was escorting the guy out of the bar when Ana and her friends finally showed up.

"Are you involved in this?" Ana asked, horrified. Her eyes moved from left to right between me and her friends. Her head didn't even move.

"I apologize, you guys," she said to them. "Valentina hasn't been out in a while. What the hell is wrong with you, you *gringa*?" she said

172

to me. "Did you forget how to bust a guy's balls on your own, without having to involve the police or hiring a lawyer?"

Hmmm . . . *Qué será, será* . . . Who knew that throwing a violent guy out of a bar was a no-no, in Miami? At last I understood that show *Miami Vice*. There I was, in a kind of blank canvas that featured lying, cheating, drinking, and people driving yellow cars bought with credit cards. It's strange but people from Venezuela have a weakness for the place. Azucena herself will tell you that taste is a very personal matter.

But before I get accused of being a *gringa* yet again, let me tell you what's wonderful about Little Havana: the Cuban food, the weather, and sightseeing at the beach. To my knowledge, they don't have express kidnappings yet. Sometimes it takes a while for new technologies to cross the border.

ANOTHER SPLIT

The following week, unable to convince any of Ana's friends that my body wasn't an extension of their car clutch to drive as they pleased, I decided to call Marc back. Marc and his other friend from Canada, a guy named Alex, turned out to be surprisingly normal people. But because they went to bed before three in the morning, Ana said they were boring. Going to dinner, talking, and walking on the beach, these things were an overdose of civilization for her. So we had a falling out.

By the time I got back to Arizona, Max had left a few messages: "Let's get together." "Let's go out." But Marc had a distinct advantage over Max: he didn't have kid pictures in his wallet. And what's more, he lived in another country, which meant, of course, that if I wanted to, I could move!

SLEEPLESS IN SCOTTSDALE

Marc and I talked on the phone almost every night—he from Vancouver, I from Arizona. I had never been to Vancouver. He said I would love it. He described the water, Robson Street, Stanley Park, and all of a sudden I was magnetically attracted to area code 604.

Marc had grown up in B.C. That is what he said. On weekends growing up he had gone skiing at a place called Whistler, a picturesque town nestled in the Canadian Rockies that just might make the Swiss Alps envious. Except, it was extremely cold in this picturesque town. I can't remember all the details leading to my arrival in Whistler one snowy November day for my job as a project manager at one of the resorts. It had something to do with Marc knowing the man who owned the company that owned the resort.

I put together a resume. I sent the resume to Marc. Marc said, "I'll send it to Alisdair." Alisdair was a sales guy. I had been to "How to Use Mimicking People as an Effective Relating Technique" with a guy named Guy Malloy, which is another way of saying that Alisdair and I spoke the same language. At least, that's the impression Alisdair got after interviewing me on the phone. Getting that job was one example of the effective use of mimicking to get your dream job. There I was, traversing five feet of snow in high heels, risking gangrene. What had I done!?

I lived in Whistler for three months, spent mostly in tears. I have never been so cold. One day, while walking to the village to buy some razors, I got lost. Why ever bother to shave your legs when you'll never see them again? That's a question I should have I asked myself before heading to the woods like Gretel. The pine trees up there are truly beautiful—that's undeniable. I think they call them firs, or furs. The problem is all the furs look the same. In no time I was lost in a dense forest that swallowed the green and red roofs of places called lodges. I couldn't tell anything apart. To make matters worse, my adventure in the Canadian forest took place after work, which meant that it was getting darker with every step I took in the wrong direction. I was pretty sure I would not be able to find my way back to the resort where I lived and worked. In desperation, I started to cry. I usually don't cry in desperation. As you know, I move instead. But that time, I cried in desperation, and then moved. As it turned out, there was no crying allowed in Canada. How was I supposed to know that at thirty degrees below your tears freeze? So I peeled these tiny stalactites off my cheeks, taking off a piece of skin in the process, and walked into a lodge to borrow a phone to call Marc, who, as if he had been born with his own GPS system, knew exactly where I was.

"Oh, you're next to the Reindeer's Lodge, I'll be right there." By the time I got back to the resort and the front desk clerk started piling towels on my feet to stave off gangrene, I knew that my Canadian period would be short-lived.

By the following Valentine's Day, I was living in New York with the Egyptologist who taught at NYU. She was as old as Tutankhamen. I thought it would do me good to surround myself with such stable people for a while.

HELLO, MY NAME IS SYBIL

New York is an ideal place for someone with an open mind and a creative disposition. New York turned out to be a museum for my wandering curiosity. One foot in Manhattan and suddenly the lyrics "Start spreading the news . . ." had been written just for me. There was Central Park. There was Broadway. There was your uncle, Ira. But it would be a while before we would meet. And there was the Jackie O. exhibit at MoMA, where Diego and I met. Perhaps the most interesting part of my New York period is how I ended up at the Museum of Modern Art in the first place.

MoMA was planning to host an exhibit, a retrospective on the life of Jacqueline Kennedy Onassis. In preparation for this, ads ran in the *New York Times*, inviting Jackie O. look-alikes to audition to be hostesses during the opening and for the duration of the exhibit. A dream job, I thought. I didn't see it so clearly at the time—that if you're not liking yourself lately, why not try being someone else? And why not Jackie O.? The only problem was that I don't look anything like the late Mrs. Onassis. Whereas her jaw was square, mine is more of a triangle. Whereas her body was petite and succinct, my height announces me a mile away. So what? A mere lack of structural resemblance in a body and a face were not obstacles enough for me; it certainly didn't mean I shouldn't try. And besides, I did have a few things in my possession that I knew no other Jackie O. look-alike would have: I spoke Spanish, Italian, and French; so did she. I also owned a strand of pearls identical to the ones she used to wear. And I had imagination! It was the imagination part that led me to the library to check out a book about the life of the Kennedys. Let's face it. If you're going to impersonate *the* former First Lady for ten dollars an hour, you need to get your story straight.

When I arrived at my room in Brooklyn Heights with my book about the life of the Kennedys, the woman from whom I'd rented the miniature abode—the Egyptologist professor who taught at NYU—praised my good taste. "What a smart girl to have for a tenant, for a change!" It isn't every day that a young woman from Caracas arrives in Brooklyn, New York, eager to impersonate a beloved former First Lady and to learn all about Camelot.

So, day after day, until the day of the audition, I sat on the Egyptologist's leather couch in Brooklyn absorbing every detail about the woman I would be on opening day at the Museum of Modern Art in New York City. She was born Jacqueline Bouvier. She rode horses. She knew ballet. Her parents got divorced when she was ten. Both her first husband and her father were philanderers. Both men were named Jack. She smoked cigarettes. She once dumped a pie on a much-hated teacher's lap. Her favorite colors were pink, green, and yellow. Come audition day, other than the executors of her estate, no one in New York City would know more about Jacqueline Bouvier Kennedy than I.

THE FASHIONABLE BUFFOON

A couple of weeks before the Jackie O. audition at MoMA, Azucena called to tell me she was coming to visit me in New York. She never visited me when I lived in New Orleans. But New York appealed to her. The French Quarter had nothing on Fifth Avenue! Azucena wanted to do some shopping, catch a Broadway play, anything that made her forget that Carlos was still upstairs and now using her expensive lavender soap. It was a perfect opportunity, I thought, to try out my new Jackie O. persona on someone as discerning as the lovely Azucena.

On the day she was to arrive in New York, I told my sister that I'd be crazed until early evening, and suggested we meet at a busy trattoria in the theater district. That it be busy was important for what I had in mind. My plan was to sit at the bar among a crowd, dressed as Jackie O. My hope was that Azucena, whom I had not seen in a while, would walk into the trattoria, survey the place, and say, "I don't see Valentina, but isn't that Jackie O. at the bar?" Never mind that Jackie O. was dead, dead.

In preparation for Azucena's visit, earlier that afternoon I went to the hair salon and asked the stylist to do my hair in a bouffant. His eyes went from the picture I showed him to my face in the mirror, again and again. He didn't say a word. After frowning fussily a few more times, he finally said, "You know bouffant is no longer in style, right?"

"Of course," I said. "It's for an audition."

"An audition?" he laughed. "Sweeeetheart, I don't mean to burst your bubble, but you're the farthest thing from Jackie O."

"Don't worry about that," I said. "I haven't done the makeup yet. And besides, I have the pearls."

"It's your moneyyy," he sang. "Let's put a smock on you and get you washed."

ALL ABOUT APPEARANCES

Can you guess what happened when Azucena saw me at the trattoria wearing a pair of Onassis glasses and a third of my face covered with a headscarf? I wish I could tell you that it took her a while to find me. Azucena has always been very composed. Some people might use the word *deliberate* to describe her. She came into the trattoria, looked left, then right, without moving the rest of her body, then made her way slowly toward where I was sitting. She then pulled up a bar stool and said, "Are you planning to rob a bank?"

But I'm not so easily discouraged. I cheerfully took off my glasses and said, "Can you guess who I am *now*?"

"What happened to your eyes?" Azucena winced.

"Jackie loved makeup," I said.

"Who's Jackie?"

"What about the pearls, Azucena? Jackie always wore pearls . . . ."

And in that very special way that my sister has of cutting whatever she deems insipid at the knees, she asked, "Do you know if they have any decent bottles in this place? I feel like a Bordeaux."

I had spent the past two months studying and preparing for this moment. Of course I was a little disappointed. But disappointment is such an unproductive emotion, *mi amor;* it doesn't really get you anywhere. For me, the big epiphany at the trattoria was that no matter how much I had learned about Jackie from her biographers, it was all about appearances. This meant what it meant—by the time of the audition I'd have to have the makeup nailed. And maybe the Onassis glasses and the headscarf together were a little much.

The other thing I learned from meeting Azucena in New York was that very rarely in our lives do the events we have imagined live up to our expectations. Why deny it? I was bummed.

NO CAMELOT

For the audition I settled on a leopard-skin pillbox hat, like the ones designed by Oleg Cassini, except that mine came from a place called Urban Outfitters. Pillbox hats, with their flat crown and straight, upright sides, are very chic. Jackie loved pillbox hats. She also loved gloves. Mine were white. But gloves or no gloves, I should have been discouraged the moment I set foot inside the museum.

For one thing, the lobby was so crowded with applicants for the job that the museum guards had to set up those ropes used for reining in cattle to make us form into lines. After a while, a woman wearing a bellman's uniform made the following, brief announcement: "Auditions on the left." This way one could safely assume that the rest of the people in MoMA's lobby were onlookers.

Even celebrity-wannabes are considered celebrities in this country, *mi amor*. This can be very encouraging. It can also be very discouraging—all that competition. I can't imagine this being the case in places like Croatia or Bosnia, for instance.

So, as a celebrity aspirant, I joined the line on the left. I should have walked straight back to the library at that very instant and return the book about the lives of the Kennedys. But I didn't study for two months to be Jackie O. to give up at the lobby of MoMA just because all her other clones looked like they had come right from the wax museum. And besides, no one ever quit a marathon at the twenty-fifth mile. These American aphorisms come in very handy, don't they?

The other thing I can tell you about MoMA's lobby that day is that had Jacqueline Bouvier Kennedy happened to walk by, she would have been scared witless. I mean, where had all these girls been hiding? And what were their lives like when they were not being identical copies of the late Mrs. Kennedy? You walk down the street anywhere in the world and no two people look alike. Here we were in a museum lobby in New York City and the place was crawling with

Jackie O's. That's when I finally got discouraged. But I stayed in line, anyway.

While waiting in line, I devised a plan to overcome the physiognomy objection: I would respond to the interviewers in French! But so that you can better visualize the humiliation I endured, let me describe the setup. Three judges were sitting behind a long table draped with a white tablecloth. Three Jackie O's at a time stood before each judge and answered a question. The first judge always asked the same question: "What makes you think you can be Jackie?"

This was supposed to be a disqualifying question. If you couldn't get past it, one of the ushers pulled you aside, gave you a Jackie poster, and said, "Thank you for your time. Have a nice day!" I still find the idea of the poster a little odd—after all, doesn't this amount to giving a person a memento of her failure?

Anyway, I should probably also tell you that I was, by far, the tallest woman in the building. So I hunched a little, in order not to lose any additional ground on account of my height. When my turn came, the first judge asked me the expected question. But I noticed he asked it a notch louder than he had up until that point. I think he wanted the other two judges to hear my response, because they both stopped interviewing the other two Jackies, perked up their ears, and looked in my direction.

"So, what makes you think you can be Jackie?"

And I said, "Parce que je parles Français."

It took less than five seconds for the judge to say, "Give her a poster."

And that is why, *mi amor*, you should always enjoy the ride more than the destination. Or is it, If you don't know where you're going, any road will take you there? Pick the lesson you want. This is a free country.

REJECTS

On my way out, a guy going into the museum held the door open for me. Once outside, I took off the pillbox hat and left it on top of a Dumpster. I knew I'd never wear it again, but maybe someone else might want it. Then I took off the white gloves and put them in my purse.

I think I was buying time. After all, I had spent several months thinking I would spend the rest of the year being Jackie O. I had no idea where to put myself now. My hair was all puffy. And my face felt sticky from all that makeup. I must have looked like I was going to a socialites' luncheon somewhere on Park Avenue. Suddenly, I felt sorry for real actors and actresses. I was pretty sure I couldn't go through that kind of rejection every day. And I was holding a poster to prove it.

I was getting ready to throw the Jackie poster away when the same guy who held the door open a minute before, said to me, "Wait! Don't throw that away."

"Why not?"

"It's a collector's item," he said.

"A poster from an audition?" I asked, incredulous.

"It is," he insisted, adding for good measure, "I came to get one for my little sister, but I was too late."

"In that case," I said, "give her this one."

"Are you sure you don't want it?" he asked.

"I'm positive," I said.

The stamp "resident alien" on my green card was reminder enough that I was a reject. I didn't need a poster to underline it. And yet, by the look on this guy's face I could tell he couldn't believe his luck. This would be a recurring theme during our marriage. Everything I wanted to throw away was a treasure to Diego.

"Where you headed?" he asked.

"To the library," I said. "I have a book to return."

A couple of months later, once we'd gotten the preliminary interrogations out of the way, Diego asked me what I had been doing at the museum that day. The answer caused him to spill his drink. He had thought I was one of the event organizers. It had never crossed his mind that a woman who laughed as if she were choking, could think, even for an instant, that she resembled in any way the woman who said, "If you bungle raising your children, I don't think whatever else you do matters very much."

Had someone bungled raising me? What was I supposed to do in New York City now that I had failed at immortalizing Jackie O. at a museum exhibit?

SAN JUAN — THE PILL

The chiropractor said it was the high heels. The physical therapist agreed. But there was no way to know for sure why my back started to take revenge on me all of a sudden. So the doctor ordered an MRI. Having your insides scanned can be an instructive experience.

At any rate, that particular MRI center was quite busy, so I had to wait a while before my name was called. After catching up on the lives of Madonna, Janet Jackson, and other lesser stars, whose lights did not shine as long, I looked around the waiting room. At one point, a woman with short, aggressive brown hair came in with her Pekingese dog. As luck would have it, the dog had an urge to bark. I ask you, what dog does not want to bark? But the woman who owned the dog hadn't been let in on that secret. So she started arguing with her Pekingese. Her bickering plus the barking turned the small waiting area into an even smaller place, from which none of us could escape.

The sign at the MRI place read, "Seeing-Eye Dogs Only." Through the foggy lens of translation I took this to mean that only dogs whose eyes were working could be here. This made very little sense, but who could know for sure? Who could tell if the Pekingese was a "seeing dog," or a "not-seeing dog"? And who would run the risk of asking, "Excuse me, is your dog blind, or are you?"

So, as her Pekingese started to bark and bark and bark and bark and bark and bark and bark and bark until it went berserk, a woman with gray hair and eyes to match said to the owner of the barking Pekingese, "Have you tried Saint John's wort?"

Because I'm from a very Catholic country, and because my grandmother used to pray for everything, the first thing that crossed my mind was, "Lady, there's no saint you can invoke to make that dog shut up. Birds chirp. Cows moo. Dogs bark. That's their full-time job." But by then, believe it or not, I had learned to bite my tongue. So I didn't say anything.

As the women's conversation progressed and these two strangers became waiting-room friends for twenty minutes, it all became clear to me. The woman with the gray hair and eyes to match hadn't meant, "Have *you*, the person, tried Saint John's wort," which turned out to be some sort of antidepressant you can buy at a place called GNC. She meant the dog, which from here on out I shall call "Peki."

On hearing about Saint John's wort, Peki's ears perked up, because, as I was to learn from you, dogs are very perceptive creatures. Peki could tell that his days as a barking dog were numbered. Peki was confused. Peki did not understand why an animal had been invited to live in the world of humans and afterward been asked to behave as part-human, part-dog. From then on, whenever Peki had the urge to behave like the dog he was, well . . . he would have to take his tranquilizers so that the woman who owned him could take him along to MRI appointments and read her *People* magazine in peace. *Pobrecito* Peki. Peki, the immigrant dog brought into the human world and asked to be part-Peki, part-John. I don't know about you, but I have a feeling that Peki might have been happier as Kung Pao Peki.

But how did we get here, anyway? We were talking MRI and now we're talking cruelty to animals. It turns out waterboarding is not the only way to torture a living creature. Saint John's wort works too. And please don't get me started on euthanasia.

THE X-RAYS SHOWED NOTHING

Who could predict that an MRI appointment would change your life? But that's exactly what happened. By then, I was due for a new Valentina period. I didn't know what that period would entail. But now that the Jackie O. audition was behind me, I was in the market for a new self.

This must happen to everyone from time to time; this getting tired of yourself. But I've figured out a way out of it. Say you're tired of being a coffee drinker. The way I see it, you don't have to die a coffee drinker. You can change that. So one morning—pick any morning of the week—instead of going to wherever it is that you get your coffee, you take a brief detour and go to a place where they sell chai tea instead.

Even if the place where you go for coffee also sells tea, I wouldn't recommend getting the tea there, mainly because you'll still run into the same people. Here's what will happen. The first sip of tea you take will cause you to ask, "Is it pee, or is it me?" But don't dismiss the tea just yet. Go back a second time, try a new flavor, and I guarantee you that pretty soon you will meet someone who knows what the capital of Nepal is. So you listen to this person, mainly because Nepal is not something that is at the top of your mind for you as a coffee drinker. A couple of weekends later, the person you met at the tea shop invites you to a party where you meet people who know how to pronounce and spell the word *Kathmandu*. As it turns out, all these people have heard of a guy named Dalai, they all know how to burn a stick of incense, and you also notice that none of them brush their hair. And before you know it, you start not brushing your hair either and you're part of an eco-tour group that is helping troubled yetis in the Himalayas. It's as simple as that, *mi amor.*

The reason I like these periodic changes is because they can be such a great source of respite. Now you're talking different interests, now you're using different words, words you would have never learned had you kept on drinking cappuccinos. But just because these people have never heard of Kerastase Hydrathérapie for stressed hair, or Nordstrom, it is not your job to enlighten them by inviting them to the semiannual sale. The purpose is to get a breather from your current self, remember?

That's how I was feeling on the day I went for my MRI appointment. So after they called my name, I entered the claustrophobic little room and I said to myself, "Pay attention, Valentina. This could be the beginning of a new Valentina period." And I did. And it was. It was really a lucky break that my back was killing me to the point of sending me straight to a place that had all the answers.

THE IDEAL JOB

My MRI exam was far from routine. Now that I was in learning mode, I wanted to talk. Unfortunately, the MRI technician did not. She was one of those efficiency experts. The first thing she did was to hand me a pair of earplugs wrapped in a little plastic bag. Only in this great country of yours, *mi amor*, does one have the luxury of individualized earplugs made in China.

"What are these for?" I asked.

"It gets noisy in there," she said, pointing to the giant white bullet, aka the MRI machine. I was to call it "the MRI machine" only once. After I became an MRI technician myself, I knew its maker, its proper name, and its serial number. But at that moment, as I prepared to enter the big bullet, I was still far removed from the realization that I was about to have a career change.

Once I was settled, I had to wait for the technician to go into a little chamber to push some buttons. This was a very claustrophobic moment, so I distracted myself by thinking I was someplace else. People with imaginations should not be allowed any idle time. My mother always seemed to know that. And it was as I was waiting for the MRI technician to push the buttons that I started thinking, "This woman is here alone. She has no boss, no coworkers. There's no one here, except for me. And I will leave in ten minutes and she will never see me again." This meant no repeated contact with clients, coworkers, or other business partners, the little encounters that tend to breed what's officially known as office politics, something for which, surprisingly, I have very little talent.

And just like that, my mind was made up. No two ways about it, this was the ideal job! And what's more, the job had a built-in bonus. This woman had to wear these doctor-type fatigues, a uniform, which meant I'd save money on clothes. And it was because of my eagerness to learn all about my new job that we had to repeat the MRI test so many times. "We have to do that one again," the technician sighed.

"How come?" I asked.

"Can you stay still for a second, please? The machine doesn't like it when people move."

Oh, no! We can't make the machine mad. "I'll pretend to be a corpse." I was full of good intentions. But then I had the urge to ask her a question. Apparently, the machine didn't like it when people talked, either. So we were there for a while.

By the time I rehooked my bra, I was so excited I was going to MRI school that I forgot I had gone in for an MRI. The thing to do now was to find out where one goes to become a button pusher. So I asked the technician, "Where do you get a degree to do what you do?"

And she said, "Saint John's." She might have been curt. She might have been short after all the grief I gave her. But she was neither. She was pleasant and forthcoming with the information. She even gave me the address! Because in her heart of hearts, *mi amor,* she knew that she would never see me again. Her good disposition served to confirm that I was onto something.

The next day, I was first in line at Saint John's. The downside was that I had to take out a loan. Small potatoes when you consider a new lease in life.

NO COMPREND-O

My MRI Technician period coincided with my decision to erase any trace of my former self from Google. It was also during that time that Diego and I started seeing each other. Given his name was Diego de los Rios, that he was from Puerto Rico, that he played Latin music at Latin clubs in New York City and spoke better Spanish than he did English, my trying to blend into the mainstream proved a challenge.

At Saint John's University, I registered under the name of Val Viloria. The admissions clerk had a bit of a problem with this. She was one of those people with no imagination, people who think that because your driver's license says Valentina, you can't chop off six miserable letters from a name you've owned since you were born. So I had to talk to a supervisor, who said it was fine to use a nickname on my application, as long as we put the real name in parentheses. So for a while my name became a parenthetical note. But there was more to it than that. In addition to the quasi-official name change, I had a little secret plan: I would stop speaking Spanish altogether. If anyone asked me if I spoke Spanish, I would politely say in my best English, "I'm sorry, my parents moved here from Nicaragua when I was a baby." Why Nicaragua and not Venezuela? Because at one point in its history, Nicaragua had a real problem—a problem called the Sandinistas, a problem that most people who had a pair of ears had heard of, a problem serious enough that it made it plausible for anyone in New York City to believe that my parents could have escaped Managua with an infant and never looked back. Back then, the idea that anyone might leave Venezuela, the tropical paradise with the Caribbean breezes where Miss Universe babes are bred for Donald Trump, would have been simply incomprehensible. Hence, Nicaragua.

My plan to hose myself down was quite brilliant, I thought. Wearing an android-blue uniform that made it impossible to tell whether I was or wasn't a mom all but guaranteed I would never be fired again for owning a pair of boobs. Let's face it, *mi amor,* no one can be envious of a woman wearing an android-blue uniform. Not unless a handsome doctor falls in love with her sense of humor. But that wouldn't happen. I would not have a sense of humor either. I would limit all outgoing communications to "Please wear these earplugs," and "have a nice day."

The only problem with my plan was that for it to work, I had to become two different people—the MRI technician whose name tag read "Val," and the sassy woman who went out with the Puerto Rican guitar player named Diego de los Rios. This minor split of sorts is the reason my MRI Technician period had to inevitably overlap with what I now refer to as my Separation of Church and State period.

So by the time Diego proposed to Valentina Viloria, Oh she of the brown eyes, I was in a bit of hot water. For one thing, no one had ever heard of her at work. Nor had anyone heard of Diego de los Rios. What I did to work around the sticky situation was head to Target, where I had once seen a product called Boyfriend in a Box.

MORE THAN I BARGAINED FOR

As these things go, Boyfriend in a Box was one of those products that delivered on its brand promise. And as far as I'm concerned, whoever came up with the idea was a genius, someone who should have gone to Harvard. But probably didn't. The Boyfriend in a Box came in three varieties—the Professional, the Athlete, and the Romantic. To better seduce you, there were descriptions of each boyfriend on the back of each box.

The product had been invented for the reason that all products sold in the United States are invented: there was a market for it. The market for this product was single women who wanted to be left alone at work. I was in the market for a Boyfriend in a Box. Each boyfriend was only about fifteen dollars or so, which I thought was a bargain, given the magnitude of the problem he was supposed to solve: to create a believable story about a woman's life. So I bought the Athlete. Not because I had ever entertained any fantasies of even bumping into anyone with the IQ of a pea shoot, but because of more practical considerations, one of them being that athletes are often away, which meant I didn't have to introduce him to anyone.

At any rate, when I got home and opened my boyfriend in a box, I grabbed his photo and looked at it for a while. The picture was of good quality and brilliantly shot from afar and with him wearing glasses. I imagine this was done in case two women bought the same boyfriend and someone was to recognize him. However, you were supposed to buy your own frame. And frames, as we all know, are supposed to do just that, frame things in different ways. There was also a story about the boyfriend inside the box: where he was from, what he liked to do on weekends, and other particulars one is required to know about someone who wins that title.

There were a few name choices befitting an Athlete, as well as a list of sports. His name and the choice of sport were left up you. You, the Athlete's girlfriend, got to decide whether Chad, or Chaz, or Chuck, played football, or baseball, or simply favored triathlons. As

Chad's creator/girlfriend, it was my job to make up a story that I could believe, so that I could repeat it believably to the people I was hoping to repel with his very existence. Given that I know zilch about sports, Chad proved a little challenging. In fact, at the office Christmas party that year I failed to convince a coworker that Chad could not be there because he was in the middle of spring training.

Much can be accomplished by keeping one's mouth shut. But that's never been my strongest suit. My strongest suit is deflection. So deflect is what I did. When Kendra—one of the technicians—looked a little incredulous about spring training, I said, "I was just joking, Kendra, to see if you were listening. As a matter of fact, Chad just got me these earrings as a Christmas present. Do you like them? Awww. Isn't Chad sweet?"

"So, how did you guys meet?"

Invisible as he was, Chad turned out to be exhausting, particularly at home. Who would have thought that Diego would be bothered by Chad? It takes a very sensitive person to be jealous of a cardboard boyfriend. Diego was.

WOULD I MARRY ME?

The problems started as soon as we got engaged. By the time Diego proposed, Chad's picture had been on my desk for more than a year. It turns out even a cardboard lie is very difficult to undo. Because how do you say to people at work, "I know you thought it was Chad the baseball player all this time, but Val broke up with him last night and tomorrow, Valentina Viloria Serrano is marrying Diego de los Rios? The bride's bouquet was made of *Aves del Paraíso*."

"What are *Aves del Paraíso*, Val?"

See the difficulty? For practical reasons, reasons having to do with my not getting arrested for schizophrenia, Chad's picture had to stay on my desk. As a matter of fact, his picture stayed on my desk the entire time I dated and was married to Diego.

When I first told Diego about Chad, he thought it was a joke. I still find it a little mystifying that the things that seem like lies aren't, and the other way around.

Take for instance, my parents. When I told them that Diego had studied archaeology but could not find a job in the field and therefore had to make a living playing guitar, they thought I had been fed weed.

"How do you know he's not lying to you just because everyone thinks archaeologists are glamorous?" Azucena put in.

"Since when are archaeologists glamorous, Azucena?"

"Since Indiana Jones, Valentina!"

And how, exactly, is one supposed to go about proving a thing like that? Except for Catherine Zeta-Jones, what bride would say to the man she's about to marry, "I won't set foot inside the courthouse until you show me your diploma!?" *¡Por favor!* The night before marrying Diego I dreamed I was camping out inside a thrift store.

HIGH HOLIDAYS

Diego and I were jinxed from the start. The week before we were going to get married, your dad, who had apparently given up hope by then, found my number in the book and told me he happened to be in New York visiting his brother. This was before your time, *mi amor*. Before you were born, there was something that used to be called the phone book and everyone was in it. The phone book precedes what you now know as an iPod search app. That was when people used to read things called books and used to wear these medieval-type instruments called reading glasses. Quite frankly, it's hard to imagine a time before Lasik surgery.

In any event, the reason Max called was because he wanted to invite me to something called Rosh Hashanah at his brother's house.

"Roshawhat?" I asked. "Is that some kind of flower festival, Max?" I had never heard of it. I mean, I had heard of Exodus, Genesis, and so on. So had Max. After all, Catholics and the children of Israel share the same Old Testament. The thing is, the version of the Old Testament sermonized to Venezuelan *señoritas* differs greatly from the version of Exodus et al preached to nice Jewish boys from New York. Rosh Hashanah might be a High Holiday elsewhere, but not in Caracas.

Isn't it the same with everything, though? Take the Vietnam War, for instance: the Vietnamese call it the American War. Take the Korean War: the Koreans call it the American War. Take the war in Iraq: the people of Iraq call it the American War.

Religion suffers from a similar misappropriation; people from various places take the same ingredients and cook up a story that tastes good to them. That's what happened with the Last Supper, in fact. Any Catholic will tell you this was a farewell dinner Christ was sharing with twelve apostles and a prostitute named María Magdalena. But get five people in a room who are wearing yarmulkes and some of them might tell you that the Last Supper was a Seder. This may sound strange, but for most Christians the tale as told in the painting by Leonardo was the real beginning of the story—not Genesis, not Exodus—for the simple reason that after Judas betrayed Christ, Jesus went on to die and then he came back. Whereas for some children of Adonai, the Last Supper was the *end* of the story, because Christ went on to die and he isn't back yet.

But that was before a guy named Dan enlightened us all by telling us that Christ was really a woman and that she's buried at the Louvre. You just can't believe everything you hear, *mi amor.* I keep telling you this. And not only had I never heard of Rosh Hashanah until Max mentioned it on the phone, but imagine my surprise when he told me he was inviting me to a dinner at his brother's place to celebrate the New Year.

"Have you checked a calendar recently, Max?" I asked. "We're in September."

But your dad, optimist that he was, simply said, "I was hoping you'd be free."

That's how I ended up at a Rosh Hashanah dinner on the Upper West Side of Manhattan with your uncle Ira, your *tía* Lilith, your cousin Devin, your cousin Josh, and the gay couple. If I had to call that evening something, I wouldn't exactly call it a success. After everything that happened I suspect Ira regretted telling Max he could invite whomever he wanted.

From the start there were issues. Max and your uncle Ira might as well have been conceived by different parents, from different countries, in different time periods, even. As for Lilith, I don't think we'd ever run the risk of running into one another at Bergdorf's. And I don't think that a gay nurse and his playwright lover were what your uncle expected to find at his Rosh Hashanah dinner table. And I haven't even mentioned the wildly inappropriate gift I had brought. Or the guinea pig that was neither a pig nor was it from Guinea. Why sugarcoat it? The evening was a full-blown disaster.

By then, my hair had grown some. I wore it parted on one side and it was no longer the strange red it had been when your dad and I had met at Zumba in Arizona. When he first saw me that night, Max didn't recognize me for a second. He also didn't know I was getting married the following week to a Puerto Rican guitar player.

All Diego had been able to afford as an engagement memento was a tiny cross, which dangled from a bracelet I wore. That night Diego had to play somewhere. It was fine with him if I went to dinner with an old friend, so long as I wasn't out to dinner with Chad, the cardboard baseball player.

It took a minute or so for Max to take in the longer, black hair. But once he got used to it, he told me I looked like some of the girls with whom he had grown up. Except for the nose, of course. My nose belongs to my dad, who in turn got his from Adonis. As for your dad, he still had those crazy curls that made you cry when he cut them off after we got married.

At any rate, after these preliminaries, Max asked me what was in the box, and I told him it was a treat from a French bakery. He was always a patient man. He could wait to see what was inside the box. I liked that about him. I liked that he wasn't the kind of person who pushed people. So we made our way to the kitchen and I set the box on one of the marble counters. That's where I met your cousin, Devin, who was cradling a furry rat in her arms.

"This is Valentina," said Max. At this, Devin smiled that tenuous, please-love-me smile of hers.

"What's your rat's name?" I asked.

"Mom, uncle Max's girlfriend thinks Pumpkin is a rat," Devin said.

"It's called a guinea pig," Max said, winking at me. I should have taken it as an omen, that when a guinea pig named Pumpkin peed on my brand-new dress, at some point I would have a Guinea Pig period. But I was unsuspecting. I was, after all, marrying someone else the following week.

How come you weren't there that night? *¡Ay, mi vidita!* That's one of those "divorce double *Jeopardy!*" questions for Alex Trebec. Back then, neither you nor the twins were allowed to come within five feet of anyone wearing a yarmulke. Your parents' divorce decree included a very specific clause requested by your mother. It was called a "no-proselytizing clause," a sort of giant "No Smoking" banner, which basically meant that neither you nor your brothers could be present at any Jewish holidays. To read the decree was to know beyond the shadow of a doubt that words such as *Passover, Yom Kippur,* and *Hanukkah* were profane. I have no idea why, *mi amor.* How should I know? Maybe your mom was afraid that "Christ has come" did not hold as much promise as "Christ will come." Who can know what kind of sawdust is flying loose inside another person's head?

What's funny is that both Ira and your dad probably grew up thinking that the Pentateuch was within walking distance from the

Pentagon. But that's the reason I didn't meet you or the twins that year. That's why I met your aunt, your uncle, and your cousins first. It wasn't because of some secret plot on your dad's part to introduce me to the family before introducing me to his kids. Though I can see why anyone might think that. The drama that comes with divorce is always much more fascinating than the actual truth. It's a little silly, though, that after people get divorced they see nothing but evil in the eyes of the person they once loved.

Not me. I try to stay on friendly terms with everyone I've ever married. Although I must confess that Jean-Pierre made it a little difficult. Still, had you guys been at Rosh Hashanah, the story his ex-wife would have told her friends might have been, "The children are being traumatized by Holocaust stories." The truth wouldn't have mattered one matzo ball. Divorce is like a Monopoly game in which the rules keep changing to make sure no one ever gets out of jail.

NOT KOSHER

Who else was at dinner that night? There was Jake, the nurse, who would become a good friend of mine. Mere seconds after we met, Jake asked me who did my hair. For some reason the question made your *tía* Lilith wince. Had she known at that moment that asking for my hairdresser's name would be the nicest thing that Jake would say that evening, Lilith might have reached for her pajamas and gone straight to bed. The only reason Jake was there was because he was involved with Geoff who had grown up in New York with both your dad and your uncle Ira. At the time, Geoff had a runaway hit on Broadway—a musical based on the lives of a group of people called the Lovin' Spoonful—people I had never heard of.

As it turned out, Jake wasn't the only person who made your aunt and uncle think that the Lord had left New York that night. You have to remember that your dad had told me it was New Year's. And even if it wasn't *my* New Year, I decided to do something special. In Venezuela we celebrate the New Year's holiday by eating *pan de jamón*, an amazing ham roll that might tempt Jesus into coming back. I looked everywhere in Manhattan but I couldn't find *pan de jamón* on either this or that side of the Hudson. So I did the next best thing, I bought ham croissants from a French bakery. That's what was in the box, except that, for some bizarre reason, everyone assumed I had brought dessert! I think that made the transgression twice as objectionable. Not only had I *not* brought Napoleons, but judging by the looks on their faces when they saw the croissants, you would have sworn I had brought stuffed cat.

Expectations are such a befuddling thing. Why would anyone assume that a woman they've never met would bring dessert rather than ham croissants? Maybe it was the ornate French label on the box. Who could know? What I do know is that when your dad brought the box to the table and I told them the story of the *pan de jamón*, your aunt Lilith's face suddenly became paralyzed. This seemed to delight Devin, whose smile was no longer tenuous.

In fact, to reward me for my unintentional mischief, Devin said to me, "Would you like to hold Pumpkin?" What??? What else was I supposed to do to atone for putting pig on their table but to hold their kid's rat?

"Of course, sweetie," I said. "Of course, I'd love to hold Pumpkin." The transfer of the rat from Devin's warm and loving arms into my cold, reluctant hands was closely observed by all. Everyone was a little nervous, not the least Pumpkin. Animals have such great instincts. Pumpkin knew I would have sent him to Peru on a skewer if I could have. All was well in the heavens until the moment I felt this warm liquid seeping through my legs and I went, "It's peeing on me."

"What's peeing on you, doll?" Jake asked. And because my hands were full of Pumpkin, as it were, I had no choice but to open my eyes wide and stare at my own lap.

"Pumpkin does that when he gets nervous," Devin explained. She really didn't have to.

As for Jake, who was sitting next to me, he was quick to say, "No one will forgive you for ruining a Lanvin. Come with me." I have no idea how he knew I was wearing a Lanvin dress, which, I might add, was Azucena's idea and for which, I'm still paying after all these years. Mercifully, Jake turned out to know what best to rub on finicky fabric and how to keep someone distracted while getting rid of the smell of rat urine, skills no doubt honed while extracting blood at the hospital where he worked. Once he was assured the Lanvin was out of danger, he asked Lilith for a hair dryer. I wonder if Jake knew that Lilith is accustomed to doing the asking herself; she glared at him as if he were an escapee from Alcatraz. A little while later she came back with a hair dryer, which she set it on a little table, and left in stony silence.

"Ham croissants?" Jake said. "That was brilliant!"

Imagine, he thought I had done it on purpose! "Why would I want to offend these people, Jake? I don't even know them."

"Doll, have you ever heard the word *kosher*? Don't you know that Jews and pigs don't get along?"

"Catholics and pigs don't get along either," I said. "But it's only on Fridays that they don't."

"That settles it," said Jake. "I know this great place in the Village . . ."

After we finished drying my dress we returned to the table, where mum was the word. To lift the funereal spirits, it occurred to me to ask Jake how he and Geoff had met. It isn't every day a gabby nurse and a pensive playwright bump into one another. I was betting on an interesting story that might distract everyone from pigs, rodents, and the beckoning smell of urine.

¡Ay, Dios mío! There was nothing to be done after the question had left my mouth. Another person might have managed an emergency lie, changed the subject, punt. Not Jake. Jake has always enjoyed sincerity a little too much, I think. He likes to see what can be flown down from heaven in times of duress. And so he said, "I knew I was in love when I found out that Geoff could suck a golf ball through a garden hose."

Why use big words? Why beat around the bush? And what were we to do when faced with such a candid display of affection? Even Geoff, the love object, blinked a few times. Max was trying very hard not to burst out laughing. Your uncle Ira didn't raise an eyebrow—he raised both of them. Sometimes I think Ira got all the judgmental genes in the family. Who can account for gene distribution? For my part, I crossed my hands on my lap and tried to channel my mother.

Not Lilith. She got up immediately under the pretense of going to the kitchen to get more wine. But we all knew she was going to the kitchen to keep from pouring a whole bottle of wine on Jake's head. There's that about your aunt Lilith—the way she makes people have the urge to run away all of a sudden. In all fairness, though, there's really no way to take words back. Anyone can say, "I'm sorry," of course. And what of it? Ever since that night, "Open your mouth at your own risk" has become something of a motto for me.

After Jake's remark everyone started to disperse, ever so slyly, toward the front door. For my part, I stood in front of the kitchen talking to your cousin Josh, waiting for the right opportunity to say, "Look at the time!" From our brief little chat I had the impression that Josh's brain had been programmed from early on with only to two themes: politics and basketball. He couldn't have been older than ten, yet there he was, urging me to vote Republican. There's always been a rebellious streak in Josh.

But anyway, it was right about then that I overheard Lilith talking to Ira. "You didn't tell me he was dating an aerobics instructor," Lilith said. At first I thought she was talking about me, because in Venezuela you'd be hard-pressed to find a male aerobics instructor.

But I knew it wasn't me she was talking about because I had clearly said during the pre-dinner inquisition that I worked in imaging, an elegant way of saying I pressed a button on an MRI machine for a living. And besides, I wasn't dating Max. It turned out Lilith was talking about Geoff.

Jake was really a nurse. But I suppose he might have passed for an aerobics instructor. He was in excellent shape and he spoke in an evenly paced pitch, which might have made Lilith's repressed unconscious hear, "And one. And two. Now squeeze those cheeks." What I really loved about Lilith and Ira's little marital spat, though, was the fact that Lilith couldn't bring herself to speak the words *blow job*. So she called Jake an "aerobics instructor." If she only knew that Jake could care less about her high-minded consideration.

It's like when some people say to me—by way of relating—Some of my best friends are South American. And I'm like, "Who are *you*?"

Right before leaving, Jake made me swear on the saved Lanvin that I would call him with my hairdresser's name and number. We hugged. We kissed on both cheeks. He winked conspiratorially. After all the good-bye fuss, Max pulled out the pin on the hand grenade and told me he wanted to see me again.

"But aren't you still in Arizona, Max?"

"Location. Location. Location." He smiled. "That can be arranged." If I had to remember your dad by one thing alone, it would have to be his delusional optimism. . . . That's why this other thing just doesn't make sense. . . .

What to say to Max? "I'd love to, Max, but there's this little problem. I'm getting married next week."

"Wow. I see . . . hmm . . . I guess that's what you call a deal killer. . . . You love the guy, Valentina?" And because they teach mind reading at Yale, *mi amor*, or because your dad was simply a genius, he looked me straight in the eye and said, "How far will you run?"

"Who's running, Max? I have no idea what you're talking about."

As we say in Spanish, *mi amor*, Max nailed me to the cross.

THE RHYTHM METHOD

It's harder to get through a Jackie O. audition than it is to get a marriage license. Even at the Jackie O. audition there was that first judge who asked the first disqualifying question: "What makes you think you can be Jackie O.?" I think the clerks at city hall should follow their example and start asking people, "What makes you think you can be married?" Perhaps that might deter some.

In order to marry Diego, I had to say good-bye to many things and many people, including Dr. Patricia Cunningham, whom you've heard me refer to as the Egyptologist who taught at NYU. Pat, as she preferred to be called, gave me a warm farewell as I gave her back her keys. I was to see Pat again, under slightly different circumstances.

But all this talk about marrying the wrong people just made me realize that you and I haven't had the birth control talk, *mi amor*. Of course I know you don't want to talk about this. But you've brought it on yourself. You're the one who started calling me "stepmother," remember? Now I have to get involved. Now I have to start going into your room to tidy things up, read your secret journal, and call your boyfriend behind your back.

Yes, I know you don't have a boyfriend. Yet. That's a minor felony, as smart and pretty as you are. But we still have to talk about you keeping your legs crossed, for when you do get a boyfriend. Eventually, everyone gets a boyfriend, even if he comes in a box. I'm positive about that. I just hope you pick the right one the first time around.

Yes, I realize you don't want a talk about birth control. You just told me that. But not everything we don't want to talk about can be avoided, Emily. If only more women in South America would stop listening to men in robes about the rhythm of their own bodies, there wouldn't be so many unwanted children and so many unwanted stretch marks. In my humble opinion, the Catholic Church is primarily against the Pill because decreasing birth rates would mean two things: there'd be less collection money, and the Muslims would get an edge. We can't have that! But the Pope shouldn't worry. Catholicism will always have an edge over Islam. Because, unlike Islam, Catholicism comes with its own insurance policy: you sin, you confess, you go to heaven.

It's a very soothing religion, to tell you the truth, appeasing as it does all those poor souls who can't help themselves, whereas Islam simply asks too much of its followers. It's just plain inconsiderate to ask busy people to stop everything they're doing, no matter where they are, and wham, drop to the ground, wrinkle their pants and skirts, look in the direction of Mecca, adjust their headscarves, and wait to do it again four more times.

As far as I'm concerned, if he's losing any sleep over losing fans, the head cheese at the Vatican should donate his Ambien to someone who really needs it. Not soon will Catholics give up all those benefits. Plus Salvation! And what about anticipatory Mass on Saturday afternoons? It's not for everyone, of course; only for people who have trouble choosing between Christ and Sunday brunch. Sometimes, a little flexibility on everyone's part is all that's needed to have peace. That's the case with Saturday Mass: people get the commitment out of the way, the Church gets its money, everyone's happy.

But we were talking birth control. If I may be a little selfish for a second, the reason I want you to keep your legs crossed is because it's bad enough to be a stepmother, *mi amor*, I don't want to be a grandmother too. I'm too young for that. Another reason to lock your knees is because you don't want to have to start switching from Monistat to Vagisil. Keep it clean.

And do me a favor, whatever you do, don't get on Seasonique, or whatever that pill is called. Anytime you hear an announcer say, "Your body wasn't meant to have twelve periods a year," you should check the bottom of your TV screen to make sure you're not watching the Discovery Channel. Genetic engineering might be fine with Grapples, broccolini, and plumcots, but only because a plum has no way of saying it doesn't want to be an apricot. Humanity may not agree on much, *mi amor*, but everywhere from Kyoto to Kinshasa people agree that twelve periods a year is pretty much the standard planet-wide. Don't ever let anyone tell you that the body of a woman, after centuries and centuries of having twelve periods a year, can all of a sudden get away with four. You're a human, *mi amor*, not an avatar. What's sure to happen during one of those four times is that you'll pee a blood clot the size of a kidney. Trust me on this.

The problem is that most people your age grew up on instant technology. I can see how that might give you the impression that you can make your period go away at the mere push of a button. But there probably isn't room on your iPhone's little screen for the fine print: ". . . this pill doesn't prevent AIDS, blood clots, or heart attacks. Tested by doctors." Maybe doctors in Guantánamo Bay!

But anyway, I know you don't want to discuss birth control. I know you think that neither your mother nor your stepmother believe that you will ever come in contact with a person of the male species. But keep in mind that I grew up among monkeys. So I'll be preaching birth control until the day the roosters come home.

I ONCE MET A GIRL NAMED VALENTINA

Val and Valentina reached an impasse on the day a woman who suspected she had breast cancer and was also claustrophobic came into the MRI center and asked if anyone there spoke Spanish. What to say to this woman? By then I had traded the blue contacts for green, only because when I looked in the mirror at the optometrist's office, green eyes and black hair looked like a more believable mainstream combination. The woman had been driven to the MRI center by her daughter. Her name was Alma Ruiz. The reason I remember her name after all these years is because on that day, I disappointed myself. You can disappoint others and say, "My bad," but on the day you disappoint yourself, you feel like shit.

The Valentina I used to know would have spoken to Alma Ruiz in Spanish because Alma Ruiz was terrified. The Val I had created, on the other hand, continued to instruct the woman in English. "Please wear these earplugs. I will now slide you inside the chamber." If only I could have soothed her in her native tongue. It was just a handful of words. Still, I couldn't manage them. The person who could have managed them was not in the room.

When I told Diego that night about what had happened at work, it finally hit me. Oftentimes I wished Diego had been the kind of person who said things like, "You're a monster, Valentina." Not Diego. Diego was one of those nonjudgmental types. He just said, "Why?"

"Why what!? You know why!! You know why I refuse to utter another *Hola* in this country. Because everyone thinks I'm a migrant worker who crossed the border illegally. Because I don't want to get fired again, Diego. Because I don't want to be called a spic again by people from Alabama who are fixing toilets in Louisiana!!! That's why, Diego!!! And because now that I've hung a shingle on my uniform that says, 'Val is open for business,' I can't very well tell everyone I'm a fraud!! That's why, Diego. That is why I couldn't say, *"Buenos días, señora. Por favor tome asiento. No tiene nada de que temer."*

"I've been called worse," Diego said.

"I don't give a damn what you've been called, Diego. This isn't the Olympics of ethnic slurs! Do me a favor, Diego. Name two people you know who can say whether your beloved Puerto Rico is a state or a commonwealth of this country."

"I can't, Valentina."

"Don't call me that."

"I thought that was your name."

"Not when you say it like that! You're insulting me, Diego. And you know it. Go ahead, name two people."

"Is that why you changed your name to Val? Because you want to be one of those people?"

"You bastard! You're the one playing Latin music to them night after night."

"That was a low blow, Valentina. You know very well why I—"

"Shut up, Diego. You know this game was rigged from the start. Just . . . shut . . . up."

LEAVE EARLY

We hadn't been married a month when we started having these bizarre fights. I can't remember feeling myself so low a creature in the order of things. Well, maybe, when I think of it, it wasn't my long-held ambition to find my best friend rocking Jean-Pierre to the beat of rhythm and blues.

But why dwell on the negative? There's so much for which to be grateful here, so much that encourages and sustains. The problem is that I've always been in such a hurry that I haven't had time to stop and give expression to all that is wonderful about being alive. A woman who knows the value of time can't very well be expected to be grateful too, can she?

So maybe I'm a little ungrateful. Well, at least I'm not hesitant. Or a dawdler. I'd much rather be bold and incautious. Bold is always much more stimulating. I've always found it stimulating to run, run, run along, and to find out by the time I get to the finishing line how truly bewitching breathlessness can be. All that quivering is good for your lungs. And who has time to count blessings, or sheep, while quivering?

And besides, I'm not a sentimental loser. The only way to stay a step ahead of the emotional landslide headed in my direction was to start thinking about a change. Moving always beats staying put, no contest. I'm always happy to leave a party that did not end up as planned.

BEING BILINGUAL

The hoped-for change of scenery came in the form of Kirsten Kramer, a recruiter at a firm called Finders Keepers. I met Kirsten at a place called the Boom Boom Bar in Soho, where Diego was playing one night. It was Kirsten who convinced me that with my skills, my resume, my looks . . .

"My God! What are you doing wearing a silly blue uniform and pressing the same button all day long? I know I'd be bored out of my mind," said Kirsten. Once we became friends, I realized that Kirsten Kramer would have done just as well in Venezuela as I have done in this country. Kirsten Kramer did not believe in stuck buttons on MRI machines. "Let's get another martini," she said. "And you're bilingual, too? Oh, my God! Here, take my card. I'll have you placed anywhere in the five boroughs by the end of the week. Isn't that funny?" she said, "I wasn't supposed to be here tonight. You either? Oh my God!"

Kirsten Kramer was a great believer in coincidence. I used to be one, too. Now I'm all about probability theory. Just about the only thing I believe in these days is the birthday paradox, the notion that in a group of randomly chosen people, some pair of them will have the same birthday. The probability that a recruiter in Manhattan and a person looking to switch jobs in Manhattan would run into each other at the Boom Boom Bar, given that they both liked martinis and Latin music, was not far-fetched at all. But all hash functions aside, the reason Kirsten and I found each other was because we wanted to.

It was thanks to Kirsten Kramer that I ended up working at a place called Human Capital, helping people who had been laid off, right-sized, and downsized to get back on their feet. There I was, a kind of expert on change management, helping people who had been displaced, replaced, and mismanaged. Not only was I perfect for the job, I was a godsend to those poor people. And they were a godsend to me! Imagine, with the money I'd be making I could pay off my education loans from my brief detour as an MRI technician.

Whatever made me think I could survive six months pushing the same button!?

The key to survival, Darwin will tell you, is adaptation. Become used to your habitat and you will evolve. Learn to run fast and you will escape predators. Grow teeth, if you must, to better grind the grass. Trade your blue contacts for green, I promise you, and you will be able to look at people like Tony Zippolo in the eye. All of a sudden, you will have a much clearer picture of things.

It was during my first week at Human Capital that I met Tony Zippolo, the displaced sportscaster from Jersey.

OUTPLACED IN THE LAND OF
OPPORTUNITY

Human Capital, the outplacement firm, worked like this. An overworked outplacement counselor who had worked there a week longer than any of the other counselors, and who had no wits left to hear the same lame story over and over again, handed me a manila folder with the names of the displaced people to whom I would have to listen over and over again until I helped them find a new job, or until they died, whichever came first. Sometimes you hoped for the latter. Death as an act of kindness, that is how I felt every time Tony Zippolo came into my cubicle, chewing tobacco, sans homework in hand, and said, "Don't tawk to me about my day."

Tony Zippolo was a middle-aged sportscaster who had been replaced by a young blonde with botulism in her lips. Her name was Hannah. And Tony, who had lived the better part of his forty-odd years on this planet by something called the Nielsen ratings, couldn't get his sportscaster head around the notion that someone who had had her chin tucked, her brows lifted, and her lips puffed was replacing him in the very important endeavor of reading sports scores to horny men, who, in another country would go by the name of Carlos Upstairs. Whenever I asked Tony for a copy of his resume, he looked me straight in the eye and asked, "Whatz yah name, again? Let me tell ya whatz goin' on. I'm whatz cawlled talent. I'm used to dealin' with images and sound. I don't deal whell with papuh. That's yah job."

"I know that's my job, Tony. But how can I help you when you won't even give me a copy of your work history?"

"My wok history? How dare-ya! Turn on the TV! Everyone knows Tony Zippolo."

"I would turn on the TV, Tony, if I had one."

"Whot? You don't own a TV? Is the pay dat bad heah? Datz impossible."

"It's not impossible, Tony. Your parents entrusted you to Hanna-Barbera Productions. The people who raised you were a bear named Yogi, a Neanderthal named Fred, and a gorilla named Magilla. My parents thought that was a crime. They're psychotherapists, you see. They filled my head with Freudian slips instead. But, all the same, Tony, I need you to make those phone calls we talked about, the networking calls."

Whenever I reminded him of the phone calls he was supposed to make, Tony would say, "I can't cawl anyore yet. I'm not supposed to be heah."

And I would say, "Tony, the minute your friends turn on the TV, they will see that it's Hannah now, reading the sports scores."

"Thatz exactly right! That woman doesn't know Jordan."

"You mean the country, Tony?"

"I've been in the locker room with Jordan."

"Who's Jordan?"

"I've been to Vegas with Jordan."

"Who's Jordan, Tony?"

"I've even taken a piss next to Michael Jordan."

"I'm sorry, Tony. I've never been to Vegas. Still, I need you to update your resume."

"Hannah's just a reader with tits," said Tony. "I'm a journalist!"

"Listen, Tony, I realize Hannah is just a reader with tits. I realize the *H* in her name doesn't stand for *human*. So why are you worried about an android? Wouldn't it be more productive to work on your resume?"

"Whatz ya name, again? Aren't ya supposed to be on my side?"

Suddenly, I missed Azucena.

OUT OF MY LEAGUE

During the first couple of months at Human Capital I met Kirsten Kramer a few times for lunch. Little by little, I started to realize that Kirsten was one of those people who never dropped the ball, to borrow a term from Tony Zippolo. She wanted to see how things were going. She wanted to know if Human Capital was what's called, in placement lore, a good fit. From her point of view, it probably was. Because the longer people like Tony remained unemployed the more money Human Capital made. That failure to find a job could be so richly rewarded was confusing to me. But in the end, what was good for her client was good for Kirsten Kramer. She was pleased that in placing me there her already good reputation had moved forward another inch. So pleased was she, in fact, that she offered to bring me to a networking event one evening.

The event was being hosted by an organization called the Junior League. And it was at the Junior League, *mi amor*, that I realized I didn't know how to spell. It was after meeting Sheri with an *i*, Cathi with a *c*, and Beverlee with two *ee*'s that I realized that the spellings of all the names I had learned thus far in this country were all wrong. The other thing I was to understand about the Junior League was that unless you carried around a box of recipes, you could not call yourself a member of the League. I should have kept it to myself. I should never have mentioned at my first Cookbook Committee meeting that boiling an egg was challenging for me.

I will tell you more about the League later. I have enough League stories to write a script for Reese Witherspoon. But now I want to tell you about Peter Malone, the person who most occupied my time during my early days at Human Capital.

Peter Malone had been laid off as the CFO of a huge pharma, to put it in his words. Practically overnight, the pharmaceutical company for which Peter Malone had successfully managed dozens of mergers and acquisitions decided he was suddenly "redundant." No matter how many times you see the word *redundant* in the *Wall Street Journal*, *mi amor,* don't let anyone tell you that it is humane to call someone that. Those cruel euphemisms are usually concocted at expensive off-site meetings held by redundant InHuman Resources departments and their consultants.

But back to Peter Malone. I had more than an ounce of compassion for Peter. Like countless others he had done nothing to deserve being called "redundant." Peter worked hard. Peter had the right degrees. Peter was a conscientious creature who arrived daily at the same building to do what was expected of him. And, according to the references I was obliged to check, did so to the best of his ability. So why was Peter Malone in my office? Besides the obvious reason that he had been replaced by a team of twelve-year-old accountants in Bangalore, that is.

One of the reasons Peter was in my office was that he couldn't talk to the person with whom he shared a bed, aka Holly Malone. In the end, Peter's predicament was better suited to being handled by someone with a psychology degree than by an unseasoned outplacement counselor like me. On the brighter side, he had been given a generous severance package which, had he lived by Diego's philosophy rather than by Azucena's, would have lasted him ten years. But nooo. Peter's daughter had not one but two horses. Horses are expensive, *mi amor.* I never realized it until Peter told me how much it costs to feed a horse. Up until that point, I guess I had always thought of horses as props in war movies. To make matters worse, the house in the Hamptons was being remodeled. And what's even worse, Holly was accustomed to throwing lavish parties, which is why Peter could not tell her all of a sudden that he been made redundant. "What would Holly say?"

Instead, Peter got dressed every morning as if he were going to work, and stationed himself in the extra chair right outside my cubicle while I tried to work with the other redundant people in my manila folder.

How to convince a man that CFO, UFO, and CEO are just initials?

AN IMMIGRANT, BY ANY OTHER NAME

It started as a game. After he found a new job, Peter told me that our little game had saved his life. I don't know about that, but maybe it saved his Lexus from being repossessed. To better help him cope with the word *redundant*—and before we got to work on his resume and all the rest of it—I made Peter repeat a little mantra at the beginning of each meeting. "Peter, please repeat after me: 'I am *not* my business card.'"

The first time I suggested this, he smiled politely and said, "I don't think this is going to work."

"Peter, please, repeat after me: 'I am *not* my business card.'"

And Peter would say, "With all due respect, Valentina, that's easy for you to say because *you* have a business card."

And I would say, "Peter, I haven't always had a business card. This is quite a new business card, in fact. I'm still trying to learn my job, and to get used to my new name." I didn't tell Peter that I was married to someone whose name I wouldn't dare take and that the Valentina Viloria-Serrano was a fairly new name for me. In fact, when the HR manager at Human Capital had asked me what I wanted on my business cards, the question hit me like a tsunami. You see, I didn't want to end up like Azucena's maids in Caracas. So I hyphenated my name to give it a little push. I knew a name like de Los Rios would forever sink me inside the immigrant swamp.

"So Peter, please repeat after me: 'I am *not* my business card.' I also want you to say the following: 'I am a father, a husband, and a man who enjoys playing golf; I was a man before a pharma told me I was redundant.' Just this once, Peter. Please say it just once. I promise it gets easier. Trust me on this." But Peter wasn't listening. "Peter, when are you planning to tell Holly that you will not be receiving a paycheck come March?"

"When I have another job, Valentina."

"Very well, then. So where's your call list? How is anyone supposed to hire you if they don't know you're looking? Just humor me this once. Please say: 'I am *not* my business card.'"

Month after month Peter continued to sit on the extra chair right outside my cubicle staring at the carpet, until one day I told him I needed the chair for something else, and sent him to the conference room to make his phone calls. I had almost forgotten about him until I saw him talking on the phone on my way back from making some copies. After he hung up, I poked my head inside the conference room and asked, "Found a job yet?"

And Peter said, "'I . . . am . . . not my business card.'" And we both laughed. And then we cried.

Now, how to convince Holly Malone that her husband was worth loving, without her shopping allowance? The battle was still uphill.

On the day I finally placed Peter at his new job at a Japanese pharma setting up shop in the States, after months and months of trying to get him to say, "I am *not* my business card," he sent me champagne and roses. Gia Leone, one of the other counselors in the office, came up to me and said, "I don't know how you do it, Valentina. How do you get your clients to send you roses?"

"Tell me, Gia, what's *your* secret to placing people who feel redundant? I'm new at this. I can always use a tip."

DIVERSITY!

Someone who doesn't know how much water it takes to boil an egg is obviously out of her depths at the Junior League. So, to better make use of the more natural "shortcoming" of being a foreigner, I was placed on the Diversity Committee instead. And what does it mean to be on a Diversity Committee, exactly? It means you're the only person in a meeting to offer Third World solutions to First World problems—such as, stop eating if you're obese. It means you're destined to shock people who, although they've heard of Caracas, simply cannot believe that maids quit without giving two weeks' notice. It means you're the only person among two hundred who has never gone to the Nordstrom semiannual sale.

An organization like the Junior League would never survive in South America. The traffic alone would make it forbidding—too many committee meetings and not enough chauffeurs like José to get you there on time.

So busy was I getting diversified that I hardly saw Diego anymore. While he was playing the guitar somewhere, I was in Diversity Committee meetings. By the night of the Nordstrom gala we had gotten used to going our separate ways. That night I returned home and found Diego sitting on a chair, wearing faded jeans and a shirt opened down to here. I was wearing a stylish black gown by some designer or other as befits a person who belongs to the Junior League.

"How was your night?" Diego asked.

"Oh, Diego," I said.

"Why are you crying, Valentina?"

"*¿Y por qué será, Diego?*"

And when people in the League asked, "What kind of a name is Valentina Viloria-Serrano?" I said, "It's a hyphenated one. How about yours? What kind of a name is Beverlee? Tell me, whose idea was it about the two *ee*'s, your mother's, or your father's?"

When in doubt, *mi amor*, redirect.

A WALK IN THE PARK
(OR, THE IMMIGRANT'S DILEMMA)

Whenever I got off the phone with Azucena, I looked lovingly in Diego's direction. Compared to living in the middle of the Amazon with ignorant maids prone to praying to clock radios, living with a frustrated archaeologist pining for Egypt didn't seem so bad. Not unless you knew that the very thought of living next to dead Pharaohs and getting sand in my eyes from the decaying Cheops, Khafra, and Menkaure made me want to head to JFK and board the next plane to Caracas.

But Diego and I were relatively happy and managed life in New York as a couple of foreigners very well, so long as we stuck strictly to the Separation of Church and State Code I had instituted. The Separation of Church and State Code meant that Diego and I only spoke Spanish to each other at home and when we were among his friends. The rest of the time, I spoke English.

It was a balancing act. Oftentimes I felt like those circus people who walk on a tightrope and hope they don't fall. Or, if they do, that they don't land on cement. The code was insurance against cross-cultural disasters. It ensured that our separate worlds would never cross.

The code worked well until the Sunday I ran into Cathi Cohen in Central Park. That day, Diego and I were in the park taking a stroll with a little stuffed bear he had given me as a present for Día de Reyes, that minor holiday I told you about involving the Three Wise Men, whom we call "magicians." We had baptized him Tito. Diego, who wanted to have children as if he'd had a biological-clock implant, had bought Tito a pair of glasses. Tito usually traveled inside my purse, but that morning I was holding him because Diego wanted to see Tito wearing his new sunglasses.

Tito in hand, we walked and talked. In looking back I can see we were actually happy that day. For one, we weren't fighting, which was rare. Even if we didn't want to, Diego and I always managed to insinuate our way into a fight. But that day I had promised myself peace in the land. So I asked Diego to tell me about his dreams, about why he liked the Egyptians so much, about why he wanted to move to Giza. Notice I didn't ask, "Why do you want to live in a grave full of skeletons who will blow sand into your eyes all day?" Still, that's exactly what I was thinking.

Sometimes you're in a relationship and you just *know,* you just know by the kinds of things that cross your mind that you're tilling on barren land. That's what was going through my head that morning in Central Park. For all the wonders hidden on the Giza Plateau, I could not see myself riding on a leprous camel along the banks of the Nile. I didn't know what period would follow the Separation of Church and State period, but I had the frightful suspicion that it wouldn't include Diego. The entire time we were together, I had some kind of latent stomachache that refused to go away. So, to distract myself from the pain, I said to Diego, "Let's carve our initials on a tree!" That's one of those absurdities that otherwise intelligent people embrace from time to time: the notion that if you legitimize something you know is broken, say by putting a signature on it, or by carving it on wood, for instance, somehow the thing will stop being broken. What you have now, instead, is *legitimately* broken.

So we carved the letters "D & V" on a tree with a Swiss army knife Diego carried around. Afterward, we smiled at our creation. We embraced. We kissed. All of it was heartfelt—maybe too much so. Diego and I were breaking our own hearts. And we both knew it. So after carving our initials on the tree, Diego asked, "Why are you crying, Valentina?"

"Because I'm so happy, Diego. Let's keep moving." So we kept walking with Tito in hand. That's when I spotted Cathi Cohen, a woman I knew from the League. I should have realized something was wrong when I started walking faster, trying to avoid her. In the end, it couldn't be helped—we practically bumped into her. The entire time we were standing there, Cathi kept staring at Diego, waiting for me to introduce him. But I didn't introduce him. Because I couldn't. It is only now, after all this time, that I can admit this to myself, that Diego—with his embarrassingly thick accent and his guitar—reminded me of everything I had to leave behind to become a made-in-China copy of a truly assimilated woman. I was bent on fitting in. Diego, on the other hand, was proud to be Puerto Rican. He never felt he had lost anything by playing to people who made fun of his accent after the lights went down. Ah, the price we pay for freedom!

In the end, I played this trick I told you about, the trick of redirection. This is how redirection is supposed to work. Someone says, "What are you doing here?" And you repeat the question and say, with a hint of surprise in your voice, "What are *you* doing here?" Say someone asks, "What are you doing this weekend?" and you don't want to answer, then you say, "How about *you*? What are *your* plans for the weekend?" And so on.

So when Cathi Cohen asked, staring at Diego, "What are you doing in Central Park?" I immediately redirected. "What are *you* doing in Central Park, Cathi?"

But because Cathi's answer was clipped, a mere "I'm just out for a walk," I asked her if she knew of a good place for brunch. "Brunch?"

Realizing the question was out of place, I looked at my watch a little frantically and said, "Oh, my God, I didn't realize how late it was!" It was only nine in the morning, on a Sunday, *mi amor.* This happened years ago. But I remember every detail as if it happened an hour ago.

So after Cathi left, Diego asked, "A place for brunch, Valentina?"

And I said, "Diego, please, let's not get into a fight. I was just making small talk."

"Why didn't you introduce me, Valentina?"

"Oh, I don't know, Diego . . . I just forgot, I guess. Is that really so important, Diego, being introduced to a woman you'll never see again?" Because how do you say to someone, "You're the only one who gets me. You're the only one I recognize. The only peace I know is when I'm in your arms. I just wish you weren't written in reverse." Who can say a thing like that and not burst into tears?

So I said, "I think Tito's thirsty. Let's get him something to drink."

Are you confused yet?

MARRIAGE AU GRATIN

For my twenty-fifth birthday my family invited me to Paris. I wish I could say they invited Diego, too. But that wouldn't even qualify as an emergency lie. What they said was, "Just you, Valentina, please." That they thought a guitar player was beneath me, they didn't need to spell out.

So I was obliged to say, "Remember, we're married?"

That's when my mother said, "If you insist."

So we all arrived in Paris—my mother, my father, my sister, Carlos Upstairs, me, and Diego the outcast. In a few short days I was to discover that nothing Diego and I ever said to each other in the heat of marital discord could compete with the insults laid on him by Azucena during that trip to Paris. On the whole, I try not to feel regretful about anything. But I do feel remorse for having accepted such a wicked birthday present. Who would have known? That a Puerto Rican guitar player would be an offense to the people who wanted to talk Montesquieu, Voltaire, and Rousseau—not because those were their favorite topics of conversation, but to prove to me, as one might to a jury during a trial, that Diego could not understand a word they were talking about. And that consequently, Diego and I were incompatible. It was twisted. But because ostracizing others by speaking to them in a language they can't understand is not an ethic I share, it would never have occurred to me that anyone could have dreamed up anything so bizarre. Wouldn't it have been easier to say, "We think you've married the wrong guy yet again, Valentina," than to waste a week and ten thousand francs to show me what a huge mistake I had made? But maybe not. It's possible that my parents' radical ways were more effective at eradicating Diego than anything they might have said. "Show, don't tell," goes the saying. Well, they showed me! After that trip to Paris, hard as we tried to resume being married to each other, Diego and I never recovered.

WRITTEN IN STONE

The Code of Hammurabi stele was one of the many things that Diego had wanted to see at the Louvre. But the first thing we came to on the ground floor was the Venus de Milo, who, as you know, lost her arms and the apple she was holding while being transported from Milos to Paris. What is to be done about sloppy museum curators?

Azucena and Carlos Upstairs were nearby, with Carlos Upstairs yawning and wondering why Azucena had taken away his Game Boy in order to bring him to a stale museum to look at four-thousand-year-old broken dolls. At some point Carlos Upstairs took up residence on one of the marble benches. But not just then. As for my parents, they had gone to another wing of the Louvre, perhaps trying to avoid the nauseating sight of their firstborn's second mistake.

Diego and I were fine with this. When we were by ourselves, away from the rest of the world and its great expectations, we actually enjoyed each other. We were still standing in front of the Venus de Milo perusing a leaflet, trying to figure out where, among thirty-odd thousand pieces of art, might a museum curator decide to hide King Hammurabi's oldest known extant set of laws. We decided it must be in the Egyptian Antiquities part of the museum. It would take weeks to do justice to a place as rich as the Louvre, so Diego and I were trying to see those things you might not want to die without having seen. We were headed to the Sully Wing when Azucena, dragging Carlos Upstairs as one does an unwilling child, placed herself within earshot of us and said, speaking of Diego, "He probably thinks he's looking at that tennis player from the States."

"The other Venus hasn't lost her arm yet, Azucena *querida*," I said.

If the world is made up of the warriors, the indifferent, and the traitors, I belong to the warrior camp. Diego, on the other hand, was content to go on living and ignoring people named after pretentious flowers. So he ignored Azucena, pretending he hadn't heard what she said. It's quite possible—and this has just occurred to me—that this is why Azucena had started her own personal jihad against Diego: because he was indifferent to her. Azucena can bear many things. She can bear someone named Ika not knowing who Martha Stewart is. She can bear almost losing her entire family to a woman who makes perfect grilled-cheese sandwiches. She can sleep next to a Game Boy addict night after night. But she cannot bear being ignored. It turned out Azucena was playing to a disinterested audience, to someone who set his sights a little higher than paying heed to her childish insults.

"Let's go find the tablets," Diego said. And what is to be done about people so peculiar, so eccentric in fact, they just don't share our view of the world? Send them to Bosnia, I suppose. Azucena could not hide her disdain for a guitar player who was on a first-name basis with the treasures of ancient Babylon. As it turned out, it was only Diego among us who knew, when he set eyes on Nike, that the Winged Victory of Samothrace had not gotten to the Louvre on her rubber-sole shoes all the way from Greece. And what's more, when Diego set eyes on the artful, flowing drapery of the Greek goddess, he got all teary. But let's leave Nicholas Sparks out of this.

To avoid any further confrontations of the banal sort, I told Azucena that Diego and I were going to walk around on our own and that we should all meet at Café Marly for lunch. This turned out to be a mistake.

AU REVOIR

Le Café Marly, as it has been known since Hemingway and Sartre warmed seats elsewhere on the other side of the Seine, is in the Richelieu Wing of the Louvre. It overlooks the Cour Napoléon as well as a pyramid that owes its glow to a Japanese architect named I. M. Pei, and not, as it is widely believed, to a guy named Dan or a girl named Audrey Tautou. All this to tell you that it's close to impossible to miss either the *Pyramide du Louvre* or Café Marly. All the same, Azucena and Carlos Upstairs were late.

So Diego and I sat down and proceeded to take in the multilingual repartee, the clinking of champagne flutes, and the clacking of silverware. And we waited. The thing to remember about Diego is that despite his knowledge of winged marble beauties, he made his living as a guitar player. And Puerto Rican guitar players in New York City simply cannot compete with the salaries earned by the people of Goldman Sachs. He was understandably alarmed when he saw a sandwich on the menu that cost the same as tank of gas. Quite frankly, so was I. Maybe that's not true. I wasn't alarmed, I was just pissed that I hadn't been able to package my degree in psychology and my MBA into a book called *Why Angry People with Accents Won't Touch Brioche*. And where were my parents? These were, after all, the people who had committed to paying five dollars for fizzy water inside a green bottle. They were nowhere near rue de Rivoli.

Diego and I were about to get up and find a croissant we didn't have to put on layaway when Azucena and Carlos Upstairs showed up at our table. As for Azucena, who should have married Jean-Pierre instead of Carlos Upstairs, she had barely sat down when she lifted two little fingers of her perfectly manicured hand and said, *"Garçon, un café si'l vous plait!"* And that is something Azucena does, something I've always envied about her. Whenever she gets to a place, all of a sudden everyone else disappears. Azucena is the kind of person who arrives late at a meeting she herself called, walks calmly to the head of the table, takes off her Chanel jacket, and says, "Catch me up."

But the *garçon* whose eye she caught was well trained. He must have been personally supervised by Jacques Barbary, the general in command of the Marly, a man obviously used to accommodating all appetites. Because don't you know it? A café au lait materialized in front of Azucena the way food does in movies. My sister sure knows how to pick them. The *garçon* was quick, capable, and ridiculously handsome. And he spoke French, to boot! Azucena had arrived at her version of the seven virgins in heaven preached elsewhere. So what will it be for lunch, *Gâteau Basque* or *Saumon a l'Unilatéral*? And where were my parents?

Now I wonder if this was part of the plan. Surely my parents realized that a ten-dollar *tarte tatin* was an extravagance for a newbie outplacement counselor in New York City. As for Diego, who practically lived merely on tips from people who liked his version of *"Lágrimas Negras,"* he would just as soon have jumped from one of the cornices of the Richelieu Wing than pay for lunch at the Marly. So we didn't eat.

And when Diego refused to pay for Azucena's café au lait, she looked at me and said, "I feel so sorry for you, Valentina." This quasi-private pity conference on my behalf took place while Carlos Upstairs admired the legs of a woman who had not left Greece for Paris four thousand years before. You can see, *mi amor*, how it might be easy to conclude, when it comes right down to it, that it's the tourists who are rude in Paris, and not the French. *Au revoir.*

BURST BUBBLES

My parents invited me to Paris to show me that a man who played the guitar in New York City could never, ever, as long as you both shall live, be able to show me such a grand time. But even after all that effort, my birthday in Paris remains stuck in my hard head as the most miserable birthday of my life. And don't think I don't realize I'm risking deportation when I put the words *miserable* and *Paris* in the same sentence. Why deny it? There are many people in this world who wish they could say they spent their birthday drinking champagne on *rue de Rivoli*. But then again, I've also met people who would just as soon drink vampire blood than endure all the *bonjours, bonsoirs,* and *bon mots.* Save for his desire to see the treasures of the Louvre, Diego was in the latter camp.

And there's something else I realized while strolling alone through some of the loveliest gardens I've ever seen. *Les Tuileries,* by themselves, glorious as they are, do not have the power to make anyone happy.

SPLITTING LIES

Who said democracy is the only road to freedom? So convinced was I that Diego should really be dusting bones under the bright Egyptian sun that after returning from Paris I called my former landlady, Dr. Patricia Cunningham, to ask if, after all those years talking mummies at NYU, she couldn't dig up the name of some useful contact person in Cairo. A couple of weeks later she called back with the name and number of a fellow professor at Cairo University in Giza. What a woman.

So, one night before dinner, I handed a little piece of paper to Diego. When I told him what it meant, he had that look on his face people have when they've been kissed for the first time and they realize they like it. There are advantages to breaking your own heart—for one, you won't be pointing any fingers. I knew I'd never see him again. And why deny it, it was devastating to lose out to Nefertiti.

"Do you want to come along, Valentina?" he might have asked. But we both knew that I was no Great Royal Wife. If you're unable or unwilling to move for whatever reason, you always have the option of moving someone else.

I saw him off at JFK.

"Why are you crying, Valentina?"

"¿Y por qué será, Diego? There's a knot in our future. Please don't look at me that way. I think it's time for you to leave. But won't you please stay?"

"It's not going to work out, is it?"

"I'm too far gone, Diego. And you're too far stuck. We're a mirror of this world . . . where we can't live. Not together, in any case. No, I don't know why, Diego. You're that organ donor I needed to live . . . but somehow after the transplant, it didn't take. My body rejected it. There's not much doctors can do about transplant failure. We weren't a good match, that's all. The problem is . . . I'm still carrying a piece of you inside. Go see if you can unearth the mystery of Smenkhkare, Diego. It's better than burying each other alive in New York City. We're headed for an emotional landslide. Better not to be there when it hits. Please trust me on this, Diego. People have epochs, just like kingdoms do Consider yourself lucky you're leaving this Valentina period with most of your vital organs intact. Oh, the heart? Don't worry about the heart. The heart is a flexible organ. Trust me on this. Trust me on this. You can trust me on this . . . Diego. I know as much about this as you've forgotten about Egypt. *Adiós*, Diego."

As it turned out, Diego and I didn't even need a good lawyer. We had nothing in our possession the other one might have wanted. We divorced in absentia.

ALIENS SELLING PIZZA

Since moving to this country I've been persecuted by a strange fear—
the fear of selling pizza. Actually, it isn't my fear. It just happened to
have stuck to me somehow. The person most afraid of my becoming
a pizza-delivery prostitute in the upper part of the Americas was my
father. I don't know where he got the idea that Americans like pizza.
But more to the point, Diego brought out the fear whole. Hard as I
tried to explain to my parents that playing the guitar was something
Diego had to do because he couldn't find work as an archeologist in
New York City . . . well, that wasn't something they were eager to
believe. As a matter of fact, on the day we got engaged and I called
home to share the good news, my father, who has never answered
the phone in his life, picked up the phone. And instead of saying,
"Felicidades, hija," by way of congratulations, he said, "So you're gonna
sell pizza now?"

"*¿Qué será, será, señor?*
Whatever will be, will be.
Pepperoni, or extra cheese?
Don't mind the gun on the pie, *señor.*
I'm just here
To deliver you to the morgue
Say, cheese!*"*

This is the jingle of a popular pizzeria in Caracas. So I guess I
can't blame my father for having that fear. Living as he does in a
tropical paradise, he hasn't been able to partake in certain advances,
such as having food delivered to one's front door. "You can't call
that progress," he'd say. Having strangers whose cleaning habits you
know nothing about touch your food with God-knows-what and
deliver it to your home on a filthy moped is not progress. We're
talking a cultural divide a little wider than the Bering Strait.

As for my mother, when her turn came, she got on the phone,
said "Hello," and then went mute. For a beat, I thought the
connection was dead, which isn't all that uncommon when calling

230

down there. But after a swift recovery my mother said, "If he's an archaeologist, Valentina, what is he doing in New York City? Why doesn't he move to Egypt?"

"Good point, Mamá. I don't know why we didn't think of that."

This was followed by, "¡Valentina, *por el amor de Dios!*" No one invokes the love of God like my mother, not even a Roman bishop on Palm Sunday at the Vatican.

Sometimes I wonder why Diego and I got together in the first place. Unfortunately, I've never come up with a very good answer. Maybe it had something to do with my mother saying, "¡Valentina, *por el amor de Dios!*" There's nothing quite like the sound of the language in which you first got into trouble. That's what happened when Diego asked, "*¿Hablas español?*" while holding the door open for me at MoMA. Everything I had forgotten since leaving Venezuela came rushing back to me like poltergeists. It took only two miserable words for everything to return. His question only needed a yes-or-no answer. But instead, here's what I said: "*Me-llamo-Valentina-y-tú-cómo-te-llamas-de-dónde-eres-y-qué-haces-aquí-desde-cuando?*" I said more than I should have said. I didn't realize it at the time, but by the time a guy named Diego practically begged me not to throw away a poster from a silly audition, I was just dying for someone to recognize me. And Diego did. Diego . . . recognized me. He didn't think I was Jackie O., not for a second. But *Sad Aliens Selling Pizza in New York* is not quite the same as *Under the Tuscan Sun*.

So let's talk about something else. Life is depressing enough as it is.

CUTTING YOUR LOSSES

After the maid Alicia Muti returned to Argentina, I had what's called in Catholic parlance an epiphany. Epiphanies are not reserved only for women who manage to remain virgins after being ravaged by angels. Perfectly flawed people named Valentina Goldman can have epiphanies, too.

It happened one day after I hung up with Azucena. It happened after I got tired of hearing that Carlos was still upstairs abusing the lavender soap, among other things. So I said, "Azucena *querida*, why don't you send Carlos Upstairs outside, pack your bags, and take your children someplace interesting, like Santorini, for instance?"

And this is what Azucena said to me. I'm still a little shaken by it, to tell you the truth. The only time I've seen Azucena cry was when she thought Lucas Enrique might be born dead. I've been her sister forever and a day, so her crying on the phone took me completely by surprise. "Valentina, I can't leave him," she said. Then came the real blow. "Not everyone wants to be you!!"

"What? And who's advocating such a travesty, Azucena *querida?* We are who we are, Azucena. Calm down." But she wasn't calm. I think she was having her own epiphany. She realized she would never leave Carlos Upstairs, because she couldn't. If she had to do it all over again, she might not pick Carlos Upstairs. Still, she would never leave him.

Strange to say it, but it was Martha Stewart who convinced me of this. Because, let's face it, *mi amor*, someone who brings a copy of *Martha Stewart Living* to a place like Caracas, well . . . that's a real optimist, that's someone who's determined to get a home at any cost. So when Azucena started going neurotic on me, when she lost the calm that is her hallmark to say, "It's irresponsible, Valentina, to keep hopping from job to job, to keep going from person to person as if life had no consequences, not taking anything seriously," and so on . . . . that's when it came to me. But I bit my tongue. Stay, or leave Carlos Upstairs? Who's qualified to diagnose something as complex as the condition of enough-is-enough? Certainly not me, for whom the word *enough* rolls so naturally off the tongue. Marriage is a staggeringly elusive enterprise. There's simply no substitute for being there, for observing the patient, listening to the stories, and trying to understand. Some people cut their losses. Others count their blessings. My mother birthed one of each. Life would be so boring if we were all the same, don't you think?

But speaking strictly about the Greek Isles for a second, did you know that Santorini is the most photographed place on earth? Yes, more than the Eiffel Tower, *mi amor.* Apparently, you can take the funicular up to the top. You can also get there by donkey, I've heard. I wonder what it's like to ride on a donkey. I don't know why I suggested that to Azucena. Gyros for lunch every day—that might be a little much for her. Am *I* thinking about moving to Santorini? The questions you ask, Emily.

9 TO 9: LIVING THE AMERICAN DREAM

After Diego left for Cairo, I was busy, busy, busy. I had important things to do. I had to get back to my office at Human Capital in order to help the truly displaced get back on their feet. So time passed the way it does when you're fooling yourself. It was only a matter of time before someone upstairs noticed that I remained affixed to my chair, days, nights, and weekends. It became impossible not to notice that I was absolutely and without a doubt the most productive outplacement counselor in the history of Human Capital. So I got a promotion. I became part of something called the President's Club. To be quite honest, up until that point I didn't even know that Human Capital had a president. It seemed to me that the place was run by Ruth, the octopus-like receptionist adept at keeping dozens of balls in the air at the same time, and by the outplacement counselors, those of us skilled at convincing people like Tony Zippolo that "downsized" and "penis size" are unrelated terms.

The President's Club landed me in Maui, Hawaii, at a resort, with all expenses paid, free massages, and free drinks in the company of other superhuman counselors like myself from other regions, people whose personal lives, like mine, did not amount, as the saying goes, to a hill of beans. Beans, as you know, despite serving to feed millions and millions the world over every single day, have been for centuries regarded as the epitome of worthlessness. So worthless, in fact, that a hill of them is considered to be less valuable than a single bean.

What can I say? It was difficult to put on a good face for the comedian Human Capital had hired to entertain us in Hawaii while we sipped on a signature drink called a Lahaina Sunset. Because what is there to laugh about, *mi amor*, when what you're holding at end of the day is a plastic cup filled halfway with Rose's grenadine syrup? How many free drinks would it take to refill a heart running on empty? And I'm afraid Hawaii wasn't the last place where I would go to be encouraged to work a little harder under the guise of free massages and free drinks. Once you're identified as a top producer, your days as a free agent are pretty much numbered.

FRIENDS WITHOUT BENEFITS

Do you remember Jake? It was Jake who helped save my Lanvin dress after your cousin Devin's rat peed on me during that memorable Rosh Hashanah where I defiled the sacred by bringing piglet croissants to the dinner table. Why does heaven hate pork, anyway? Hasn't word gotten to Saint Peter that pork is "the other white meat"? Why not forbid chicken wings every other Sunday, for instance? On second thought, that might cause a revolt in this country. What would people eat during the Super Bowl?

In any event, since that fateful High Holiday that began my Yiddish education on hearing the word *treyf,* Jake and I shared a hairdresser whose name was Hans. Hans was a genius. Hans could take broom bristles and turn them into silk. Even so, Jake and I rarely ran into each other at the hair salon. Instead, we met at a rare assortment of places, all suggested by him. Jake is that singular creature whose pulse beats to the latest trend in any area of human endeavor—a museum in the meat-packing district with no doors, a restaurant where all the food is blue, a coffee shop where all the chairs are shaped like cribs, and so on. It was from Jake that I learned about these secret restaurants with no name that were always buzzing at two, three o'clock in the morning with an odd community of sleepwalkers.

There was this one time when Jake was craving a midnight snack, so he called me up and we ended up at one of these places. We had just been seated when a very attractive woman wearing a see-through blouse waltzed into the place. And by see-through, *mi amor,* I mean the blouse was like glass at an aquarium. I didn't think Jake had noticed the woman with the al fresco breasts. Perhaps because I knew he leaned in a different direction. Well, it turned out he had. And he had some friendly words for her: "Darling, just because you can doesn't mean you should!"

Since breaking up with Geoff, Jake was enjoying that much-underappreciated feeling of coming and going as one pleases. And because nurses with his qualifications were in such high demand all over Manhattan, Jake could pretty much name his own hours, which in turn meant he had a lot of free time to spend on his hobby of discovering new and interesting places. I can't remember how many times Jake, knowing I was working late, called me at the office and said, "I know you're trying to raise the GDP of this country all by yourself, doll, but why not let's go 'cool-hunting' tonight?"

So we did. And what better playmate for someone so inept at finding a reliable member of the opposite sex than a friend whose eyes roved strictly in the direction of the new, new thing? I liked spending time with Jake. The only problem with Jake was that telling him to keep something to himself was like an invitation to put it on his Twitter feed. It was Jake who called your dad and said, "She shipped the second one to Cairo. This is your chance!"

STATUS CHANGE

Two months later 1 was introduced to a new junior counselor who was to take over some of my accounts.

The reason downsized people are called "accounts" is because the companies that made them redundant in the first place have accounts with companies like Human Capital. Try as I might, I was unable to place Tony Zippolo anywhere. My new boss at Human Capital was all about "resource management." Apparently I was spending too much time on Tony for little return, so my boss had the brilliant idea of passing the sophomoric Tony off to a junior counselor, a kid fresh out of college whose name was Andy Postle. Well, I didn't want to pass Tony off to anyone with the last name Postle, or to anyone else for that matter. It wasn't fair to either of them. And besides, I took pride in the fact that most of the time I could place any qualified candidate within two months, maximum three. In Tony's case, there were extenuating circumstances. After six months, Tony was still unemployed. How to tell Andy that in order to place Tony he had to convince the guy that words like *piss, schlong,* and *tits* were not standard interviewing argot? How to tell Tony that when you're trying to convince a potential employer to exchange your time for his money, it's better to stick to words like *return on investment?*

Andy and I were going over Tony's file when Ruth, the octopus receptionist at Human Capital, came in to my now-bigger office and handed me a note. It was the natural progression of things. Since becoming part of the President's Club I was no longer in a cubicle, which is a lot to say for a foreigner in New York City. Everyone knows that space is at a premium in the Big Apple. Ask Ivanka Trump to quote you the price per inch. "Dinner tonight, gorgeous?" said the note from Max. There was also a phone number where he could be reached.

I read the note twice and then put the little piece of paper on my desk. Since the Rosh Hashanah ham croissant faux pas, Max and I had exchanged a couple of stay-in-touch-just-in-case e-mails. And that was about it. I had not told Max that I was right in the middle of a status change. I didn't know, of course, that Jake had been playing yenta behind my back.

As it turned out, Max was fresh out of a sticky situation himself. Apparently, he had been seeing a cardiologist on and off, a woman who, like him, had two children under the age that allows free movement. Speaking of which, I've never quite understood what it means to "see someone on and off." Blame it on the price of oil, but in South America we have only two switches. "On" burns. "Off" doesn't. Apparently, Max and the cardiologist with the two daughters had decided to turn on the Off button. It became a little tricky, it seemed, to coordinate the lives of two working adults of dating age— plus the cardiologist's ex and whomever he was seeing, plus four children—and to find a day in which two of those adults might see each other unaccompanied.

I didn't know any of this when Ruth handed me the note. So I didn't call Max back, which isn't like me at all. You've known me long enough to know that I always call people back. Even if it is just to say good-bye.

ARGUABLY

Come now, Emily. Why are you crying? *Ay, Dios mío.* You know I don't know what to do when you get like this. Of course I'm not going to leave you. You're the one who's going to Ecuador, remember? *Por Dios, niña.* I know you miss your dad. So don't say things like that. Please don't use the word *hate.* I hate that word. I miss him, too, *mi amor.* That's why I'm sitting here talking to you. You're a little piece of him . . . Emily, please . . . come back here. *¡Qué angustia! Niña, por Dios,* this is hard enough as it is for you to start saying you hate your father. I know he left without a proper good-bye . . . Trust me, I know, I know all about life's little practical jokes. Sometimes the person keeping the only thing you want *en esta puta vida* refuses to take your calls. Refuses to answer your letters. Refuses to call back even to say, "Valentina, I got every single one of your letters and I don't have time to answer them. Not now or ever."

I'd give your mom anything she wants. I'd move out of this house and give it to her if she'd only tell me why Max went to see her that day. Do you know how many times I've imagined Max walking into Helen's kitchen that morning after he left here? But I can't even do that. I can't even imagine that because I've never been to your other house. I don't even know what the kitchen looks like. So I get to sit here replaying the nightmare I've invented for myself over and over and over . . . until another bill arrives in the mail.

It's not that I'm jealous that he did it there instead of here, believe me. When it came to your mom and dad I always knew we weren't talking Rick and Ilsa in *Casablanca.* Even that insensitive police report said there was an argument involved. Well, tell me something I don't know! Wake me up when Helen calls, will you?

I know what you're thinking: "naive Latina." You need to stop calling me that, Emily. I officially stopped being "naive" when your dad told me he was going to work one day and I never saw him again.

THE CATCH

After Max told me about the cardiologist with the two daughters, the one he was seeing "on and off," I asked him if he wanted to have any more kids. And you know what he said? He said. "I have three perfect children, Valentina. It would be greedy to ask for more." Isn't that beautiful?

Still, I've never been sure about Zachy and Zach being perfect—two twin boys playing video games all day and talking only to each other always seemed a little strange to me. But then again, they weren't mine. And who knows? It's possible those video games prepared them for trading stocks on Wall Street. Do you think Zachy and Zach have telepathy? And do you think they can get into trouble for insider trading because of it?

I worry about your brothers sometimes. Believe it or not, that's one of the reasons I agreed to see Max again. Not because he said he had three perfect children, but because having children and living in a different city meant he wasn't actually available, not to me anyway. Getting my hand stuck on a sock full of marshmallows has never been an aspiration of mine. But never say "never," *mi amor*. I ended up doing the "on and off" thing myself. I agreed to see Max whenever he was in Manhattan to see his brother, or whenever he was in the city on business, which turned out to be quite often.

Why sugarcoat it? I'd rather sit naked on a cactus than marry a man with kids. So Max had a lot of convincing to do. He knew that otherwise I might move to Russia before he could pop the question. So he invited me to Russia instead.

VI. THE RUSSIAN ROULETTE PERIOD

THE TED BUNDY ARGUMENT

My Russian Roulette period consisted of playing with a loaded gun. Your dad was the gun. The bullets were called children. I can see how someone else, say someone from Utah, who views progeny from multiple wives as a kind of blessing, might consider this Russian-roulette analogy one of the sorrowful mysteries of the rosary. But as my normal grandmother used to say, "There are all kinds of laborers in God's little vineyard."

One of the reasons I'm sharing this, *mi amor,* is to flatter you. Don't you think it's a compliment to say to someone, "You're the one responsible for bending the mind of a professed child-agnostic like myself?" In Catholic parlance, Emily, our friendship is what's called "a miracle." Before you came to enlighten me about wayward dogs and the swimming patterns of dolphins, people often asked, with a cautious lilt in their voice, "What do you have against children, Valentina?"

In case you're wondering, it has nothing to do with fear of milk oozing out of my boobs at inconvenient times. Stranger still is that children themselves have nothing to do with how I feel about them. But come to think of it, children themselves have everything to do with it. You see, *mi amor,* children are what I call "delicate." And all things delicate must be handled, well, delicately. And as you very well know, I can't seem to stay put. Let alone stay still. And I've dropped the ball more times than I care to remember. So I never thought I'd make a great handler. But that was before I met you and the twins. Now I think I'm an okay handler—not great, not terrible, just someone who knew when to lock herself up and what kinds of pills to ingest in order to prevent a tragedy. The way I saw it, the likelihood of leaving the hospital with a baby named Joey, and turning that baby into Ted Bundy in a very short period of time, was very high.

As it turns out, this is more difficult to do than one might imagine. Most people are not great handlers. And yet, how many Ted

Bundys do we have? When you stop to consider all the mishandling of children at the mall, just to name a place, we have fewer Ted Bundys than we could have. These days I think that the Ted Bundys of this world might have come defective from the factory. Because, with all the hissing, yelling and shushing directed at kids, the ratio of Ted-to-Parent ought to be at least 1 to 1. But no. It is in fact, much lower than that. This continues to surprise me.

Whatever the case, I concluded early on that people not equipped to handle crystal ought to stay away from crystal vases. My views on this extended to stepparenting as well, which explains why when you called me a stepmother at your violin recital, I experienced a kind of paralysis of the frontal lobe. All this to say that your dad— any "dad"—was not in the cards for me. I have no idea what Jake saw in us, exactly. Maybe he just wanted a good laugh.

The person I truly pity, though, is Geoff. Jake just got bored with him. And poor Geoff didn't see it coming. Apparently, a perfect day for Geoff involved locking himself in the basement, polishing an act or two on one of his plays, and consuming a gallon of coffee. The sad thing is it didn't even have to be good coffee. This used to horrify Jake. And when a play is finished, when it leaps from the paper onto the stage, Geoff would just as soon cut off the hand that wrote it than go on the road to start promoting it.

Once we figure out what to do with your dad's ashes, I'm going to call Geoff to check on him. Still, I just don't understand. It's just not something I would want . . . to be scattered all over the place. When I die I want to stay in one place, for once, and once and for all. I hate to admit it, *mi amor*, but after a while the moving gets to you. I mean, look at my skin. But that's what your dad wanted, so I guess we'll have to get on the phone with NASA pretty soon. As a starting point, of course. I'm pretty sure we'll be put on hold before getting transferred all over the place.

But back to Geoff. As you know, Max and Geoff were *como uña y sucio*, as we say in Spanish. I know it's not the most pleasant of images, to be compared, in your closeness to someone, to the way you are to the dirt under your nails. But it gets the point across. But anyway, when they were kids, Max and Geoff used to go sledding quite often. They went to a snow-covered golf course called Oak Grove. That's what Max said.

This is something I still have a hard time imagining, sledding on a golf course. Until that time in Whistler, during my brief Canadian period involving frozen tears, I had never seen snow. How can the sky be so blue and all of a sudden all this frozen dust starts falling and falling, relentlessly, until there's enough of it to cover an entire golf course? Snow is a difficult concept to concretize when you're from the Tropics. When snow starts falling, it seems to me, it does so as a kind of revenge.

But let me get to the point here. Among your dad's things in the garage there's a red metal sled. It's the one he and Geoff used to take to the golf course when they were kids. I remember asking Max about it because it reminded me of a film I had seen. The film is called *Citizen Kane,* in case you're wondering. So when I first saw the sled in the garage, I said, "Oh, a mini-Rosebud."

And Max said, "How do you know about Rosebud?"

"Max, everyone in the world knows about Rosebud."

So . . . I was wondering, *mi amor,* if you might want to have the sled. I know Max would be very happy if one day one of your kids ends up riding on the Flexible Flyer sled. No. Of course I'm not encouraging you to have children, especially after what I just told you about Ted Bundy. That would be a conflict of interest, or something along those lines. And besides, it's bad enough to be called a stepmother—I don't think I'm ready to add Grandma to the mix. That would be more than I can handle just now—a little *pichurro* calling me *abuela.* I'm too young for that.

FROM RUSSIA WITH LOVE

Now let me tell you how Max and I ended up at a brothel in Moscow. Don't look at me that way. It was an accident. We weren't exactly brothel connoisseurs.

The entire Russian adventure was without precedent in many, many ways. In order to get there in the first place, I had to ask for an advance on my vacation at Human Capital, which, due to my excellent performance, was easy as pie—that is, if you discount the snide remarks from envious colleagues. For his part Max had to consult your mother, as well as a small legion of lawyers and mediators, to be able to leave the country for a couple of weeks, at a time when every step he took immediately appeared on milk cartons.

Strange as it may seem, your mother and her lawyers proved less difficult than my parents. When I called to share the good news that I was going to Moscow with a man I had known for seven months the second time around, my father called me a "concubine." And, I might add, he said this long-distance. "Only concubines travel with people of the opposite sex while unmarried," said my dad. Telling him that I knew Max from when I lived in Arizona, and that I had met your cousins, your uncle, and your aunt didn't help my case. "A concubine sanctioned by pimps is still a concubine, Valentina." And while my father fretted about his twice-divorced daughter's vagina, my mother put in her two cents about murder and the KGB in a country most people remember from the Cold War.

All these concerns resulted in your dad having to fax a letter of explanation to my father's office in Caracas, along with copies of the plane tickets, dates of return, and so on. "That's not a problem," said Max. "I have to do the same for Helen." Your mother always wanted copies of everything. It was her mission to bring to life that catchy slogan from Kinko's: "The new way to office." How about the new way to live? For a time, Max practically lived at Kinko's.

For my part, I had always wanted to visit the land of *Doctor Zhivago*. But divorce has a way of putting a damper on everything. By the time I boarded the plane to Moscow, I was so exhausted, I wished I were back in my office instead.

The reason we were headed to Moscow in the first place was because at the time Max was working on a big development there, a forward-thinking venture that owed much to Perestroika, a restructuring of sorts, the brainchild of a guy named Mikhail Gorbachev. Perestroika was a project that neither Pasternak nor Dostoyevsky could have imagined in their wildest fictions. Your dad's company was working on a joint venture with a man whose name was Konstantin. It involved building a members-only casino in the middle of Moscow. Think Monte Carlo surrounded by Mogadishu. What is to be done about the rising middle class the world over? For all I know the place is still there. Because eventually, the Up & Down Club, as the project was called, was built. And I say "eventually" because we were fortunate enough to have to return to Moscow a few times. Did I really say "fortunate?"

Building in Russia turned out to be a little tricky. It's not like this country, where you can hire a few men from Mexico from a temp firm called Manuel Labor, send them to Home Depot to pick up some drywall, and by the end of the week you have an entire strip mall. Yes, I know how much you hate strip malls. Still, you need to know that a strip mall in a week is not the standard in the rest of the world. In the rest of the world it might take five, six years to get up a few stories of a building. And that's not counting the embezzlement, which might set the project back a little longer. But let's suppose you can get the men in the truck, say, from a place called Beslan. Now think of the difficulties involved in building a posh casino in a place where you can never see the sky and where until very recently people were standing in line waiting for bread crumbs.

When Max first told me about the project during our fourteen-hour plane ride to Moscow, I thought it was a joke. Your dad always had a wicked sense of humor. Quite honestly, until I actually saw the Kremlin, I thought the whole trip had been an excuse to have wild sex in Siberia under the guise of a business trip. It turned out I was wrong. Once we got there, I hardly saw Max. He worked around the clock like a madman. He knew Helen wouldn't enjoy getting a fax from his lawyer that said, "Mrs. Daub, I'm sorry to inform you your ex is stranded in Moscow with a sexy Venezuelan. You get to keep the kids for an extra week."

YOU'RE NOT A CITIZEN. AGAIN!

Checking in at the hotel was the stuff of Russian spy novels. No Latina I know would willingly surrender anything she owns, especially a hard-won American passport. When the front-desk clerk at the hotel informed us she'd be keeping our passports, I said, "No, you won't. Give it back, please."

Max, who had been to Moscow before, said, "It's all right, Valentina, this is standard operating procedure here."

"Well, Max, I'm not from here. And I'm not moving until she gives me my passport back."

At this, the woman said, "Then you have to leave."

"You can't be serious, lady; it took us fourteen hours and a dozen faxes to get here!"

"Max, these people are soooo backward."

"It's all right, Valentina."

"Max, this was *such* a bad idea. Has anyone told this woman the Cold War is over?"

"It's all right, Valentina. Let's go check our room."

"I'm not moving until she gives my passport back, Max. That's all there is to it."

Some might consider it unwise to argue with the people who dreamed up the KGB. But as you know, there are no white flags on my ship, *mi amor*. The following day I waited in the lobby until there was a shifting of the guard at the front desk. Even in a place like Russia, where no one has ever heard the words *labor* and *law* used in the same sentence, there's the occasional shifting of the guard. So I put on my best smile, walked up to the new clerk, and told him I needed to look at my passport for a minute. When he produced it, I snatched it from him. Sometimes that's all that's required to get what you want, a little persistence. And of course, when you're on an errand as urgent as retrieving your American passport in a former outpost of a Communist regime, you have to have that look in the eye that says, "Don't fuck with me. I, too, know someone at the Kremlin."

THE COLOR OF RED SQUARE

During the day, while Max was working with Konstantin on plans, permits, and what have you, I was assigned to a tour guide, a woman whose English did not serve her very well but who knew on which side of Red Square rain might fall on a given day.

Is Red Square red? No, it's not. On second thought, the bricks on some of the buildings do have a reddish tint. One might be inclined to think that the name Red Square has something to do with all the Bolsheviks of this world favoring the color red. Owing, for instance, to all the blood they've spilled. But no. In Russian, the word *red* can mean either "red" or "beautiful." Nor is Red Square, square. I remember it being rather rectangular, in fact. In Spanish, we work around this architectural conundrum by calling squares *plazas* rather than *cuadrados*.

But square or not, while the tour guide talked, I perked up my ears. Russia hadn't been in the plan, but you never know if you might have to move there one day, say, due to a massive emotional landslide. I didn't know, for instance, when I was a young woman in Venezuela reading *The Idiot* in translation, that one day I would be in Fyodor Dostoyevsky's backyard with a Jewish divorcé who would assign me to a tour guide while he was busy building a casino. When I was growing up, *la Unión de Repúblicas Socialistas Soviéticas*—"URSS" to us, "USSR" to you—was off-limits to the rest of the world. It wasn't until a time that has gone down in history as "the Khrushchev Thaw" that foreigners were allowed to visit Russia. No one in the Western Hemisphere ever dreamed of setting foot in the land of Peter and Catherine the Great. I personally never thought I'd live to see the day of the fall of the former Soviet Union. To put it in context, *mi amor*, that would be like one day the United States being only Texas and the rest of the states little countries of their own. Texas might not mind, but what about the little people?

All this to tell you that when I saw the colorful domes of the three cathedrals just outside the Kremlin gates, I felt a mini-bout of hysteria. Saint Basil's Cathedral, the one with the carnivalesque domes shaped like giant onions, had been constructed by Ivan the Terrible. The story goes that once the architects were finished building it, Ivan the Terrible had them blinded so that they could never build something so beautiful again. No matter where you train your gaze, *mi amor,* the history of humanity is filled with such "lofty sentiments," isn't it? I had seen these domes in pictures. I had read about them in Pasternak and Tolstoy. Russian architecture from that period is unlike any other you have ever seen, or are likely to see, except maybe at Epcot Center. It is majestic. It is imperial and imperative. I was in awe. But it wasn't the kind of quickie awe people feel and then dismiss in the time it takes to say, "I'm in awe." This was the kind of awe that makes you feel like a church mouse when compared to something truly magnificent. And it was while standing in the middle of Red Square that I finally understood, in my stomach and not just in my head, why Diego could not live unless he lived ten feet from Nefertiti. So I burst into tears in front of the tour guide.

This happens sometimes. Sometimes I have these delayed reactions to things that have been long sealed and delivered. Sometimes I wake up in the middle of the night, all these years later, and say, "I left my country! What have I done?" But the tour guide *chica* didn't mind my crying. She just stood there, looking at her notes. She was probably used to tears whenever people got that close to the guy who set the standard for Stalin, Hitler, and Mao. Or maybe she was thinking, "What to do about the hysterical South Americans?"

It was an odd situation, to be sure. I had read more about Russia than Condi Rice has forgotten. But all of it had been in Spanish. So when I asked the guide about Lenin, she said, "You mean Vladimir Ilych Ulyanov ladi-ladi-la?" and proceeded to spew out all the man's names, patronymics and all, in Russian. The guide *chica* knew much about a lot of things, but there were many things I asked that she knew nothing about. She didn't know, for instance, about Mikhail Bulgakov. She didn't know that this man was revered elsewhere for having written *The Master and Margarita,* one of the masterpieces of the twentieth century. But then again, it's quite possible she knew all about the story of the devil arriving in Moscow one day to join a conversation between a critic and a poet about the existence of Jesus Christ, but did not wish to admit it. It's understandable. People who have lived under strict regimes are tight-lipped about certain things. No one in their right mind is going to stroll down Red Square with a cup of Kaffe Starbucks in hand and say, "KGB. Burned manuscripts. Discuss." That only happens on *Saturday Night Live*.

STRANGELY FAMILIAR

Except for the weather, nights in Moscow eerily resembled nights anywhere in the Tropics. Max and I would arrive at a restaurant to find the men around the table sitting next to their mistresses. Hardly anyone spoke English, so Konstantin had to translate. Seeing that the women were so much younger than the men and that most of them had blond hair, I thought to ask, "Are these their mistresses, Konstantin?" Max nearly choked.

Not Konstantin. Konstantin looked me straight in the eye and said, "Of course. Their wives are home with the children, where they should be."

"Max, can I have a little more vodka, please?"

Later that night: "Valentina, the questions you ask."

"I just wanted to confirm, Max. You saw it was no big deal. Konstantin knows what's what."

It was Konstantin, as a matter of fact, who asked me—after everyone had filled up on horse carpaccio—if I wanted a man.

"Excuse me?"

And Konstantin said, "I can have any man you want sent to your room tonight."

"How to put this, Konstantin? My father doesn't approve of my being here, but still . . . I came here . . . with a man."

That was a mouthful to get out, *mi amor*. Given that Konstantin shared the same mind-set as the men of South America, I thought it might be a trick question, to see how I'd respond. What if I said, "Yes, Konstantin, I want a man," and he ordered a death squad to shoot me in front of Lenin's Tomb? Apparently, his question was genuine. Konstantin was a conscientious host; he wanted his guests to feel welcome. Max told me he had always been offered women in Russia, as a matter of fact.

"Did you ever take him up on it, Max?"

"Now that you mention it, Valentina, I forgot to tell you that I have a child with a Russian prostitute."

"Just checking, Max. I don't want a fourth stepchild showing up at our wedding without an invite."

"Who said anything about getting married, Valentina?"

"My dad, Max. This isn't *Hiroshima, Mon Amour*, you know. I can't stay a concubine forever."

ARE THOSE REAL?

The following day, we left in a bullet-proof limousine. The ride, at a hundred miles an hour, skipping through obstacles and sidewalks, never stopping as if our lives depended on it, was the longest period of time I've ever been without words. I've told you about the express kidnappings in Caracas, which is to say, I was vividly reminded of these and thought it would be nice to have known our destination in advance. When we finally arrived at Konstantin's mansion in a gated neighborhood in the middle of nowhere, six bodyguards with machine guns, three on each side of the limousine, materialized from the woods and escorted Max and me into the house. As it turned out, our lives *had* depended on it. There had been a clear and present danger after all, which is why we needed three bodyguards apiece. It had to do with Konstantin's side business.

I've told you about murder at the mall. I've told you about the maid from Ecuador who prayed to the clock radio. I've told you about the caterer named Mozart. So why was entering a mansion in Moscow such a surprise? Konstantin made no bones about the art on the wall. He was proud of his paintings. Those were the Rembrandts, Vermeers, and Van Goghs that were missing from a handful of the world's museums. It wasn't the same old sky that night, that's for sure. I thought I was hallucinating one of Van Gogh's starry nights. For a beat, I missed Tony Zippolo and his talk of fake tits. There were no fake tits on any of the walls. Those were originals.

ARE THOSE REAL? PART 2.

Our ending up at the brothel owed everything to propinquity. And to hunger. And to the weather. And to a childhood dream.

Having grown up reading about Mikhail Baryshnikov's defection, I had always wanted to go to the Kirov. But we were in Moscow, so we went to the Bolshoi instead. When the most revered dancer of the world's oldest and greatest ballet company defected to Canada after one of his performances, newspapers all over the world practically stopped printing other news. This made an impression on me. Baryshnikov's defection would continue to have an impact throughout the rest of my adult life, in fact. It might have been seeing this perfect image of purity suspended in midair, the image of a man aspiring to different heights, that stamped my mind with the idea of possibility. It's always hard to pin down the source of inspiration, isn't it? A Venezuelan *señorita* inspired by a dancer from the Kirov? Go figure.

So, after the performance at the Bolshoi, Max and I were hungry. Rain was coming down as it must have done when Noah took his ark to sea. And it was freezing outside. So we ran toward a neon sign that both of us thought indicated a restaurant. What else could it be? So conveniently located near the theater? So we went inside. And it was as we waited for our menus that the first item on the menu appeared before us: a woman in her leather panties, suspended from a pole. Without offering any incautious details, all I can say to illuminate the situation, is that Max had been raised by your grandmother as a nice Jewish boy. So when he saw the woman in her panties suspended from the pole, he turned to me and said, "She sure is nimble."

"Nimble, Max? She's naked!"

At the conclusion of her dance, the girl left the pole and came to talk to us. And what did she say to us, exactly? She spoke the only words she knew in the language of commerce. She offered to show us around. In English, of course. For some reason Max and I later struggled to explain to each other, both of us got up that very instant and said, "Sure, why not?" So there we were, following a naked woman around a naked corridor. Naturally, we were curious. But when we actually saw the row of doors with chipped, cheap paint, leading to identically smelly rooms, we realized we'd seen all we needed to see to know that we would go to bed hungry that night.

"Excuse me," Max said. "Excuse me, miss, I don't mean to interrupt the tour. But we have to go now."

GUINEA PIG

As tends to happen whenever you take a couple of days off, as soon as I returned from Moscow, every single one of my clients made themselves redundant at the same time. Max himself was busy with the Moscow project, which, as I've already told you, took a lot longer than a similar project might in a place like Arizona, for instance, where you can build year-round and there's an endless supply of workers eager to cross the border. Sometimes Konstantin would come to New York, and he and Max would meet there; they took turns crossing the ocean. Sometimes the three of us would go to dinner. During that time Max and I talked on the phone a lot.

By then Kirsten Kramer and I had become friends. It was to Kirsten that I expressed my reservations about a long-distance relationship with a man who was attached to three people under the age of twelve. It was Kirsten's idea that I go down to Arizona to see for myself, in order to get a little closer to the fire and see if I could withstand the heat. It wasn't in the plan that I would meet you or the twins during that trip. But who was counting on Henry's death?

Until that point in our relationship, "the children" had been a concept, not unlike the way "factorization" is a concept until you actually put pencil to paper and say, "What are we supposed to do with all those extra brackets?" From experience, Max knew that plans for a building are not the same thing as the finished building. Therefore, in the same way, he knew that kids "at" the house is not the same thing as "in a house with kids." So when I went to Arizona, I stayed at a hotel. Before that day, Max had always taken extra care to spare me the frenzy that precedes most single parents' attempts to leave the house to go on a date. He was always careful, he later confessed, to ask lots and lots of questions of you and the twins beforehand. Questions such as, "Do you have all your homework? Do you have your tennis shoes? *Both* tennis shoes, Emily?" You, in particular, seemed always to be leaving things behind. "My homework is at the other house" was apparently a favorite refrain of yours for a while. For your dad, all those questions functioned as a kind of disaster insurance so that he wouldn't have to leave in the middle of a movie, say, to bring back to the other house whatever had been left behind.

For the most part, this worked. But death is an entirely different thing. Death does not take turns at people's houses, the way divorce does. Death is far from accommodating. I myself was to experience this in the flesh. I was at my hotel waiting for Max to pick me up when he called to tell me that he'd be late. As if I hadn't realized it already! Tardiness is one of those things that can unleash my murderous instincts. And besides, I had traveled down there all the way from New York. As far as I was concerned, I was the one being inconvenienced, which is another way of saying that I was in no mood for excuses. At the same time, I was looking for any excuse to avoid becoming inextricably involved with Max. Why not have a fight about him being late? Fights about trivial things always come in handy when you're looking for a way out.

So when Max called to tell me that he was running late, I said, "This is the last straw. I'm headed to the airport."

"Valentina, please don't do this. It couldn't be helped."

"What couldn't be helped, Max? You knew full well I was coming here this weekend."

"Well, with kids, sometimes . . . things happen. . . . I wouldn't stand you up without a good reason."

"Now you're 'standing me up,' Max? I thought you were just running late. This is it. I want no part of this. I need a life I can count on!"

Done! I started packing right after we hung up. Wouldn't you rather spend the night at the airport without a plane ticket than wait for a guy who's running thirty minutes late? Imagine my surprise when I saw Max at the lobby of the hotel surrounded by three little people, one of whom was holding a shoebox that looked as if it contained something precious. I will never forget the day I met you and the twins. I remember finding it eerie that the three of you had identical blue eyes. I remember staring at three pairs of lights and thinking, "I didn't know Jews came in blue." I also remember a pair of these lights going off when I asked, "What's in the box?" and you burst into tears.

"Henry's dead!!!!!!!!!!!!"

I wouldn't be surprised if the bellman at the Westin still has nightmares about that earsplitting wail. For my part, I held on to my carry-on, afraid to ask, "Who's Henry?" I can't say why, exactly, but I pictured Henry as some kind of plastic, sci-fi midget from a Burger King commercial.

So when you said, "Henry's my guinea piggggggggggg," and proceeded to sob as if choking on desert sand, I vowed never again to call a guinea pig a rat, whether I stayed with Max or not. That's how the five of us ended up at a place called Arby's with a dead guinea pig in the trunk of the car. I didn't know, until that day, that the backyards of all faiths in North America were strewn with little guinea pig carcasses.

For some strange reason I didn't care for the roast beef sandwich with the special Arby's sauce. Max and I had planned to go to an Italian restaurant.

FLYING HIGH

It took a guinea pig in a shoebox for me to fully take in the concept of "children." The thing I clearly had to do, come Monday morning in New York, was to break up with Max. The clouds had parted at last. Still, how to break the news to Max became the source of much soul-searching. In the end I settled on a letter.

Letters are my preferred method of communication when I have to deliver something final. You might remember that I'd been writing a letter to my parents on the plane to Miami when I met the Canadian guy who said my handwriting was elegant. Well, now I was to write an elegant letter to Max telling him that the heat of the desert didn't agree with me. It was far easier to write the letter if I continued to replay the image of the dead guinea pig in the shoebox. The letter took days to write, as I recall. I kept writing different versions and throwing them away. Because how do you say to someone, "It's not you . . . I like you fine. . . . there's just this little problem called 'your children'?" One had to use tact. Meanwhile, I didn't dare answer the phone. In the end I mailed one of the versions. But certain kinds of news are medium-agnostic. A letter, a phone call, a telegram—it hardly matters. People will react the way they will react, and there's not much you can do about it. The only thing you can control is *your* end of the situation. You can't keep a man from saying, "I won't accept this." That's what Max said after reading the letter.

For good measure he also told me I was making a mistake. "Really, Max? I guess only time will tell." And in order to clear his mind after realizing things were really finished between us, Max decided to take the three of you to Alaska.

"I hope your kids like salmon, Max."

After the breakup I was ready for a big change. To be honest, I was burned out on sad stories from people who had been wrongfully terminated, dismissed, or otherwise made to feel redundant. While I figured out what to do next, I told Ruth, the octopus receptionist, not to put any of Max's calls through. I didn't want to hear the case he would make when he returned from Alaska with his mind sharp as the tip of an iceberg. Your dad was always good at making a case. The last thing I wanted was to get confused.

A couple of months later I gave notice at Human Capital and went to work for an advertising agency on Madison Avenue as a senior account executive. This time I managed real accounts, not people who were called "accounts." Practically overnight the world seemed awash in possibility again. But as tends to happen, people who speak several languages usually wind up with jobs that involve some travel. I traveled close to fifty percent of the time, which is another way of saying that I only slept in my own bed half the year. This was fine with me. Who can think of dead guinea pigs when you're flying high, above it all?

CATCH-22

After José died sitting on one of the good chairs, there were no more chauffeurs at my sister's house. Who would pick up the children after school became a source of much anguish for Azucena. She couldn't pick them up herself, because she was tied up in Marketing Committee meeting. And let's not forget that she was the sole breadwinner. What if she lost her job? Despite working sixteen-hour days, Azucena has always been afraid of losing her job. It's hard to get your head around a thing like that, but I assure you, insecurity is as real as a pimple between your eyes. What about taking the bus? It's a fair question. But Caracas isn't Fallujah, *mi amor*. You can't put a couple of kids on a bus and hand them a pair of AK-47s.

Try as she might, Azucena could not find a reliable chauffeur. Many people can drive a car, but how many of the people who can drive a car in Caracas are not murderers? It's only a tiny variable, but it makes a huge difference. You can see how a question like that might keep a working mother up at night. And what about Carlos Upstairs? Why didn't he pick up his kids after school? When he wasn't claiming he was going to humiliate himself by being the only man among women in a school yard, he was telling Azucena that picking up Sofía and Lucas Enrique after school interfered with tennis doubles. Seeing that she was facing a catch-22, Azucena called on my mother, who, as you know, is as afraid of murder at the mall as Azucena is herself. As luck would have it, it was on the day my mother took Sofía to the mall after school that the girl was snatched from her. Lucas Enrique was at soccer practice that afternoon. That's the only reason he was spared.

CHECK

I was just back from a business trip to San Francisco when I received a telegram at work. I doubt you've ever seen a telegram. I don't even know if they make telegraph machines anymore. They must. I'm sure that a branch of the army or the navy still uses a telegraph for some military purpose or another. A "telegram" is a little piece of paper with a very brief message written on it. Think of it as an expensive Tweet.

The only telegram with which you might be familiar is a singing telegram, and only because I once sent you one for your birthday. Yes, the gorilla. I had forgotten about the gorilla. I still have that photo of you opening the door and staring at the dancing gorilla. Do you remember what you said afterward? You said, "I guess I'm naturally attractive to monkeys." You've always had knack for the unforgettable remark.

In any case, the telegram I got at work was a lot shorter than a gorilla singing "Happy Birthday." It was a one-liner, in fact. All it said was, "Happiness is possible." Never trust a telegram, *mi amor*. What of substance can be said in so few words? When in doubt, look to the Bible. The Bible doesn't come in telegram format. If it did, all those parables and teachings might boil down to something like this: Bad news at the end — Apocalypse. That's what I was thinking after reading your dad's telegram: Bad news at the end.

It wasn't Jake who betrayed me that time. It was Ruth, the octopus receptionist from Human Capital, the one I had sworn to secrecy as regards my next move. But Max always had a way of turning the uncooperative into the suddenly willing. I've never been able to extract anything out of an unwilling subject the way Max could. He might have taught a thing or two to the good people of Abu Ghraib, had they been open to more congenial methods. It takes talent to know how many drops of water will cause a spill. And to know what you want, of course.

CULTURE CLASH

It's really a shame that the "no-proselytizing" clause in the divorce decree kept you from going to Devin's Bat Mitzvah. I wish you could have been there, if only so that I could have seen your face when Lucas Enrique said to Devin, "I love your breasts!" In no time, my wise little nephew became the talk of the party.

He was only five years old at the time, which made his giving voice to such a lovely sentiment even more of an accomplishment. But how to bridge a cultural divide wider than the San Andreas Fault? Lucas Enrique was startled to learn that his gallantry went unappreciated when Devin called him a "little pervert." The poor boy was raised to appreciate female beauty and to call a spade a breast when he sees two. And what about Jake saying to Devin's boyfriend, "I'm dating a brunette, too. But with different equipment under the hood."

Were there pictures of Devin's Bat Mitzvah? Sure there were, though I can't think of where they might be. There's this picture Max took of Lucas Enrique hopping onto the rising chair that was supposed to be for Devin. No one seemed to mind: so long as the boy was high up on a chair he might keep his mouth shut about mammary glands. I remember a group of men raising him up and everyone clapping and singing "*Hava Nagila*." All eyes were on this handsome Venezuelan prince, who was smiling as if he had won the ride of a lifetime at the amusement park. Lucas Enrique has Azucena's smile. It's the kind of smile that, when aimed in your direction, makes you feel you're the Chosen One.

How come we never showed you the photos? *Mi amor*, there's such a thing as common sense, even if it isn't all that common. What were we supposed to do? Show you pictures of people singing and dancing, and tell you that you missed the time of your life? And besides, Helen would have had our heads on a plate with Bull's-Eye barbecue sauce. The mere insinuation of a boy raised on a chair while other people sang "*Nagila*" might be construed as proselytizing. And who wants to spend a day in court because some people wearing little hats are singing a Ukrainian song no one can understand?

Your mother needn't have worried, though. Her people have a much, much better marketing team than your dad's people. I used to tell this to Max, that for Judaism to take off, the good people of Adonai needed to get the services of someone on Madison Avenue. Why bother to deny it? The Christians have a much better marketing machine. And they have their story straight. The guy's name was Christ. Christ was nailed to a cross. Christ died for me. I am called a Christian. End of story. And it's a simple enough story that anyone, no matter how ignorant or uneducated, can repeat it and get others to believe it.

The same is true of Buddhism. The guy's name is Buddha. He teaches something called Bikram. Come to Bikram anytime. If you miss a class, you can always come back the following week as something else, say a bird. Why do you think the JewBu population is growing at twice the rate as the number of people buying Zumba shirts?

Now, for the sake of argument, consider this: The name of the guy we're supposed to follow, well, he actually goes by a couple of names. We can't tell you what those names are because, well, we have not yet reached an agreement about the Sadducees and the Pharisees. At this point in time, we can no longer sift out the Midrash from the balderdash, though we do agree that it isn't kosher to say the name aloud. So if you write it down, well, you have to write down "G-D," so as not to offend.

What is this, a game of Scrabble? Or are we playing Jewish Hangman? What the sons and daughters of Israel need, *mi amor*, is more people like Madonna on their side, wearing bracelets. But all bracelets need to say the same thing: *"¡Viva Kabbalah!"* And everyone needs to agree on whether "G-D" is coming back and in what calendar year he or she is planning to do so. I ought to say a mea culpa for all this. I do like the atonement being once a year: Yom Kippur is definitely more sensible than confession every Saturday. Or than praying to a woman who remained a Virgin during and after an ordeal that most normal women would consider traumatic. But whose forgiveness to ask, *mi amor*?

BUSINESS AND PLEASURE

During one of my trips to San Francisco for a meeting with a client, Max suggested we make a weekend of it. And so it was. Like smoke coming out of a genie bottle, all of a sudden we're inside a red convertible headed to a place called St. Helena. That's something I always admired about Max, his sense of adventure. I know what you're thinking: "Look who's talking!" But I'm not adventurous in the way Max was adventurous. I'm either "on" or "not on" vacation. I've never been one to mix business with pleasure. As a matter of fact, Levi Strauss had been my client for nearly a year, and not once did it cross my mind to rent a car during a business trip and head to Napa Valley — that big farm where they grow the grapes.

It was there, in fact, that Max and I had a very long conversation. With the top down, I might add. We must have talked for hours because by the time I looked at my face in the hotel mirror later that night, I had a tan. The long and the short of it was that Max proposed we resume dating seriously. His argument was that true love was hard to find. For good measure, he added that he was prepared to entertain whatever ideas, notions, or concepts I had regarding living with, visiting, or occasionally seeing . . . a man with children. In the end, I agreed.

I was always on the road, anyway. It wouldn't hurt to have the occasional dinner with someone you know will not give you gonorrhea. Good lawyers know exactly what Max was doing. Once you get someone to agree to the smaller points, well, they're still listening. All that needs to be done then is to wait for a good time to deliver the closing argument.

To resume dating seriously meant what it meant. So little by little I started to teach Max the right words to curry a woman's favor—*mi vida, preciosa, divina, dulcito, mi cielo, cariño, bonita, muñeca, hermosa, nena, reina, y tesoro.* For all that, *reina* has it every time. You can get almost anything if you call a woman *"mi reina."* But you have to say it like you mean it. And make your voice a little deeper. And grab her chin while you say it. And look her in the eye.

"Come on, Max. Try it."

"And what is the equivalent?" Max wanted to know.

"Well, Max, how best to put it? Men, being simpler creatures, there's only one term of endearment for them: *Papi*."

The marriage proposal a year later was not exactly a surprise. What took Max by surprise was that I said no. In response to my refusal, he had this to offer: "The jeweler said engagement rings cannot be returned."

"What kind of argument is that, Max? That's between you and the jeweler."

THE SNATCH THAT BROKE
THE CAMEL'S BACK

No matter how riveting a turn in my life is, Azucena has always managed to trump it with her own intriguing news. "My dad is a thief, *tía*!" That's what Sofía said to me one day when I called to talk to her mother.

"The kids are watching too many telenovelas, Azucena. Is the girl making this up, or has Carlos Upstairs resorted to outright stealing now?"

I first heard the story from Sofía. Then I heard it from my mother, who put it a little differently. My mother, never one to lower herself by cursing or by raising her voice beyond the level of a whisper, put it thus, "That fucking bastard!"

"Hmmm . . . Must be serious," I thought.

Here's what happened. After claiming he wasn't going to humiliate himself by being the only man among women in a school yard, Carlos Upstairs changed his mind and decided to go pick up Sofía after school one day, except he didn't bother to tell anyone. He got there in time to watch Sofía getting inside my mother's car. In his Game Boy brain he was due for a car chase. So he followed them to the mall. And the next thing you know he surprises them from behind and snatches Sofía from my mother. It was at that point that the poor girl started crying and screaming, which isn't like her at all. Azucena has strictly forbidden her daughter from being a wimp by issuing a very simple dictum, *Por favor*, Sofía, no tears. My niece has the driest eyes of anyone in her age group.

In the end, the ordeal at the mall brought the family much-needed relief. For my part, I could finally stop proselytizing about the example Azucena was setting for her kids. As for my sister, she finally stopped believing in the myth that children learn everything in school. At last she realized that while kids learn math and civics from their teachers, they actually learn the world by looking at the people who unexpectedly dropped them on this planet, whether those people sweat all day at Big-O-Tire, or read comic books in bed.

Don't get me wrong, *mi amor*. I'm not glad this happened. But I am glad that it opened Azucena's eyes. Admittedly, it was only a smidgen, but it was enough for her to see that it was not OK for an able-bodied law school dropout to sit in bed all day while the woman paying the bills was oppressed in her own home.

As for my mother, owing to her exemplary work with schizophrenics, she began to worry that Sofía might be scarred for life. Not to worry, mother. Sofía, Oh she who intimidates her teachers, knows what's what. As you can see, the girl needed no assistance in calling her father a thief.

It was Lucas Enrique who broke everyone's hearts. On learning the details of what had happened from his little sister, Lucas Enrique ran upstairs and dared to interrupt the goings on in Gotham City. "I'm never going fishing with you again!" he bellowed. *Pobre niño.*

Who can predict which little drop will be the one to make an already full glass go *splash*? It was when Azucena asked him to explain, when Carlos Upstairs said he had a right to his daughter whenever and wherever he *coño* pleased, that Azucena finally decided to send Carlos Upstairs outside. Who would have thought? Pubic hair isn't worth much these days. What with all the women getting Brazilians down there, it takes a guy snatching his own daughter to finally get his Game Boy privileges revoked.

DINOSAUR EGGS

"How do you like your eggs?" It's an important question. Just as important as "Would you marry me?"

"Maybe I will marry you, Max." That's what I said to your dad when he proposed the second time. It's not a very convincing answer, is it?

When you were younger—and you still do this from time to time—I noticed that you, too, were fond of the word *maybe*. And who can blame you? Back then, you were afraid people might not like you. Well, as you no doubt have discovered, no matter what you do, no matter how hard you try, no matter how conscientious, how thoughtful, or how sweet you are, there will always be people who won't like you, no matter what. The reason is not important. What's important is to be true to yourself.

As luck would have it, the secret to being true to yourself is hidden inside a seemingly simple question: How do I like my eggs? Say you like your eggs poached, and someone suggests you try them scrambled. Now you can say, "No, thank you, I don't like scrambled eggs." Say you like Sprite, and you're invited to a party where someone offers you a line of coke. Now you can say, "No, thank you. But I'll take a Sprite, if you have one." That way, after you leave the party, you're not the girl on the front page of the newspaper the next day, the one who died from the overdose.

Incidentally, the time to ask yourself: How do I like my eggs? is not when you're ringing the doorbell at the party where they're passing out the lines of cocaine. For this to work, you need to ask this question way, way in advance. And you have to remember the answer. It's people who don't know the answer to that question who tend to get into trouble.

I hate to say it, but that's what happened to your poor cousin. Because whenever someone asked Devin, "How do you like your eggs?" invariably the girl answered, "I don't know. *You* tell *me* how I like *my* eggs." All that sampling from so many different menus finally made her sick. That's one of the reasons Devin keeps going in and out of rehab.

But lest you think I've put egg on my face for no good reason, there's also a time to ask yourself if you're willing to entertain the *possibility* of trying eggs some other way. That's what your dad was asking me to do when he proposed the second time around. He was asking me to reconsider whether or not I wanted to sleep under the same roof with people who like dinosaur eggs in their breakfast cereal. That's why I was a little ambivalent. That's also why I said, "Maybe." "Maybe not." "Maybe, yes." "Yes, Max, I will marry you. On one condition. . . ." The condition was that we not live in the same house. Or in the same city.

After he was done looking at me as if I were on earth for an interplanetary visit, I reminded him that he had been the one to offer that he was willing to entertain any ideas, concepts, or notions about living with, visiting, or occasionally seeing a man who lived with three people marching forward toward adolescence, and nothing to stop them. All I was doing was extending the argument to marriage. It was his turn to ask himself how he liked his eggs.

HOT COUTURE

Last week Azucena finally left her office at a reasonable time, because she had to go to a fashion show. With the traffic, the street barricades, the demonstrations, and the planning one has to do around the kidnappers in Caracas, she knew she had to leave around mid-afternoon for a show that was scheduled to start at six in the evening.

By now you know how hectic Azucena's life is. It isn't very often that the editor of *Caracas Spectator* can actually experience what she peddles on the pages of the best-selling magazine in the country. And here's where I think Anna Wintour should perk up her ears. Because, after listening to Azucena's *relato* about the fashion show, I think the BULLET-PROOF designer collection might be a unique feature in the September issue of the North American edition of *Vogue*.

As I've told you, Azucena is calm personified. Had she not been born under the riotous Caracas skies, I think my sister might have been very much at home in the peace of Kathmandu—after their own riots subsided, that is. Unlike me, who finds everything shocking, devastating, disturbing and downright horrifying, my sister is able to look at everything that should not be in this world and say, "Tell me something I don't know," as she takes a sip of Dom Perignon. As it turned out, despite her being the editor of the most prestigious lifestyle magazine in the country, Azucena did *not* know that the models at the fashion show were going to be shot. The models themselves didn't even know. Apparently the owner and president of the company that makes bullet-proof designer clothing in Brazil—a man by the name of Orlando Seneca—had the brilliant idea of keeping certain parts of the show a surprise. I told Azucena that this kind of fashion show could never have happened here. At the mere mingling of the words *gun*, *fashion*, and *show*, there'd be a line of lawyers at the door singing that catchy song, "Class Action Lawsuit."

But after what happened at the show, Orlando Seneca's is not a name I will soon forget. I might even buy a Seneca suit to wear during future visits to Venezuela. It was understandable, I suppose. Orlando Seneca was giddy with the knowledge that he had come up with the inspired notion of bullet-proof designer clothing in a country where everyone, although they are fairly well assured that they will meet their murderers at the grocery store, still wish to die fashionably nonetheless. So, to demonstrate the quality of his designs, he brought in a couple of hired guns to shoot the final set of models on the runway. But lest you misunderstand me, I don't mean "shoot" as in "photo shoot." Some of the models, Azucena tells me, were wearing gowns so gorgeous that it was hard to believe they were actually bullet-proof.

Only Azucena would notice such details. My sister has a discerning eye. She also has her composure. Up until the moment of the shooting, as a matter of fact, there was this lilac gown that had caught Azucena's eye. She had even considered buying it for *Spectator's* Christmas party. That's what she calls the place where she herself calls the shots: *Spectator.* Azucena is put off by the word *Caracas,* so she chopped off the word from her employer's masthead.

I'm telling you, *mi amor,* we are so different. I've never understood any woman who thinks she can make a statement by wearing something in lilac, least of all at a Christmas party. Unfortunately, the model wearing the lilac dress was shot first. That spoiled everything for Azucena. Most people remained seated in a state of "let's wait and see." And that is perhaps the most telling detail of all; that a real shooting at a fashion show at the Ritz-Carlton in Caracas would garner such a response. At any rate, so fine was the craftsmanship of the dress that the only casualty was the organza. The stuff underneath the gauzy organza—whatever that material is— well, that fabric did its job. As for the model, once she got over the initial shock of being shot in the line of duty, she continued to the end of the runway, composed, as models ought to be. She was a professional.

It was at that point that Seneca himself jumped onto the runway *a la* Rudolf Valentino and asked one of the gunmen he had hired to shoot him in front of the audience. It seemed Seneca knew a thing or two about the brevity of life in Caracas. After being shot, he smoothed out his tuxedo and walked to the microphone. And with one of those winning smiles that Latin men learn in the crib, he said,

"*Damas y caballeros*, for quality-control reasons I had to agree to being shot. Thank you for your indulgence." And he proceeded to take orders for the collection.

Azucena thinks it will be a hit. But the reason I think Anna Wintour should stay tuned is because this could be the first time in the history of Venezuela that a fashion trend travels up north instead of the other way around.

OTHER DESIGNS

Speaking of what to wear on special occasions, let's go back to your dad's marriage proposal, and my counterproposal to him. As you well know, a room of your own is an invaluable thing. Ever since your parents got divorced, you, yourself, have had two rooms, one at each house. That's the argument I used with Max. I said, "Max, all of us already have the rooms we want, decorated in the way we want them. None of us want to move and start splitting weekends between Pottery Barn and Best Buy, do we?" It was a brainless argument, but I got him to see the light. That's why, after we got married, you guys stayed in Arizona while I, your father's wife, continued to live in New York City. I was the wife who visited from time to time—more like the aunt everyone is always happy to see because they know she won't be staying long. I thought the setup was ideal.

But how to sell the deal to our parents? This turned out to be the tricky part. You and your brothers did not need convincing. No child I know wakes up in the morning and when someone asks, "What will it be for breakfast, Tommy?" the kid answers, "Oh, I was craving a stepmother."

Ironically, it's the people we think we know who often pull the rug out from under our feet. It was my mother's question when I called to tell her that Max and I were engaged to be married that took my breath away a little. "I've been meaning to ask you, Valentina. What are they like?"

"What's who like? The kids? They're very cute, Mamá."

"No. I mean the Jews."

"What? Mother, I thought you had not one but *three* college degrees. What kind of question is that?"

"Oh, I don't know. . . I guess everyone is curious. You're always surprising us like this, *hija*."

By "everyone," my mother meant her entire side of the family and everyone on my dad's side of the family who had been reading their Bible. "And then God blessed them and said, 'Be fruitful and multiply.'" As if these creatures needed reminding! Had anyone kept track of all the ex-wives? All these people I had not seen in years—by choice, I should add—were suddenly coming to our wedding because they were "curious." I agree with my mother that they're curious—as in odd, strange, and peculiar. But our real wedding, the one just between the two of us in the Sacromonte, that's the one that will always count for us . . . for me, anyway.

WHAT TO BELIEVE?

Ours was a match made in a cave. The walk through the green hills of Granada while looking up toward caves the color of chalk was the stuff of Gypsy folk tales. Max had always wanted to get married in Granada. I never asked him why he didn't do it the first time around, but I can guess. The idea of getting married inside a windowless cave doesn't appeal to all brides. The first thing I noticed on entering the dark cavern was that there were hundreds of pots and pans hanging from the very low ceilings, so the place felt a little claustrophobic. I was always curious about how Max came upon all these eccentric ideas—weddings in caves, ashes cast out into space. . .

We were married by a Sephardic rabbi, who conducted the entire ceremony in Hebrew. Perhaps because I didn't speak the language, I didn't get cold feet, or have a chance to panic about the impossibility of living up to marital injunctions dreamed up during the time of the Roman Circus.

So as I jumped onto the stage with the *gitanas* and grabbed your dad's hand to come dance with us, I said to no one in particular, "*Diosito*, make this moment last forever." In some of the pictures from that day, which we never showed anyone, it's hard to tell who's who. I, too, wore a ruffled red skirt, just like the Zambra dancers on the stage. Some days I can still hear the finger cymbals.

I don't know exactly when it happened, when Max lost the thread of his dream. He was the delusional optimist, the one who believed in blue butterflies. I was the Doubting Thomas. I remember telling him I had never seen a blue butterfly, therefore they must not exist. He told me they were called Mission Blues. It was I, in fact—just as I was about to sign the *ketubah* we planned to frame in one of our houses—who noticed the "Spanish" rabbi's name at the bottom of the document. "Look, Max," I said, "his name is Jeff."

"Jeff?" Your dad was in disbelief.

And I said, "Pray tell, rabbi, where are you from?"

"New Jersey," he said.

"Where are the Mission Blues?" I asked, looking at Max.

After we came back from Granada, no one believed we had actually gotten married. Isn't that why it's called "eloping"? Azucena thought she had accidentally flipped the channel to a cheap telenovela from Bolivia. My parents thought it was crass that we had eloped to Granada without telling anyone. The twins shrugged as they shrugged at most anything that wasn't a video game. And you? You took us by surprise, yet again. You had wanted us to get married so that you and I could play Parcheesi uninterrupted until the end of times. Remember our Parcheesi marathons? Even so, you were so upset at seeing a wedding ring on your dad's finger that you stopped talking to him for days.

At first Max was surprised. Then he was crushed. As for your grandparents . . . well, they wanted something a little more official.

"Is a hotel official enough, Max? And why is our marital status so interesting to everyone?"

In the end we decided to host a wedding at the Biltmore Hotel. So in answer to my mother's question, I said, "The only difference between Jewish men and other men, Mamá, is the penis. But not to worry, we won't be serving foreskin stuffed with goat cheese at the wedding; it's being catered by the *goyim* of the Arizona Biltmore. So everything will be kosher." But that's how our phony ceremony turned into a Judeo-Spanish version of *My Big Fat Greek Wedding*, with the other rabbi, the priest from Venezuela, and my uncle, my uncle, my uncle, my uncle, my uncle, and my aunt Zulay.

LAST NAME CHANGE

Your cousin Josh made an impression on my family. It isn't every day that Latin boys in tailored suits get to meet a skinny boy named Josh whose underwear is hanging out and who calls himself LeBron for no apparent reason.

As for the priest my parents brought in from Venezuela saying his part of the service in Spanish, I'm sorry to say I can't remember a word of it. But I'm sure he was talking Miracle Whip—Christ turning water into wine at a wedding in Cana of Galilee, as if the people of Galilee couldn't afford a good Shiraz. To be honest, I can't remember much about that day. The bride had only one thing in her mind: "Who are these people?"

Now you know the truth, *mi amor*. Now you know how someone who started out as Valentina Viloria Serrano becomes Valentina Goldman and proceeds to heed coyote howls for the rest of her days. How will you remember your step-*madre*? Oh she of the blue eyes? Oh she of the brown eyes? The woman who escaped Mardi Gras for fear of Monistat? How does, "my stepmother the MRI technician" sound? What about "my stepmother the singer?" Ahhh, you didn't know I could sing, did you, Emily?

CONJUGAL VISITS

Once all the wedding *mishegas* was behind us, I returned to New York, where I still had my job at the ad agency and a room of my own, as was Virginia Woolf's wont. That was how the arrangement was supposed to work. And for a while, it did.

For my birthday later that year, your dad flew to New York. I remember he brought a big box with him, though I didn't have the slightest idea what might be inside it. One of the advantages of living apart from the person you're married to is that your life seems forever shrouded in mystery. It was through our odd little arrangement, as a matter of fact, that I discovered that to get over any disappointment he was feeling, major or minor, Max bought luggage. He had new luggage every time he came to New York. When I had seen about half a dozen different pieces, I finally asked, Max, "Do you think this is a full-blown fetish?"

And he said, "If I were very, very rich, *tesoro*, I would buy different luggage for every trip."

"And what would you do with it afterward, Max?"

"I don't know, Valentina. I have no idea where the very rich store their luggage."

"Just curious, Max, what exactly is it that you like about luggage?"

"It's the pockets. Do you realize, *mi vida*, that some luggage has pockets for your wet bathing suits?"

"No, Max, I didn't realize that. What's wrong with a Ziploc bag for my wet bathing suits?"

"You don't always carry a Ziploc bag with you."

"Say, Max, do you think your luggage fetish is as bad as those people who look at porn on the Internet?"

"No, *mi reina*. It's nothing that serious."

The Spanish lessons were paying off. By the end of the first year of our marriage, Max had learned every single term of endearment by which Latin men make women believe they are their one and only.

"By the way, Max, what's in the box?"

The box. That box. Wow! *Cri-cri* chocolates, *bolero* chocolates, *toronto* chocolates, chocolate *turrones,* and more chocolates—a treasure trove of candy bars I had not seen since childhood. It's as if after you move to Ecuador and decide never to come back, *mi amor,* your Ecuadorian husband were to call Zachy or Zach and get the names of your favorite candy bars, to wit—Crunch, Sugar Daddy, Twix, Milky Way, and all that other good stuff you taught me how to eat.

Max got the chocolates from Azucena. My sister and your dad were that rare case where people sincerely feel they are the other's sister or brother and not just another "in-law." Max was a brother to Azucena and a great *tío* to Lucas Enrique and Sofía. Lucas Enrique still has that baseball signed by Derek Jeter that Max got for him in New York.

I know, *mi amor.* . . . I know how hard this is. But let's do try to remember your dad for everything he was, and not by this one instance alone. I don't think Max would have liked for us to start playing klezmer music all of a sudden. Acceptance is the only recourse when there's no understanding. As the yoga teacher explained just the other day, acceptance is a kind of letting through and letting go at the same time. I suppose we can choose not to accept this, but I wouldn't recommend it. What happens when we refuse to accept certain things—say, that your parents hate each other, or that you're homeless in a foreign country, by way of random examples—is that those things end up taking residence inside you, kind of like shrapnel. And I don't know about you, Emily, but I don't want to start beeping at every airport in the world as if I were a terrorist on the run, do you?

So whenever you hear that diamonds are a girl's best friend, now you have evidence to the contrary. Now you know that to make a woman truly happy on her birthday, the only requirement is chocolate.

Every time Max left New York, he would say, "Dream a little dream of me while I'm gone." We need to take him up on that, *mi amor* . . . and dream a little dream sometime.

A LITTLE CONDOM GOES A LONG WAY

Perhaps because I didn't live with you at first, it didn't occur to me that you, your brothers, and I were unwilling performers in someone else's circus. It took me a while to realize that questions that I had once considered polite were now all but illegal. There simply was no way to ask, "How was your weekend, Zach?" and not be risking a court order. "What do you mean, 'How was my weekend?' What exactly are you trying to find out, Valentina? Are you suggesting I couldn't have had as good a time at the other house? Or are you trying to find out if I *did* have a good time at the other house so that the Divorce Olympics may begin?" It's inevitable. Once parent A finds out that parent B makes excellent brownies, parent A will quickly learn to bake double-chocolate brownies with Swiss chocolate. And God forbid a child ever utters the word *mom* in front of dad, or vice versa. After a while even a Muppet is smart enough to realize that all conversations with the children of divorced parents will go the way of a penis in a marriage.

All that pussyfooting. And to get nowhere! I couldn't say, for instance, "Is that a new shirt, Emily? Blue is a nice color on you." Even the most sincere compliment could easily degenerate into, "Dad, Mom says you owe her two hundred dollars." Talk of money, by the way, was the only dispensation to mention the words *mom* or *dad* in front of the other parent.

The thing to do, then, was to channel Eliza Doolittle and to stick to only two topics: the weather and one's health. But then again, maybe not; talk of health carried its own inherent risks. A kid might momentarily lower her guard and say, "Mom's not feeling so well lately." And Dad might say, with glee in his eyes, "Really?" while secretly praying that Mom had a rare strand of the avian flu so he could finally stop paying alimony. And if clever children quickly come up with nonflammable terms, such as "the other house," and learn to play down any notions that you actually have another parent at that other house, well, what is to be said about the adults running the circus?

I hate to admit it, but every time you asked, "How was your week, Valentina?" my guard immediately went up.

Then it was my turn to say, "Let's see what's on TV, Emily."

Because, let's face it, had I actually answered your question and told you that your dad and I had gone to Las Vegas because the tickets were cheap, the only reasonable thing to expect a few days later was some kind of nastygram that said, "You bastard, you're gambling away the kids' college money with that whore!" Always, it seemed every conversation was missing a vital part. And everyone knew it.

"Can we please have a normal conversation around here????" But on second thought, "Has anyone seen a condom around here?" might have been a more fitting question.

REASONS TO LOVE

During one of his visits to New York, Max showed up at my doorstep with two bags that did not match. Given his luggage fetish, I was immediately on the alert. And for all that, it was the photos—more than the oddball bags—that shook my world a little.

After dinner that night, Max invited me to the couch and said, "Come here. I wanna show you something." He then proceeded to take out every single one of the pictures he had ever taken of you and the twins. As you know by now, my parents are very practical, no-nonsense people. Neither owns a camera, nor do they like photos. At first I didn't think anything of it, just a guy showing me some pictures. But after seeing the evidence of sooo many memories issuing from those bags, I came very close to getting sick from thinking I had been robbed of my own childhood.

In time, though, I came to understand something you once told me when I asked you what it felt like to have parents who were divorced. Do you remember what you said? "Valentina, I don't know anything else." It seems we only know the lives we're shown. I suppose it's not until we become adults and start comparing notes with strangers that we find out that other people used to bake cookies for bearded men who don't exist but who climb down chimneys once a year, nonetheless.

Max used to joke that had I had children of my own, they might have enjoyed shooting people from the rooftops of tall buildings. On the contrary, Max, my children would be astronauts. My children would not waste their precious development years wondering why their parents and a bearded man from the North Pole, of all places, have identical handwriting. Or why a rabbit, which they studied in biology as a mammal, lays chocolate eggs for one week a year. Please tell me, Max, what purpose does the Easter Bunny serve except to confuse a child? I do not like lies, Max. Someone needs to research the impact of that kind of deceit on people's psyches. It's heartbreaking, really, the way adults actively participate in the warping of a kid's mind. But there was no convincing a man who loved blue butterflies that a deer named Rudolf, the Tooth Fairy, and the boogeyman were creepier than all the ghosts and goblins from Halloween put together.

It was through the photos in the bags that I learned about the earlier years, the times when I had not been around. All I can say is that I had never seen so many pictures in my life. The twins riding their bikes. You swimming at the pool. You and Max in Alaska. You, the twins, and Max in Alaska. A bear from Alaska. A school of fish from Florida. Max at the pool somewhere. You getting out of the water at yet another pool. You in another-color bathing suit diving into a pool. Pools, pools, and more pools. Pools all over the place. Emily likes to swim, does she, Max? Until I met you in person, mostly I had seen you in colorful bathing suits, surrounded by . . . *Ay,* Emily, *por el amor de Dios,* please don't say it didn't matter. Of course it mattered. *¡Dios mío, niña!* Of course your dad loved you. I have the pictures to prove it. Why do you think I'm telling you about the bags of pictures when my condo in New York didn't even have a photo of our honeymoon? Come, now . . . I know it gets a little confusing, sometimes. Some days I still feel that I've had breakfast for dinner and the other way around. But I promise you . . . I promise you, Emily . . . Please trust me on this . . . Peter, please repeat after me: "I am not my business card." . . . Emily, please repeat after me: "I was precious to my dad." *¡Por Dios santo!* Give me a minute. . . .

WHO, ME?

"This isn't going to work." That's what I told Max when he called to tell me that your aunt had fallen down the stairs in Ohio. In the time it takes for a phone to ring, a woman falls down the stairs, her sister has to go take care of her, and the kids have to move in with their dad until the second coming of Christ. Amen.

"Can I ask you a question, Max? Why wasn't What's-her-name hanging on to the handrail? I have a job, Max. I can't move to Arizona!"

And because life is wicked that way, my job at the ad agency in New York was turning out to be the best job I'd ever had. When you've had as many jobs as I've had, *mi amor,* that's quite an endorsement. For the first time in my life I was working with people who did not suffer from stab-in-the-back disorder. All of us traveled, which is to say we rarely saw one another. Whenever we happened to be in the office at the same time, we compared notes on car rental fiascos and delayed flights while filling out expense reports. There was also the occasional surprise of meeting new hires upon return from business trips.

Most jobs get stale after thirty days. But I'll always remember the ad agency as being very fresh. Back then Max was traveling like crazy, too. More than once we crossed paths at an airport. And even I have to admit that meeting one's husband at the airport and buying some caramel corn together before boarding our respective planes is a little out of the ordinary. Some of our good-byes were lamentable. Other times I felt unbelievably lucky. I couldn't believe I trusted someone enough not to follow them around as if I worked for Interpol. Happiness is possible. That's what Max had said in his telegram. But contrary to popular belief, happiness is not a lifestyle on sale at Pottery Barn. I wish I could say otherwise. I wish I could say, "Emily, there's a planet Happiness. You might consider moving there one day." In the end, happiness consists only of moments, stolen moments at that. No one was counting on Helen's sister falling down the stairs. No one could have predicted that you and the twins would have to move in with Max all of a sudden, and for an unspecified period of time. When I married your dad, it never occurred to me that anything could change so drastically as to merit the complete overhaul of our arrangement.

Max had once told me that once you put kids on this earth, they are yours for the duration. They might move to Tanzania to follow their lifelong passion of photographing elephant stampedes. But one day they can pick up the phone and say, "I've seen enough elephant stampedes, I'm coming home." And what are you going to do?

"What are *we* going to do, Max?" I was panicked. All of a sudden "married with kids and wife in New York" became a mouthful for Max. I suggested he hire a nurse, a governess, a kid consultant— professionals whose job it is to know the difference between rice puffs and that other kind of cereal that stains the milk with ink. But Max was opposed to having his children handled by strangers. In fact, the only time you guys were ever left with a babysitter, it was because it couldn't be helped.

That time, your dad was away and I was in jail. I'll tell you more about that later, about how I ended up spending the night at the Pima County jail. That's not a night I remember fondly. Who wants to get arrested?

But anyway, whenever Max and I talked, I heard the stress in his voice. At first I thought it was the static on the phone. But when he said, "I can't do this by myself much longer," my heart skipped a beat. And then he said, "I could use your help down here, Valentina."

"What? Isn't the sister getting better, Max? Did she break something when she fell down the stairs?" I never knew your aunt's name; it was one of those unmentionables. I only knew her as Helen's sister. The only thing I knew for sure was that "unspecified period of time" meant exactly that.

"I need a life I can count on," popped into my head now and again. "This isn't going to work," played like a stuck record every hour of the day. At first, I was in denial. After hanging up with Max that time, I called one of my clients—something routine. I refused to believe that my life was about to turn into some version of tic-tac-toe. Then I was angry. I didn't know whom to blame. "This isn't going to work. This isn't going to work," was the only constant. I was not unlike a woman who knows she's pregnant but who keeps pleading with the little piece of paper to please, please turn the other color. But the color never changed. And I couldn't very well say to my boss at the ad agency, "Elizabeth, I'm going to Arizona for an unspecified period of time. I can't tell you how long, Elizabeth, but will you hold my job for me in the meantime?" The thing to do was to get a divorce. And to move.

"Is there a world atlas in this office, by chance?"

VII. MUFFINS AT 11

A NUT TO CRACK

His name was Andrew Rosenthal. The reason I picked him, in particular, was because of all the pictures of old women from India hanging from every wall in his office. I would later learn that he had taken all the pictures himself. I interviewed two other therapists; you can say I was qualified. But I settled on Dr. Rosenthal because, quite frankly, I needed someone who could illuminate some issues. I wanted someone to tell me, "No, you're not crazy for wanting to move to Chernobyl rather than to help the man you married raise his kids in Arizona." I know that sounds vapid, and I know you shouldn't judge a therapist by his photos, but I'm pretty sure I wouldn't have hired a therapist who had photos of Linda Evangelista on the walls, even if that would have been more pleasant to look at during the interminable sessions, which, owing to the urgency of the situation, sometimes went on for hours at a time.

Pretty soon it became clear that Andrew Rosenthal had not obtained his degrees from a mail-order catalog. One day, after I had been in therapy for a couple months, Dr. Rosenthal suddenly changed our regularly scheduled appointment. I was horrified. I'm not afraid of sweeping change, say, moving to Islamabad and wearing a headscarf as my only accessory. But little changes to my routine, those freak me out. On the day we were supposed to meet, Dr. Rosenthal's secretary called my office to tell me that he could only see me at eleven. Eleven? I can't even begin to tell you about eleven. Eleven is a ridiculous time of day. Eleven is stuck in the middle between productive hours, such as eight, nine, and ten, and the lunch hour, noon. Eleven is simply too fungible. Unfortunately for me, Dr. Rosenthal knew his buttons. And he knew when to push them. To this day I have no idea what gave the man the impression that I would have a mini nervous breakdown about a tiny time change. If tardiness is the monster, *mi amor*, changing the time is the offspring. All sorts of things can happen in sixty minutes. There's a reason there's a disturbing TV show with that name.

At the end of the day, Andrew Rosenthal made a prediction that came to pass. When his secretary called to tell me about the time change, I told her it was impossible. I told her there was *no way* I could meet him at eleven, not on that day, not ever! That's when she put him on the phone. Apparently, Dr. Rosenthal had seen much, much worse than some control-freak foreigner. He always reminded me of those airplane pilots who got started in air combat and then go fly commercial. I was the passenger throwing a tantrum about a seat change. Andrew Rosenthal knew I wouldn't die from it, so after telling me that his schedule was full until Israel and Palestine agreed to build a mall on the Gaza Strip, he asked me to please bring a muffin to our next session.

"What kind of muffin?"

"Any muffin."

"At eleven?"

"Yes, Valentina, at eleven."

"This isn't going to work out, Max. I don't seem to be getting any better. And my therapist is nuts!"

CHILDREN NEED THEIR MOTHER

It's inevitable. Sooner or later, all divorcées dye their hair red. The natural progression of things for a working mother fresh out of a divorce is to try to figure out when to squeeze in potential dates. But how does a busy, finicky mother of two find the time to conjugate? It wouldn't be easy, that's for sure. Still, now that Carlos was outside, there were many minds on the case of trying to find Azucena a boyfriend—her friend at work, her friend not at work, her best friend from high school. Even her new chauffeur, a brazen man named Pingo, suggested a friend or two. It was hard to believe that Azucena would be tongue-tied about Pingo's generous offer. How about this? "Pingo, as a general rule I'm not attracted to smugglers with STDs. But thanks for thinking of me."

Even Carlos Outside was trying to get Azucena a boyfriend. The reason: so that she'd get off his case about paying alimony and child support, something he contested, claiming he was the one who needed support for putting up with her all those years.

A custody battle in the balmy Tropics is no mean thing. For one, the children are always assigned to the mother. Case closed. The mother will have to fight the now ex-husband for everything from diapers to visiting days. Case closed. In a place where the leaves of palm trees are fanned by the Caribbean breeze, everyone from the presiding judge down to the clerk who puts people under oath agrees that children need their mother. The fathers, on the other hand, are free to visit whenever they want—once a year, or never, the choice is theirs. Men need freedom in order to remake their lives. And who can remake anything with two kids in tow? This kind of setup also ensures that children pine away for the parent who's never around—the fun-loving dad who's not telling them to do their homework, to brush their teeth, or to stop watching Brazilian telenovelas. Familiarity does breed contempt, after all—for the mother.

As for Azucena, who insisted on raising Lucas Enrique and Sofía to be neither pimp nor prostitute, well, she made life more difficult for herself by always bossing her kids around when she happened to be around. Afterward, she felt guilty for being a bitch, so she bought them expensive presents. And after that, she worried that she was spoiling them, and possibly turning them into versions of Carlos Outside. That's when she herself decided it might be a good time to engage the services of a good therapist. She had started, quite literally, to pull out chunks of her own hair.

"Why not color your hair, instead, Azucena? That always does the trick for me."

THE PERFECTION OF PLASTICITY

The matter was urgent. So Azucena's therapist ordered her to go on a date, any date. It was an easy enough assignment, but one that Azucena, an overachiever of sorts, could not manage to fulfill. Besides Lucas Enrique and Sofía, my poor sister had other equally weighty matters on her mind.

"Valentina, I'm fat. Valentina, I can't show my Yanomami Indian boobs to any man."

"How about showing them to a woman, then, Azucena *querida?*"

"Valentina, I'm serious. Have you any idea what a pair of kids can do to a pair of boobs?"

You might be headed down to Ecuador, *mi amor*, but you haven't done enough eco-travel through the Amazonian rainforest to know that Azucena's tribal reference meant that her breasts had sagged to their lowest point possible—her stomach, perhaps. As for the Yanomami women, despite *National Geographic's* best efforts to promote their existence, no one had contacted them yet to let them know that a short plane ride from Ciudad Bolívar to Caracas and they too, could be in the hands of a competent plastic surgeon who could give them a lift after years and years of running rings through their nipples. But how dare I compare the lovely Azucena to an Indian woman? The man who did no longer lives with her.

I have a sticky memory of a family vacation during which Carlos Upstairs refused to be in a photo with his own wife and newborn child. It was only a Polaroid, so I wouldn't call it "a Kodak moment." By then Max had infected me with the business of preserving family memories, so I bought one of those cameras you can throw away after you get the photos, and took it with me to Trinidad. I shouldn't have insisted. But everyone in our family is glad that I did. Sometimes there's no other way to get a double exposure than to insist. When Carlos, still Upstairs, refused to be in the photo with Azucena and the newborn Sofía because he was embarrassed to be seen, in his words, with a Yanomami Indian, time stopped for us all.

The thing to realize about Carlos Outside is that either (a) he has been given an incredibly malfunctioning brain, or (b) he was playing his cards right by humiliating his wife out loud so that we could all hate him, thereby freeing him to ask Miss Universe out on a date. With him, it's always been hard to tell.

My father, who had been reading the paper by the pool, stopped reading for a second to look up. My mother, who was laying out on one of those stretchers, took off her glasses to make sure the person who had called her once-anemic daughter an Indian woman from the Amazon, and the husband, were one and the same.

As for me, I said, "There's a tidal wave coming. . . . How about you go sailing this afternoon, Carlos?" I secretly hoped he would drown. Then, as Lucas Enrique's godmother, I could tell the boy later on, "We tried to stop him, *mi rey*, but your daddy insisted on going sailing when the weather turned, and now he's dead, dead, dead. Boo-hoo-hoooo. What a tragedy!"

By the time the therapist entered Azucena's life, some time had passed since my days of playing family photographer in Trinidad. And for all the leaves in the rainforest, I could not convince Azucena that—gravity problems aside—she still had the face of a goddess. And that when a man truly loves you, he doesn't look at your boobs. But all my sound advice was falling on ears stuffed with tropical mold.

"You've been away too long, Valentina. Guys down here have their pick of any Miss Universe who can talk sports cars."

"Really, Azucena? Are there really that many smart women down there? I guess things *have* changed. But trust me, Azucena *querida*, you don't want that kind of man."

"But I doooooooooooooooooooooo, Valentina."

"Very well, then. You get what you pay for. So call the plastic surgeon already."

STOP

Need I say that when I arrived at Dr. Rosenthal's office at eleven on the dot, muffin in bag, I was pissed? But I *had* followed directions. Anyone raised on the words "consider the consequences" will always follow directions, even if once she gets there, she will read her therapist the riot act. So Andrew Rosenthal and I had our first confrontation. Good therapists will sometimes cause these staged of confrontations, *mi amor*. It is their job to do so. It is their job to show you what stupidity looks like in a mirror, and if you're smart enough to recognize it, then you can help bring about the much-desired change in your own life. Then there might be hope for you.

We were getting close to the end of our session when Dr. Rosenthal, who I thought hadn't noticed the little bag I carried in with me, asked me to munch on the muffin while we wrapped up.

"Excuse me? I thought the muffin was for you," I said.

"No," he said, "the muffin is for you, Valentina. . . . What do you think would happen if you relaxed a little?" he asked. "What do you think would happen if you gave eating a muffin at an unexpected hour a chance? What do you think might happen, Valentina, if you stopped running away from everything?"

"I hate you!!!!!!!!!!!!!!! That's what I said." So he handed me a box of Kleenex and returned to cleaning his glasses. Now that I had no mascara left, now that I was practically naked in front of this crazy guy, what else was there left for me to do but to take a little bite of the damn muffin? It was a humiliating moment. To add insult to injury, Andrew Rosenthal massaged his goatee while I posed as a feeding rodent. No gentleman, he; not even a hug! When at last he deigned to speak, it was to ask me, "How does it taste?"

"I will NEVER eat another muffin at eleven for as long as I live. Do you hear? Every normal person in the world knows that muffins are eaten between seven and eight o'clock in the morning, Andrew. But I get your point. I totally get your point."

"That will be five hundred dollars, please."

DEFYING GRAVITY

What would Azucena's eventual boyfriend be like? Would he work for a living? Would he like Lucas Enrique and Sofía? Or would he want more children, thereby making Azucena's boobs sag once again, even *after* the plastic surgery? In my mind I was already past the operation, past recovery, meeting my new brother-in-law over Cuba Libres somewhere. Not Azucena. My sister was busy giving self-torture a good name.

"Valentina, what if there's a power outage during the operation? What then? And how long can I afford to be out of work, anyway? I'm the editor-in-chief now, Valentina. I don't have the luxury of going to recover in Aruba, like some women here do. And besides, they've stopped renewing passports down here, so I guess that's a moot point . . . But still, that means I'd have to recover at home. And who's going to keep the kids now that Carlos . . . ?"

I've often wondered if it's intentional, or if it was the childhood anemia that scarred Azucena for life with the odd desire to drive others mad right along with her. No pun intended, but my sister is a tough nut to crack. So in order to get her mind off the boobs, I thought I'd talk politics with her. Azucena hates politics. But thanks to Hugo Boss she lives in a country now dubbed "the next Cuba," where talking politics is always in fashion. So I said, "Does anyone need new boobs in the next Cuba, Azucena? At the rate things are going down there, you'll never be seen again, naked or clothed."

"Valentina, you are *such* a downer."

"Well, Azucena *querida*, are new boobs really a necessity? Last time I saw you, you looked fine. How about buying a push-up bra, and going on a diet to get rid of five miserable pounds? Afterward, you, too, can Google the difference between a Ferrari and a Maserati, and become one of those busty women you told me about who can also talk sports cars. Then you'd be ready to go on a date with one of those men who go for melons and revved-up engines."

"Are you even listening to me, Valentina? This is a major decision. This is isn't like going to the nearest butcher and saying, 'Cut.'"

"I'm sooo sorry, Azucena. I didn't mean to treat you like a piece of meat."

SIDE EFFECTS OF SADISTIC MEDICINE

To further postpone the assignment her therapist had mandated of going on the date, Azucena went to see a nutritionist. That's one of my sister's favorite tricks. Just when you think she's not listening, it turns out she is! Now dieting was back on the table. It's easy to see how after a while some of her friends just give up. "Why doesn't so-and-so call me anymore?" Azucena asks, mystified. "Hmmm . . . have you tried inquiring about the new admissions at the local asylum, Azucena? Perhaps your friend has just checked in."

As for the nutritionist, I was all for it. I've always said it, ask the same question of different professionals and you'll get answers befitting their professions. When you say to a plastic surgeon, "I'm fat," you'll be shown a knife collection. When you say the exact same thing to a sports trainer, you'll be asked to circle the city on foot until the fat on your thighs has coated the pavement on every street. And when you tell a nutritionist, "I'm fat," you'll be told that Switzerland has been wiped off the map, which means: no more Swiss fondue, Swiss chocolate, or Swiss raclette for you.

As it turned out, the nutritionist Azucena went to see was of a different school of thought altogether. He had done his residence in a new field called Sadistic Medicine. To my surprise, my little sister had not had enough of being cut down by Carlos Outside when he was upstairs. So she got a referral from a friend and went to see this celebrity nutritionist whose specialty was helping women lose weight by asking them to take off their clothes in front of a giant mirror and humiliating them into thinness. Only in the balmy Tropics would women pay for the privilege of having a tall, dark, and evil man shake his head and say, "Look in the mirror. Would you come near you if you didn't have to?"

That's when it finally hit me that I was living in the wrong hemisphere. That's when I thought, "Why not return home to direct a show called *Tropical Survivor*? Why am I circling the globe working for an ad agency, hardly ever sleeping in my own bed?" Because when Azucena called to tell me that she couldn't go back to the nutritionist a second time because she was ashamed to show "that handsome man" her body again, that's when I said, "Hand me a tranquilizer, will you?" Men have no idea.

BROKEN VOWS

A few days after Andrew Rosenthal made me eat a muffin at the wrong time in New York City, I called Max to give him the good news that I was reconciled to the idea of moving down to Arizona. I didn't want to use the word *resigned*—that's too close to saying, "I have no choice." *Reconciled* implies so much more maturity. *Reconciled* says, "I'm prepared to accept . . . ," whereas *resigned* says, "I can't believe my life has come to playing knock-knock-who's-there with coyotes howling in the background." So I gave notice at the ad agency and moved to Arizona to do the one thing I'd vowed I'd never do, so help me God.

VIII. WONDERING IN THE DESERT

THE NEW ORDER OF THINGS

During the first five minutes in Max's house I suddenly understood why antidepressants were, as we used to say at the ad agency, a "growth market." I was far from the immaculate order of my condo in Manhattan, that's for sure. My initial reaction was to run. But you don't want to start skipping through piles when you're wearing stilettos; you might break an ankle, or worse. Then you'd have to stay on hold with the insurance company for so long that you might swear off wearing high heels altogether.

How could I have known that never again would I sleep, uninterrupted, for eight hours in a row? I had no idea—and this is just as well—that in a few days I would witness a screaming match between you and Zach, and that the end result would be an entire bottle of chocolate syrup deposited on the carpet. I knew nothing about the hobbies that flourished for a week or so as a result of trips to Hobby Lobby, only later to be abandoned in the basement, along with fifty pounds of construction paper and half-used bottles of Elmer's glue. I was unsuspecting about the mean girlfriends and didn't know there'd be unreturned crushes that would break my heart too. More than anything, I could not understand how more mothers didn't end up in mental institutions.

Innocent of all that was to come my way, I just said, "The kitchen is nice and airy, Max. Where do you keep the Windex?"

I had betrayed Virginia Woolf. It was all I could do not to burst into tears.

I'M HERE ABOUT THE BLOW JOB

Unlike Christ, who was free to roam around, even if he did choose to go barefoot, I went to the desert to stay put. I wish I could say I went there to wander. But no, I was there to wonder. That was the whole point: to stay put and to wonder about things beyond my comprehension. Your dad was away on a business trip and your aunt was still bedridden in Ohio when I read about the problem at Dillard's.

"It was in the paper today, Max."

"What was in the paper, Valentina?"

"Max, the article said that if your daughter is spending too much time at the mall, you'd better start asking questions."

"Why, Valentina?"

"Max, it says here she might be in a dressing room at Dillard's giving oral sex to a young man. Apparently, Max, teenagers have figured out that Dillard's dressing rooms are never supervised. How to broach the subject with Emily, Max?"

"Hmmm . . . I need to call you back, Valentina. My client just got here."

"Max, Max, Max, please, don't hang up. This is important. Would it be all right, Max, if I talked to Emily about—? Maaaaax!"

I stood by the phone, waiting for your dad to call back. But I knew that those planning meetings were marathons and that sometimes he couldn't call back right away.

After waiting for a while I decided to go upstairs and see if I could glean any clues. But on the way, I poured myself some gin, because I never knew what might greet me on the way up. And also because a lady at the gym had said that juniper berries, which gin is made from, have a calming effect.

When I finally opened the door to your room, hoping you really were working on that UFO project at Sarah's and not spending time in the dressing room at Dillard's, I visually took in the room's contents. Suddenly, the desire to go in and start cleaning up got a hold of me. But I knew I shouldn't. One of the first things Max did when I moved in was to instruct me that I was never to move a single object in your or the twins' rooms, no matter how tempted I might be, under penalty of death. So as a way to stave off the anxiety that chaos produces in me, I always kept the doors to your respective rooms shut. I couldn't handle not being able to see the color of the carpet, or if the room even had a carpet for that matter.

That day, I remained in the doorway and surveyed the stuffed animals against the wall. These were no ordinary stuffed animals. They had names; interesting names, too. You would never name a stuffed animal something affected, such as Bambi. You named your guinea pig Henry, and your stuffed animals Grace, Homer, and Leonardo. And it was after looking at the wall of stuffed kittens, mini-gorillas, piglets, lions, and baby tigers that I said to myself, "Nah, nine is too young for blow jobs. Let's see what's on TV."

Still, the next time I went grocery shopping, I bought a box of Trojans and put it in the cracker drawer in the kitchen.

"What are these for?" you asked.

"Ooops, I have no idea how a condom got in the cracker drawer. But feel free to take one of each. Just in case. You never know who you might run into at the mall." I was trying to act natural, to stay calm before the concept of preteen sex. But I don't think I fooled you, did I?

WHAT'S EATING YOU?

Whereas I had successfully moved on and now enjoyed quiet sunsets in the desert, Azucena was still stuck.

"How about doing some math, Azucena? You have an MBA. This might be an area of potential growth for you. Try this: eat less, weigh less. Granted, it's not as sexy as dieting with the evil nutritionist, but it might work."

"That's easy for you to say, Valentina. You have no idea how demoralizing it is to eat only a single grape while your child smacks his lips eating a cheeseburger."

"Hmmm . . . I'm afraid you can no longer use that argument with me, Azucena *querida*. These days I'm surrounded by McDonald's wrappers. How about joining a gym?"

"A gym, Valentina? At what time? And with the traffic down here . . . ?"

"Then how about taking your therapist's advice? How about going on a date *just as you are*? For your information, Azucena, there are men in both hemispheres who think Nicole Kidman looks like a giraffe. These days, men are infatuated with the Kardashian butt. Had you been keeping up with the Kardashians, you, too, would know that here in the United States there's even a name for your condition. It's called 'generous hips.' See? When you add in the word *generous*, it doesn't sound so bad, does it? It even makes you feel lucky, as though you're a bit richer, say, than all those anorexic women on magazine covers."

OBJECTS OF AFFECTION

On the night of Azucena's first date in years—purely by coincidence, you understand—Carlos Outside bought a couple of little turtles for Sofía and Lucas Enrique. What the cute little turtles couldn't have known was that by the time my sister bore children, she had seen enough pets. The yellow volleyball frog she claims not to have seen, the dead *gallito* she heard about, the fox that scared away one of the maids, the tiger that came to replace the fox, and the parrot that said *"puta"*—all had left their mark.

"What should we call the turtles, Mami?" Sofía asked, cooing at the little things inside the glass bowl.

Azucena called them "dead." When she got home from her date and found two slimy reptiles swimming inside a crystal vase that Martha Stewart had pronounced strictly for fancy flowers, she carefully picked up the vase and flushed the turtles down the toilet. And when Sofía started crying, Azucena said, "No pets. No tears, Sofía. I can't stand people who cry. And whose idea was it to put them in the Baccarat vase, Sofía? Was it your dad's? The vase is infected now!"

Sofía was too young at that time to say, "Mami, I would have put my pet turtles elsewhere had this been a normal household where people keep containers made of materials other than crystal." Unfortunately for the little turtles, there's never been any plastic in Azucena's house. Plastic smells. Plastic stains. Plastic looks cheap. Plastic is an invention her children would have to wait to see at a World's Fair someday.

Meanwhile, I was busy planning a Tupperware party. But that was the least of my problems.

UNDER MY SKIN

More often than not, Max could not help himself. And because he simply could not help *not* being a woman, I would have to ring up my mother in Caracas to ask her for advice. You have no idea, *mi amor*, how many times I called my mother to ask for guidance in times of duress. She would know what to do, I thought. She had, after all, raised two healthy daughters—a fugitive for whom no place on earth was far enough to hide from emotional landslides, and a workaholic who was terrified of going out on a date.

It was to my mother that I posed the question about the tattoo. "Mamá, Max's daughter is thinking about getting a tattoo. How do you suggest I tell her that when you look up the word *tattoo* in the dictionary, the word *whore* comes up as a synonym?"

"*¿Un tatuaje,* Valentina?" my mother asked in disbelief. "Is that something the girl's mother does? Whom did Max marry on first nuptials?"

"I don't know, Mamá. The only thing I know is her name. There aren't even pictures of the woman anywhere. She's like a ghost. They hate, hate each other, so they talk through lawyers."

"Really, Valentina?"

"*Sí,* Mamá. They call themselves evolved here, but don't you think not talking to a former spouse is a little unsophisticated? I mean, there are certain things you shouldn't leave in the hands of lawyers. Things such as needles under the skin require a conversation between those involved."

"Maybe she's doing it for shock value," said my mother.

"For shock value, Mamá? Freud didn't have all the answers, you know."

"*Ay, Valentina, eso sí está complicado.*"

"I know it's very complicated, Mamá; I wouldn't have called you long-distance if it weren't serious. This is much more serious than you think. American children are raised to talk back to their parents.

It's mortifying to hear a mere *pichurra* say to her father, 'This is none of your business.'"

"I don't believe you, Valentina. Stop exaggerating."

"Why would I be exaggerating, Mamá?"

"Well, *hija*, if it's not the parents' business, then whose business is it?"

"I don't know, Mamá. This is one of those culture-shock things. And if she can say to her parents, 'Don't butt in,' what do you think she's going to say to me, the guest mother, when I mention the word *tattoo*? She'll throw me out of the house, Mamá! Do you think I should take my condo in New York off the market?"

"*¡Ay, Dios mío, hija, qué angustia!*"

"You're telling me, Mamá! I've taken to regularly having a little bit of gin right before the kids come home from school. Things are always very tense around here. You have no idea how tense."

"Be careful, *hija*. Be careful you don't become an alcoholic. Your aunt Zulay lived there for a while and she told me alcoholism is practically an epidemic there."

"*Ay*, Mamá, *tía* Zulay is exaggerating. I've never met an alcoholic the entire time I've lived here. And I've just about circled the country. Anyway, I have to go. I hear Emily downstairs."

Was I really worried that you'd throw me out? *Mi amor. Mi amor.* You have no idea. While you and the twins were in school, I used to watch that show with the judge on TV. One time, I swear to you, there were two brothers divorcing their parents. It was a very real fear for me. Oddly enough, it was all that law I learned on television that came to the rescue when it came to down to adjudicating the tattoo. In the end, you and I settled it through plea-bargaining. As you know, we each made our case before the other until we traded your forgoing the tattoo in favor of getting one pierced ear. I still remember telling you, "Just one pierced ear, Emily, *por favor*. I'm begging you now. Leave the Maori Indians alone. Self-mutilation is a tribal practice, *niña*, whereas you live in a country that is considered to be the leader of the free world. So please own up to your position on the globe and leave self-mutilation to the people who started it. At one point there were Indians in Arizona, too, but do you see a trace of them, other than the street names? Very well, then. There's no need, really, to start sticking needles under your skin. To say nothing of the fact that mutilation is not kosher. How am I going to explain this to your father? 'Max, you went away on a business trip and I couldn't even keep the girl away from an inky needle?' There simply aren't enough Yom Kippurs in a lifetime to atone for a tattoo. Your dad is working very, very hard to send you to a good school, Emily. You need to do your part."

What did my poor mother know, in the end? My mother had never been presented with such challenges as being sued by a twelve-year-old for invasion of privacy. She had no idea that the only way to approach the subject of self-mutilation is straight on.

A REFRESHING GLASS OF HIS OWN URINE

Azucena's date took us by surprise. He was not at all what we had expected. He was on time. He was well dressed. He didn't curse. He didn't live with his mother. As it turned out, he lived with his wife!

"Where did you find him?" My mother wanted to know.

As for my father, he's always favored action over talk. So when Azucena said she had accepted the date knowing the guy was married and then quoted her therapist as having said, "That's not your problem, it's his wife's," my father said, "I should offer the guy something to drink. How about a glass of his own pee?"

During the date, What's-his-name had been nothing if not a gentleman. He took my sister to dinner at a new Japanese bistro with a French twist. The place was called Japoix, or something along those lines. According to Azucena the tuna foie gras was fantastic. "*Foie*-what my ass," said my father. "Not in my house!"

That's when Azucena was supposed to remind him, "This is *my* house, Dad." This scene, and others like it, Azucena's therapist had predicted. The therapist had also predicted that once they knew their mother was eating foie gras elsewhere, either Lucas Enrique or Sofía (or both at same time) might become a touch jealous.

It was Lucas Enrique who said, "If he touches you, I'll kill him." Sooner or later all those TV shows featuring lethal weapons finally start to pay off. Unfortunately for Azucena, because she had once been an anemic child, she couldn't shake the reputation of being helpless, so everyone was trying to help her out by offering their two cents on her burgeoning romance with a man who was otherwise engaged.

Stranger still was the fact that What's-his-name was also into classical music. He also liked to travel, although apparently not with his wife. All told, he seemed to have a whole lot in common with Azucena. And what's more, he didn't mind the five extra pounds.

In the end, What's-his-name turned out to be the breath of fresh air *I* needed. Now our Sunday Skype calls were devoted to something else entirely.

"Valentina, I can't do this. I'm not wired to be somebody's mistress."

"Really, Azucena?"

IMMACULATE CONCEPTION

"Max, Max. Wake up!"

"What is it, Valentina?"

"I just had a dream."

"What about?"

"I dreamed I was pregnant. Well, it was more of a nightmare."

"Can I get you some water?"

"No, it's all right, Max. I'll be okay." Of course I'd be okay. By then we both knew that a pregnancy would be *the* Immaculate Conception. Who can have sex with abandon when in the room next door sleeps a girl who might be going to Dillard's under false pretense?

"On second thought, Max, didn't your doctor just prescribe some little pills for you so that you could sleep on the way to Moscow? Can I have half of one? Just to take the edge off. Just half, Max."

I should have asked him why he was taking those pills in the first place. They weren't for sleeping on a plane, I'd bet.

OTHER DESERT CREATURES

"What are you doing that for, Valentina?"

"Doing what, Max?"

"Pressing down on the tips of your shoes like that."

"Checking for scorpions, of course. The pink ones are the worst, Max. I know you hired those spraying people, but scorpions are very sneaky. Trust me on this. I grew up with scorpions. And things are weird enough around here as it is . . . ." Later that day, after driving Max to the airport, I got arrested.

Blame it on the training. The arresting officer might have been sent to Diversity Training to become color-blind, so he wouldn't beat up the people whose color he didn't like. But for all that, he still lacked the understanding about what it really means to be an alien. He hadn't had the benefit of an exchange program called Seeking Common Ground, so he didn't know that some picky local customs aren't necessarily crimes elsewhere. Go to Uganda. Go to Rwanda—but you don't have to visit Africa if that freaks you out. Go to Rome, and you will find that your driver's license is not tied to an accounting system. All you get in Rome by way of accounting is a highway sign that blinks whenever there's an update: *"Un morto,"* or *"cinque morti"* depending on how many people had died so far that day. The highway patrol keeps track of casualties and posts the changing numbers throughout the day as a kind of deterrent for people for whom speed might be a problem. And that's about it.

How was I supposed to know that every time I got a speeding ticket, some "bureau-drone" elsewhere was taking points off my driver's license? Or that speeding was such a big deal, for that matter? How many times did I tell the policemen that I did it out of habit? "Officer, if you slow down anywhere in Caracas, you'll get murdered. It's as simple as that." Some officers were more understanding than others. Overall, I found that very few of them had a sense of humor. Some even thought—when I told them that if you dared stop at an intersection in Caracas, you'd get rear-ended—that I was using innuendo to offer them a sexual favor.

After dropping Max off at the airport, I was driving like a madwoman to try to pick you up at school, when all of a sudden I heard a siren. At first I thought it was an ambulance, so I went a little faster to get out of the way. Point of reference is everything, *mi amor.* That's when the "ambulance," too, started going a little faster, trying to catch up with me. The stern voice yelling over the loudspeaker came out of nowhere: "STOPPP THE VEEHHICCLE." I was going so fast, the wind stretched the man's voice a little. In the end I was arrested for a misdemeanor. But don't let anyone tell you that there's a difference between a misdemeanor and third-degree murder. A jail is a jail. Regardless of the crime, you cannot get an upgrade on your cell. Not unless your name is Martha Stewart.

PLEASE HURRY

We started out on the wrong foot, I think. To move things along a little bit, I told the officer there was someone waiting for me. In fact, I clearly remember telling him that "a little person" was waiting for me. Well, what do you know? The guy took forever to check out my driving record. I'll bet anything that's a strategy they teach them in the police academy: to keep people waiting for an unreasonable period of time, as a wicked way of forcing submission. By then I knew I'd be really, really late. While the guy sat in his car playing with his gun, I started imagining the worst. I imagined you were standing in the middle of the school yard all by yourself, feeling abandoned or worse. In Caracas, you'd already have been kidnapped—that's a given.

After I moved to Arizona, Max handed me a phone and told me to keep it with me at all times. "In case the kids call," he said.

"I can't, Max. I can't be in the middle of doing something and waiting for a potential phone call like that. Life's stressful enough as it is without having to carry a phone around, waiting for a kid to call you and say, 'Guess what? I just got stung by a bee.' Then what? No, thank you." So to make sure I'd never get a call like that, I always left my phone at the house.

But anyway, after an eternity and a half the policeman finally came back and told me he had bad news.

"What's the bad news, Officer?"

"Is this your vehicle, Miss?" It was all he could do not to call me a thief. But as I told you, he had attended sensitivity training. And besides, with so many people crossing the border, officers in Arizona have to be extra careful about word choice.

"Whose vehicle would it be? Do I look like the kind of person who'd be driving someone else's car just for fun?" It was like talking to a burro.

"Miss, the name on the registration and the name on your driver's license don't match."

"Oh, that! Don't worry about that, Officer. That's a long story. I'm here temporarily and I haven't gotten around matching all the names. But one of these days . . ."

"You're under arrest for driving a stolen vehicle."

"You're joking!"

PRACTICAL JOKE

Last week I got a call from Azucena. Ever since she's been dating, she doesn't call as often. I didn't even hear the phone ring when she called. I must have been in the shower. That's probably why she had to leave me a voice message. Azucena hates leaving voice messages. She'd much rather hijack a person's sanity in real time.

Apparently, she's still going out with What's-his-name, and now he wants to take her on a trip. I have no idea where he might be thinking of taking my dear sister for a tryst. But for his own sake, I hope he's thinking five stars, and somewhere above the clouds. If there exists in any living creature a delicate dissatisfaction with the world, a yearning for all that spells excellence, it has made itself at home in Azucena. I hope What's-his-name is smart enough to realize that if he says, "Motel 6," Azucena will have *him* arrested for a misdemeanor. But talk of a tryst on my voice mail wasn't the real surprise. Azucena always leaves surprises till the end. . . .

"I'm thinking about sending you the kids, Valentina. Call me back."

Ha-ha-ha. It's really too bad there isn't a laughter ringtone tied to Auto Reply. A feature like that should sell well, I think, and not just during Halloween. And do you think that anywhere in her message, Azucena asked, "How are you doing, Valentina? I hope you're having a lovely Friday afternoon." That's just as well. She might not have known what to say were I to mention the ashes in the fridge. Hard to believe, isn't't? How difficult it is for working mothers the world over to find a decent guy and the time to get away. I'm starting to think that single motherhood might be a swindle.

PAYING YOUR WAY

When it comes to traffic problems, most countries give you the option of paying the officer, paying the judge, or paying both. The choice is yours. Then everyone can get on with their day. I never bribed anyone in the United States before. Throughout South America, though, carrying bribe money is as essential as eating daily from all the food groups. From the day you obtain your driver's license, in fact, you're encouraged to think of police officers as living toll booths. The problem with trying to bribe the officer who told me I was under arrest for driving a stolen vehicle was that I didn't know the going rate in the United States. In most of South America you might be able to bribe a highway patrol officer for, say, ten dollars. It used to be cheaper, but with all the toppled regimes and whatnot, rates have gone up. Civil servants in most parts of the world are underpaid. That's just a fact of life. So you don't want to insult them by not offering a substantial enough bribe. This is a particularly sensitive issue in South America, where the Latin temper might flare up and rather than taking you to jail, the officer might decide to kill you and solve the problem *that* way. Anyway, I was pretty sure I didn't have enough money to bribe the North American officer.

Max used to always say," Valentina, you need to carry more cash."

"Why, Max, I have a credit card?"

"In case of an emergency. You just never know."

"Max, there are no emergencies in this country. Tell me, Max, what kind of emergency can anyone possibly have in a place with so many rules?"

Well, there I was, in the middle of an emergency, and not enough money. That's when it occurred to me that because everything is more efficient here, the officer might accept a credit card. Still, I was pretty sure that one policeman in an industrialized country would be much more expensive than two policemen in the Third World. That's just logical. It's a better standard of living all around, and that extends to every aspect of society, including the highway patrol. The problem was that I didn't want to call further attention to the fact that I was an alien by offering the wrong amount. Then I'd be in real trouble. Trust me, you don't want a policeman from an industrialized country saying to you, "Is that all you got?" the way they're used to remarking to fellow officers at urinals.

So when the officer told me to get out of the car, I wasn't sure what to do about the bribe just yet, but I was pretty sure I didn't want to get out of the car. As I understood it from the judge on TV, my own car was under my own jurisdiction. So long as I remained inside, I was safe. So I didn't get out. And when I didn't, the officer put a checkmark on a little tablet he carried with him. From my sitting position inside the car I couldn't read that he was checking "resisting arrest." So I asked him what he was doing. That did it. The minute I opened my mouth, he immediately blurted, "You have the right to remain silent. Anything-you-say-can-and-will-be-used-against-you, ladi-ladi-la." You've heard it a million times on *LAPD*, or whatever that show is called.

Despite his best efforts to tolerate me, the officer's voice was a little tighter when he asked me to "please step out of the vehicle" one more time. When I still didn't budge, he called for help. In seconds, another policeman, who just as well might have been hiding under a cactus, came out of nowhere. I was in deep trouble now. I definitely didn't have enough cash in my wallet for two officers. I was tempted to ask, "Do you guys take Visa?" But I was late enough as it was, so I figured that if I got out of the car, we could wrap things up and then I'd be on my way. But no. The minute I got out of the car, they turned me around and handcuffed me.

After they were done frisking me—something that happened a lot more slowly than "as seen on TV"—I turned back around and told them I had a way to prove that I was the owner of the vehicle. Obviously, I was bluffing. By then I couldn't even remember what version of my name was on what application. That's when Officer Number 2 asked, "Have you read her the Miranda?" or something to that effect. So while the two of them were getting high on rules and regulations, I squeezed my hands out of my handcuffs. As you know, I have tiny, elegant wrists, so it was no trouble at all. Who could have guessed that that would earn me yet another checkmark? And therewith things went from bad to worse.

In the end I had to leave my car where it was because they took my keys away. It was very unnerving, to have to leave my car on the side of the road, not knowing if I'd ever see it again. In Venezuela, you'd never see it again. The arresting officer would sell your car to his cousin, who would paint it a different color, drive it to Medellín, and sell it to Cuca's boyfriend at the drug cartel for a small profit. End of story. But this is a developed country where everything is handled by the book. So nothing of the sort happened. In time I got my car back. There wasn't even a scratch on it.

NEITHER HERE, NOR THERE

The drive to jail was really annoying. One of the officers stared at my newly handcuffed hands as if I were a child who needed supervision. That's when it occurred to me to test his patience. If I was going to be treated like a common criminal just because my names didn't match in some database at headquarters, well then, I would act a little strange, unsettle him a little bit. So I asked, "Does that turn you on, Officer, a woman in handcuffs?" Another checkmark! I would learn the meaning of all the checkmarks a year later when I was in front of the judge, who proceeded to read every single count ever so slowly, as if I were some kind of child molester, or worse.

By the time I was given my allotted phone call, I had a series of misdemeanors piled on top of one another, though I didn't realize it at the time. The one saving grace was Max. When I called him to tell him I was in jail, he didn't go all ballistic, as some other husband might have done. Your dad had infinite patience. It was something I always admired in him, given I can't count patience as one of my virtues. If he could wait to see what was inside the box at Rosh Hashanah only to find out that it wasn't Napoleons, he could wait to find out what his wife had done that would merit getting a call from jail. So he didn't ask. The only thing he asked was, "Are they treating you OK, baby?" And quietly took care of sending a babysitter your way.

But what do we know in the end? That was my little epiphany on the day I got arrested. There's so much to learn from *Don Quixote*. So, rather than thinking that I, a woman named Valentina, was being fondled under the pretense of being frisked, I decided to travel in my mind to a place called El Toboso and think of myself as Dulcinea instead. This little flight of fancy did the trick; it offered me twice the protection. Dulcinea was, after all, in Don Quixote's imagination. And he, in turn, lived only in Cervantes's mind. None of it really happened. I was never in jail. Because I was never arrested in the first place.

In the end it doesn't really matter how long any of us stick around. Regardless of time done, we won't amount to much; we're predestined to remain insignificant, subordinate to all we can't understand, pretty much in the same way that Don Quixote was prey to the fantasy that he might be a gentleman. Everyone knows he was no gentleman. After all the years living in this country I've finally come to understand that obedience is a virtue valued here. But even if you manage to obey the rules, you're still an outsider. Since when does obedience put bread on the table? And besides, you still have the accent. But maybe there's something to be said for dying bereft of everything, yet obedient.

Now that your dad is gone I've been thinking about going back home. But I'm a little confused about where home is just now. After all these years here, something tells me I'd be even more of an alien there. Feminism isn't one of those words that go in one ear and out the other. A concept that powerful tends to stick. All this to tell you that if I were crazy enough to go on a date with one of those charmers who call on Azucena, I'd probably be arrested there too. Not for speeding, of course. For murder, *mi amor.*

HEALING SMILES

I finally gave in. I couldn't bear it much longer, so I went through your dad's things. And what I found out was a little more than disconcerting. I wasn't really looking for e-mails to his high school sweetheart or anything that lame. I just wanted an explanation. Most normal people want an explanation. I would even have settled for just a hint at that point.

So I decided to comb through your dad's e-mails, even though in real life I'm not the sort of person who likes to pry. For one, I hate surprises. And besides, when it comes right down to it, most people's in-boxes are really boring. Well, that's only a supposition. I don't know that for a fact. But then I came across the e-mail from Giovanna Fox. *¡Ay Dios mío!* That's when my fingers started trembling a little. For starters, I had never heard Max talk about anyone named Giovanna. So I hesitated before opening the e-mail, especially because the subject line read, "Operation Smile." Oh, shit! This is it, Valentina. Brace yourself.

Dear Max, thanks for putting a smile on my face. Click here to watch.

I was about to say, "You bastard," when purely by accident, you understand, I clicked on the link. The song at the beginning of the video was from the Beatles, who, as you know, were your dad's favorite band. *"Here comes the sun . . . and I say it's all right. Little darling, it's been a long, cold, lonely winter . . . ,"* and then, boom! The face of this deformed kid fills the entire computer screen.

Needless to say I was a little shaken. I mean, who shoves a camera in front of a kid with a cleft palate and says, "Smile for the camera, Matumba." The video closed with the following: *"Our Mission: To heal children's smiles and transform lives across the globe. Join our online community."*

Now I get to go on torturing myself, thinking I hardly knew the guy I married. Max never mentioned, not even once, that he had an interest in facial deformities. It just goes to show you that sharing a bed with someone means absolutely nothing. *Nada. Nada. Nada.*

But who knows? Maybe it was spam.

CURSE YOGA

"Get yourself together, Valentina. . . ." It seems these days I have to have these little chats with myself more and more often. I need to stop doing that. I'm too young for dementia.

Max used to think it was charming that I had to give myself instructions from time to time to avoid doing something that might land me in jail. I'd be at the grocery store, for instance, and someone with twenty items, for example, would waltz in front of me in a lane that says "Ten Items or Less," and I'd have to stop to have a little chat with myself. "Valentina, I would say, this person is probably illiterate." "Valentina, this person in front of you is not buying kashi in bulk just to torture you." "Valentina, this person may have no hair left, but that doesn't mean he just had a lobotomy and is fresh out of the cuckoo's nest. So calm, down!" Max was charmed by the fact that I'm the kind of person who can say to herself while looking into a mirror, "That's enough, Valentina You're not a cripple. You don't live in Darfur. Can you even spell Darfur, Valentina? You'll have to do much, much better than abandonment by suicide to get any sympathy from anybody. Nobody cares about people who have been abandoned, Valentina. You're the only dumb ass who actually reads those silly signs the homeless now flip around to extract pity from dumb asses like yourself. So shut, the fuck up!"

These mini-sessions work wonders, *mi amor*. You should try self-coaching sometimes. I know, I know, Max used to hate it when I cursed, too. But it helps me get through the rough patches.

There are two services that I think would be in great demand for people in our situation. One is Curse Yoga. The other one is an automated message service from Facebook. It would work like the automated reply message that says, "Sorry, I'm out of the office right now." But in this case the automated message will read, "My bad." And much like flood insurance, if you have any doubts whatsoever about how your life might turn out, you can pay for the service in advance on the day you put up your Facebook page.

You'd be surprised how many people out there love to play Jesus to the lepers in their head. I think that such a service would be very, very popular. And very Christian. Don't you think? It would make everyone feel good. Those left behind would be comforted in the knowledge that it was the other person's bad, not theirs. And the deceased would feel good on the day they sign up for the service. Ever since moving to this country I've become fond of happy endings.

EXILED

You once saw us kissing as you were coming down the stairs. Later that evening, at dinner, you asked us if we were soul mates. An odd question, I thought, especially from a ten-year-old. Max and I looked at each other. We didn't know what to say. I don't know about soul mates. I do know that sometimes, not always, when in the presence of another, everything seems to expand and all of a sudden there's room for everyone and everything. It's usually a wordless moment. Maybe that's what you saw that day when you were coming down the stairs—that Max and I were separate and one at the same time. It's not something you can call up at will. The opposite is a kind of exile. That's why I'm a little mad at him just now.

THE EDGE OF MADNESS

I keep having this recurring dream involving blueberry muffins and a former coworker. So Kante and I—that was his name—are sitting at Bloomingdale's eating blueberry muffins. He's wearing a smart black suit and a blue silk tie. Kante was from Lagos. Yes, *mi amor*, that's in Africa, of course; Lagos is the capital of Nigeria.

But anyway, Kante was the epitome of what people call tall, smart, and handsome. What doesn't track for me, though, is why Kante and I are eating blueberry muffins. And at Bloomingdale's, of all places. If Max were here, he might be able to tell me what this odd dream means. I haven't heard from Kante in years. We worked together on the Levi Strauss account. And in all that time I never saw him eat a muffin—blueberry or any other flavor. I'm the muffin freak. As for Kante, he was one of those people who always kept it together no matter what. The earth could be shaking under his feet and he could make it stop just by looking at it.

Maybe the dream is not really all that strange. I've always liked muffins, provided they're eaten between seven and eight in the morning. And I always admired Kante for his calm. I just don't understand why both should show up after all this time. And keep coming back night after night. Dreams are too close to the edge of madness for me. Jung used to write them down. But who needs dreams when you have a perfect life like mine?

Should *you* see a therapist? That's a really good question, Emily. Certainly not in Ecuador. The language barrier alone will be enough to give both you and the therapist migraines. Trust me on this. When I was learning English, I used to get these massive migraines that would last days. But if I may touch on Ecuador for a second. Here I am, pouring my heart out about the perils of South America—the express kidnappings, the rolling blackouts, murder at the mall—and you're still bent on going down there. And I haven't even scratched the surface.

Have I told you about dengue fever? You will die with your bones aching from an innocent mosquito bite. Well, maybe the mosquito is not all that innocent. But still. And what about rabies? You cannot, under any circumstances, Emily, come near a dog when you're down there. Do you hear me? And never pet a bat either. Bats are almost worse than dogs, because you can't see them. They live in the dark. Above all, avoid contact with people in crowded areas. Oh, and I forgot about *mal de Chagas*. If you can help it, avoid staying in houses made of mud, adobe, or palm thatch. My advice? Sleep under a steel roof. Steel is really the only safe material, given it is nonporous.

And only because you're an accomplished swimmer, I won't tell you about the poisonous jellyfish down there. The problem with jellyfish, *mi amor*, is that they sneak up on their victims. One minute you're cruising along under water and the next thing you know, there's a slimy tentacle attached to your leg. I'm not even going to tell you how to peel off a jellyfish tentacle from your skin. That way you'll have no choice but to stay out of the water.

Please don't get me wrong. It's not that I don't understand the need to get away every once in a while. Trust me. I'm the one who told you that the secret to happiness is to keep moving. But why South America, *mi amor*? When half that continent has pending visa applications with the state department here? Nobody's ever happy with what they have. My hairdresser says that all the time—you have curly hair, you want it straight. How about going to New York, instead? Your uncle Ira said you could stay with them for a while. Or how about visiting the twins? A visit from their sister might be the thing your brothers need to survive the pressures of day trading in this economy. Zachy might even welcome you. Zach, on the other hand . . . Hmmm . . . I know what you mean about your uncle. Ira has always had more questions than answers. And they're usually questions no one wants to hear. I can hardly believe it's been almost a year since that phone call . . . I could swear I just talked to him this morning.

"Hi, Ira, Valentina here. Something really bad has happened."

"Can you please be more specific, Valentina?"

"Give me a minute, Ira. I don't know exactly how . . . to say this."

In looking back, I think I might have been in shock. I don't even remember dialing his number. As a matter of fact, it wasn't until he asked me if Max had left a note that I lost it a little. "My God, Ira, don't you think a gun to your head in your ex-wife's kitchen is as good as a note?" That's what I felt like saying. What I really said was, "There was no note . . . "

People always want a note . . . as if a note could explain . . . This isn't the damn Junior League!!! People are so dumb, *mi amor*. Hand me a Kleenex, would you? Shit!

KRAZED

About the only surprise of our marriage was that weird e-mail from that Giovanna Fox woman. Don't get me wrong, *mi amor*, I want to go down kicking and screaming, the way pretty women do in the really thorny telenovelas. But what am I supposed to do when your mom has sealed her lips with Krazy Glue?

Do you want to know what I really think? I think Helen has a guilty conscience about something. That's why she won't talk. I mean, I can understand her not wanting to talk to me. But why not put her own daughter's mind at ease? And do you want to know something else? I think Max went there with the intention of having a chat, not a friendly chat, mind you, but an adult conversation about something having to do with money. Money was the only thing those two ever talked about. And I'll bet you all the papayas in Brazil that things got out of hand. I'll bet Helen called Max one of those charming names she used to call him. And that when she saw the gun, she said, "You're just bluffing, Max. Spare me." And Max said, "Wanna bet?" Unfortunately, all of us lost that bet.

But let's do something more useful than speculate. Let's go back to your question about the therapist. . . . Say you have this favorite Chinese restaurant. Mine is a little dive in a strip mall, not too far from here in fact. It's called Jade Dragon. I know you hate strip malls, *mi amor*. I've never understood what you have against strip malls. Any mall where you can shop free of murder is good enough for me. So let's say that whenever you have a craving for Chinese, you go to Jade Dragon. Say you always get the same thing—the Kung Pao Chicken, for instance. And this Kung Pao Chicken is usually served to you by the owner's daughter, a polite, young woman whose name is Yuan Lee. Now, Yuan Lee, having lived at Jade Dragon since she first learned to say, "Have a nice day," knows all the secrets about the place, including the fact that your favorite Kung Pao Chicken is really Kung Pao Poodle. Sorry, *mi vidita*. I know how much you like dogs. I'm just trying to tell you what it's like to know too much. I'm trying to tell you that given Yuan Lee's insider knowledge of the family business, she probably has a different perspective. I'll drink a bottle of soy sauce if Yuan Lee isn't a vegetarian.

Well, it's the same with every profession. I know more than I care to know about analysis to be able to recommend it to anyone in good conscience. A good friend might be better than a good therapist, in some cases. I also know that you and I are going to have to get through this, somehow. But I don't know exactly how just yet. I don't have all the steps that are going to get us from your mother's kitchen back to here. Take a state of fugue, for example—a rare case of reversible amnesia triggered by trauma. People affected by this are temporarily unable to recall their past. Sometimes, they even assume a new identity for a bit—change their name, that sort of thing. Now you tell me, how is a therapist who doesn't know the first thing about Emily Goldman supposed to know what she has and has not forgotten? How does the therapist know that when Emily says, "I'm going to Ecuador," Emily isn't playing Prisoner's Dilemma for one? How is *any* therapist supposed to know when Emily Goldman says, "I hate my dad" and "I miss my dad," which of the two statements is true?

Should you see a therapist? It depends, *mi amor*. You should probably see a therapist if you're confused about something and you don't think you can sort it out on your own. Now, if you're in a world of hurt about your dad leaving without an explanation, I wouldn't recommend seeing a therapist for that. Not unless you're so depressed you can't leave your bed in the morning. But you *did* leave your bed this morning, because you're here with me. Feeling hurt is a fitting response to this variety of loss. You *should* be in a world of hurt. Does anyone really need a therapist to tell them that it's no fun to sleep with a hundred spiders? That's just common sense. The hurt will eventually pass.

No, it doesn't mean you'll forget you ever had a dad. Or that you'll forget that your dad took a different kind of exit route than most people. It would be grand if the human brain had an Off switch, like that "dating on-and-off" option. But that's not going to happen any time soon. What will happen is that the pain, which seems to have made the world very, very small all of a sudden by forcing you to concentrate on the pain and nothing but the pain to the point of making you want to move to Ecuador, will eventually leave you alone for longer and longer stretches of time, until one day, you will open your eyes, and you'll be able to see the other things that you can't see right now because the pain keeps reminding you to focus on it. Pain is both selfish and intolerant, *mi amor*.

Now, if you're confused, that's a different story. If you're confused, a competent therapist might be able to help you sort out the confusion. So can a good friend. So can writing things down in a journal. Just make sure you know what you want in advance. If you go Freudian, you'll have to get unconfused on a couch and possibly have to talk about why you have the urge to pee. If you go Group Gestalt, you'll have to discuss your parents' divorce by holding the hands of strangers somewhere in California. If you go Jungian, you'll have to analyze that dream you had last night about the twins playing video games, and all its potential ramifications, at length. But be forewarned. Carl Jung himself was convinced that he was two people—a schoolboy living in his own era, and an influential man living in the eighteenth century.

I don't know, *mi amor*, the more I think about this, the more I keep thinking . . . Kung Pao Poodle.

MARISOL MURANO

A SPOONFUL OF MARRIAGE

Do you know how I knew something was wrong? It was the extra teaspoon of sugar Max put in his coffee that morning. He told me he was going to work. I still find it hard to believe. Max and Helen hadn't spoken in years. In fact, Helen got her alimony payments by direct deposit. I've never been fond of banks taking money automatically out of my account. But even so, I have to admit that something like direct deposit is an invention made-to-order for divorce victims.

I should have said something to Max about the sugar. But after years and years of getting the impression that I always open my mouth at the wrong time, I decided to keep my mouth shut for a change. But what if he was yelling? "VALENTINA, LOOK! I'M PUTTING AN EXTRA TEASPOON OF SUGAR IN MY COFFEE. DO SOMETHING!"

It's just as possible that he was distracted, that with so much weighing on his mind he reached for a second teaspoon of sugar and wasn't even aware of doing it. How to know for sure? I should have asked him. But I've never liked women who nag. What if I came across as accusatory? "Are we having extra sugar in our coffee these days, Max?" Or what if I came across as ridiculously obvious, which my mother warned me never to be? "You never want to be obvious, Valentina. Obvious is ridiculous." I remember thinking about my mother, in all her silent glory, that morning. That's what kept me from saying, "Max, I notice you're putting an extra teaspoon of sugar in your coffee." Marriage is hard enough as it is to add ridiculously obvious to the list of grievances. And there's something else about marriage—the fact that, after a while, you stop noticing the other person. It's no one's fault, really. I'm not even saying there's anything wrong with it. There's a chair I love in the den. I always read on that chair. You know the one I'm talking about. If something bad were to happen, say a desert fire, and that chair were to burn down, I don't

336

know what I'd do. Still, I hardly give that chair a second thought when I'm not sitting on it.

You want to know what my only regret is *en esta puta vida?* That the one time in my life when I should have said something, I kept my mouth shut. I should have asked Max about the damn sugar when I had the chance.

THE SILENT TREATMENT

If there's anyone qualified to figure this out, it's someone with an undergraduate degree in psychology and an MBA. But an education isn't worth much these days, especially from Tulane University. And I'm not just talking about Katrina. Did you know they used to call it "Jewlane"? The only reason I wasn't horrified is because I was too busy learning real English to start translating prejudice after school. But even if I didn't have an MBA, *mi amor*, I can still read the world *foreclosure* in a letter from a bank. I know how Max must have felt. I get to look at those letters piled up on his desk every single day. I'm to the point that I'm going to tell the mail guy he has the wrong house.

So your dad went to Helen's that day to talk about alimony. He went to see her with the best intentions, and things just went haywire. Things always get that way with an ex. It's only in *Sex and the City* that women start melting on the sidewalk when they see the guy who betrayed them with their best friend. Trust me on this, *mi amor*. I've been divorced twice. The only difference between me and Helen is that I leave them before I kill them.

ASHES TO ASHES

Take a deep breath, *mi amor.* Breathing always helps at times like these. But let's not take him out of the fridge, not just yet. I don't want him to get cold. Let's look up Lockheed Martin first.

Have I told you I once applied for a job there? The people at Lockheed sure have it together. If they can get a satellite into outer space so that Lucas Enrique can watch *Rambo* in Caracas, I'm sure someone there knows how to shoot ashes into space. The people of Lockheed know that outer space is a demanding environment. And if they can throw Congress into orbit, *mi amor,* why not a person? Then we can resume talking about Ecuador . . . after we send your dad on his way. Let Lockheed Martin's missiles go ballistic, not us. One thing at a time . . . so that we can keep our wits about us. Let's get this thing done, then we can resume talking about to whom we shall entrust your brain for the next few years.

You have a good brain, Emily. It would be a shame to let it go to waste. Please promise me you'll think about college after you come back. You're coming back, aren't you? . . . I know of a great program in Rome. Don't look at me that way, as if I were talking "arranged marriage," or something evil. What's wrong with going abroad? I went abroad . . . to the land of opportunity, no less. And look how well everything turned out for me. I'm sitting in a desert . . . looking at a cactus in the backyard . . . talking to my beautiful stepdaughter . . . about . . . how to . . . get this done.

Give me a minute, *mi amor.* Just give me . . . a minute, please.

Don't go anywhere, Emily. I'll be right back.

SHARE *VALENTINA GOLDMAN*

I hope you enjoyed reading *Valentina Goldman's Immaculate Confusion* by Marisol Murano. If you would like to tell your friends about it, please click on the link below for a hip way to share info about the book.

http://www.bit.ly/ValentinaG

Rob Simon, Publisher
Hipso Media

PS: If you want to learn about new titles, new authors, special discounts and what's hip at Hipso Media, please sign-up to join our free Hipso Book Club.

join@hipsomedia.com.

NOTES

"Tragedy is a cosmic matter" is from Charles Simic, *The Unemployed Fortune-Teller: Essays and Memoirs* (University of Michigan Press, 1995).

"It's not personal. It's strictly business" is from the film *The Godfather*, directed by Francis Ford Coppola, screenplay by Mario Puzo and Francis Ford Coppola.

"Start spreading the news" is from the song "New York, New York," which is from the film *New York, New York*, directed by Martin Scorsese, lyrics by Fred Ebb.

"Then God blessed them and said, 'Be fruitful and multiply'" is from Genesis, 1:28. New Living Translation of the Bible.

"Here comes the sun . . . and I say it's all right. Little darling, it's been a long, cold, lonely winter" is from *Abbey Road*, lyrics by George Harrison.

"To heal children's smiles and transform lives across the globe" is from Operation Smile, www.operationsmile.org.

A NOTE ABOUT THE AUTHOR

When she was 18-years-old, Marisol Murano moved to the United States to attend school so that afterwards she could return to her native Venezuela to get married and have kids. None of this happened. Instead, she ended up getting one more degree than she had expected—a Master's degree—which eventually landed her a boring job in an exciting city: New York.

After a few years running the corporate rat race, she woke up to this one day, "Even if you win the race, you're still a rat." That was the end of her banking career and the birth of her first novel: *The Lady, The Chef, and The Courtesan.*

Marisol was the first to be surprised when her first novel— launched at BookExpo America—was named Latino book of the Year, Original Voices from Border's and was picked as a BookSense selection. She was further surprised when it was translated into several languages.

A second career detour led her to become a chef. Between novels, Chef Marisol now travels the world conducting culinary demonstrations on exotic cuisine. She authored a cookbook based on recipes she collected during her travels, *Deliciously Doable Small Plates from Around the World.* In fact, *Valentina Goldman's Immaculate Confusion* was born at sea in a split-second of confusion when during a culinary demonstration a woman raised her hand to ask: "Did you always know you wanted to be a chef?"

Life is stranger than fiction, indeed.